Praise for *Into the Storm*

"Anderson expands on familiar concepts with high-tension battles and skillful descriptions of period attitudes and dialogue" —*Publishers Weekly*

"Outstanding . . . nonstop action . . . extremely high-level achievement at both world building and characterization." —*Booklist*

"Combines a love for military history with a keen eye for natural science." —*Library Journal*

"Readers who enjoy series similar to John Birmingham's Axis of Time trilogy, Eric Flint's 1632 series, or classics like Jules Verne's *Mysterious Island* should find this book enjoyable. Many questions are yet to be answered, and I can hardly wait to read the answers." —SF Revu

"Succeeds on many levels . . . exciting . . . a great adventure in an alternate world. . . . This gripping read is hard to put down." —*Romantic Times*

Also in the Destroyermen Series

Crusade

DESTROYERMEN
INTO THE STORM

TAYLOR ANDERSON

A ROC BOOK

ROC
Published by New American Library, a division of
Penguin Group (USA) Inc., 375 Hudson Street,
New York, New York 10014, USA
Penguin Group (Canada), 90 Eglinton Avenue East, Suite 700, Toronto,
Ontario M4P 2Y3, Canada (a division of Pearson Penguin Canada Inc.)
Penguin Books Ltd., 80 Strand, London WC2R 0RL, England
Penguin Ireland, 25 St. Stephen's Green, Dublin 2,
Ireland (a division of Penguin Books Ltd.)
Penguin Group (Australia), 250 Camberwell Road, Camberwell, Victoria 3124,
Australia (a division of Pearson Australia Group Pty. Ltd.)
Penguin Books India Pvt. Ltd., 11 Community Centre, Panchsheel Park,
New Delhi - 110 017, India
Penguin Group (NZ), 67 Apollo Drive, Rosedale, North Shore 0632,
New Zealand (a division of Pearson New Zealand Ltd.)
Penguin Books (South Africa) (Pty.) Ltd., 24 Sturdee Avenue,
Rosebank, Johannesburg 2196, South Africa

Penguin Books Ltd., Registered Offices:
80 Strand, London WC2R 0RL, England

Published by Roc, an imprint of New American Library, a division of Penguin
Group (USA) Inc. Previously published in a Roc hardcover edition.

First Roc Mass Market Printing, February 2009
10

Copyright © Taylor Anderson, 2008
All rights reserved

ROC REGISTERED TRADEMARK—MARCA REGISTRADA

Printed in the United States of America

PUBLISHER'S NOTE
This is a work of fiction. Names, characters, places, and incidents either are the
product of the author's imagination or are used fictitiously, and any resemblance
to actual persons, living or dead, business establishments, events, or locales is
entirely coincidental.
    The publisher does not have any control over and does not assume any re-
sponsibility for author or third-party Web sites or their content.

For my darling daughter, Rebecca Ruth.
Everything I do is for her, after all.
In return, I get her humor, wit, companionship,
inspiration, and unqualified adoration.
Not a bad trade.

ACKNOWLEDGMENTS

First, I must thank my parents, Don and Jeanette Anderson, who tolerated my various early eccentric pursuits—albeit sometimes with dubious, strained smiles and rolling eyes. Parents always want the best for their kids, and many of the paths I chose in life were untrodden, dark, and overgrown. At least they didn't have to worry that I was running with the "wrong crowd," since I spent most of my formative spare time in the woods with a flintlock and a bedroll. They didn't just sit back and watch, though, and therefore must take a measure of responsibility for the example they set. My dad taught me about old radios, Fort Worth Spudders, flying—and honor, of course. My mother taught me strength of will and character. I might sometimes feel compelled to substitute "stubbornness and obstinacy" for those more noble-sounding traits, but which is, after all, more virtuous and practical?

I have to thank MMCPO (SS) Tom Postulka, USN, a good friend I miss a lot and who, even though a submariner, sparked my interest in four-stackers a dozen years ago. Erik Holland, USN (ret.), is a quintessential "snipe," and his stories of engine-room life on diesel-electric Fleet submarines have kept me laughing and learning for years. SCPO Jeff Fairchild, USN (ret.), may be a "Nukie Puke," but he's helped me out of a few jams too. Lt. Col. Dave L. Leedom, USAFR, and Mark Wheeler reminded me how fun flying can be. (Bad) Dennis Petty, Jim Goodrich, Col. Alan Huffines, USAR, and Lynn Kosminski convinced me that maybe I could string a few words together after all—in spite of the harm many of my professors did by stifling all literary allusions in my earlier, purely historical work.

Other people who've helped me in so many ways include (but are certainly not limited to) Robin and Linda Clay, Mark Beck, Brad Fisher, USMC (ret.), Dennis Hudgens, Michael Dunegan, Walter Baldree, Sgt. 1st Class Dex Fairbanks, USA (ret.), Riqui and David Wartes, Preston Furlow, and Cortney Skinner. Special thanks to Dr. David Bererra and all the nurses and staff at Harris Southwest Methodist Hospital, and of course, to my long-suffering, beautiful bride, Christine.

Last, but certainly not least, I have to thank Russell Galen and Ginjer Buchanan.

Ginjer is the best editor I know and has always been gracious, friendly, and supportive. She and her staff are a pure pleasure to work with.

Russell Galen is the best agent in the business. His patience, professionalism, encouragement, and friendship truly are the steam that moves this ship through the water. To say "I couldn't have done it without him" is ridiculously insufficient praise. I rarely find myself at a loss for words, but I simply cannot express how much I appreciate his help. Thanks, Russ.

BORNO
(Borneo)

SULAR

BAALKPAN
(Balikpapan)

THE SQUALL

Exeter
Encounter
Pope

B'MRANDO
(Madura)

BAALI

JAAVA
SEA

JAAVA

ARYAAL
(Surabaya)

CHIL-CHAAP
(Tjilatjap)

- - - - Loss of HMS EXETER

HMS ENCOUNTER & USS POPE - 3/1/1942

THE SQUALL - Evening of 3/1/42

Actions, March - July 1942

WALKER & MAHAN

SALISSA alone

MAHAN alone

WALKER looks for MAHAN

WALKER alone

WALKER & SALISSA

- IJN Battlegroups

A&B - Cruisers & DDs, C - Amagi & DD

Walker & Mahan vs Amagi & DD

Walker & Salissa vs 6 Grik

"Battle of the Stones"

U.S.S. WALKER   DD-163
NAVIGATIONAL CHART FLAGS LABEL
Naval aug. 6, 1942

Scale 1/99=372x76

-- Possible tracking of Grix Map Symbols --

- On Dark Areas: Extent of enemy conquest.
▲ Lemurian territory
• Lemurian population center.
Closed Triangle - Single Grix ship?
▲ 3 Grix ships?
▲ Blood Sands? - A place of battle.
HH - Lemurian Home
• - Patrol/area for Grix squadrons

In their Mather P. Reddy, Lieut Comd'r. USN

Arabia

África

Ceylon

Madagascar

They were running. There was no other word for it, no comforting euphemism to make the sting less sharp. In fact, it seemed impossible to wring the slightest sense of purpose from the confusion, privation, terror, and bone-numbing weariness they'd endured since the very day the war began on December 7. Now, three months later, they were running away ("limping" might be the better term) and they hadn't even had a chance to lick their wounds. The tired men and elderly ships of Destroyer Squadron (Des Ron) 29 had hurled themselves repeatedly at the implacable juggernaut that was the Japanese Imperial Navy while their numbers were ruthlessly slashed by disaster and disrepair. It was a tragically lopsided contest, a feeble gesture of defiance against overwhelming odds. In the end, a gesture was all it had been. Now all that remained was to flee—and it was probably too late.

Lieutenant Commander Matthew Patrick Reddy, USNR, the captain of USS *Walker*, stood on the starboard bridge-wing and tried to maintain at least a semblance of dignity in his rumpled and sweat-stained shirt. His left hand clutched his hat to his head against the thirty-knot breeze while his right tried to keep the half-filled mug of lukewarm coffee from slopping onto his uniform.

Red-rimmed eyes squinted from what was normally an almost embarrassingly boyish face, but at the moment a general covering of brown stubble and a fatigue-slacked expression made him look older than his thirty-two years. Not quite thirty-six hours earlier, he and his exhausted crew had participated in the largest surface action of the war to date: the Battle of the Java Sea. For once, the forces were evenly matched—in numbers, if not quality—and they thought they'd had a chance. But from the beginning, nothing went right. The battle finally ended sometime in the night with the ruthless slaughter of virtually the entire force under Admiral Doorman's command. While the enemy grew ever stronger, the scattered Allies were picked off in ones and twos.

Walker wasn't there when the poor old *Houston* and the staunch *Perth* were surrounded and hammered to the bottom. All the destroyers had been ordered to Surabaya to refuel and had thus been granted a short reprieve. *Edwards*, *Alden*, *Ford*, and *Paul Jones* departed for Australia as soon as their bunkers were full, and nobody knew if they'd made it through the gauntlet or not. The remaining destroyers were ordered to wait for the British cruiser *Exeter*, the only capital ship to survive the battle, and escort her to Ceylon after she completed temporary repairs. Matt spent that day of short intermission sending out parties to scrounge anything they might use, but little turned up in the bombed-out remains of the Dutch naval yard. The searchers discovered some belted .30-cal, eighty rounds of four-inch-fifty for the main guns, two condemned torpedoes, a little food. It wasn't much. All the while, emergency repairs to *Walker* were under way. Even if Matt had found the time, he couldn't have slept through the racket.

Now, standing on the bridgewing, he allowed a huge yawn to escape and hoped it made him look calm instead of just worn-out. The morning sun was bright, and the beauty of the vast, calm, almost violet sea was marred only by the distant hump of Bawean Island and the tiny cluster of American and British destroyers guarding *Exeter*'s wounded flanks like battle-weary army ants escorting their injured queen to a new home. As far as Matt knew, he was looking at all that remained of the Allied Forces in the American, British, Dutch, Australian—or ABDA—defensive area. He knew they'd been the last ones out of the tangled mass of wreckage and half-sunken hulks that Surabaya, Java, had become. ABDAFLOAT's initial force was composed of two heavy cruisers, seven light cruisers, twenty-three destroyers, and about thirty submarines and assorted support vessels. Now all that was left were three battered, Great War–vintage U.S. "four-stacker" destroyers, one British destroyer, *Encounter*, and the badly damaged heroine of the River Plate, HMS *Exeter*. The massive Japanese fleet that destroyed or chased off the rest of their comrades now had them alone to concentrate on. USS *Pope* (DD-225) and HMS *Encounter* screened *Exeter*'s starboard side, while USS *Mahan* (DD-102) and Matt's own *Walker* (DD-163) screened to port.

He glanced up at the lookout standing in the little tub near the top of the mast. Rodriguez, electrician's mate 3rd class, appeared transfixed, staring through heavy binoculars at a point far astern. From where he stood, Matt couldn't see anything yet, but he knew the two Japanese heavy cruisers and the destroyer that had pursued them since 0700 were still behind them. Rodriguez could see their smoke and they were getting closer.

When they'd slipped out of Surabaya the night before, they intended to run the Sunda Strait into the Indian Ocean and make a dash for Ceylon. Blocked by the enemy, they reversed course across the Java Sea to run east along the Borneo coast. Their quick about-face gained them breathing room, but the enemy cruisers launched observation planes. Two circled even now, high above and beyond reach of their meager antiaircraft defenses. All they could do was watch while the planes kited lazily overhead and reported their progress to every Japanese ship within range of their radios.

The convoy was limited to twenty-seven knots by *Exeter*'s damage, but Matt knew *Walker* couldn't steam much faster herself. The daily litany of mechanical casualties plaguing his ancient ship read more like a shipyard inventory than a morning report. *Pope* and *Mahan* were in no better shape. The stress of constant steaming and frequent combat—in addition to ordinary wear and tear—had placed a heavier strain on *Walker*'s machinery and equipment than she'd endured in all her twenty-three years of service. *Walker* had gone beyond her design, and Matt was very much afraid that she, as well as her crew, was being pushed beyond her capability.

He hadn't commanded her long, only four and a half months. As a reservist, even one from the Academy, he'd been treated pretty rough by the Navy. He'd worked his way into the exec's slot on a Benson-class destroyer (a major step up in the peacetime Navy), but he'd lost the posting to an older regular officer and found himself on the beach. He knew it wouldn't last and he was right. War was brewing all over the world, and it was just a matter of time before the United States got involved. When he got the letter, he expected—hoped for—a posting to one of the new Fletcher-class destroyers, possibly as gunnery officer. That would have suited him fine. Much to his surprise, he was given a command. But not of one of the sleek, lethal, modern destroyers he yearned for. No, he was to command one of the decrepit and almost defenseless antiques with which he was familiar, but found far from satisfying. Even more disheartening, his "new" command was attached to the Asiatic Fleet.

USS *Walker* had toiled with the Asiatic Fleet for more than six years and in that time she'd never been back to the country of her birth. She was 314 feet long and not quite 31 feet wide. Her long, sleek, needle-shaped hull and the four slightly raked funnels that provided the unofficial moniker for her class gave an impression of speed. And she was fast—by the standards of 1919—having made thirty-six knots on her trials. Even now she wasn't what one would have called slow, but the effort required to maintain her maximum speed was . . . excruciating.

Her ancient boilers were choked with sediment, and her steam lines sprouted leaks with unpredictable capriciousness. Her wiring was so corroded that most of it didn't do anything anymore. Much had been spliced or bypassed, and unidentifiable bundles of wires ran all over the ship. Her hull plates leaked rust through cracked and peeling paint, despite constant work by her crew to keep it chipped and touched up. The plates themselves were only two-thirds as thick as they once had been. She stank of sweat, smoke, grease, paint, fuel oil, steam, and strangely, hot linoleum. Her round bottom made her roll horribly in anything but the calmest seas, and she rattled and groaned and vibrated so badly you could feel it in your teeth. Her blowers produced a loud and decidedly asthmatic wheeze, and the general cacophony of abused machinery made hearing difficult in the remotest areas of the ship.

Her main battery consisted of a meager quartet of four-inch guns—only three of which could possibly bear on a single target—and none of which could elevate high enough to engage aircraft. There was one little three-inch antiaircraft gun on the fantail, but its range was so short it was used mostly for firing illumination star shells. The only even marginal antiaircraft defenses she had were two .30-caliber machine guns on the fire-control platform and two .50-caliber guns on the amidships deckhouse. Hanging over the fantail where it tapered sharply to a slightly rounded vee were two old-fashioned depth-charge racks. Her real teeth consisted of twelve 21-inch torpedoes carried in four triple-tube mounts between the number four funnel and the aft deckhouse. The torpedoes, and her once-respectable speed when delivering them, had been the reason for her creation so long ago. But like everything else in this new war so far, the torpedoes had been a grave and costly disappointment.

Matt had always heard that new captains often overlooked the shortcomings of their first command. But the first thing that sprang to mind when he saw her riding at anchor in Manila Bay, besides a general feeling of dismay over her apparent condition, was that the white-painted letters "163" on her bow seemed much too large.

Matt had been to the China Station and the Philippines—the Asiatic Fleet's area of operations—only once before. He'd been an ensign aboard another four-stacker during the buildup over the *Panay* incident, when the Japanese "accidentally" bombed and sank an American gunboat on the Yangtze River. Even then, the men, ships, and conditions of operation in the Asiatic Fleet made quite a negative impression. Equipment- and personnel-wise, the station was the abused, ugly dog of the Navy. The men were considered the dregs of the service, and the ships were third-rate obsolescent relics that, it was joked, were kept in the Asiatic Fleet because they weren't worth the fuel to steam home to scrap. When he assumed command of USS *Walker* he'd studied the log and fitness reports of his predecessor, Captain Simmons. As expected, the crew's reputation for hard drinking and carousing was confirmed on the pages he read. But to his surprise, there was also a subliminal thread of tolerance, amusement, and even protectiveness among the author's words. Discipline had been strictly maintained, but it was quickly clear that Captain Simmons had liked his crew. Judging by the initial reserve with which Matt was received, the feeling was mutual. He wondered at the time how difficult it would be for him to "fill the Old Man's shoes" and how much trouble he'd have making the men conform to his own expectations. Even on more agreeable stations, change often provoked the most friction when a new captain took command. And he hadn't "come up" in the Asiatic Fleet.

Despite his apprehension, there was little friction after all. Perhaps it was his quiet competence and uncomplicated, black-and-white sense of duty that left no doubt among the crew where they stood. Or maybe it was his quick discovery that these men were not dregs—at least most of them weren't. Ever since the Depression, the Navy had been particular about the recruits it accepted. A fair percentage of the misfits may have gravitated to the Asiatic Fleet, but for the most part, the men were at least as professional as their counterparts on other stations. They just led an entirely different life than was the norm in the rest of the Navy. They were forced to cope with worn-out equipment and keep their ships combat ready with little more than the proverbial baling wire and chewing gum. It was only natural that they might vent more steam than their peers on stations with less stress, a better climate, and fewer "diversions" than had been the case in China or the Philippines. He could discipline and punish them for their rowdiness and debauchery during a night on the town, but in his heart he couldn't condemn them for it. Their ability to fix anything, or at least make it "sorta" work, in difficult circumstances appealed to his sense of independence. Whatever the reason, much quicker than he'd expected, he'd been elevated to the exalted status of "Skipper," and he realized he liked them too.

Now, captain and crew together had been tested in the cauldron of combat, and Matt's black-and-white concept of right and wrong had come under serious assault. They'd dodged air attacks and experienced the unexpected exultation of "victory" in the Makassar Strait. They'd seen the senseless waste of lives in the Badung Strait caused by confusion and miscommunication. They'd lived through the frustration and horror of the Battle of the Java Sea, while their comrades on other ships and in other navies died for a purpose that began to elude them. No one questioned the War; it came without warning or mercy. It was real, it was all-consuming, and it was here. Why they were fighting it here was the unfathomable question.

Leaving the Philippines was tough. A lot of the guys had Filipino wives and sweethearts, and to them it was home. Some planned to retire there. But after the Air Corps was slaughtered in the opening days of the war, the only things left that had wings had red circles painted on them. Clearly, if the air belonged to the Japanese, remaining in the Philippines was suicide. No one wanted to leave, not even Matt, who still hated being stationed there. But he hated being "run off" even more. Maybe it was his Texas upbringing, or the "Spirit of the Alamo" or something like that, but he'd been perfectly willing to fight to the last even though the withdrawal made good sense.

Shades of gray appeared when *Walker* and Des Ron 29 were redeployed south to defend the Dutch East Indies. It was clearly a hopeless cause. Air cover was still nonexistent, and there weren't enough ships to stop what was coming. The Dutch oil fields were the Japanese objective, but leaving a few old ships to try and slow them down would only provide them with target practice. If they had to make an Alamo-like stand, why couldn't they have done it in the Philippines? Their "home" waters, so to speak?

Java belonged to the Dutch, and it was understandable that they'd want to keep it, but it was impossible. Reinforcements weren't coming. It made more sense to Matt to pull everything out and save the men and ships until they had enough to knock the Japanese on their butts for a change. Of course, he wasn't an admiral or a politician, and the very condition of the Asiatic Fleet proved that its survival wasn't a priority to those who were. He admitted he might've felt differently if Java was his home. The Nazis had Holland, and Java was all that was left. He *had* felt differently when the Philippines were at stake, and he hadn't even liked it there. It was all a matter of perspective. He knew he was relatively young and inexperienced, but he couldn't shake the thought that if it was strategically wrong to defend the Philippines, it was wrong to defend Java too. Maybe he was just bitter. The same people who expected them to fight to the last in the Dutch East Indies hadn't lifted a finger to support the United States in the Philippines.

After the disaster in the Java Sea he thought even the Dutch would realize it made more sense to fight their way back in than be destroyed getting kicked out. As far as he knew, they hadn't sunk a single Japanese ship during the battle. Except for *Exeter* and the aged destroyers, AB-DAFLOAT had ceased to exist. He was mistaken. Word was that Admiral Helfrich, the Dutchman who'd replaced Tommy Hart as ABDA's commander, still planned offensive action even after Admirals Glassford and Palliser told him they had nothing left. The Dutch had no monopoly on stubbornness; the British hadn't showed much more sense regarding Singapore, and thousands of Americans were trapped in the Philippines, cut off from any support. But it was past time to leave. ABDA had done its best with what it had. There'd been willing cooperation, but no coordination. Without air cover or reconnaissance, or even a common language, they'd been like blindfolded kids running around on tricycles with a steamroller bearing down. It was a disaster.

He often reflected on the certainty he'd felt regarding an eventual war with Germany, and he admitted that before he got out here, he'd never given much thought to the Japanese. Evidently nobody had. Now his entire consciousness was devoted to preventing that underestimated foe from shredding his ship and her crew and sending them to the bottom of the Java Sea.

With a gauging glance at the stately *Exeter* off the port quarter to ensure that *Walker* was holding proper formation, he stepped into the pilothouse. The gunnery officer, Lieutenant (j.g.) Greg Garrett, looked anxiously from the port bridgewing and Matt waved him back. The tall, lanky young officer nodded solemnly and resumed scanning the sea toward the dark smudge in the north that was Borneo. A good kid, Greg. He was conscientious and industrious, if just a bit intense. They were still at general quarters, as they'd been since the morning watch, and Garrett's battle station was normally on the fire-control platform above the pilothouse. Matt had told him to rotate himself and his team out of the wind and sun periodically. The main battery was useless against air attack, and it would be a while before they were in range of the Japanese cruiser's eight-inch guns. Longer still before they could hope to reply. Even so, when it was Garrett's turn to take a break, he merely descended to the pilothouse and kept doing what he'd done above—watching and waiting. Matt understood how the younger man felt. The atmosphere of anxiety and tension was thick. Everyone anticipated the cry warning of enemy ships or planes.

The stocky, broad-shouldered form of Lieutenant James Ellis clomped metallically up the ladder from the main deck below, and Matt arched an eyebrow at him. He liked Jim Ellis, and they were as close to being friends as their rank difference allowed, but Jim was much farther from his battle station at the auxiliary conn on the aft deckhouse than Garrett was from his.

"Yes, sir, I know," Ellis said, anticipating the reprimand as he maneuvered Matt out of hearing of the others in the pilothouse. "But those nurses and their flyboy chauffeurs want to know if there's anything they can do. That Army captain"—he tilted his nose up with unconscious disdain—"actually tried to come up here and bug you. Chief Gray said he'd have to wait your convenience." Ellis grinned. "That wasn't good enough and Gray offered to sit on him—physically. Then he sent for me." Matt smiled in spite of his jitters.

Before they cleared Surabaya, they'd taken aboard a rather motley assortment of passengers. First to arrive was an unkempt and harried-looking Australian, a Mr. Bradford, a construction engineer for Royal Dutch Shell. He introduced himself as a "naturalist," but paid his passage by intervening on their behalf with the harbor officials, who didn't want to fill their bunkers. They'd argued that the fuel would be better used by Dutch ships, staying to defend Java. Courtney Bradford countered with the fact that there was only one Dutch ship left, a destroyer, and she was getting the hell out just as fast as she could. Perhaps it was their lingering respect for a corporate superior, or maybe just the final realization that everything really was falling apart. Whatever the motivation, *Walker* left Surabaya with her bunkers overflowing.

Next to come limping aboard was a sergeant from *Houston*'s Marine contingent. He'd been wounded by a bomb that had killed dozens and wrecked the old cruiser's aft turret. Left ashore in a hospital with a lacerated leg, he missed her final sortie. He didn't intend to become a guest of the Japanese. Upon his arrival, he was roundly scolded for bleeding on the deck and sent below to the surgeon.

Finally, motoring out to catch them in a "borrowed" boat just as they were preparing to get under way were six Navy nurses and two P-40 pilots who'd escaped the sinking of the old *Langley* the day before. *Langley* had been ferrying P-40 fighters in for the defense of Java, but she was caught fifty miles short. Bombed into a smoldering wreck, she was abandoned, and one of *Walker*'s sisters, *Edsall*, was forced to finish her with two precious torpedoes. The majority of *Langley*'s personnel shipped south on the oiler *Pecos*, but in the confusion, the nurses and airmen were left behind. They persuaded the driver of a Dutch army truck to take them to Surabaya, and they arrived just in time to come aboard *Walker*.

Matt hadn't seen them. He'd been aboard *Exeter* conferring with Captain Gordon's executive officer. When he returned, he was informed of the ship's newest passengers by a leering Jim Ellis and a scandalized Lieutenant Brad "Spanky" McFarlane, the engineering officer, whose strict observance of Navy custom—if not always regulations—filled him with a terrible conviction that women on board would certainly doom the ship. That Army aviators accompanied them would probably send them to hell as well. Matt was inwardly amused by the diverse reactions, and it never occurred to him to set them ashore under the circumstances. He only wondered briefly where they'd be kept. Since then, he hadn't seen them and they'd been forgotten.

"What's his name?"

"The Army captain? Kaufman, sir."

"Very well, send him up, but by himself. And, Exec," he added ominously, "we don't need the distraction of women on my bridge. Clear?"

Lieutenant Ellis grinned hugely and went to fetch their visitor. Matt stepped onto the bridgewing as the Air Corps captain clumsily appeared. He prepared to return the salute he expected, since they were technically out-of-doors. It didn't come. His eyes narrowed slightly and the other members of the bridge crew exchanged shocked, knowing expressions.

"Lieutenant Commander Reddy? I'm David Kaufman, Captain, U.S. Army Air Corps."

The man stuck out his hand and Matt took it briefly. His initial impression was that the lack of a salute and the use of his specific rank instead of the appropriate, if honorific, title of "Captain" were due to ignorance. A Navy lieutenant commander was equivalent to a major in the Army. But the emphasis Kaufman applied to his own rank warned Matt that his guest didn't see it that way and might try to intimidate him if he could.

"What can I do for you, Captain Kaufman?" he asked, placing emphasis on the "Captain" as well, but in a way he'd address a subordinate. Kaufman glanced at the hostile expressions of the seamen on the bridge and modified his tone. His next words were less condescending.

"I just thought if there was anything I or Lieutenant Mallory might help you with, why, just let us know." He smiled smugly, and the patronizing inflection returned as he spoke. He acted like he'd granted a favor.

"What can you do?" Matt asked simply. "Besides fly airplanes. I assume you can fly airplanes."

Kaufman's face reddened, and he realized he might have overstepped. "Yeah, I can fly airplanes," he said with a quick, brittle smile. He held his hands out to his sides. "But I'm fresh out. You don't have one I can borrow?" His attempted joke fell flat and he just shrugged. "I can fire a machine gun."

Matt turned to Garrett, observing the exchange with wide eyes. "Mr. Garrett, perhaps the captain and his lieutenant might assist your crews on the thirty-cals on the fire-control platform? If we come under air attack they'll need to be supplied with ammunition." He grimaced. "Since we lost most of our mess attendants when we left the Philippines, it's hard to spare men for that chore." He looked the aviator square in the eye. "Thanks for the offer. You're dismissed." With that, he turned and peered out the pilot-house windows at the number one gun down on the fore-deck. He sensed Kaufman's furious presence behind him for a few moments more, but with an audible sigh and a few muted chuckles, the rest of the watch relaxed and he knew Kaufman must have left. *I shouldn't have let him rile me*, he scolded himself, but he made a quiet snort of amusement anyway. Then he spun—"Exec!"

Ellis's head popped back into view. "Skipper?"

"Those women are nurses, you say?"

Ellis leered again. "Absolutely."

Matt shook his head. "If they want to help, send them to Doc Stevens in the wardroom. And spread the word! They'll be treated with respect. Any man who inflicts himself on them will go overboard for the Japs. Understood?"

Ellis nodded, his leer now slightly wistful. "Sir."

"Very well. And, Exec?"

"Sir?"

"Keep them off my bridge."

Ellis slid down the ladder, firehouse style, and caught up with Kaufman, who was striding purposefully through the amidships deckhouse. His handsome, square-jawed face was clouded with anger. Ellis touched his sleeve and Kaufman spun. He recognized Ellis and forcibly composed his expression. He stood six inches taller than the burly exec, but Ellis was more muscular. A tolerant smile never left his face. Fitzhugh Gray strode up, adding his pudgy but powerful presence to the group. He handed each man a Coke, already opened, and slipped a church key onto the cap of the one in his own massive paw.

In a service where everyone had multiple "names"—real name, nickname, and sometimes multiple titles—Gray had the most. He was the chief boatswain's mate, and the highest-ranking NCO on the ship. Although he was technically subordinate to the most junior officers, only the captain and the exec would have dreamed of giving him an order. Time in grade, as well as personality, made him the "senior" chief aboard, and he was usually referred to as just "the Chief" by the crew. The other chiefs and officers often used the outdated but still honorific "the Bosun." Only the captain or the exec ever used the respectful diminutive "Boats."

"Going to be another hot one," Gray said, wiping his forehead with his sleeve. "Course, if the goddamn Nips get us, I guess we'll be swimmin'. Them that can swim. I think I'd rather be sweating than swimmin'. I guess you fighter jocks don't give as much thought to swimmin' as destroyermen do." It was just a friendly jibe, but Kaufman was still annoyed by Gray's earlier threat, and what he perceived as the captain's humiliating treatment of him.

"What's that supposed to mean?" he demanded hotly. Gray looked at Ellis and rolled his eyes. At that moment, Lieutenant Benjamin Mallory joined them. He was already drinking a Coke and he held it up.

"How about this, Captain?" he said. "These destroyer pukes have a Coke machine! Far as I can tell, it's the only thing that works."

Rebuffed by Kaufman, Gray began to bristle. Ellis recognized the lieutenant's friendly banter, however, and turned to him. "That's right, boy," he said with a grin, "and if you airedales had done your job in the Philippines, we'd still be sitting fat and happy going up and down with the tide in Cavite. Nothing to worry about but keeping the Coke machine stocked while the yard-apes worked on these worn-out boilers." He stomped his foot on the deck for emphasis, indicating the forward fireroom below.

Mallory didn't laugh. "I'm afraid you got me. I wasn't there, of course, but I heard the fellows didn't do so good." Ellis saw Gray take a breath and prepare his tirade about the ineffectiveness of the Air Corps, a topic much discussed. The Japanese air cover and the American lack thereof had been an extremely sore subject since the war began. Ignored now, and glad to be, Kaufman strode away. Mallory started to follow, but Ellis stopped him.

"By the way, Captain Kaufman asked if we could use a hand, and the captain said if you could keep the ammunition flowing to the machine guns it would help."

Mallory nodded thoughtfully. "Sure thing. Not much else we'd be good for on a ship. Show me where you keep the bullets and I'll haul as many as you need." He looked wryly at Ellis and gestured over his shoulder with his chin. "He didn't like that much, did he?"

Ellis smiled and shook his head. "No, son. I think he expected us to put him in charge."

The corner of Mallory's mouth quirked upward. "Kaufman's really not such a bad guy, but I guess he is sort of—" He caught himself and shrugged sheepishly. "I'll do anything I can to help."

Ellis slapped him on the back, and the powerful blow nearly knocked Mallory into the Chief. "I know you will. Boats, have somebody show this man where we keep the bullets. I better get back where I belong."

Nurse Lieutenant Sandra Tucker pushed aside the pea green curtain and led her entourage into the wardroom. She was petite, measuring only five foot three, and her long, sandy-brown hair was coiled tightly about her head. When it came down, it framed a face that may not have been classically beautiful, but was striking in a pretty, "girl next door" sort of way. Her large green eyes projected an impression of naive vulnerability, but anyone making that assumption would have been mistaken. At twenty-seven, she'd been a Navy nurse since '35, and in that time she'd encountered every excuse, pickup line, real and imagined ailment, injury, and malingerer's complaint possible in a bored but active peacetime Navy. She was smart, confident, and even tended toward an arrogant streak when in her realm of expertise. Her mild conceit was understandable, since she was an outstanding nurse and often made a better doctor than the doctors did. She'd assisted in a variety of surgical procedures and performed everything from appendectomies to amputations by herself, since many of her postings had been in remote areas where emergencies were handled on-site. When war loomed, she and her companions volunteered for the Philippines. She had friends there,

and that was where she figured nurses would be needed.
She knew she was good at her job and genuinely wanted to
be where she could make the greatest contribution. That
was why she'd become a nurse in the first place. Right now,
although she was the highest-ranking officer in the wardroom, it became quickly obvious that she wasn't in charge.

The ship's surgeon, "Doc" Stevens, was a tall, cadaverous
man in his mid-forties. He and Pharmacist's Mate 3rd Class
Jamie Miller were sitting at the green-topped wardroom
table with the Marine sergeant, Pete Alden, playing dominoes when Sandra entered with the five other nurses.

The wardroom was the officers' dining room, but it also
served as a surgery when the ship went into battle. The long
dining surface became an operating table, and a large light
hung above it by a fixture that could be lowered near the
patient. Except for the dominoes, all superfluous articles
had been stowed, and various gleaming surgical instruments lay neatly arranged and ready at hand.

The pharmacist's mate looked to be just a boy, like most
of the crewmen Sandra had seen, but the Marine was a
large, well-muscled, and deeply tanned thirtysomething.
He regarded the nurses with a frankly appraising eye. The
imposing surgeon grimly played a domino and glanced at
them as the nurses crowded through the opening.

"I sort of expected to see you ... ladies here." His Mas-
sachusetts accent was strong and nasal. "I bet you nurses
want to be nurses, right?" He shifted in his chair and
rubbed his chin. "I never had a nurse before. Not counting Jamie here, of course. Tell me, Sergeant," he said, addressing the Marine, "have you ever had a nurse?" Alden
looked at him, astonished. The nurses were, after all, officers. Stevens shook his head. "Never mind, Sergeant. Of
course you have. You're a wounded hero, after all. I'm sure
you had nurses all over you." Sandra's face clouded and
she began to snap a reprimand. Doc Stevens's look momentarily silenced her protest. "I know you're officers and
I'm just a lowly Warrant. I don't give a damn. I know about
you nurses; wouldn't even give me the time of day if I came
squirming into your nice, clean, modern hospital. Well, this
is *my* hospital! If you want to stay here and help, that's fine.
There'll probably be plenty to do. But if you want to give

orders or get in the way, you can turn around, climb that ladder and go play dollies under the depth charges because I don't need you." He stopped long enough to smile at their expressions. "I've got Jamie. He makes a pretty good nurse, even if he looks dreadful in a dress."

Sandra's eyes narrowed, and for an instant she hesitated. She'd faced this kind of attitude all her life and it was particularly pervasive in the military. Her father had perhaps been the worst, refusing to accept that she might do something with her life other than wait for "the right guy" to come along. His restrictions and expectations might have been couched more gently than Stevens's, but they were no less corrosive and condescending. And wrong. She'd proven that. She straightened her back and forced a smile.

"Surgeon's Mate Stevens, is it not?" she asked, and her voice held an icy calm. Stevens arched an eyebrow, but jerked an aggressive nod.

"Your captain asked that we report to you and that's what we've done. I know this is your 'hospital' and I'm prepared to defer to you." Her voice took on a dangerous edge. "But since you insist on wallowing in your 'lowly Warrant' status I'll remind you I'm a LIEUTENANT in the United States Navy. My ensigns might not pull rank on you, but I SURE AS HELL WILL! You're clearly not a gentleman, so I won't appeal to you as one, but as a superior officer I insist you get up off your skinny ass and show the respect due my rank or by God, I'll have you up on charges for insubordination!"

Her voice had risen as she spoke, until her final exclamation was uttered as a roar that her small form seemed incapable of producing. Jamie Miller's chair hit the deck as he rocketed to attention. Even the wounded Marine struggled to his feet, his face a study of embarrassment mingled with respect. Doc Stevens remained seated a few moments more, but finally he stood also, an expression of mocking insolence on his face. He threw an exaggerated salute.

"Your orders, ma'am?" The question dripped sarcasm, but Sandra smiled in anticipation of his reaction. She looked at Jamie. "You!"

"Pharmacist's Mate Miller, ma'am."

"Mr. Miller, stow those dominoes and disinfect that table this instant. We could have casualties at any moment." She looked at the blood-soaked bandage the Marine wore. "Are you even fit for duty?"

"Yes, ma'am."

"Hmm. I doubt it, but we'll see. We'll have a look at that leg presently, circumstances permitting."

Stevens cleared his throat. "And what about me?" he demanded, surly. Sandra was sorely tempted to upbraid him again, but instead she smiled sweetly and indicated the rest of the nurses.

"You, MISTER Stevens . . . will tell us what you want us to do next. This is your 'hospital,' after all."

Matt had already forgotten his encounter with Captain Kaufman. He had far more important concerns. A Morse-lamp message from Captain Gordon was composed of only three words: "Enemy in sight." *Exeter*'s lookouts had a higher vantage point than Rodriguez, but just a few moments later Garrett held his earpiece tight against his head and looked up.

"Sir! Rodriguez sees them too. Still dead astern, but coming up fast. They must be making thirty-five knots!" He sounded incredulous. Matt nodded. Even without *Exeter* slowing them down, *Walker* couldn't outrun them. Not anymore.

"Very well, Mr. Garrett. Return to your station. Mr. Rogers?" he said to the first officer. "Relieve Rodriguez in the crow's nest, if you please. If we can see them, they can hit us. Lieutenant Flowers"—he addressed the navigating officer—"take the conn."

Flowers spoke to the man holding the brightly polished wheel. "I relieve you, sir."

The seaman relinquished his post. "Mr. Flowers has the conn," he responded and looked around, at a loss. Matt motioned for him to put on a headset.

"Sound general quarters again. We've been at battle stations all morning, but somebody might be fooling around in the head."

The rhythmic, ill-sounding *gong, gong, gong* of the general alarm reverberated throughout the ship.

*   *   *

In the aft fireroom, Brad "Spanky" McFarlane, the engineering officer, wiped sweat from his narrow face and shook it off his hand to join the black, slimy slurry on the deck plates. In the space containing the number three and four boilers, it was at least 130 degrees. He barely heard the sound of the alarm over the thundering blower and the roar of the burners as atomized fuel oil was consumed at a prodigious rate.

"Gotta get back to the forward engine room. That's the second time they've sounded GQ. Maybe they mean it this time."

Firemen Isak Reuben on the blower control and Gilbert Yager on the burner nodded, but paid him no further attention. They were both entirely focused on their tasks. Their two jobs, and that of the water tender, required careful concentration. Too much fuel and not enough air, and black smoke billowed from the stacks, earning an instant reprimand from the captain and the scorn of their fellow "snipes." Not enough feed water in the lines, and white steam rose overhead. Too much water, not enough air and fuel, and water instead of steam sprayed into the turbines. That could damage the delicate blades. Isak and Gilbert were magicians at their jobs and the very best he had, but McFarlane didn't know what to think of them otherwise. They were inseparable, but rarely talked to anyone else. They were both wiry, intense little men, and neither seemed to mind the hellish temperatures in which they worked. Even off duty, they lingered in the vicinity of their posts—which annoyed the men on watch. They never caused any trouble, but they didn't make friends and they didn't play on the ship's baseball team. They just kept to themselves. The other snipes called them the White Mice, or just the Mice, because of their similar, almost rodent-like expressions and because they never went above deck if they could help it. Therefore, their otherwise perpetually sooty skins had an unhealthy pallor. The only explanation McFarlane ever got was that if they spent too much time in the "cool" air on deck, they'd lose their tolerance for the temperatures in the fireroom. McFarlane shrugged and stepped to the air lock. They were squirrels, sure enough, but they were his squirrels.

He cycled through the air lock into the forward engine room. He was shaped much like the Mice, and he barely had to squat to step through. The large compartment was filled by the big turbines and a maze of steam lines and conduits, but he moved among them with practiced ease to the enclosed intercom by the main throttle control. "Throttle manned and ready," he said into the mouthpiece. The talker on the bridge acknowledged, and Spanky looked at the other throttlemen. They looked back with almost pathetically hopeful expressions. They were all so young, and the faith they placed in him and their "new" captain made him feel uncomfortable.

He wasn't much of a poker player. He disliked games of chance. He felt at ease only when he was totally in control of everything it was his business to control. Right now his business was the engines, and cantankerous as they were, he could handle that. He couldn't influence the outcome of anything beyond the confines of his engine room, and in a way he was glad. Deep inside, however, was a feeling like the one he hated whenever he did play poker: knowing that his destiny, or at least a portion of his pay, was at the mercy of the cardboard rectangle held carelessly in the dealer's hand and knowing that luck alone would dictate how it affected him. He understood the sense of frustrated helplessness plaguing the young sailors nearby. It gnawed him too. But he couldn't let it show—just as the captain couldn't. All he could do was hope for an ace. Somehow, they'd drawn the right cards so far, in spite of their deficiencies, but the Japanese kept stacking the deck. He hoped Captain Reddy had some card tricks of his own, because that was what they'd need to survive this call.

Matt squinted ahead against the sun. It no longer streamed directly through the windows, but it was bright enough to make everything washed-out and fuzzy. Suddenly, exactly where he looked, two closely spaced geysers of spume erupted directly in their path, two hundred yards ahead. This was followed by the superfluous report of his talker that the enemy had opened fire. The columns of water thrown up by the eight-inch shells were at least as tall as the mast. Matt glanced at his watch and took note of the time.

He was glad to see that his hand was steady. His carefully hidden anxiety of a few moments before had subsided now that the first shots had been fired. Large, grayish-brown clouds enveloped *Exeter* as her own eight-inch guns replied to the Japanese salvo. The overpressure of the report shook the pilothouse windows. The waiting was over, and Matt felt a surge of exhilaration edge out the anticipation even further. It was much like the baseball games of his youth, he reflected. He sometimes got so keyed up for a game that he felt physically sick. He didn't know why, but he suspected he was afraid he would screw up somehow. He played third base, and in his mind's eye he always saw himself missing the critical catch and thus allowing the other team to score the game-winning point. The idea of such humiliation was worse than enduring the real thing, and always, as soon as the first pitch was thrown, his nervousness was forgotten. He supposed this wasn't a dissimilar context, although if he screwed up here much more than a game was at stake.

Exeter's salvos came faster than Matt would have expected, and he noticed with a sense of admiration and vicarious pride that Captain Gordon had replaced *Exeter*'s naval jack with an enormous battle flag, much like the little destroyer *Electra* had done in the Battle of the Java Sea when she charged the enemy fleet all alone. That action saved the crippled *Exeter* from destruction by forcing the enemy to maneuver to avoid *Electra*'s torpedoes, but the resulting fusillade of enemy shells obliterated the gallant destroyer. It was one of the bravest things Matt had ever seen, and he'd seen a lot of courage in the last few months. Unfortunately, he thought bitterly, most had been futile.

The enemy shells became more concentrated, and the great plumes erupted continuously around the veteran cruiser. The impacts seemed to have increased in number as well.

"Sir, *Exeter* has sent a radio message. I guess they don't think we'll see their Morse lamp through the splashes." It was Petty Officer 1st Class Steve "Sparks" Riggs, the comm officer, who had scampered down from the fire-control platform above.

"What does she say?" asked Matt impatiently.

"Two more Jap ships, heavy cruisers at least, and three

destroyers bearing two one five! The heavies have opened fire. *Exeter* says her fire control is out—no hits yet, it just quit. They've gone to local control of the main battery." Matt's sense of exhilaration turned to dread. Without her fire-control equipment, *Exeter* was nearly as helpless as her escorts. "Captain Gordon wants us to take formation with the other destroyers astern and make smoke."

Matt nodded. "Acknowledge. Confirm *Pope* and *Mahan* received as well. Make the adjustment, Mr. Flowers," he said, addressing the helmsman. "I'm going topside for a look. You have the deck."

"I have the deck, aye, sir."

Matt turned and climbed briskly up the ladder to the platform above. Now, except for the mast and the four slender funnels beyond it directly astern, he had a full 360-degree view of the panoramic drama of which *Walker* was, so far, such an insignificant part. Garrett stepped from the range-finder platform.

"More Japs, sir! They just popped out from behind that squall. Do you see? There!" He raised his long arm and pointed far astern, off the port quarter. "There's more and more rain squalls," he added hopefully. The deck tilted as *Walker* heeled into a sharp turn to starboard. The blowers lost their intensity briefly, as Flowers reduced speed to join *Walker*'s partners forming in *Exeter*'s wake. Off to the west-northwest, a number of indistinct ships were visible to the naked eye, not far from the coast of Borneo. That landmass appeared as a hazy smear, but it was actually closer than it seemed. The shoreline was obscured by the same squall that had concealed the Japanese ships.

"I see them, Mr. Garrett," he said in what he hoped was a confident tone, but he felt like he'd pronounced their death sentence. There were now two distinct battle groups in pursuit and far above in those loitering planes he knew even more forces were being called. It would probably not be long before attack aircraft arrived as well. He leaned over the speaking tube. "Let's make a little smoke, Mr. Flowers."

Immediately, his orders were relayed to the torpedomen, who sprang to activate the smoke generators. At the same time, in the boiler rooms, the burner batters exchanged the sprayer plates to increase the flow of oil through the burners. Slowly at first, but building rapidly, a huge column of sooty black smoke gushed from the funnels and piled into the clear morning sky. It was joined by the smoke of the other three destroyers, rapidly creating an opaque wall between them and the enemy. The incoming fire began to slacken, and Matt stared aft at the huge cloud they were creating. It seemed to blot out the entire western horizon. Lieutenant Garrett glanced at him when he chuckled quietly. "I always get a hoot out of doing that."

They continued east-southeast under a black pall. The enemy barrage was less accurate, but it didn't stop. The cruisers were in direct radio contact with the spotting planes overhead, correcting their fire. The Allied squadron tried to zigzag subtly, to increase the correction error, but they couldn't deviate much from a straight heading because the enemy was already faster and zigzagging slowed them down. All they could hope for was a squall of their own to hide in, to stretch the chase until dark. Then they might change course unnoticed and lose their pursuers. Matt had little hope of that. It was now only 1100. Whatever fate awaited them, it would certainly unfold before the sun went down.

Lieutenant Rogers's excited voice screamed from Garrett's headphones. "Surface target! Starboard quarter! Four Nip destroyers out of the smoke. God, they're fast!" The ordnance strikers on the platform swung the gun director.

"Gun crews, load!" Garrett shouted into his mouthpiece.

"Fire on the nearest target as soon as you're ready, Mr. Garrett," Matt said, and stepped back to the speaking tube. He looked to see how the other destroyers, in line abreast, were maneuvering. "Conn, starboard ten degrees."

At this speed, *Walker*'s range finder was useless because of vibration, but Garrett estimated the range to target. "Fire up-ladder. Range, nine five-double-oh!" The shouted commands came rapidly and Matt heard the tinny replies of the gun crews leak from Garrett's earphones. He couldn't help but feel a surge of pride in his crew as they went about their duties with calm, well-drilled precision. After the range, bearing, and apparent speed of the target were fed into it, the mechanical fire-control computer reached a solution.

"Surface action starboard. Match pointers!" Garrett instructed the three crews whose weapons would bear. He listened as they reported their readiness and looked at Matt. "The guns are ready, Captain."

"Commence firing."

"Three rounds, salvo fire. Commence firing!" He leaned forward and stabbed the salvo buzzer button. The nerve-racking, jangling *raaaa* sound was almost instantly overwhelmed by the simultaneous concussion of three 4-inch guns. Even before the first rounds fell, the buzzer sounded again and the second salvo was on the way. Splashes kicked up beyond and astern of the closest enemy destroyer, but seconds later more splashes rose among the ships when their friends opened fire as well. The third salvo seemed to have the range, but it was still behind the enemy.

"They're even faster than I thought! I guess I didn't lead them enough," Garrett said apologetically. He fed corrections into the computer. Somebody got a lucky hit with the first salvo, and the third Japanese destroyer belched black smoke from her curiously raked 'stack and slowed out of line. Men cheered and even Matt felt like pumping his fist. It looked like the hit came from *Pope* or *Encounter*. The remaining enemy ships continued the charge. They opened fire from the twin mounts on their foredecks, all three shooting only at the damaged British cruiser.

"They're making for *Exeter*. Get on them, Mr. Garrett!" To Matt, the enemy strategy was clear. They were trying to get in a few licks on the primary target and slow her down still more. Her escorts would then be forced to leave her or stand and fight. Either way, the result would be the same. Another salvo slammed out from *Walker,* and this one looked on target, but there were no explosions. Either they were still shooting long, or the shells were passing through the thin-skinned Japanese ships without detonating.

"That's it!" shouted Garrett into his comm. "No change! No change! Rapid fire! Let her have it!" The geysers erupting around the advancing enemy now resembled those that had bracketed *Exeter* a short time before, if not in size, then surely in volume. The Japanese couldn't know that *Exeter*'s fire control was out, and Matt had to admire the courage of their approach. They began to angle for *Exeter*'s starboard side. Knowing their gunnery was in capable hands, Matt realized his place was in the pilothouse. Without a word of distraction for Garrett, he dropped to the quarterdeck below.

"Captain on the bridge!" somebody shouted.

"As you were. I have the deck, Mr. Flowers. You keep the conn."

"Aye, aye, sir. You have the deck. I have the conn."

"Skipper." PO Riggs spoke up. "Captain Blinn on *Pope* sends to execute a starboard turn in column and prepare to fire torpedoes." Blinn was senior to both Matt and Captain Atkinson on *Mahan* and had authority over the three American destroyers.

"Very well, acknowledge. Mr. Flowers, bring us in behind *Mahan* when she makes her turn."

Ensign Bernard Sandison, the torpedo officer, stood on the starboard bridgewing and adjusted his headset while an ordnance striker fiddled with the connection linking the antiquated torpedo director to the two mounts on the starboard side. As the four destroyers accelerated to block the enemy thrust, his eyes burned when they turned into their own smoke screen.

"Sir," commented Flowers, "*Exeter*'s firing torpedoes." He pointed at the cruiser, now off their port bow. Puffs of smoke drifted aft from her amidships tubes, but the splashes when the weapons hit the water couldn't be distinguished from those of enemy shells. Then, as they looked on, there was a small reddish flash between *Exeter*'s two funnels. A column of black smoke rocketed skyward and a cloud of escaping steam enshrouded her amidships. Except for the racket of the blowers and the wind, there was stunned silence in *Walker*'s pilothouse, broken only by someone's soft, pleading murmur.

"No, oh, no . . . no."

Matt didn't know who said it. It might have been he. Somebody cursed. *Exeter*'s speed dropped to nearly nothing, as if she'd slammed into a wall. Shells rained down and more began to hit as she wallowed on helplessly at barely four knots. The Allied destroyers executed another turn, in column, and ran up *Exeter*'s starboard side, placing themselves between the doomed cruiser and the oncoming enemy ships. Through the thinning haze of the smoke screen, the Japanese cruisers were visible, much closer than before. At the head of the line, smoke and steam spewed from *Encounter* as her torpedoes leaped into the sea. The two American destroyers ahead followed suit.

"Engage as they bear with the starboard tubes, Mr. Sandison."

"Aye, aye, sir!" he replied, and cried into his microphone: "Torpedo action starboard! In salvo! Fire one, fire three, fire five! Fire seven, fire nine, fire eleven!"

Matt peered around the chart house. The amidships deckhouse was in the way, but he saw the cutoff-looking muzzles of the pair of starboard triple launchers angled out thirty degrees from the side of the ship. As he watched, the first three 21-inch-diameter, 2,215-pound MK-15 torpedoes thumped out, one after another, the sun shining on their burnished metal bodies as they plunged into the sea with enormous concave splashes. They disappeared, but a moment later dense trails of effervescent bubbles rose to the surface in their wakes. There were only three, however.

Sandison looked at his captain with an apologetic, frustrated expression. "Sir, there's a casualty on the number-three mount. They don't know what it is yet, but the torpedoes are secure."

Matt swallowed a curse. It probably wasn't anybody's fault, just worn-out equipment. "Very well, Bernie. Let me know what you find out. Light a fire under it, though. I want those torpedoes!"

"Captain!" cried the talker. "Lookout reports torpedoes in the water!"

Matt looked at him blankly for a second. Of course there were— Then realization struck. He ran to the bridgewing and shouldered Sandison aside.

"JAP torpedoes!" he yelled over his shoulder. "Right full rudder!" *Walker* heeled sharply. "Signal to all ships—torpedoes inbound! Lots of torpedoes! Am evading!" During his brief glance, he saw over a dozen wakes. He looked back at the incoming streams of bubbles, which contrasted sharply with the dark, deep water. They should be relatively easy to avoid in daylight, but there were so many. They might blunder into one while maneuvering to miss another. *Walker* was only thirty feet wide, and Matt instinctively turned directly toward the oncoming weapons to present the smallest possible target. The rest of the column of destroyers disintegrated into chaos as they maneuvered independently as well.

"Lord, looks like the Nips just flushed a covey of quail," said Flowers as dryly as he could manage.

"Rudder amidships!" With gratifying alacrity, *Walker* steadied, and the cant to the deck disappeared. *She may be old,* Matt thought with an unusual sense of proprietary satisfaction, *but she still handles like a rumrunner.* Nimbleness wasn't a trait usually associated with four-stackers, but Chief Gray had told him an extra three feet of depth had been added to her rudder as an experiment. It worked, but there were objections to the added draft and, as far as Gray knew, only a couple of her sisters were ever altered.

"Here they come!" someone yelled. Almost everyone in the pilothouse but the helmsman rushed to the bridge-wings and looked anxiously at the water as a pair of torpedoes raced by on either side of *Walker*'s frail hull. The one to starboard passed less than a dozen yards away. A young seaman's apprentice named Fred Reynolds, a boy who looked all of thirteen, grinned at Matt with a pallid expression and then vomited over the rail. The malicious wind made sure that most of the spew wound up in his close-cropped hair. The salvo buzzer rang again, and the number one gun fired alone. The report stirred the bridge crew from the momentary relief of having dodged the torpedoes, reminding them that they were steaming directly toward the enemy.

"Where the hell do you think you are? Watching toy boats in a duck pond?" bellowed Chief Gray as he ascended the ladder. He gave Reynolds a malevolent glare and pantomimed dumping a water bucket on the deck. The boy wiped his mouth and staggered back to his station. The rest of the bridge crew followed suit. Matt winced inwardly. He'd been as guilty as the others, but Gray just winked at him and sighed theatrically when no one was looking. Matt nodded grimly and turned.

"Left full rudder! Helm, tack us back onto the tail of the column as it re-forms!"

There was a loud *clang* above their heads, and Lieutenant Rogers's voice blared from the crow's nest speaking tube. "JESUS CHRIST! A shell just took a notch out of the mast about two feet under me!"

The salvo buzzer rang and three guns fired again. Matt looked down at number one and was surprised to see a young man in Army khakis carrying four-inch shells from the wardroom below to replenish the ready-lockers.

"That's Mallory," said the Chief, reading his mind. "He came aboard with that other officer. *He* seems a decent sort." Matt nodded his understanding and noted Gray's obvious opinion of Captain Kaufman.

The column shook itself out. But their relief over evading the torpedoes was shattered when they were brutally reminded of the one member of their group that couldn't evade anything. A towering column of water spouted directly under *Exeter*'s aft funnel on her starboard side. She heeled hard to port and then rolled back into a pronounced starboard list. A heavy secondary explosion sent debris and smoke high in the air.

The salvo buzzer rang. *Wham!*

They couldn't worry about *Exeter* now. Waterspouts were rising around *Walker* again, and there was another loud noise somewhere aft.

"Damage report!"

Ellis's voice came over the intercom. "Nothing serious, Skipper. A new hole in the aft funnel. The shell didn't explode. It must've been armor-piercing—and it's not as if we have any armor."

Raaaaa! Wham! Cheers erupted from fire control when a big explosion rocked a Japanese destroyer. It veered hard out of formation, smoke obscuring the bridge. The other two enemy destroyers finally broke off their attack and retreated behind a smoke screen of their own, toward the protection of the remorselessly approaching cruisers.

"Skipper." The grim voice was Riggs. "Signal from *Exeter* to all ships. Captain Gordon says thanks for the help, but he'll take it from here." Matt strode to the port bridgewing and stared at the once-handsome ship that had seen so much action in this war before the United States was even involved. She'd hounded the *Graf Spee* to her doom, but past glory meant nothing now. Lifeboats were in the water and men were going over the side. He took a deep breath.

"Acknowledge. And send, 'Good luck, *Exeter*. God bless.'"

Shells still pummeled the helpless cruiser as *Walker*, last in line, sped impotently by. Matt slapped the rail in frustration. "God help them," he muttered. *God help us*, he added to himself. Another huge explosion convulsed *Exeter*, and she rapidly rolled over onto the boats and men in the water. He could see the red paint of her bottom come up on the far side as her superstructure disappeared into the sea. And still the shells fell. The number one gun was silent now, no longer able to bear on their pursuers, and he saw the grim expressions of its crew as they watched *Exeter* go down.

"Skipper . . ." It was Riggs. "Signal from *Pope*. She says to resume line abreast and continue making smoke. She also wants to know if we can increase speed."

"Acknowledge, and tell her we'll try."

The next hours were like a feverish nightmare. They gained some distance on the cruisers, but they never moved completely out of range. Periodic savage salvos churned the sea around them, and all the destroyers were damaged, mostly by near misses. An eight-inch shell detonating close aboard made a hell of a concussion and *Walker*'s riveted seams leaked in a dozen places. More enemy aircraft arrived, and they finally cut the smoke, figuring it just made them easier to spot from the air. Only fighters had appeared so far, but they were carrier planes and they strafed the lonely ships repeatedly. They soon decided to wait for the bombers and cruisers to finish the job after one of their number fell to the destroyers' machine guns. It narrowly missed *Mahan* as it plunged into the sea.

A few tantalizing squalls marched across the horizon, but it seemed they could never reach them. Matt vigorously rubbed his eyes and looked at his exhausted bridge crew and their haunted expressions. The trauma of watching *Exeter*'s destruction—the most powerful member of their group—had etched itself on their faces, and he knew they believed it was only a matter of time before they all met a similar fate. One by one.

Encounter's turn came next, and with appalling suddenness. Another ranging salvo of eight-inch shells screeched in, the sun glinting off the projectiles in flight. Geysers of spume marched across the sea—and across the British destroyer. In the blink of an eye, for all intents and purposes, she was gone. When the spray cleared, all that remained was twisted wreckage, already awash, and a few men scurrying about on the buckled deck, throwing anything that would float into the sea. The three tired greyhounds raced on. There was nothing they could do. Matt knew it on a rational level, but deep down he felt an overwhelming sense of shame. His jaw muscles tensed, and he ground his teeth as he forced himself to watch what was left of *Encounter* slip farther and farther astern. Chief Gray stood beside him, watching too.

"I'm getting sick of leaving people behind," he growled.

Matt nodded. "It could just as easily have been us. And we wouldn't want them hanging around to get slaughtered picking us up." The Bosun shook his head, but Matt would have sworn there was a damp sheen in his eyes.

"With your permission, sir, I'll see if Spanky and his snipes need a hand with anything, like patching holes, or keeping the screws from falling off." Matt felt the corners of his mouth twitch upward by themselves. Gray must really be frustrated if he was willing to descend below his holy deck and help engineering do anything. He shrugged at his captain's look. "Hell, Skipper, if they sink the bottom half of the old girl, the top half goes too."

"That's true, Boats, but Spanky's keeping up with the problems below for now, and I'd rather have you up here to direct damage control for the deck divisions if need be."

"Yes, sir."

Rogers's voice piped down from above. He was still in the crow's nest, where he'd been almost all day. "Skipper, there's a promising cloud off the starboard bow. Looks like it's working up to rain pretty good." Matt raised his binoculars.

"Sir, signal from *Pope*," supplied Riggs. "Make for the squall."

"Acknowledge. Helm, right ten."

The cloud hung before them, growing darker by the moment. A new flurry of enemy shells kicked up spray as their pursuers noticed their course change.

"Jap planes! Bombers! Six o'clock high!" came the shout from the crow's nest. "Three pairs of 'em! I thought they were those observation planes, but they're comin' right in!"

Almost immediately, there came the *thump thump thump* of the little three-inch gun on the stern, throwing up shells in the path of the oncoming planes. Matt craned his neck upward and saw them, dark specks growing larger fast. Two angled for *Walker* through the small black puffs of smoke. He looked toward the cloud and saw it had started to rain. Harder and harder it fell, only a couple of miles away. They'd never make it. He looked at the planes, trying to judge their angle of attack and praying he could predict their release point. "Steady as you go, helm!" he ordered tersely. "Make them think we're easy." He waited. He couldn't see the furtive glances exchanged around him. *Wait. Wait! NOW!*

"Left full rudder! All ahead flank!"

Walker heeled so sharply it was difficult to stand, and she surged forward with an audible groan. Two small objects detached themselves from the pair of descending planes. They grew rapidly larger until it seemed they'd fall right on the ship. Two thunderous explosions ripped the sea less than a hundred yards off the starboard beam and fragments spanged against *Walker*'s side. The heavy bellow of the .50-cals and the lighter clatter of the .30s sent tracers chasing the fat-bodied dive bombers as they pulled out and thundered away. Their ungainly fixed landing gear seemed only inches above the water. Glaring red circles clearly contrasted with the white-painted wings.

"Damage report!"

The machine guns stuttered to a stop as the planes flew out of range.

"Just some scratches in the boot topping."

"How about the other ships?" Matt asked, looking for himself. They seemed okay as each emerged from the spray of bomb splashes.

The squall was closer. Still at flank speed, *Walker* strained with every aged fiber to reach the camouflaging shroud of the torrent ahead. To starboard, *Mahan* labored to keep up. Farther away, her interval doubled since the loss of *Encounter*, *Pope* blurred as she dove into the opaque wall of rain.

The bombers were re-forming and Matt urged his ship forward as she stretched her tired legs. Suddenly the bow disappeared as it parted the edge of the storm, and within seconds the windows were blanked out and a heavy drumming sound came from the deck above. Water coursed onto the open quarterdeck behind them, and small smiles of relief formed on several faces.

"Secure from flank, all ahead two-thirds. Come left ten degrees. The Japs can't see us, but neither can our sisters. Let's put some space between us."

"Jesus," muttered Sandison, and dabbed sweat from his face with his sleeve.

Lieutenant Garrett, along with the rest of the fire-control team, was soaked to the bone and water poured off his helmet, obscuring his view. No one had any idea where their consorts were. They'd altered course several times to accomplish the dual necessity of staying within the squall and continuing in a general direction away from the enemy. Garrett and his division did their best, straining their eyes to spot another ship or warn about upcoming "light" spots, but realistically they would probably run into one of their sisters before they saw her in time to turn. It was growing lighter ahead, however, and there were no "dark" areas to advise the bridge to steer for. He huddled over the speaking tube when he raised the cover to prevent too much water from pouring in.

"Bridge. We're breaking out of the squall."

With almost the same suddenness that they'd entered it, they drove out of the squall and into the afternoon sunshine. They all blinked their eyes against the glare, and the water on the decks and in their clothes began to steam. Then, less than five hundred yards to port, *Mahan* emerged and seemed to shake herself off like a wet dog as she increased speed. Men immediately scanned for enemies.

"Oh, my God, Skipper! Look!" shouted Sandison. The Bosun swore and Matt shouldered in beside him on the starboard bridgewing. He felt like his heart had stopped. There, about four miles off the starboard beam, *Pope* was enduring her final agony. She wallowed helplessly, low by the stern, while aircraft swirled like vultures in the sky above. Massive waterspouts rose around her as the spotting planes summoned the cruiser's fire upon their carrion.

"Skipper! Can't we . . . I mean, is there . . . ?" Young Reynolds clamped his mouth shut, realizing the pointlessness of his appeal. Then he looked at his captain's face and was shocked by the twisted, desperate rage upon it. With an audible animal growl, Captain Reddy spun back into the pilothouse. Ahead, about seven miles away, another squall brewed. It was huge, and darker than the last one, almost green, and it blotted out much of the horizon. For some reason, it seemed to radiate an aura of threat nearly as intense as the force that pursued them so relentlessly.

"Make for that squall!" ordered Matt in a tone none of the men had ever heard him use. It was the voice of command, but with an inflection of perfect hatred. "Signal *Mahan*. We'll keep this interval in case we have to maneuver. Helm, ahead flank!"

Another squall, lighter, was a little to the left of the one they were heading for. It was dissipating rapidly, though, as if the first was somehow draining it, sucking its very force. As it diminished, two dark forms took shape.

"Holy Mary," muttered Gray, crossing himself unconsciously.

Before them, racing to prevent their escape into the looming rainstorm, were yet another destroyer and a massive capital ship. There was a collective gasp.

After a moment spent studying the apparition through his binoculars, Matt spoke. "That, gentlemen, is *Amagi*." His voice was harsh but matter-of-fact. "She's a battle cruiser. Not quite a battleship, but way heavier than a cruiser. I know it's her"—he smiled ironically, but his expression was hard—"because she's the only one they have left. Built in the twenties, so she's almost as old as we are"—he snorted— "but they've spent money on her since. Major rebuild a few years ago. Anyway, I remember her because I was always impressed by how fast the Japs could make so much metal move." He sighed. "I guess it's fitting, after everything else, she should show up here. They *really* don't want us to get away."

He turned and spoke to Riggs in a voice that was white-hot steel. "Signal *Mahan* to prepare for a torpedo attack with port tubes. Mr. Sandison, speak to your division." He crossed his arms over his chest and his hands clenched into fists. "We can't go around her and we can't turn back. That leaves only one choice."

Gray nodded with grim acceptance.

"Yes, sir, we'll have to go right through the son of a bitch."

Blowers roaring, haggard destroyermen performing their duties in an exhausted fugue, the two battered, venerable old ladies slightly altered course and together began their final charge. Matt noticed that even Captain Kaufman was on the foredeck now, hauling shells. Lieutenant Mallory and two ratings scurried up the ladder behind, each festooned with belts of .30-cal. It was clear to everyone that getting past the two ships ahead and disappearing into the strange, ominous squall was their only hope. It was equally clear that it was impossible.

Ahead waited *Amagi*: 46,000 tons of cemented armor plate. As they watched, she began a leisurely turn to present her full broadside of ten 10-inch guns. Her secondary battery of 4.7-inch and 5.5-inch guns was entirely superfluous. The sleek new destroyer at her side was all but forgotten despite her guns and deadly "Long Lance" torpedoes. The additional threat she represented was almost laughably insignificant under the circumstances. She could have taken them by herself.

The shriek and splash of incoming shells proved the cruisers behind hadn't forgotten them either, and the growing drone of propellers indicated the bombers had seen them too.

"Looks like every Jap in the Java Sea's in a race to sink us," mumbled Gray.

Five miles away, *Amagi* opened fire. She pulsed with flame from one end to the other as she salvoed her big guns. Seconds later, the rattling roar of ten-inch shells thundered toward them. They sounded deeper than the eights, Matt reflected absently. Then he stepped into hell.

*   *   *

The first salvo fell short, but it threw up a wall of spray that drenched Greg Garrett and his team and probably soaked Lieutenant Rogers way up in the crow's nest. Rogers had fallen silent, and Garrett tried to adjust the fire of the number one and three guns, but he couldn't bloody *see*. *Walker* pierced the spume raised by *Amagi*'s main guns, but the splashes from the secondaries and the cruisers behind were uninterrupted. He thought of all the times he'd shot turtles in the stock tank behind his grandmother's house— now he knew how they must have felt. There was a loud *bang* behind him and he twisted to see chaos on the amidships deckhouse.

A roar overhead made him turn to see a dive bomber pull up and blow by, its wingtip a dozen yards from the mast. An enormous explosion convulsed the sea to port and bomb fragments whined off the rail and the range finder. Tracers rose to meet the plane and something fell off it. Another mighty salvo rumbled in, the splashes seeming to concentrate on *Mahan*. He half expected to see a twisted wreck as the spray fell away, but somehow she staggered out of the trough and shook herself off. Water sluiced from her. Her aft deckhouse was wrecked, and her number four funnel lay on a crushed lifeboat davit. The searchlight tower had fallen as well.

Something went *crump* forward, and a 5.5-inch plowed a furrow in the starboard bow and ricocheted into the sea. The big anchor chain that normally disappeared into the well trailed over the side from the bollard. Another salvo bloomed ahead, less than three miles off. *Damn we're close!* he thought as the shells almost sucked the air from his lungs as they passed—just barely—overhead to thrash the sea astern. He peered through his binoculars during a momentary respite.

"There they are! Right there!" he shouted into the speaking tube. "I mean, surface target! Bow! Estimate range five five double oh!" The salvo buzzer sounded more shrill than usual before the pathetic report of their own guns. Greg held on tight as *Walker* turned sharply to starboard. *Amagi* seemed almost motionless, the destroyer tucked under her skirt like a timid child. Beyond them, much closer now, the squall beckoned. Dark and alive with a torrential green rain.

Another salvo slashed out from *Amagi* just as six torpedoes chuffed from their tubes and lanced in her direction. Black smoke poured from the stacks again and Garrett felt a sense of anxious elation now their torpedoes were on the way. With any luck . . . A thunderous crash and a fiery cloud of hot, black soot and steam swept him to the deck.

Walker heaved when a ten-inch shell on a virtually flat trajectory punched through the forward fireroom. It didn't explode, but the sudden decompression of the compartment caused the burners to fireball. The flames didn't kill the men, but the steam from ruptured lines did. The destroyer's speed dropped and Matt turned to Chief Gray, but he'd already left. His gaze returned to the shattered pilothouse windows, sweeping past the speaking tube that led to the crow's nest. Blood dripped from it to join a widening pool. Electrician's Mate Janssen's blood was there too, as well as Rodriguez's. Rodriguez had been carried to the wardroom. Janssen was dead.

"Sir, forward fireroom's out of action! Mr. McFarlane bypassed with the main deck valve. He says our speed should be restored—almost—momentarily."

"Very well."

Mahan emerged from the smoke and spray astern cutting a wide, looping turn to port. Back toward *Amagi*. Matt stifled his instinctive command to signal her when he saw the reason why. The gun on her foredeck stood vacant and exposed, the splinter shield shot away. Behind it, the entire bridge superstructure was askew, torn and shattered and gushing smoke. After a single horrified glance, he doubted a soul had survived inside it. Her port torpedo tubes were rigged out, so at least maybe she got off her salvo, but otherwise she was a wreck.

More men lost. His men now. Since Captain Blinn was lost to them with *Pope*, he was senior. He'd ordered the torpedo attack—it made no difference that there wasn't any choice. Those men now steaming blind and helpless at flank speed directly toward the enemy were under his orders. But what of *these* men? Chances were, with *Mahan* headed straight for her, *Amagi* would concentrate on the helpless destroyer. The fire aimed at *Walker* had already slacked. She could almost certainly slip into the squall. He rubbed his forehead vigorously and looked into the wide-eyed, expectant faces of the men around him. They wanted him to do it: to give the order to turn back. They were willing it. Didn't they understand it was death? They had a chance to live—all they had to do was abandon *Mahan* to *Amagi*'s fury.

No, they couldn't live like that and neither could he. They'd run far enough. It didn't matter anymore where they were. The fight was here and they would face it. Shades of gray no longer existed. Everything was a stark black and white once more. Was that what it all boiled down to? Had the entire Asiatic Fleet been sacrificed just because it was there? The salvo buzzer rang and numbers one, three, and four let loose, but he didn't even hear. Finally his gaze fell upon Reynolds. The boy was the youngest and most junior crewman on the bridge. The look he returned was ... pleading.

"Come about! Bring us as close alongside *Mahan* as she'll bear." He gestured at the bombers above. Three of them flew lazy circles, watching, as if afraid to descend into the line of fire. "Maybe we can at least keep them off her."

"Skipper, the Jap cruisers behind us are out of the squall. They can see us now."

"Good. Let 'em watch," Matt snarled. Some of the men giggled nervously. "How much longer for the torpedoes, Mr. Sandison?"

"Ten seconds."

Walker finished her turn and sprinted after *Mahan*. The sea frothed around her with the strikes of enemy shells. She staggered from another impact forward.

"Time?"

"Three ... two ... one ..." Sandison looked up from his watch with a wretched expression. Damn! More duds—or whatever it was that had been wrong with the torpedoes since the war began. They were nearly even with *Mahan* now. Her speed was dropping off.

"See if—" Matt was interrupted by a bright snap of light, and he looked up in time to hear the detonation of the single massive explosion that disemboweled the Japanese destroyer. The ship hung, jackknifed, her bow in the air and her stern already slipping. The flames were bright against the dark squall beyond. Wild cheering erupted and Matt cheered too—but they'd missed *Amagi*. She was turning toward them in case there were more torpedoes in the water, and therefore, for a moment, she couldn't fire. Shells fell in earnest from the cruisers behind, but *Amagi* suddenly blurred. The squall was moving over her. Toward them. They were a mile away.

"Skipper! Get a load of this!" shouted Flowers. He was looking to his left, at *Mahan*. A column of spray collapsed on her deck and a man struggled through the cascade. He pointed at them with his right hand and held that arm up. Then he patted his chest with the left and brought it from below, across the bottom of his elbow and up alongside the other. Then he vanished in more spray.

"What the hell?" muttered Sandison.

Mahan dropped back and they saw men on her wreckage-strewn deck heaving on the exposed steering cables. She sheared to the right and narrowly avoided colliding with *Walker*'s stern. With a burst of speed, she lanced forward along the starboard side. The same man as before stood between the two torpedo mounts, still rigged out. He pointed at them exaggeratedly.

"My God, they're still loaded!" shouted Sandison. Matt ran onto the bridgewing and held up his own right arm. Then he took both arms and brought them up, diverging on either side of where his arm had first been. The man on *Mahan*'s deck held up an "OK" sign and scurried away.

"Left twenty degrees!" Matt shouted. "We're going to run up both sides of her! We may not have any torpedoes, but the Japs don't know that!"

Amagi had crept out of the squall, but just barely. It was almost as if the storm followed her. Now she was pointed directly at them and water peeled from her bow as she surged ahead. They were so close and the angle was such that only a couple of her secondaries would bear. *They're still plenty big,* thought Matt, *and as soon as we come alongside, the entire secondary broadside will come into play.* It would happen in less than two minutes.

Mahan moved farther and farther to starboard. With the loss of her forward fireroom, *Walker* could barely make twenty-five knots. *Mahan* looked like a wreck, but she was keeping up. The roaring bombers swooped to attack in spite of the incoming shells. Machine guns clattered above and behind. The salvo buzzer rang. Antiaircraft rounds raked *Walker*'s bridge as the two four-stackers streamed past *Amagi*'s bow. Lieutenant Flowers spun away from the wheel and collapsed to the deck, and Matt jumped into his place. The maelstrom of fire and the kaleidoscope of images were beyond anything they'd experienced yet. *Amagi*'s side was alive with flashing muzzles, and *Walker* drummed with impacts as numerous as the raindrops of the previous squall.

Simultaneously, *Walker* heaved with the close impact of a pair of bombs, and the plane that had dropped them slanted unnaturally toward *Amagi*, trailing smoke. It impacted with a monstrous fireball directly atop her amidships turret. Two more explosions rocked *Amagi* from the opposite side and she heeled sharply toward *Walker* with the force of the blows. The salvo buzzer rang. *WHAM!*

Another bomb detonated and shells from the other cruisers still fell. Some even struck *Amagi*. Amid this tempest of fire, smoke, overpressure, and death, they were finally consumed by the squall.

E lation surged in Matt's chest as the green deluge—tinged with the reflection of explosions and flames—descended upon them. In spite of himself, a shout of exultation escaped. Instead of the comforting, drumming rain on the deck above, however, a shocking . . . silence . . . stunned his senses. He heard surprised shouts on the foredeck and then confused murmuring of the bridge watch, but for a moment there was nothing else. He spun to look past the chart house. As the rest of the ship . . . materialized out of the greenness behind them, he began to hear it—the ship itself. The reassuring thunder of the blowers as they roared into being, the shouted obscenities of the number two gun crew amidships. On and on, until he heard the tumult as far away as the fantail. But other than the increasingly alarmed voices of his crew, the normal sounds of his ship, and the loud ringing in his ears caused by the din of battle, there was nothing.

But there *was* rain. The rain he'd expected to pound his ship at that very moment was there—but it wasn't falling. It just hung there, suspended. Motionless. He raised his hand in wonder amid the pandemonium, waved it through the teardrop shapes, and felt their wetness on his hand. He moved out from under the shelter of the deck above and felt the rain as he moved through it, saw it wet his ship as their forward motion carried them along. Just as his initial shock began to give way to an almost panicky incredulity, the screws "ran away," like when they left the water in re-

ally heavy seas. The sound lasted only seconds—at least
Spanky was on the job—but it drew his gaze over the side.
He blinked in uncomprehending astonishment. The sea was
gone. Down as far as he could see, past the boot topping,
past the growth-encrusted red paint of the hull, into the
limitless greenish-black nothingness below, were only un-
countable billions of raindrops suspended in air. Before the
enormity of it could even register, the deck dropped from
under his feet and a terrible pressure built in his ears. He
grabbed the rail and pushed himself down to the wooden
strakes of the bridge—anything to maintain contact with
something real. What he'd just seen couldn't possibly be.
His stomach heaved and he retched uncontrollably. He
heard the sounds of others doing the same as the sensation of falling intensified. Then there began a low-pitched
whine, building slowly like a dry bearing about to fail. It
built and built until it became torment. The pressure increased too. He dragged himself back into the pilothouse,
careful not to take both hands off the deck at once. He
scrunched through broken glass and blood until he reached
his chair, attached to the angled right-forward wall, and he
slowly climbed up the braces.

His eyes felt like they were being pushed into their sockets, but he saw that everyone else on the bridge was down.
Reynolds met his gaze with an expression of controlled terror. Riggs sat on the deck with his palms over his eyes. Matt
looked through the shattered, square-framed windows and
saw men on the foredeck crawling amid empty shell cas-
ings, or trying to hold on to something as if they, like he, felt
they would fly away from the ship like a feather if they let
go. And all around there was nothing but the wet, greenish void. The screeching whine continued to grow until it
drowned the noisy blowers. He held his hands over his ears
with his arm linked through the chair, but it made no difference. The sound was inside his head. Again he fought the
urge to vomit.

Abruptly, with terrifying suddenness, the deck swooped
up beneath him like a roller coaster reaching the bottom
of a dip and rocketing upward. With a thunderous roar, the
raindrops that had remained poised for what could have
been only moments, plummeted down and became the del-

uge they should have been from the start. Exhausted from straining against the impossibly contradictory sensations of weightlessness and gravity, he collapsed into his chair and stared numbly out at the now perfectly normal squall. *Walker* coasted along, her engines stopped, losing way on the rain-stilled sea.

Matt gathered himself while the men picked themselves up and stumbled back to their stations. In their confusion, they sought the comfort of their responsibilities. He didn't know what had just occurred, but he knew that, for now at least, he must do the same. Later the time would come for questions. He still had a crew and a ship to save, and to fight with, if need be. The cries of alarm began to grow again, but then, with unspeakable gratitude, Matt heard the booming voice of the Bosun rise above the tumult.

"Stow that girlish gab! Where do you think you are? You! Yeah, you, Davis! Secure that shit! Form a detail and clear these goddamn shells! Look at this mess! LOOK AT MY BEAUTIFUL DECK! You'd think a bunch of goddamn hogs or even *snipes* been rootin' around up here. You think you've been in a battle? I've had scarier fights with the roaches in the wardroom! Quit pukin', Smitty. You sound like a frog!"

Matt listened as Gray's abuse moved aft. He cleared his throat and rubbed his lips with wet hands. He tasted blood. Riggs stood, shakily, holding the wheel, and Matt nodded at him. "Damage report," he croaked, his voice a harsh rasp. He cleared his throat. "Damage report!" he demanded more firmly. "Why've we stopped?"

The blowers didn't sound right. Sandison was on the bridge phone, listening intently as reports came in.

"Lieutenant McFarlane shut down the engines," he reported. "Water's coming in, but the pumps can handle it—when we get them back. Forward fireroom's out of action. Fires are out in the aft fireroom. It's full of smoke from raw fuel on the burners and they're venting it now. As soon as they can get in, they'll relight the fires. Should be just a few minutes." Sandison's voice had a cadence to it as he repeated the information he heard.

"We took a lot of hits forward and there're lots of casualties," he added grimly. "Doc's dead. He was working on Rodriguez when a shell came through and just . . . took him apart. Lots of the wounded were killed in the wardroom. One of the nurses is dead." His face turned ashen. "She was standing next to Doc. The other nurses have been helping out. Mr. Garrett reports one dead and two injured on the fire-control platform and he thinks Mr. Rogers is dead. There's . . . blood running down the mast from the crow's nest. He sounds a little rough." Sandison replied to Garrett and then listened to other reports, nodding as he did as if those making them could see him.

"There's water in the paint locker, but"—he shrugged—"there's always water in the paint locker. Probably mostly rain. We were real lucky with the hull—at least below the waterline. Most of the leaks are coming from loosened plates, from near misses. A lot of the shells hit us on flat trajectories and just punched through the upper hull. A few lighter shells exploded. The number three gun's out of action with four men killed . . . but all the big stuff must've been armor-piercing and didn't hit anything substantial enough to make them blow."

He listened a little longer and then looked at Matt. "Jesus, Skipper, we have a *lot* of holes."

"Anything on the horn? Anything from *Mahan*?"

Sandison shook his head. "Radio's out of whack, sir. Radioman Clancy just reported there hasn't been a peep since we entered the squall. Before that there were lots of distant distress calls, merchant ships mostly, under attack and begging for escorts." He cleared his throat. "Just static now. Something probably came unplugged."

Matt took a breath. "Casualties?"

"Don't know yet, sir, but . . . a lot."

The captain removed his hat and ran fingers through sweat-matted hair. "Torpedoes?"

The ensign shook his head guiltily. "No sir. Just the ones in the three mount, and with everything that's been . . . I'm sorry, sir, I just don't know."

"Very well. Secure from general quarters. There's too many men just standing around with so much work to do. But keep the crews on the guns and a sharp lookout. See if we can get some hot food into these guys." He stifled a jaw-racking yawn that wasn't quite an act. "And I need more coffee. Also, as soon as Lieutenant Ellis is able, have him report to the bridge." He paused and added in a softer tone, "Ask the Bosun to detail some men to bring Mr. Rogers down."

The rain continued and Matt yearned to be under way, making as much distance as they could under cover. There was no way of knowing *Mahan*'s fate. They'd taken as much pressure off her as they could, but he didn't know what to think about how that turned out. Evidently *Walker* had returned to help *Mahan* while she was making a suicide charge to let *them* get clear. Hopefully, the confusion saved them both. But even if *Mahan* had made it, she would be in bad shape. Maybe even sinking. Then again, she could be miles away by now. Either way, there was nothing he could do for her. *Amagi* was badly hit, that much he knew. How badly was anybody's guess. Enough to retire? Hopefully. Enough to sink? That would grant his fondest wish. But whether *Amagi* swam or not made little difference, because the other cruisers were still coming. He didn't think they would give up, not when they still had spotter planes to guide them. They couldn't be far away.

When *Walker* regained steam pressure, she must press on. All they could do was pray that *Mahan* had escaped. Matt suddenly wondered if the other destroyer had experienced the same phenomenon *Walker* had. He shuddered, and glanced quickly around the gloomy pilothouse. He didn't think anyone else had seen what he had, and he couldn't completely banish the suspicion that he'd been teetering on the brink of madness. It had to have been a hallucination, brought on by exhaustion and the stress of combat. The motionless raindrops were certainly explainable, he assured himself. They'd passed into the most intense squall he'd ever seen. Squalls were by nature extremely unstable. Who knew what sort of strange winds might exist within one? Sudden gusts that could capsize a ship weren't unheard of. Why not some freakish updraft? His nervous fingers tried to reshape his sodden hat. That still didn't explain what he'd seen when he looked over the side. Nothing could explain that. It couldn't have happened—must not have happened.

"Skipper, Mr. Garrett says the squall's passing."

The volume of rain had diminished and it was perceptively lighter. Matt stirred and turned to see a woman's face peering at him fearfully from the ladder at the back of the quarterdeck. All that was visible was her rain-drenched hair, head, and shoulders. Her big brown eyes widened in surprise when they met his and her mouth formed an O of alarm. The white of her uniform blouse was stained and sooty, her cheek smeared with grease and blood where she must have wiped it with her hand. Immediately, and without a word, she raised a shiny coffee urn and placed it on the deck. She gave it a tentative shove in his direction as if it were an offering to a terrible god and then vanished down the ladder.

"Coffee's here," he muttered, then blinked and shook his head. He moved from his chair and was surprised his legs supported him. "Get Spanky on the horn. I want those engines *now*!"

They were fully exposed to the midafternoon sunlight by the time they had steam to move, and then only with the starboard engine. The water beneath the fantail churned and foamed as the screw began to turn. The deck vibrated horribly and pieces of broken glass fell from the empty window frames. The pressure was rising on number four, and soon Ensign Tolson, who'd replaced Bob Flowers, wouldn't have to fight the unbalanced thrust of a single screw. The squall still raged astern, but it was dissipating. They all expected the menacing forms of Japanese cruisers to emerge at any moment, and every eye watched the sky for spotting planes or bombers. If only they hadn't lost the boilers, they'd have been long gone by now.

Jim Ellis was on the bridge. There was blood and soot on his uniform, and his eyes were puffy and swollen. His customary ebullience was tempered by the horror he'd seen, and he spoke in a soft, somber tone. "The ship's a wreck, Skipper. Just about everything topside is shot to hell. We're in better shape below, if you can believe it, but we're still taking water, and the faster we move, the more we'll take. Hell, most of the water's coming in through holes above the waterline. Waves slopping in." He sighed. "You know, my granddaddy was at Manila Bay. His brother was at Santiago Bay. He always said there'd be days like this, only he always made it sound more fun."

Matt nodded wearily. "Dad was on a can just like this in the North Atlantic, during the last war. They chased a few subs, but they never saw anything like this. Somehow I think his stories may have been closer to the mark. He didn't have fun. I can't imagine many things more miserable than one of these four-stackers in the North Atlantic. At least I couldn't until the last couple of months." He paused. "And today, of course. Especially today."

They'd been talking quietly, but Matt glanced around the bridge to ensure that no one could hear before lowering his voice still further. "What did you think of our ... experience, right after we entered the squall?"

Jim looked at him with a hesitant frown. He clearly didn't want to talk about it, and his expression seemed to accuse Matt of breaking some unspoken compact by even mentioning it. "Yeah, well, that was different," he managed at last. "I'm, ah, thinkin' it was an updraft or something."

Matt nodded agreement. "Me too. In fact, that's how I'll instruct Mr. Tolson to enter it in the log. But ... did you ever happen to look over the side?"

Lieutenant Ellis pulled back, as if recoiling from a slap. The look on his face was sufficient to confirm he had indeed seen the same thing as the captain, and Matt's guts twisted.

"Just a little," Jim whispered.

Matt glanced around again. "How many of the crew, do you think, might've seen it?"

"Not many. Hell, probably none. They were pretty busy at the time. Then with the screwy raindrops ... I figure most everybody was looking up."

Matt massaged his temples. "Damn. I only asked because I hoped you'd confirm my suspicions that I *didn't* see anything." He took a deep breath. "Well, whatever it was, it's over now. We're back in the real world where all we have to worry about are the Japs."

The corner of Jim's mouth twitched. "Yes, sir, but if it's all the same to you, I'll—"

He was interrupted by Quartermaster's Mate 2nd Class Norman Kutas, who'd replaced Sandison as the talker. "Mr. Garrett reports surface target, bearing one seven zero! Range five five double oh!"

They rushed to the starboard bridgewing and brought up their binoculars. A dark form was taking shape behind them as the squall dispersed. It was bows-on and listing to port. Smoke poured from amidships and slanted downwind. Even at this range, tiny figures were visible on the foredeck, wrestling with a fire hose.

"Oh, my God, Skipper," breathed Jim. "It's *Mahan!*"

Walker made a wide, slow turn to avoid having more water pour through her perforated sides. Once pointed at her sister, she sprinted to her. Everyone was at least secretly terrified by the prospect of turning back. But one man dressed in dark khaki, standing on the foredeck, silently cursed the ill luck that showed them *Mahan*. If they hadn't seen her, hadn't known she was there, they could have continued on. That would have salved his conscience—not seeing her—even if he knew she was there. But there she was, in obvious distress and at the moment with no enemy in sight. He fumed. Of course that upstart on the bridge would risk all their lives. He'd been safer in Surabaya! And the way he'd been treated was an outrage! He was an officer, by God, a fighter pilot! And to be forced to perform manual labor—and be physically threatened to do so—alongside common sailors was beyond the pale. Heads would roll for this, he decided. He had friends and he'd remember. Now if they could just *go!* But there was *Mahan*, damn it. They were all going to die for the sake of a ship that was already doomed. He shoved an empty shell casing savagely over the side with his shoe.

What Captain Kaufman didn't realize was that most of the destroyermen on DD-163 wouldn't have cared if *Amagi* still stood between them and their sister. They hadn't expected to last this long, and the deck was stacked against them whether they went back or ran away. They might as well die doing the right thing.

They ran down on *Mahan* and hove to upwind. Jim Ellis took the conn and kept *Walker* poised forty yards off the other destroyer's beam. Matt went on the bridgewing with a speaking trumpet and stared at the other ship. She looked doomed. She was low by the bow and her forward superstructure was a shattered wreck. Smoke gushed from the ventilation hatches above the aft fireroom and men directed hoses into them. More smoke still wisped from the first two funnels, so the forward fireroom must be okay, but her aft deckhouse and auxiliary conn were wrecked, so her only means of maneuvering was still the exposed steering cables. The number four funnel was gone, probably rolled over the side to clear the deck, and the searchlight tower had fallen across the number one torpedo mount, crumpling the tubes. Men on the amidships deckhouse manned the guns, but everyone else seemed too busy trying to save their ship to even talk to Matt.

He glanced at the sun, nearing the horizon, and he willed it to move faster. He looked up at Lieutenant Garrett's disheveled, blackened form on the platform above, and the younger man returned his glance with one of confusion. The squall had finally spent itself and all the lookouts were tense and alert, but so far there was nothing. Matt wasn't about to complain, but he couldn't believe the Japanese had simply given up. Even if the cruisers had turned away, the aircraft would have continued to search. Of course, some were carrier planes. Maybe they were low on fuel, or didn't want to land at night. The spotting planes might have returned to their ships as well. He frowned. Even so, they'd mauled *Amagi* badly—at least he hoped they had. He thought two of *Mahan*'s torpedoes had struck her at the end. She at least should still be near, unless she'd continued on at full speed, and he didn't know how she could have unless she was even tougher and faster than he thought. Maybe she sank. Now that was a happy thought.

All these considerations came in an instant, just before he turned back to *Mahan* and raised the speaking trumpet.

"Is your fire under control?" The trumpet projected his tinny voice across the intervening distance. "Will our hoses help? Can you steam? Where's Captain Atkinson?" He thought he already knew the answer to his final question. A bedraggled form moved to the rail. It might have been the same man who had helped coordinate their charge, but it was impossible to be sure. The man cupped his hands and shouted.

"I'm Lieutenant Brister. Engineering. Captain Atkinson's dead. The whole bridge crew's dead or badly wounded. I think we've about got the fire licked and we can steam, but I had to use the men on the steering detail for damage control. If you can spare some men, I think we can get under way."

The entire bridge crew? "Who's in command?"

"I guess I am, sir."

"Lieutenant Brister's a fine officer," commented Matt as he and Ellis watched the whaleboat motor across the short distance between the ships. They'd sent half a dozen seamen under Bosun's Mate 1st Class Francis "Frankie" Steele, of the second deck division, as well as Signalman Ed Palmer, with one of the portable Morse lamps. None of *Mahan*'s lamps had survived the destruction of her bridge and auxiliary conn. At least now they'd be able to communicate.

Jim nodded. "Yes, sir. He deserves a commendation for keeping his ship afloat, not to mention fighting her so well. He's gonna have his hands full, though."

"Yeah, he's not a navigator or a bridge officer. I hate to lose you, but maybe you better go across and assume command."

Jim frowned. "Well, sure, if you say so, Skipper, but we've got damage of our own."

Matt waved away his objection. "Lieutenant Dowden can handle it. He knows what to do, and the men like him. Besides, he's the assistant damage control and repair officer. With Richard dead, it's his job." He looked at Ellis with a sad smile. "Go on, Jim. *Mahan* needs you. We have to get her under way as soon as possible, and if anybody can speed that up, it's you."

Jim quietly watched several ratings sweeping and mopping debris. "Aye, aye, sir. I guess I just hate to leave the old girl in such a shape." He smiled wryly and looked at *Mahan*. "I never expected my first command to be the best ship in the Navy, but this is ridiculous." Matt barked an unexpected laugh at how closely his exec's thoughts mirrored his own when he first assumed command of *Walker*. Of course, *Mahan* was in worse shape than *Walker*, and *Walker* had taken a terrible beating. Comparatively speaking, Jim had more right to complain.

"I'll just run down and get some things and as soon as the boat returns, I'll go." He stood awkwardly for a moment, then thrust out his hand. "Take care, sir . . . Matt."

Matt shook his hand and squeezed his friend's shoulder. "You too. Report as soon as you have a handle on what shape she's in. Holler if you need help."

Jim grinned. "Same here." He looked around. "Even money who hollers first." They both chuckled, and then Lieutenant Ellis stepped back a pace and saluted. Matt returned it and after Jim left the bridge he sighed and sat tiredly in his chair. "Pass the word for Mr. Dowden."

The whaleboat returned and the coxswain, Tony Scott, was unhappy to learn he had another trip to make. He was strangely uneasy. The water didn't seem quite right. He was wrung out, like everybody, and the weird experience of the squall had left him unnerved. But what had him on edge right now was how many things kept bumping into the boat. He was accustomed to the occasional thump of a fish, or a shark, but they were out in the middle of the ocean and things wouldn't stop bumping his boat. It was constant. Nothing big had struck it, and occasionally he glimpsed a silvery swirl alongside, so he knew they were just fish. But why the hell were they bugging his boat? It was like the bright white bottom paint was attracting them. He shuddered with a premonition that it might draw other, larger things as well. Jim Ellis tossed down his seabag and swung over the side, descending by way of the metal rungs welded to the hull. As soon as Ellis was aboard, Scott advanced the throttle and steered for the other destroyer, hoping to make his second run as fast as he decently could.

"Skipper," reported Sandison, "lookout sees something 'screwy' in the water, dead ahead, about two miles. Wait a minute! He thinks it's a submarine!"

"What's the status of the whaleboat?"

"Alongside," supplied Riggs. "They're hoisting it aboard now."

"Very well. Signal Palmer on *Mahan* we're investigating a possible submarine. Sonar's still out?"

"Yes, sir," said Lieutenant Dowden, puffing up the ladder. "Jim, I mean, Mr. Ellis, had us working on it, but . . . We still might get it working if—"

"Just put it in your report." More worn-out equipment.

"Sir, Mr. Garrett sees it too, and damned if it don't look like a sub to him," said Kutas. "He says there's debris and people in the water around it. Might be a sub taking on survivors from that Nip can we sank."

"The whaleboat?"

"Secure, sir," said Riggs, standing on the port bridgewing, watching the work.

"Sound general quarters! All ahead full. Maybe we'll catch 'em on the surface."

Spanky was inspecting the damage in the forward fireroom. Eight bodies had been removed, and he shuddered at the memory of the scalded men. Men he knew. Machinist's Mate 2nd Class Dean Laney and Dave Elden, shipfitter, trailed behind him with clipboards. Dwindling daylight seeped through the two holes made by the ten-inch shell, one on either side of the compartment. The boilers had escaped destruction, but steam lines and conduit were shredded.

"It's a miracle it didn't hit a boiler," observed Laney. Mc-Farlane grunted. "Yeah, but a wrecked boiler'd be the least of our concerns. It probably would've exploded if it had, and blown the bottom right out of the ship." The other men nodded solemnly.

"Not much we can do right now, Spanky," said Elden. "She needs yard time bad."

"I know. Let's see if we can get at least one back on line as a spare, though. I don't like steaming on two boilers. 'Specially if one's number four. I don't trust it. Anyway, if either of the boilers in the aft fireroom craps out, we'll be down to one, and we'll be a sittin' duck for the Japs."

The general alarm shattered the relative quiet of the ravaged compartment.

"Jesus H. Christ!" groaned Laney when the grating beneath his feet tilted and the ship surged ahead. "Not again!"

"Didn't they tell you?" McFarlane growled, as he hurried for the air lock. "There's a war on."

"Surface action, bow!" shouted Garrett over the comm. "Estimate range two two double oh. Target is stationary. Match pointers!" Most of the soot had washed away, but the back of his neck still hurt where the steam scalded him when the fireroom was hit. Fire control was still a mess, but it was back on line. He watched a dark shape, barely on the surface, like a flooded-down submarine, ease slowly through a group of men in the water. He didn't feel good about firing on helpless men, even if they were the enemy, but he was about to give the order when a strange thought occurred. He leaned over the speaking tube without taking the binoculars from his eyes. "Skipper, something's not right."

Matt snatched the headset from his talker and spoke into it. "What do you mean?"

"Sir, something *is* screwy. The sub's moving a little, but there's no conning tower. And the men in the water seem to be trying to get away from it. I see splashing. There're not many men, sir, just a few, but they look . . . upset." For several moments, as they drew closer to the object, no one said anything. "Skipper . . . ? Do you think it's one of our boats? Maybe that's why the Japs don't want to get aboard. I've heard they won't surrender."

"I don't think so, Greg. I'm looking at it too. It doesn't look like any sub I ever saw. We have quite a few boats out here, but none look like that."

Reynolds was in the crow's nest and his voice suddenly crackled on the line. "Holy *shit* . . . Sir! That's not a sub. It's a great big stinkin' *fish*!"

Garrett blinked. He'd seen a submarine because he expected to see a submarine. As soon as Reynolds spoke, he realized the young seaman was right. "Jesus Christ! Skipper, it *is* a fish, or whale or something and it's . . . I think it's *eating* those Japs!"

"Commence firing!"

"Aye, aye, sir! Gun number one, range is now, ah, one four five oh! Match pointers! Commence firing!" He was so distracted by . . . whatever was swimming lazily about, snatching the struggling sailors, he didn't press the salvo buzzer. The gun on the foredeck boomed, and a split second later, a geyser erupted a little beyond the target.

"Gun one, correction! Down sixty, three rounds, resume firing!" Three shells slammed out as fast as the breech was opened and another round loaded. A tight group of water-spouts erupted on and around the creature; a tinge of red intermingled with the spray. The thing heaved itself from the water and in the gathering gloom Garrett got an impression of a long, pointed flipper, like a right whale. But he also saw an elongated, tooth-studded snout like a croco-dile's, snapping viciously at the spume as the beast slapped back into the sea. Two more large flippers churned the surface and propelled the monster beneath the waves.

"God a'mighty."

As they drew near the few remaining men, clinging desperately to floating debris, the surface of the sea churned again with hundreds of silvery shapes schooling around the survivors. Garrett watched in horror as the fish struck. They looked like tuna, but acted like piranha. They were close enough now he could hear the screams.

"All back two-thirds! Right ten degrees rudder!" Matt yelled. He leaned through the shattered window and shouted at the foredeck below. "Boats! Get those men out of the water!" He looked at Tolson and spoke in a more normal tone. "Rudder amidships. All stop. Keep them in our lee." He looked down from the port bridgewing. The sea churned with a horrifying frenzy that brought to mind an old reel he'd once seen of a cow carcass thrown into the Amazon. He'd been fascinated as he watched the voracious fish reduce the carcass to a mere skeleton within moments. Now he fought to control his stomach as hundreds of much larger fish attacked the struggling Japanese in much the same fashion. What were they? He was no expert on marine life by any means, but he'd never seen such a thing. By the expressions on the faces of his men, neither had anyone else. Only Chief Gray seemed immune to the shock. He went about his assigned task with a single-mindedness that Matt could only envy, as though huge sea monsters and man-eating fish lurked in the water every day. Which they did, he supposed, but not like this.

In spite of Gray's efficiency, before he could assemble a party to throw lines to the survivors, there was no one left to save. A froth of flashing fins and teeth marked the spot where the final swimmer had disappeared. The rest of the swarm began to disperse or snatch tiny morsels drifting here and there. Alone upon the gently rolling sea, an overturned lifeboat bobbed with two forms precariously balanced. One seemed unconscious, and the other hovered over the first with a split and badly gnawed oar in his hands. He now regarded the destroyermen with inscrutable Asian eyes. His stoic face hadn't changed expression since he had battled the carnivorous fish and the submarine-sized cross between a whale and a crocodile. *We're just different enemies,* Matt thought. He turned and saw another face peering anxiously from the ladder, aft. This one belonged to the Australian engineer whom he'd only briefly met.

"May I, ah ... come up there, sir, for a word?" Matt nodded, and the tall, portly man puffed to the top of the ladder. His sparse, graying hair was plastered to his skull with sweat, and he ran his left hand over it as if feeling for the hat he held in his right. Noticing that everyone on the bridge wore a hat or helmet, he plunked his back on his head. He glanced at the foredeck, where men were throwing lines to the enemy seaman on the boat and trying to convince him to take one.

"Oh, dear. Unimaginable. After what that Jappo's been through, he still won't surrender. I don't suppose you have anyone who can speak to him? No, of course not." Matt looked at him and quirked an eyebrow. He'd noticed before the man's strange habit of answering his own questions.

"Actually, Mr. Bradford, we may surprise you. Quite a few old China hands aboard this ship. Some may have learned a few words."

"Indeed?"

In the end, their translator was not a "China hand" but

Lieutenant Mallory, the Army pilot with Captain Kaufman. He spoke a few terse phrases in what could have been Martian for all Matt knew, but the stubborn Japanese sailor finally let his oar slip into the sea and caught the rope. Matt looked up at Garrett. "Get some weapons to those men before they hoist those Japs aboard." He raised his voice to be heard by the men on the deck below. "Where'd you learn Japanese, Mr. Mallory?"

The young officer shouted a reply. "I grew up in Southern California, sir. My folks ran an orange plantation. Lots of Japs in the citrus groves."

"Why wouldn't he take the rope?"

"He said his family, his ancestors, would be ashamed if he surrendered."

"That's nuts! Didn't he see what happened to the others?" Matt shook his head. "How'd you talk him into it?"

Mallory hesitated. "I didn't, sir. But he agreed to let us 'rescue' his officer since he's unconscious and can't decide for himself. I told him we'd let him kill himself later if he wants."

"Jesus," someone muttered. Chief Gunner's Mate Sonny Campeti arrived on deck with several Springfields. He quickly passed out all but one, which he kept for himself. The others stood back, their rifles ready, while three men pulled on the rope. The burly Japanese sailor held the other end, bracing himself upon the keel as best he could. Occasionally a jostling wave caused him to glance anxiously at the unmoving man beside him. The supine form's uniform was dark blue. The boat bumped against the hull, and another rope was lowered. Quickly and professionally, the man tied it around his officer's chest under his arms and then stood back, balanced precariously, as the destroyermen hauled the unconscious man to the deck. Without another glance at the men above, he sat down on the boat and put his hands on his head, lacing his thick, powerful fingers together in his hair.

Chief Gray looked up at Matt with an expression that said, "Now what?" and the captain raised his speaking trumpet. "Is he alive?" Gray felt the man's neck for a pulse and nodded. Except for a small gash on his head, there were no obvious injuries. "Take him to the wardroom, under guard."

"Aye, aye, sir."

"What about the other one?" Mallory asked.

"I don't know. Maybe we can lasso him, or something. We can't just leave him here—Jap or not."

"Goodness gracious!" exclaimed Courtney Bradford. He stood next to Matt, looking into the sea. The captain looked at him, then followed his gaze. The dark blue water became much darker directly beneath the boat. Suddenly the creature they'd driven under, or one just like it, rose to the surface, and its gaping, crocodilelike jaws snapped shut on the capsized boat. The thing was enormous! Matt knew the boat must be twenty-five or thirty feet long, and the jaws were very nearly that long themselves. As the boat splintered, Matt heard a shriek and saw the terrible jaws close on the Japanese sailor's legs. Even then, it sounded more like a scream of pain, not terror. He shuddered. The roar of the machine gun just above his head deafened him and an instant later, the bigger .50-cal, amidships, joined in—as did a couple of men with rifles. He hoped a few thought to finish the stubborn Jap, but amid the geysering splashes he couldn't tell. The creature writhed and slammed into the ship hard enough to make him grab the rail. With a huge splash and a swirl of flippers, it disappeared from view.

"Goodness gracious," said Bradford again, his voice subdued by awe.

Matt stood transfixed, but for only a moment. Then he bellowed to the men below. "Boats, get somebody down there to check the hull for damage. Whatever the hell that was, it bumped us pretty good." For a moment nobody moved, but finally the Bosun stirred.

"Get the lead out, you miserable girly saps! The Skipper gave an order! Ain't you never seen a sea monster eat a Nip before? Shit!"

With that, Matt turned, walked woodenly back to his chair, and sat. Out there, off the port bow, the sun finally vanished entirely beneath the blackening sea, and he removed his hat and plopped it on his lap. He felt like the reserve of adrenaline that was supposed to last his lifetime had been completely tapped out that day. He was so tired. Finally he sighed and rubbed his face.

"Mr. Tolson, take us back to *Mahan*. Hopefully, she's ready to move. Secure from general quarters, but keep men on the machine guns for a while." He yawned tremendously and glanced at the men looking at him, still stunned by what they'd seen. "It's been a hectic day," he whispered.

*T*hey ran south all night at twenty knots. The two operational boilers on each ship could have carried them faster, but with all their damage, twenty knots was a sufficiently hair-raising speed. Repairmen labored on, exhausted, trying to accomplish tasks while under way that ordinarily required a yard. Shoring timbers pushed warped seams together and shipfitters welded them instead of waiting for rivets. They had too far to go. Matt briefly considered returning to Surabaya, but with all the enemy activity, they'd probably wind up trapped. Ceylon was still within reach, fuel-wise, but the only reason that had been their original destination was that its yard facilities could handle *Exeter*. With the British cruiser lost, there was no reason to go there. Wiser to make for Perth, Australia, where some of their sisters had gone.

It was a cloudless night, but the moon was the merest sliver. It provided just enough light for *Mahan* to follow their wake. Matt pitied her shorthanded, exhausted crew. *Walker* had lost more than twenty killed herself— almost a quarter of her complement—and another eight were seriously wounded. But *Mahan* had more than sixty dead. She was a floating morgue. Most of her casualties occurred when a ten-inch shell destroyed her bridge. Other men were lost in the aft deckhouse and fireroom.

It was a miracle that either ship had survived. The only things that saved them were getting in close where *Ama-*

gi's main guns couldn't engage . . . and the Squall, of course. Matt shifted uncomfortably in his seat at the memory. The Squall had been unusual in itself, but then a whole string of strange events followed. The ravenous fish, the "sea monster" (he couldn't think of anything else to call it). Then there was the odd lack of radio traffic. The radiomen and electrician's mates had studied the equipment carefully and found nothing wrong, but everyone was exhausted and they must've missed something. It was that simple . . . Matt's eyelids fluttered open again, and he shook his head to clear his blurry thoughts. Instead, his chin slowly drooped until it rested on his chest.

The midwatch would be coming on soon, he thought muzzily. *At least some of the men could sleep. Poor Richard. Up in the crow's nest all day long, only to die when they were so close to safety. He'd done his duty, but he'd missed the sea monster. Jim missed it too, as had everyone on the other ship. They were lucky. At least it won't swim in their dreams. It's already in mine and I'm not even asleep.*

He was snoring lightly. Garrett, his neck and hands covered with gauze, had the deck. He stepped quietly over to stand beside his captain, lest he fall from his chair. He caught the eyes of the other tired men and held a finger to his lips.

Matt came awake in a blurry, gray dawn. He blinked, rubbed dried grit from his eyes, and looked around. Lieutenant Dowden was nearby, conversing in quiet tones with the Bosun. Matt felt a surge of irritation at being allowed to sleep, but it was immediately replaced by a vague sense of guilt at having done so. Wry acceptance followed. At least now he could face this new day without dropping from exhaustion.

"Coffee?" he croaked.

Almost before the word was uttered, Juan Marcos appeared at his elbow, steaming mug in hand. Juan was the officers' steward and the only Filipino who hadn't—understandably—jumped ship when they left the Philippines. He beamed as his captain took the cup and nodded his thanks. Raising it to his lips, Matt took a tentative sip. "That's good," he said, and sipped again. "Very good, Juan. Best coffee you've ever made."

A wounded expression clouded the Filipino's face. "But Cap-tan Reddy, I did not make it!"

Matt glanced at Gray, who suddenly looked away. "Well . . . of course I just woke up and it's my first cup. I'm sure it just tastes so good because I really needed it."

The Bosun coughed to stifle a laugh. Juan took good care of them, given his limited resources, and no one would have dreamed of hurting his feelings. But his concept of good coffee was . . . different from everyone else's.

"No, Cap-tan Reddy. I'm sure it is very good. Better than mine." Juan spoke with brittle formality. "One of the nurses made it. The *señorita* nurses," he added darkly as if to say it might taste good, but would probably poison him. "Now you are awake, I will bring you a breakfast I doubt they could match!"

Matt chuckled. "I'm sure you will, Juan. I'm starved!" The Filipino summoned all his dignity—a most impressive quantity—and left the bridge. Matt raised an eyebrow at Chief Gray and shook his head. He then turned in his chair to glance astern.

"She's still hangin' tight," Gray said, referring to *Mahan*. Matt could just make her out in the grayish pink morning half-light. He stood, stretching his arms over his head. He felt like he'd been thrown from a horse, but except for minor cuts from broken glass, he'd escaped the previous day's battles without injury. "Where are we?"

Dowden stepped to the chart table, and Matt and Gray joined him there to peer at the map. "Here, sir," Dowden said and pointed. "Just about exactly."

Matt looked at the indicated position and then stared out the windows. It was difficult to tell, but he thought he saw a landmass ahead. "I'm not enthusiastic about running Lombok or Bali Strait in daylight," he said. "If the Japs are here ahead of us, it would be simple for them to put a stopper in the bottle. There're only so many holes in the Malay Barrier. Even after all the running around we did yesterday and last night, we're only about three hundred miles from where we started. They could easily have beaten us here."

"Yes, sir," agreed the Bosun. "And they don't even need ships." He pointed at the map. "A couple of planes patrolling here, or here, and they'd have us. They couldn't miss us. We're in no shape to dodge dive bombers."

Matt rubbed the stubble on his chin and nodded thoughtfully. "What's this?" He pointed to a sliver of land off the northeast corner of Bali.

Dowden leaned closer. "Ah . . . Menjangan Island. It looks like it's only about two and a half miles long. The chart shows a narrow channel between it and Bali that's about a mile wide."

"What if we eased in there and hunkered down for the day, and then ran Bali Strait tonight?" Matt mused aloud. Dowden looked unconvinced, but Gray was thoughtful.

"Looks like plenty of water. The channel shows a hundred forty feet. There's about three fifty all around. The currents look okay." He looked at Matt. "Bali Strait wouldn't be my first choice in the dark; it's so narrow. But the Japs might think that too. It sounds good, Skipper."

"Yeah, but we know there's Japs on Bali," added the captain darkly. "After the fiasco in Badung Strait, there was nothing we could do about it. That should have been different." He sighed. "It all depends on how far they've advanced. We know their force wasn't very big and they'll be concentrating on securing airfields." He deliberated. "Bali's pretty big and they went ashore on the far side of the island. Worst case, they might've sneaked a few observers in to watch the strait, but I can't imagine they'd waste their time watching that little gap beside Menjangan. It doesn't go anywhere." Dowden was nodding now. Their only other option was a daylight run through a very confined stretch of water.

"We lie doggo for the day," Matt decided. "It'll give us a chance to patch some holes. Besides, I'd like to get with Jim. I need a real report on *Mahan*'s condition, as well as our own." He stared at the map a few moments more. "I wonder what kind of cover Menjangan has. A lot of these little islands are just jungles poking out of the sea. That'd be perfect for our needs. Some are barren volcanic rocks too." He looked around the pilothouse questioningly. "I've never been there." Dowden and Gray were both shaking their heads, and no one else spoke up. "Send for Mr. Bradford. Maybe he knows."

"Aye, aye, sir."

The Bosun followed Matt to the bridgewing, where they stood silently staring aft at *Mahan*. Matt grimaced. "By the way, Boats, how are our other 'passengers' making out?"

Gray arched an eyebrow and then snorted. "Well, Skipper, I've been a little busy, and they might've strayed from my immediate presence a time or two . . ."

Matt chuckled. "But, Boats, you're not just a chief, you're *the* Chief. The Bosun! You're supposed to know everything that happens on this ship."

Gray grunted noncommittally. "Yes, sir. Lieutenant Mallory pulled his weight. He helped out a lot hauling ammo and if it weren't for him, I guess we'd've had to leave the Nip. He'll live, by the way." He glowered. "On the other hand, Kaufman's a wonder. He ran around all day, gettin' in the way and tryin' to tell everybody what to do. Finally, Campeti got fed up. He handed him a four-inch shell and told him he could carry it to the number one gun or he'd cram it . . . down his trousers . . . and throw him over the side."

Matt started to laugh, but the humor was replaced by anger at the self-important idiot who'd harassed his men during battle. He forced himself to maintain a placid expression but was shocked by how quickly his outrage flared. "What about the nurses? I heard one was killed."

Gray nodded. He put his hands in his pockets, but quickly withdrew them. When he answered, his voice held genuine regret. "Yes, sir. She was a pretty thing too. Leslie Runnels, or Ranells, or something. She was helping Doc with Rodriguez when they got hit. Rodriguez'll be okay, though. The cut on his leg wasn't very big, but they nearly didn't get the bleeding stopped. Cut an artery, I guess." He was quiet a moment, but when he continued, he was shaking his head. "The shell that got Doc and the nurse couldn't'a missed Rodriguez by a foot. The other nurses took over and did just fine. Their lieutenant—Tucker's her name—just jumped right in. I looked in a time or two, bringin' guys in, mostly, and there she was, shells slammin' through the ship, smoke and blood all over the place . . . and her stitchin' and cuttin' and giving orders as calm as you please, and her no bigger'n a button. I don't know what we would've done without her. Would've lost more men for sure." He stopped. "They went through hell, though, all of 'em, and that's a fact. We had a lot of wounded—and them losin' one of their own . . ."

"I'll have to thank her. Thank them all." Matt took a deep breath and let it out. "I have a rough idea of our casualties. I want the specifics, names and such, when I take a report from each division. A lot of letters to write . . ."

Courtney Bradford chose that moment to ascend the ladder and present himself. "I understand you need a pilot for these mysterious seas? Of course you do, and I'm just the fellow! The marine life around Menjangan is exquisite! Simply exquisite! There are no shallows, you know, just a sheer underwater cliff with all manner of fascinating creatures clinging precariously to it! Once I lowered a net and dragged it up the side and was amazed by what I found. Amazed!"

"Yes, well," replied Matt, taken aback. "I'm afraid we won't have time for sightseeing. I'd forgotten, though. You said you were a naturist?"

"Naturalist, actually. It's a hobby of mine. I planned to write a book one day." He shook his head wistfully. "This confounded war has certainly inconvenienced me, let me tell you!"

"What exactly does a naturalist do?"

"A naturalist, dear boy, is one who studies nature. It's a dreadfully inclusive term, but I'm a dreadfully inclusive naturalist. Most of us tend to have a specialty, but I have broader interests, shall we say. I'm not really an expert on anything, but I know a little about quite a lot. In fact, my book wasn't to be a treatise on any particular thing, per se, but more a general discussion of the various fauna of this region as a whole, don't you see? Of course."

They'd moved into the pilothouse as they spoke, and the rest of the watch were surreptitiously straining to listen to the strange Australian.

"Tell me, Mr. Bradford," asked the captain in a serious tone, "in your studies, did you ever happen to hear about that . . ." He hesitated, searching for a term. Somehow "sea monster," however appropriate, didn't strike him as a responsible description. He finally settled for "creature" regardless of its inadequacy. "I failed to ask you last night before you left the bridge."

Bradford looked pensive and glanced at the others within hearing and lowered his voice. "No, Captain. Not ever. And that school of fish! Abominable! I've never even *heard* of such a thing. Unless, of course . . ." He paused and removed his hat, fingers massaging his brow. "Have you ever heard of the plesiosaurs?" he asked hesitantly. Matt blinked, and Gray just shook his head. "They're quite fascinating, actually. A particularly formidable specimen of a type of plesiosaur was once found near Queensland. It's called kronosaurus, I believe, and its head is nearly eight feet long!"

With an audience including the entire bridge as his voice began to rise, Bradford warmed to his subject. "Quite horrible, I'm sure! Great long fins, or flippers, you might say, and a long mouth full of unusually terrifying teeth! Consummate predators, not unlike killer whales, I should think. Surely you remember hearing about them now?"

Matt shook his head and smiled. "No. I'm glad somebody has, though! That must've been what we saw. You sure described it well enough. They must be awful rare, or you'd hear more about them."

Chief Gray looked at Courtney Bradford with the skeptical expression of a man who's been told a fish story. "I been in the Navy almost as long as this ship," he rumbled, "and I never heard of 'pleezy-sores,' or whatever-the-hell-you-called-its."

Bradford stared at them, astonished. He resembled nothing more than a paunchy owl that awakened hanging upside down from a limb it knew it had been standing on. "No! You don't understand! It cannot *possibly* have been kronosaurus! They've been extinct for tens of millions of years!"

Matt looked at Bradford and took a deep breath. He shifted his shoulders uncomfortably. He definitely didn't need this endless procession of mysteries. He'd hoped that Bradford could sort them out.

"Extinct, as in all gone?" muttered Gray in an ominous tone.

Bradford was nodding. "Precisely. Extinct means precisely that. I didn't mean to imply ..."

"Hmm. Well. Boats, I assume you have duties? Very well. Mr. Bradford? We're going to hide out between Menjangan Island and Bali until nightfall. I hope you'll be available if we have questions. I'm going up top for a while." With that, Matt nodded at the two men and stepped to the ladder.

As he climbed, he heard the Chief mutter, "Real cute. If I ever hear you call the captain 'boy' again, I'll toss you in the wake!"

In spite of his concern, Matt couldn't help but grin as Bradford sputtered and protested and apologized at once. *Gray thinks he was spinning an educated fish story,* he thought, *but I'm not so sure. We definitely saw something eat those Japs, and it was damned real. Every now and then, something turns up that scientists thought was extinct forever. Maybe this*—he didn't even try to pronounce it—*is one of them?*

On the fire-control platform, he exchanged greetings with the morning watch and peered ahead at the landmasses looming before them. The flanks of both islands were shrouded in fog, but it wasn't too dense. It was unusual in these seas, but it shouldn't hazard navigation and it might help conceal them from planes. After a while he returned to the pilothouse.

Mahan followed closely behind as they crept carefully—with just a few suggestions from their guide—into the narrow, hazy strait that separated Menjangan Island from Bali. On the foredeck, the Bosun bellowed commands at the special sea and anchor detail. The anchors were dropped, and several men from each ship motored ashore on Menjangan with a heavy hawser. The bridge crew watched anxiously as the boats became vague shapes in the fog.

"You did instruct them to stay out of the water, I'm sure?" asked Mr. Bradford in a nervous tone. Matt glanced at him.

"You don't think there might be more of those fish here?"

Bradford shook his head. "There shouldn't have been any where we saw them."

Matt grunted agreement. "I wouldn't worry. After yesterday, I doubt anyone wants to get wet."

The anchors held well enough and they could have stayed right where they were, but Matt wanted to snug up as tight to the bank as they could and camouflage their ships with foliage from shore. It was strangely quiet. The roar of the blowers had faded to a steady rumble. There was only the slightest breeze, and the gentle swell of the strait lapped innocently against their battered hull. Men brought thin mattresses from below and spread them on deck to sleep away from the stuffy berthing spaces. Others continued making repairs. As always, Matt was struck by the contrast.

His destroyermen were capable of amazing feats of courage and endurance while on watch, but only because when they weren't, they could sack out anytime, anywhere, and in any situation. Many of the men shuffling about looking for a place to stretch out had been awake for thirty-six hours and more. Most who were busy had managed at least a little sleep during the night. He watched as two "snipes" emerged from below, squinting, as if even the fog-filtered morning light hurt their eyes. Beneath the grease and sweat-streaked soot covering them, he saw their pasty skins and realized they were the two firemen everyone called the Mice. He didn't remember ever seeing them above deck. They looked around, very much like mice that had just chewed through a wall into an unexplored room. Finally, they climbed the ladder onto the amidships deckhouse and crept to the ready ammunition locker behind the number two gun. They lay down on the bare deck and were probably asleep before they'd even finished moving. Of all the men, the damage-control parties and the engineering division had suffered the worst, he thought.

He joined Lieutenant Dowden, staring intently in the direction the boats had gone. They were visible in the thinning fog, tied to the rocky shore, but there was no activity. The island beyond the landing faded into haze, but they had the impression it was covered by dense brush and stunted trees. A prickly sensation of apprehension crept into his chest, but he shook it off. They would be searching for trees large enough to secure the hawsers to. Perhaps it was taking longer than expected to find any suitable ones.

From the island, they heard a muffled shot. Then another. They both raised binoculars and tried to pierce the haze. Three more shots thumped from shore, and without lowering the glasses Matt shouted up at the platform above. "Make ready on the starboard .30-cal, but hold your fire until I give the word!" The canvas cover on the gun was snatched away and a new belt of ammunition prepared.

Gunner's Mate 2nd Class Dennis Silva, ordinarily gun captain on number one, was on the trigger. He was probably the best they had and would have been a credit to the ship—if he weren't more often an embarrassment. He was tall and powerful and kept his hair burred so short he might as well have shaved it. Aboard ship, he was usually competent and professional, but ashore he was completely unable to behave. He always reminded Matt of a quote he once read: "Maleness gone berserk." That described Dennis Silva to a T. Matt would have restricted him to the ship for life, but he'd just go AWOL (he'd done it before) and wind up in more trouble than he could be rescued from. He was *Walker*'s Hercules—a valuable man, but he required . . . supervision. Now Silva peered at the boats like the rest of them, his hands on the weapon, but the muzzle was pointed up and away. One of his minions, Tom Felts, held the belt of linked cartridges.

"I see them!" exclaimed Dowden, pointing. Emerging from the gloom were several men. Two were helping a third. They reached one of the boats and piled in, pushing off from shore. There were a couple more shots and then the rest of the shore party ran down and hurriedly cast off the second boat. Matt heard the motors cough to life, and then the boats were speeding back toward *Walker*.

"I don't know what they're shooting at, Silva," Matt called above, "but keep that shoreline covered."

"Aye, aye, Skipper."

A few minutes later, both boats bumped alongside and the men climbed out, sending the injured crewman ahead. Matt was surprised to see a couple of the nurses waiting for him on deck. Bosun's Mate 1st Class Carl Bashear, who'd commanded the party, lingered over the wounded man and spoke to one of the nurses. Then he puffed up the ladder to the bridge.

"Skipper, we couldn't secure the hawsers," he said. He was breathing hard and his black hair was plastered to his skull. Even with the haze, the temperature was already over eighty degrees and the humidity was horrible.

"I can see that. What happened? Who got hurt?"

"Lizards, sir! It was *lizards*. Big ones."

"Impossible!" snorted Courtney Bradford.

Matt shot the Australian a look that silenced him. "What do you mean? What lizards? What were you shooting at?"

Bashear's breathing began to slow. "Damned if I know what I mean, Skipper, but there *were* lizards. We'd split up and were looking for some good trees to tie off to, and a couple more to drop in the water to make a pier. All of a sudden, Leo Davis takes to hollerin' that somethin' had ahold of him! Me and Vernon and Scott ran over there, and sure enough, this big-ass—'scuse me, sir—this dern big lizard has chomped down on Davis's leg and is draggin' him off."

Bradford was about to burst. "But—but—" he stammered. Matt held up his hand and motioned Bashear to continue.

"Yes, sir, thank you, sir. Anyway, ol' Davis is carryin' on that he's bein' ate, so we took to shootin' at the lizard. Me and Scott had rifles." He stopped a moment, and thankfully took a long gulp from a Coke the Bosun handed him. He smacked his lips. "Well," he continued, "it turned him loose and come at us." He shrugged. "We shot it some more. I'm pretty sure we killed it. Anyway, we grabbed up Davis and headed back to the boat. All of a sudden, there's *more* lizards, so we shot at them too. I guess we nearly didn't make it. All we had was the shells in the guns. And like I said, Skipper, those lizards was *big*."

"Preposterous!" sputtered Bradford. "The only 'lizards' that might attack a man are on the island of Komodo. That island, sir, is two hundred nautical miles from here. The great reptiles inhabiting it are found there and on a couple of small neighboring islands. Nowhere else. Certainly not Menjangan! My God, man! I've been here myself, and there are no such creatures! I don't believe there are even the smaller monitors."

Bashear eyed the Australian coldly. "You callin' me a liar?"

Gray interrupted. "These Komodo lizards—"

"Dragons, sir. We in the scientific community call them Komodo dragons. *Varanus komodoensis*, to be precise." Bradford sniffed.

"I don't care if they fly and blow fire out their ass," Gray growled impatiently. "Are they poisonous? One of my men was bitten."

Bradford blinked, his contention forgotten. "Oh, dear. Yes indeed, they're extremely poisonous—or rather, their bite is highly septic. We believe it has to do with bacteria in their mouths—" The Chief merely glanced at Bashear, who interrupted Bradford again.

"Skipper, with your permission . . ." Matt waved him on and Bashear hurried away.

Bradford turned and walked onto the starboard bridge-wing and peered at the island, which was becoming more distinct. Suddenly he stiffened. "Oh!" he exclaimed. "Oh, look! Someone lend me a glass, I beg you!" The assistant gunnery officer, Ensign Pruit Barry, shrugged and handed him his binoculars.

"There! Oh, there! There are *two* of them!" Matt joined him and raised his own binoculars for a look. On the beach, in the dwindling mist, was a pair of extremely large lizards. They appeared to be ten or twelve feet long from their blunt-nosed snouts to the tips of their whip-thin tails. They crept down almost to the water and seemed to stare at the pair of destroyers, their beady eyes fixed on the ships. "Oh, my goodness, they *are* big!" chortled Bradford excitedly. "They're the largest I've ever seen. And their color! Green and red! Amazing!" Then, as they watched, one of the lizards raised itself onto its hind legs until it gained a nearly entirely erect posture. It stood with its head bobbing up and down as if testing the air. Bradford gasped.

"My God! Oh, Captain, I must go ashore! Look at that! It's standing up! My God! This must be an entirely new species! Never before seen! Just think of it!" Matt lowered his binoculars and turned to the man. "Captain," Bradford continued, oblivious to Matt's stare, "I insist you allow me ashore! I must have a closer look!"

When Matt spoke his voice was quiet, but he couldn't hide his incredulity. "Mr. Bradford, have you entirely forgotten yourself?"

The Australian wrenched his gaze from the beach and regarded Captain Reddy. His mouth hung open as if to protest, but then it clamped abruptly shut. With a mournful expression, he nodded. "Of course, Captain. Of course." He sighed. "I apologize. It's not every day a man of my interests observes a new species, particularly one this important." He glanced wistfully at the island. "Just one more debt I owe those miserable Jappos."

Matt nodded understanding. "I think we're all keeping score." He turned to Dowden. "It doesn't look like we'll be able to secure to the island. We'll remain at anchor here. Every pair of eyes not otherwise occupied will watch for aircraft, and I want to be ready to move in a hurry."

Matt suddenly reflected with surprise that he'd already begun addressing Lieutenant Dowden as *Walker*'s executive officer. With Jim gone and the other senior officers dead, he was the obvious choice. He'd been Jim's assistant and he'd filled in for him often enough. In many ways, execs had the hardest job on any ship, and this wasn't the time to appoint somebody unaccustomed to the role. He was just a "jay gee," and very young for the job, but with a war on he'd likely be a full lieutenant by the time they got to Australia anyway. He would do fine. Besides, the only other possibilities—within the chain of command—were Alan Letts, the (j.g.) supply officer, Garrett, and Spanky. Spanky and Garrett were essential where they were and Letts was . . . a disappointment. He was a good guy and knew his job, but he wasn't very industrious. *Walker* needed a go-getter right now, and the willowy, blond-haired lieutenant from Tennessee certainly fit that description.

Matt mentally shook his head and continued. "Chances are they won't spot us, though. They'll be looking at the strait. Signal *Mahan* and ask Mr. Ellis if he's comfortable coming across for an hour or so, or whether he'd prefer to report by Morse lamp."

*   *   *

Matt sat on the bunk in his small cabin and tested his freshly shaven chin with his fingers. It had been difficult negotiating the razor around the painful glass cuts scattered across his face. Satisfied, he finished dressing and looked in the mirror over his desk. *Better,* he thought. The quick shower he'd indulged in had helped. His eyes were still red and there were circles underneath them, and he was still so tired that when he blinked it seemed his eyelids moved too slowly and then tried to stick together. He sat back on the bunk and listened to the growing conversations in the crowded wardroom. If only he could lean over and lie down. Just for a minute. The cramped, uncomfortable bunk was the most inviting thing in the world at that moment.

Someone knocked on the doorframe. "Sir?" said Garrett hesitantly. "Everybody's here." Matt sighed and rose to his feet. Squaring his shoulders, he stepped through the doorway and down the short corridor into the wardroom. Most of his officers and department heads—many new to their jobs—were there. Ellis and a bandage-swaddled ensign named Tony Monroe had come from *Mahan*. Monroe was assistant navigation officer and aside from Perry Brister, her chief engineer, the sole surviving officer. Brister remained on *Mahan* to continue repairs—and so there'd be at least one officer aboard her if they had to move in a hurry.

Three of the nurses and the Army pilots were also in the room. Courtney Bradford leaned against the far bulkhead since there were too few chairs, and Juan circulated through the crowd filling coffee cups from the two carafes in his hands. Everyone was sweating in the stifling heat, and cigarette smoke eddied and vented away through the punctures in the hull that made up two of the wardroom walls. In the general hubbub, the captain wasn't immediately noticed. Garrett shouted over the din:

"Captain on deck!"

Everyone came to attention, with the exception of Captain Kaufman, who continued leaning against the bulkhead with an expression of hostile disdain.

"As you were, gentlemen . . . and ladies," Matt added for the nurses' benefit. Even exhausted, he noticed that the nurses were young and attractive, and he recognized the one who had brought coffee to the bridge and made a small nod of appreciation. One of them, though, the lieutenant, returned his gaze with a frank appraisal of her own.

What Sandra saw was a very tired young man who'd been violently forced to shoulder extraordinary responsibilities under very stressful—and unusual—circumstances. They all knew their predicament, or at least thought they did, and it was no secret that there'd been strange goings-on. She detected uncertainty beneath his veneer of confidence, but whether that reflected the situation, the unusual events, or the heavy burden of responsibility for two badly damaged ships and all their people, she didn't know. Instinctively, her heart went out to him. She was a nurse, and she knew when a man was suffering, even through gritted teeth. Though his injuries were superficial, the wounds to his ship and her people were reflected in his eyes.

Matt had the uneasy feeling, looking into her green eyes, that the nurse lieutenant saw beyond his facade of calm, and he quickly turned his attention to the room. "First, our own condition: I don't have all the details yet, but I have some idea. We can steam, our leaks are under control, and we have fuel for a twenty-knot run to Perth. Since our plans are contingent upon *Mahan*'s capabilities, however, I think Mr. Ellis should start."

Jim nodded and cleared his throat. "Thanks, Skipper." He looked around the compartment. "*Mahan* took a hell of a beating. She's not sinking, but everything topside is a wreck. Half her crew is dead and there're twenty wounded. Some seriously." He looked at the surprise on the assembled faces. "Yeah, that's a pretty lopsided number," he said grimly. "Most of the casualties were on the bridge and in the aft fireroom. Everybody in the pilothouse or on the fire-control platform was killed. She has no fire control at all. Guns two and four are okay, and we can use them in local control, but that's it. Number one might be repaired, but we haven't really even checked." He sighed wearily. "The machine guns amidships are okay, so we're not totally helpless from the air, but all torpedoes are expended and I'd rather not push her past fifteen knots. She can make that, the forward fireroom's fine, it's just . . . well"—he gestured at the beams of light entering the wardroom through the holes—"you know.

"Anyway," he continued, "*Mahan*'s shorthanded as hell—only about forty effectives, not counting the guys I took aboard—but she's not finished yet. Whatever you decide, Captain, we'll do. We might just want to take it a little easy. I also really hope we don't have to fight again." He chuckled wryly. "At least not as briskly as yesterday." His last comment drew scattered chuckles, but the mirth was tempered by the realization of what that fight had cost.

"What's the status of your wounded?" Matt asked.

"Mostly stable, but we could use a hand. The pharmacist's mate is dead, and the surgeon's run pretty ragged."

Matt nodded, and glanced at the nurses. They were a study in contrasts. The one who'd brought coffee—he'd learned her name was Karen Theimer—seemed nervous, jittery, almost fragile. She blinked constantly as her eyes quested around the compartment and her hands squirmed against one another on the table. The one beside her, Pam Cross by her name tag, was almost as short as Lieutenant Tucker and outwardly as self-possessed, but her eyes told a different story. The other two nurses, Beth Grizzel and Kathy McCoy, weren't present. The sandy-blond lieutenant was still watching him, which was understandable. Everyone was. But once again, her expression of appraisal left him uneasy. Besides, she was a knockout. He managed to smile at her. "You must be Lieutenant Tucker."

She stood from her seat at the table. Since the captain didn't sit, she wouldn't remain seated while speaking to him. "Lieutenant Sandra Tucker, sir."

"Lieutenant, I apologize for not greeting you when you came aboard, and I'm sorry I haven't had a chance since, but I'd like to thank you now for all the help you and the other nurses have given us. I'd also like to extend my deepest regrets for the loss of Ensign Ranell." Several heads bobbed, and there was a general murmur of condolences.

"Thank you, Captain Reddy. I'm sorry too. I'm sorry for Leslie, and for all our losses. My nurses and I stand ready to help any way we can."

"Thank you, Lieutenant. As a matter of fact, that raises my next subject, and that's to ask if you'd feel comfortable detaching a few nurses to *Mahan*."

"Of course, Captain. I'm willing to go, but I'd ask you to allow my nurses a choice." She smiled ironically. "Not that there seems much difference in the relative seaworthiness of either ship, if you'll forgive my saying so."

Matt smiled back at her amid the ensuing chuckles and good-natured indignation. "Absolutely. They can choose, but you may not. The needs of the service, not to mention the needs of my crew, dictate that I break with tradition— as well as virtually every regulation I'm aware of—and appoint you acting medical officer. Under the circumstances, we'll consider it a separate department."

"Yes, sir." She grinned. "I wouldn't enter it in the log, though, if I were you." Matt grinned back.

"Perhaps not." He paused, watching her sit, admiring her poise and apparent calm. *Gray was right,* he thought. *She's something else.* He cleared his throat self-consciously and addressed the others. "Next on the list, Lieutenant Dowden is acting exec in Mr. Ellis's place, for as long as he commands *Mahan*. Rick Tolson is acting navigation officer. Larry? You and Rick better pick assistants. Think hard about it, but give me your recommendations as soon as possible." He turned to Chief Gray. "How about the deck divisions?"

Gray's brow furrowed, and he tucked his hands behind the belt encircling his ample girth. "Like we talked earlier, we're still afloat. But I'm running shorthanded too." The deck division's noncombat occupation was general maintenance, and it served as a labor pool. He glanced at Lieutenant Ellis, who now had some of his men, but it wasn't an accusation, merely a statement of fact. "All the leaks are under control. We welded a lot of seams, which'll have the yard-apes throwin' fits, but there's no way to replace rivets out here. The big holes are all above the waterline. If we don't run into heavy seas, we'll be okay. We're workin' on covering those holes too, but it's slow. Some are pretty big and there's nothing for it but to patch 'em." He cocked an eyebrow. "Not a lot of plate steel just layin' around. If we had time, we could cut patches out of *Mahan*'s aft deck-house, but for now we're sort of working our way up. I figured the stuff close to the waterline had priority."

Matt was nodding. "Very well. Anything to add?"

"Nothing big. About a thousand little things are in my report. Mostly the same stuff the old girl throws at us every day, times ten."

"Mr. Garrett?"

Lieutenant Garrett now wore a real bandage on the back of his neck to protect his scalded skin. Thankfully, his injuries weren't more serious. He fidgeted and cleared his throat, and Matt suppressed a smile. He'd been the personification of cool professionalism during the action, but now, in this setting, he was more like a schoolkid than a naval officer.

"Uh, main battery's operational and responding to fire control." He paused and shrugged. "The range finder's wrecked. A big chunk of shrapnel just about chopped it off—but it wasn't any good anyway. The ready ammunition lockers have been replenished. There's something wrong with one of the .50s, but Gunner's Mate Silva says he'll have it working by this afternoon."

"Tell him to get a move on. That one gun represents a quarter of our antiaircraft defense. What about torpedoes? Ensign Sandison's working on them now, correct?"

"Yes, sir. He still doesn't know what the problem was. A connection on the mount, maybe? He was drawing them out of seven, nine, and eleven, and intended to put them in one, three, and five, unless you'd rather disperse them."

"No, that's fine. What's the status on the two torpedoes we picked up in Surabaya?"

"They're not sure what's wrong with them. They were condemned. Hopefully it's something we can fix. One looks pretty beat up, though."

"Thanks, Greg. Have Sandison keep me informed about his progress. Now, let's see. Engineering? Spanky, let's hear from you."

"Yes, sir. Well, we took a beating, sure, but it looks like most everything's under control. We might even get number two boiler back on line. We'll keep her going if the water stays out. Twenty knots, at least." Matt smiled at

Spanky's qualifier and started to ask a question, but the engineer wasn't finished. He shook his head and continued in a quiet tone. "Honestly, sir, I don't know how we made it. This old girl'd had enough before the war even started, but I guess she's tougher than we thought. She deserves a lot of credit." He shrugged. "God should get the most, I guess. I didn't see it, but there's talk of a weird squall . . . Anyway, I'm not real damned religious, but that's where most of the credit should go."

Matt controlled a shudder at the thought of the Squall. Somehow, he didn't think God was responsible for that. But who knows? He looked at McFarlane and saw the engineer staring back.

"A lot of credit should go to Captain Reddy."

There was a general murmur of agreement to the unexpected compliment, and Matt felt his face heat. He didn't think he deserved much credit at all. Spanky was a good officer, though; he knew how important it was for the crew to have confidence in their captain. For the captain to have confidence in himself. Deserved or not, he appreciated Spanky's gesture.

"Thank you, Mr. McFarlane." He paused to sip coffee from the cup Juan handed him, breaking eye contact with the engineer. It was his own white porcelain cup, the one he always used in the wardroom. He had another just like it on the bridge. As always, his eyes strayed to the black printing around the side: CAPTAIN—USS WALKER—DD-163. With mixed feelings he took a breath.

"We'll stay here for the day, at anchor, and make whatever repairs are practical." He looked back at McFarlane. "Maintain full steam, but I want no smoke. We'll keep double lookouts and the machine gun and three-inch crews will remain at their stations at all times. I know the three-inch isn't good for much, but a puff of black smoke in the air might make enemy planes think twice. I intend to run the strait tonight, as fast as we can manage. Hopefully, we'll have some torpedoes by then. Jim, I know you'd rather go slow, but I want every turn you can make, at least through the strait."

Ellis nodded. "We'll keep up, Skipper."

"Good. Once again, we'll lead. Stay close, though. There'll

be almost no moon, so it'll be dark. Sonar's still out, but we won't waste time zigzagging. The strait's too tight for that anyway. I think, even with all our problems, we have a good chance—if we make it fast and sneaky."

He took another sip of coffee and looked at the faces in the room. He'd rather just ignore the next subject, but he didn't have that choice.

"That brings us to the last item of business." He noticed several people shift uncomfortably. "Everyone knows, in addition to our other problems, there've been ... strange events. The crew's talking about it, and they have enough to worry about without a bunch of mysteries." He let that sink in for a moment. "On the other hand, if you discourage the talk it'll just make them worry even more. You must all assure the crew by your words and actions that we're taking care of the problem, whatever it is, and it's not something to concern themselves with. Do I make myself clear?"

There were nods.

"That may be easier said than done." Captain Kaufman spoke for the first time. He stepped forward and put his hands on the table. "What's the dope on the radio?"

Matt gritted his teeth. "It's still not working."

"That's not what I hear. I hear it's working fine, but we're not receiving anything but static. Have you tried to transmit?"

Matt looked at him incredulously. "Of course we haven't tried to transmit! We might as well paint ourselves pink and steam through the channel in broad daylight. It's obvious the Japs have carriers between here and Australia. The reports before we left implied they did, and we've since seen carrier planes. That means they're ahead of us and behind, and can easily triangulate our position. It's equally obvious, despite what you've heard, that the radio can't be working—otherwise we'd hear something. They don't know what's wrong with it, but there must be a problem. Checking the radio by giving away our position seems sort of counterproductive, don't you think?" Matt's voice rose as his annoyance grew. "And frankly, Captain Kaufman, as to your earlier statement, if you find it difficult to suppress your fears in front of the men, I prefer you not go around them."

Kaufman's face turned purple. He looked around, surprised to see almost everyone, even the nurses, regarding him with hostility. Only the bandaged ensign from *Mahan*—Monroe—seemed sympathetic. He barely heard Gray whisper to Lieutenant Garrett: "Ought to be in the chain locker with the Nip." He was practically sputtering with rage, and he started to reply, when they all became aware of a commotion on deck. It might have been going on for a minute or two, but with the confrontation the wardroom hadn't noticed. Now they heard running feet and rising voices.

Bernard Sandison burst into the wardroom, wide-eyed and gasping. "Beg pardon, Skipper, but you better come on deck."

"Are we under attack?"

"No, sir. Not under attack, but . . . just please come and see."

As one, spurred by the ensign's cryptic statements, the assembly crowded for the passageway. "Make way!" the Bosun bellowed. "Make way for the captain!"

All the officers, including Nurse Tucker, scrambled up the ladder to the pilothouse. Everyone else climbed onto the amidships deckhouse to join most of the crew already there, or along the port rail below. In fact, the port side was so crowded that *Walker* was heeling noticeably. As soon as he gained the bridge, Matt heard Gray bellowing for the men to return to their duties before they capsized the ship. It was no use. For once, even the Bosun's legendary wrath was wasted. Matt snatched his binoculars from Ensign Tolson and looked toward Bali—the direction everyone was pointing and staring. He adjusted the objective slightly.

The fog to the south had almost entirely dissipated and he clearly saw the northeastern coast of Bali less than a mile away. It was a scenic view, about what he'd expected from descriptions he'd heard and pictures he'd seen. Beyond the dark volcanic beach was a rocky shoreline, choked with a lush hedge of vines or brush. Beyond this boundary, a broad coastal plain rose steadily upward to the flanks of a distant mountain. He'd read the slope was terraced and had been for hundreds of years. Mr. Bradford had commented on it as well. He saw no terracing, but everything else seemed as it should. Except one thing. Upon the plain before him, in the middle distance, was a small herd of what could only be described as dinosaurs, grazing slowly along.

Ridiculously, the first thing that popped into his mind was that they were smaller than he would have thought, about the size of Asian elephants. But the long necks and whip-like tails protruding from the otherwise quite elephantine bodies were exactly what he'd have expected of an artist's rendering of, say, a brontosaurus. He heard a small sound and glanced aside.

"Somebody grab Mr. Bradford. He's about to faint."

Jim Ellis leaned close and whispered nervously in his ear. "We're *damn* sure not in Kansas anymore, Skipper."

Matt grunted distractedly as the amazing creatures ambled unconcernedly along, much like cattle feeding on grass, except these animals took as many leaves from the trees as they did grass from underfoot. "Personally," Matt whispered back, his voice shaky, "I liked the black and white part of that movie the best. Everything that happened once it went to color gave me the creeps."

The Mice filed tiredly back to their stifling lair. There was way too much commotion on deck to rest. No good ever came from leaving their boilers. One of the water tenders looked up as they entered.

"What the hell's going on up there? We run aground or something? Why are we heeling over?"

Isak looked at him with bleary, disinterested eyes. "Dinosaurs on Bali," he said simply. Then he and his friend lay down next to the hull, where the water outside kept the plates slightly cooler. They wadded up a pair of greasy life jackets for pillows and promptly went to sleep.

All over the ship, men slowly returned to their duties or tried to rest. Some talked nervously among themselves, and others said nothing at all, pondering the implications of this latest mystery. A few might have panicked if not for the steadying influence of the older hands, but mostly the destroyermen took it in stride. It was just one more thing. What was one more thing after all they'd been through? They didn't know what was happening and they knew it wasn't right, but most were too tired to care. Men from Mars flying by on giant blue chickens would probably not have elicited a more prolonged response—but they probably would have been shot at if they came too close.

Dennis Silva was thinking just that. He manned the .50-caliber machine gun on the port side of the amidships deckhouse. He'd been almost finished putting it back together when the commotion began, and he'd been one of the first to see the creatures. Now he stood, still watching, with just a few others. The first group of "bronto-sarries" had moved along, but there was a steady stream of other, equally improbable animals. A smaller group resembling the first ones they'd seen appeared.

"Boy," exclaimed Silva, "I'd sure like to shoot me one of those!" Tom Felts and Paul Stites looked at him.

"What the hell for?" Stites asked incredulously.

Silva shrugged. "Ever'body and ever'thing's been pickin' on us lately. I feel like pickin' on somethin' myself for a change."

Felts shook his head. "I wouldn't pick on one of those damn things. Hell, Dennis, what if they can swim? You'd have prehistoric monsters down on us too! Ain't the Japs enough?"

Stites peered over the side at the water speculatively. "You think them things are really dinosaurs? I mean, there ain't supposed to be dinosaurs on Bali, is there? I thought they all died off."

"Course there ain't *supposed* to be none here." Silva guffawed. "There ain't supposed to be none anywhere! All that's supposed to be here is a bunch'a nu-bile young native girls runnin' around without shirts."

Stites and Felts both looked at the island. "Well, where the hell are they?"

"Better ask the Skipper, fellas." Silva's grin went away, and when he spoke again his voice was uncharacteristically subdued. "I bet he don't know either."

For the first time since she could remember, Sandra didn't know what to do. She didn't have an answer or a solution or even a suggestion. That hit her almost as hard as anything else. Seeing the creatures on Bali did something to her that nothing else had ever accomplished: it shook her sense of pragmatic self-assurance to its core. She was still on the bridge, although she doubted she was supposed to be, but no one asked her to leave. There were no more critical patients to treat, and the seriously injured had been transferred to their berths, where the other nurses and their shipmates fussed over them and tried to make them comfortable. If not for the possibility of air attack, she would have already asked to have them moved on deck for fresh air. *Maybe I should move them up,* she thought, but the latest shock left her unable to concentrate. She'd always prided herself on her ability to adjust to any situation; that was what good nurses had to do. But this! What was going on?

She looked at the captain. He was deeply involved in a whispered, serious conversation with several officers. After the initial excitement, the ship grew eerily quiet. She looked aft. Now the mist had cleared and the sun beat down once more, and most of the men had resumed their duties, or the perpetual quest for shade. Now and then, however, she saw men glance furtively at the island as if to confirm they'd actually seen what they thought they had. She looked again herself. Sure enough, the bizarre animals were still there. The place was teeming with them. She shuddered. She was *not* imagining things. If she was, so was everyone else.

She looked back at the group of officers and saw the fatigue in their expressions—the tired, bloodshot eyes and haunted looks as they too glanced nervously toward Bali now and then. Captain Reddy looked little better than the others, but she admired the way he hid the fear and uncertainty he must feel. He just stood there, listening attentively and nodding occasionally. When she heard his murmured words, she was encouraged by how calm he sounded. She found it ironic and unsettling that, shortly before, she had been evaluating his steadiness from a perspective of self-confidence. Now she looked to him for reassurance.

Courtney Bradford had recovered himself, and now leaned against the port bridgewing rail, oblivious to the concerns of others and staring in rapt fascination through binoculars. She moved beside him.

"Are they truly ... dinosaurs?" she asked in a quiet voice.

He nodded vigorously. "Of course! They do seem rather small, compared to what we were given to expect by the scale of most assembled fossils. But indeed, there can be nothing else to call them. Obviously, they shouldn't be here! I've studied the charts, and I've been here before. That island *is* Bali. The only difference is the lack of agricultural terracing and, well, the dinosaurs, of course! The terracing is strange enough. It hasn't been very long since my last visit, and I can assure you that even with a concerted effort and heavy machinery, the terraces couldn't possibly have been removed so thoroughly as to leave no trace they ever existed. As for the dinosaurs?" He shrugged and smiled happily. "I have no explanation."

"But surely ... what could've happened?" She pointed across the water. "Those things have been gone for millions of years! You don't think ... " She couldn't finish.

"Once again, I have no idea," Bradford replied cheerfully. "Perhaps that disconcerting squall had some unusual effect beyond what we experienced? Perhaps. Time travel?" He snorted. "Hardly. If the Squall did something to us, it didn't send us back in time! Time travel is, of course, impossible. Besides, during the age those creatures"—he waved toward land—"roamed the earth, the shorelines were shaped quite differently. Warmer temperatures, higher water ... These islands are frightfully volcanic. They might not have even existed!" He pointed shoreward again. "That *is* Bali! So whatever is afoot, we're in the *now,* if you follow my meaning? Of course you do."

"But if this is now, *where* is it now? And where is the now we should be in?" Her voice was almost pleading. "Dinosaurs on Bali are impossible too, aren't they?"

"Precisely."

They didn't run the strait that night. Instead, they remained at anchor and continued repairs while the officers pondered what to do. It was clear now, beyond doubt, that something extraordinary had befallen them. Bradford's argument that they hadn't been transported back in time was gratefully accepted, for the most part, but that left the burning question of what *had* happened. Was this simply some bizarre phenomenon localized in the vicinity where the Squall had occurred? Or had they been transported somehow to an entirely alien world? No. That couldn't be. The stars were right, the sliver of moon did exactly what it should as it traversed the heavens overhead, and the charts showed them to be exactly where they were—anchored snugly between Bali and Menjangan Island.

But that couldn't be. Nothing that had happened since the fight with *Amagi* and their subsequent entry into the Squall had been normal. The moon, the stars, the sun itself, and the very air they breathed—the smell of the sea upon which they gently rocked—all testified to their senses that nothing had changed. But there were monsters in the water and giant lizards on the land, and that couldn't be.

Despite all their planning in the wardroom that day, no one knew how to proceed. If they'd been transported to another time or place, what about the Japanese? Were they still in danger from attack? If they went to Perth, would it even be there? Like any good destroyer commander, even in the face of such profound questions, Matt immediately began to worry about fuel. What if the phenomenon extended to Australia? Where would they get fuel? If it was even possible that Perth was gone, should they risk wasting all their fuel to get there? These were the questions he pondered now. The immediate concerns. What they would do in the long run hadn't even entered his tired mind.

Like most destroyermen in the Asiatic Fleet, Matt had no family back home, besides his parents, to concern him. A lot of the old hands left wives and sweethearts in the Philippines, but most of them had already resigned themselves to the fact that there was nothing they could do for them while the Japanese ran unchecked. Even when they steamed away from Cavite that last time, Matt was struck by the stoicism of most of the married men. They knew they might never return. If they did, that would be good. If they didn't, they'd keep fighting until they did. It was all very matter-of-fact. Whatever had occurred when they entered the Squall had created a whole slew of distracting implications, and he wondered how the men would react to leaving their whole world behind? He wasn't yet prepared to deal with that. Right now, his primary concern was for the safety of *Walker* and *Mahan* and their crews—and how best to use their fuel.

Utter fatigue finally forced him to turn in, but before he did, he ordered Jim to shut down one of *Mahan*'s boilers. *Walker* would keep both hers lit, just in case, but henceforth, they would conserve fuel any way they could. It was all he could do. Perhaps after some sleep he would think of something. Maybe he'd wake from this terrible dream and find that all he had to worry about, once more, was the Japanese. He stripped off his sweat-sodden uniform and lay on his bunk. The small, rattling, oscillating fan on the bulkhead labored to move the dank, stifling air. He was so very tired, but a vast tension clutched his chest. Even as he reached to turn off the light, the ghosts and monsters of the last few days began to gather around.

Captain Reddy was sitting in his chair on the bridge when the forenoon watch came on at 0800. The familiar routine of the watch change had a soothing effect that helped dispel the unpleasant aftereffects of unremembered nightmares that had plagued his sleep. Lieutenant Garrett relieved Larry Dowden, who immediately went in search of a cool place to rest. Garrett looked like he'd had a difficult night too, and he acted for a moment as if he had something to say. But then he stepped onto the port bridgewing where Courtney Bradford stood. The Australian was waiting impatiently for the morning fog to disperse so he could view Bali's wonders once more. Matt stood and stretched, and then went back to stare at the chart. He heard the sound of someone climbing the ladder at the rear of the pilothouse and checked his watch. Right on time.

"Morning, Jim."

"Morning, sir," Jim Ellis replied.

"Sleep well?" Jim made a wry face and stifled a yawn, theatrically. Matt chuckled. "Look, I've made a decision you're not going to like, but I don't see any alternative." Matt's former exec looked at him questioningly. "I'm going to take *Walker* to Surabaya and have a look around. If everything's as it should be, we'll still have fuel for a slow run to Australia. If the ... phenomenon has affected Surabaya like Bali, we can only assume the same is true for Perth, if not the whole world. If that's the case . . . Well, we'll figure out what to do. If Surabaya's unchanged, or we run into Japs, we'll turn around and collect you. *Mahan* will remain here until then. I'll leave three of the nurses and all the most seriously wounded with you." He grimaced. "I know you're shorthanded, so I won't leave you the prisoner to guard, but I will inflict Captain Kaufman on you. Maybe you can get some work out of him. I think his lieutenant will be a help, at least." He motioned toward Bradford. "I don't know whether to leave him here to gawk at the animals or take him along. He might prove useful again if we have to scrounge for fuel."

"I don't like you leaving, sir, but it sounds like as good a plan as any. *Mahan* would just slow you down and give you something else to worry about in a fight." Jim grinned. "As for Mr. Bradford, I'd just as soon you take him. I'd have to watch him constantly to keep him from swimming ashore, sea monsters or not. As you said, if I don't have men to guard a Jap, I sure can't keep up with him."

Matt chuckled. "Very well. We might as well get started. If we're not back in three days, proceed to Perth alone. Alor will be our rally point. If we don't meet you there . . . we're not coming."

The unusual mists had mostly cleared by the time the personnel were transferred and *Walker*'s anchor chain clanked and rattled through the hawse and into the well. The special sea and anchor detail directed a spray of seawater from the fire hose on the chain as it came aboard. Matt stepped out on the starboard bridgewing and peered at the enigmatic Menjangan. He noticed the wind had begun to swing the bow toward it, now that the anchor had cleared the bottom.

"Starboard engine ahead slow." He spoke quietly, but his voice carried to the helmsman.

"Starboard ahead slow, aye," confirmed Tony Scott. Matt sighed. The routine of ship handling soothed the tension of their predicament. The anchor came aboard as the ship twisted to maintain her position and the men on the fo'c'sle leaned against the safety chains to hose the mud and weed off the anchor. It was a procedure he'd witnessed many times, but for the first time he truly appreciated the efficient and matter-of-fact way the deck-apes accomplished it. He was glad to see that no matter what happened, some things never changed. Things like duty.

Suddenly the intercom buzzed, and the bridge talker opened the circuit to the lookout, Alfred Vernon, in the crow's nest.

"Bridge! I have a surface target! Bearing three five zero! Range . . . damn! It's hard to tell. The mist is still heavy in the strait. I make it six zero, double zero! Whatever it is, it's *big*!" Vernon's voice was pitched high with excitement.

"Sound general quarters!" shouted Matt. "Signal *Mahan* to head for the rally point. We'll . . . distract whoever it is and catch up tonight!"

In the aft fireroom, Spanky had just returned the coffeepot to its place near the burner when the general alarm sounded. Then the bells rang up AHEAD FLANK and all hell broke loose. He dropped his cup reaching for something to hold on to, and it shattered. The stern crouched down as the big screws bit and *Walker* surged ahead. The Mice and the water tender worked frantically to keep water out of the turbines. The blowers roared and raw fuel gushed straight into the stacks. Isak swore when the coffeepot fell to the deck, sending scalding liquid sloshing across his legs. Men scampered about, sliding the loosened deck plates back where they belonged as the ship picked up speed, but began settling back into a relatively normal and only slightly nerve-racking acceleration.

Spanky looked around at the aftermath of chaos and wiped sweat from his brow as he checked for blown gauges. "Bloody hell!" he muttered. "I guess the Skipper didn't take the hint when I asked him to take it easy."

*C*hack-Sab-At was sulking. High in the air, at the very top of the first great wing—almost a hundred fifty tails above the main deck of *Salissa* Home—he could concentrate on nothing but his rejection. He should have known. Selass had flirted with him only as a means of attracting Saak-Fas, first son of the clan chief controlling the center, and most prestigious, of Home's three wings. He realized now, with a measure of embarrassed bitterness, that he'd fallen for her ruse, as had his rival. Her pretense of favor easily convinced Saak-Fas to take her to mate before it came Chack's turn to choose. No matter. He was young and not without prospects. He had a wide choice of eligible mates. He was a first son also, and though his sister was older and closer in line to succeed their mother as clan chief of the forward wing, he expected to go far. He was the best wing runner on all *Salissa* Home and when a new Home was built in a season or two, he would climb to the top of its center wing and become fas chief himself.

Or maybe not, he corrected himself glumly.

Selass might truly dislike him enough to see to it that her father, the High Chief of *Salissa*, did not grant him that honor. It wasn't unheard of. The hereditary nature of the wing "nobility" was rarely interfered with, and each of the three wing clans of Home was virtually autonomous. Except, of course, in how they cooperated with the other clans to move Home from place to place. If a clan chief were incompetent, or unable to agree with one or both of the other wing clans—or the Body of Home clan, for that matter—the succession could be altered. High Chiefs always rose from the Body of Home clan and were supposedly impartial to the bickering among the wings. They had the power to confirm or deny all successions and, indeed, the power to banish.

Keje-Fris-Ar was sovereign over them all and literally held the power of life and death. If he began to dislike Chack, life—which until that very morning had seemed so full of promise—might reveal progressively more disappointment as time went by. Subconsciously, Chack knew Keje was a good and benevolent ruler. He would not countenance any personal vendetta based on a scornful daughter's whim. But Chack felt sorry for himself, and he was in no mood to limit the depths of his misery. It didn't help that, try as he might, he couldn't shake the vision of Selass's soft silver fur and green eyes from his mind.

He glanced far below at the surface of Home and saw the many Body of Home people performing their daily chores: salting fish from the morning drag or tending the plants that grew from under the protective overhangs ranged entirely around *Salissa*. Life went on as it did every day, day after day, during fair-weather times. The People were happily heedless of his puny disappointment, for the People *were* happy, for the most part. Few water monsters were a threat to anything as large as Home, and only the worst storms were noticed. The only threats were the rare mountain fish, land, and of course, the Grik.

Mountain fish were few and encountered only in the deepest regions of the Great Seas, where Homes of the People rarely ventured. Land was easily avoided. The Sky Priests, with their mystical instruments and scrolls, saw to that. If weather hindered the path they decreed, the sharp eyes of the wing-tip watchers—the post that Chack stood—would see danger in time for the Body of Home clan to deploy the great fins that could move them against all but the most furious sea. If even that failed, then they had the huge copper feet, two at each end of Home, that could be dropped into the sea attached to a great cable. There had never been a blow—not even a strakka—that could conquer the feet.

The People really feared only the Grik. The Grik were the Ancient Enemy, who cast them from paradise long ago. So long had it been that even to the Sky Priests, it was just "Long Ago." But the People escaped the Grik, and it had been so long since any had been seen that they'd become creatures of legend, of myth, of nightmare—boogeymen to frighten younglings into performing their chores. If they did exist, they dwelt safely across the Western Ocean, upon which no vessel could pass. That was what the People believed for generation upon generation—until the Grik came again and an ancient, almost instinctual dread was revived.

They hadn't been long in these waters, but there were more of them all the time, and they were liable to appear anywhere in their ridiculously small and fragile Homes. Homes that only a few hundred could travel upon, but Homes that were amazingly fleet and maneuverable and had very sharp teeth. Homes that always attacked. In Chack's first seven seasons, he'd seen only one of their tiny Homes, and it had attacked them—only to be beaten off. But the shock of that day lingered still. That such a small thing with such frightening creatures would attack without thought or warning—and with such dreadful ferocity—still troubled his sleep. The next seven seasons carried him into young adulthood, and he'd seen no less than six more Grik Homes. Each time one appeared, it attacked without fail. They never managed to do more than inflict minor damage, but always a few of the People were slain repelling them. One such had been Chack's father. It made no sense. The Grik had to be at least a little intelligent, else they couldn't have built the fast little ships. But to attack Homes of the People from their much smaller craft was like flasher-fish against gri-kakka. They could wound, but nothing more. The priests taught that Grik were creatures of the land. Perhaps that explained their madness.

Chack didn't pretend to understand them, any more than he understood the treachery of females. He glanced at his sister, Risa, on the wing support a dozen tails beneath him. She watched him with concern in her large amber eyes—and impatience. He knew Risa loved him; she was his very best friend. But she also thought he took things much too seriously. She made a joke of everything except her duty, but there was a difference between giving and taking a joke—and becoming one. Her body language told him more than words ever could: he was acting a fool. He blinked rueful acknowledgment and resumed scanning the skyline. They were in a confined area and as good as the priests were at laying a course, it was instilled in wing-tips from birth that they could never be too careful. Besides, it was in confined areas that the Grik usually chose to attack.

He was studying the hazy shoreline with just that thought in mind when he first saw something strange. A large puff of black smoke appeared above the haze that lingered between the small island and the large one. There was a sudden impression of rapid motion and a white froth grew on the water. A smallish shape, advancing impossibly fast, appeared atop the foam, under a diminishing cloud of smoke. He clung to his perch for a few moments more with his jaw hanging slack. *Nothing* could move that fast! He blinked his eyes. Of course it could. He saw it. He reached over and grabbed a line.

"The Grik! The Grik come!" he shrieked at the top of his lungs, and dropped down the rope toward the surprised and alarmed upturned faces.

"I can't tell yet!" answered Vernon in the crow's nest to another urgent query. "There's too much haze," he continued excitedly. "It's big, though. God, it's big! Bigger than that cruiser we tangled with!"

Dowden clambered up the ladder to the pilothouse, wiping sleep from bleary eyes. "What is it, Captain?"

"Don't know yet, Larry. Something in the strait." Matt smiled grimly. "Sorry to wake you. I have the conn, Mr. Garrett. Take your station, if you please. Torpedoes?" Ensign Sandison scrambled to his position at the starboard torpedo director.

"They're ready, Captain."

"All stations manned and ready, sir," supplied the talker.

Matt brought his binoculars to his eyes. The haze in the strait was still thick, but it was thinning rapidly under the combined assault of the fully risen sun and a freshening breeze. Even on the bridge they could see a large dark shape, and it did appear larger than *Amagi*. Matt knew then that all their toil, sacrifice, and suffering, the gallantry and heroism of his fine crew, had been for nothing. Whatever lay ahead could only be a very large Japanese ship, and as soon as it saw them they would die. His only plan was to gain the attention of the enemy, fire *Walker*'s last torpedoes and run like hell under a cloud of smoke back in the direction of Surabaya. Maybe they could distract it from *Mahan* and the other destroyer would escape.

The talker asked the lookout to repeat himself. "Captain?" he said hesitantly. "Vernon says he's a little above the haze now and he can see a fair amount of the target, which is also above the haze. He says it ain't no Jap warship he ever saw. It ain't nothin' he ever *heard* of."

"Explain!" snapped Matt. Every eye in the pilothouse was fixed upon the talker.

"Sir, he says it's got sails."

All binoculars were instantly in use as the bridge crew scrutinized the apparition more closely. Sails. Whatever it was, it was *huge* and it had *sails*. Lieutenant Garrett's voice came over the comm, calling out range estimates and instructing his gun crews. "Range six four five oh. Bearing two five oh. Speed fo—four knots? Captain, I have a solution. Request permission to commence firing."

Captain Reddy tore his gaze from the ship that was rapidly resolving into something . . . remarkable, and strode to the intercom himself. "Negative, Mr. Garrett. I repeat, *negative*! Hold your fire. Continue to track the target, but hold your fire!" He looked at Sandison. "You too, Bernie." He returned to stand beside his chair and raised his binoculars again. Wind rushed in through the empty window frames and threatened to take his hat, but he didn't even notice. It was a ship, all right. Bigger than a battleship. Bigger than a carrier. Hell, it was bigger than anything he'd ever seen. And rising high in the air, at least three or four hundred feet, were three huge tripods that each supported enormous semi-rigid sails much like those of a junk, but bigger than any junk's that were ever conceived. "Engines slow to two-thirds. Left ten degrees rudder. Let's see what we have here."

The great ship was threading the channel—with evident care, considering its size—on a heading taking it into the Java Sea. There was silence on *Walker*'s bridge as she drew closer and details became more defined. Matt didn't even notice Sandra Tucker and Mr. Bradford join him to gape at the leviathan. It was double-ended, sharp at bow and stern, and looked like a gargantuan version of the old Federal iron-clad *Monitor*, except the straight up-and-down sides reared a hundred feet above the sea. Instead of a turret, there were three large structures with multiple levels, like wedding cakes, forming the foundations for the great tripod masts. In a sense, they looked like the pagoda-style superstructures distinctive of Japanese warships, except they were larger and were, like the rest of the huge ship, evidently made of wood. Bright-colored tarps and awnings were spread every-where, creating a festive air, and from what he could see of the deck from his low perspective, the space between the structures was covered with pavilion-like arrangements of brightly striped and embroidered canvas.

The ship was easily a thousand feet long, but most out-landish of all were the hundreds of creatures lining the rails and in the rigging and leaning out windows in the "pago-das" to stare right back at them.

"Bring us alongside, Mr. Scott." Matt's voice sounded small, and he cleared his throat, hoping for a more authori-tative tone. "No closer than a hundred yards. Slow to one-third." He glanced at the talker. "Try to raise *Mahan* and tell her to hold her horses." Perhaps they'd repaired her radio. Jim was optimistic.

"Sir!" cried Sandison. "What about the Japs? Won't they hear us transmit?"

An explosive giggle escaped Tony Scott, but he managed to compose himself. Matt let out a breath he must have been holding and gestured out the windows with his chin. He smiled hesitantly. "Mr. Sandison, I don't believe there are any Japs. Not anymore."

*   *   *

The chattering voices grew progressively quieter as the strange vessel approached. Excited exclamations and panicky activity all but ceased. Chack and Risa were on the catwalk above the gardens that ran around the ship. They squeezed through to the railing for a better view. The thing was close now, less than a hundred tails distant. Though small compared to Home, it was longer than any Grik ship ever seen, although maybe not as wide. There was a single tall mast toward the front and a much shorter one at the back, but neither carried a wing of any sort! It had checked its mad dash and now matched their speed, moving parallel to their course. The white froth it threw aside as it dashed through the waves diminished to a whisker.

No wings—and yet it moved effortlessly in any direction, regardless of the wind! As it kept station off their beam, Chack had the impression it was going as slow as it possibly could and strained to surge ahead against some invisible bond. Four tall pipes, or vents, towered from the middle, and occasional wisps of smoke curled away. Perhaps the pipes were wings? He couldn't see how. If so, must they light fires in them to make them work? When he first saw it, there was much smoke and it went very fast. Now it was slow, but there was little smoke. Perhaps. He felt a twinge of superstitious dread. Fire was another thing the People feared, and only the cookers and lighters were allowed to use it. All it would take was one careless moment and all of Home might be consumed. To harness fire and use it so made him feel uneasy. The thing boasted few colors, except for a tattered, striped cloth that fluttered at the back. Other than that, it was dull, like a stormy sky, with brownish streaks and smudges here and there. It also looked like it had been bitten by a mountain fish, as there were holes, large and small, all over.

Chack's thoughts were interrupted by the arrival of the Guards, who arrayed themselves along the railing every five tails or so, pushing spectators away. Most hadn't bothered to don their light armor, but all had their axes and crossbows, which they strung when they took their positions. Chack felt a twinge of guilt. He was in the reserve Guard, as was every able-bodied person on Home. But he hadn't even thought to arm himself, so anxious was he to get a look at the stranger. He thought about fetching his weapons now, and even started to leave, when the chattering grew louder again. He squeezed back through the people that packed the rails. Risa grasped his arm. "They are *not* Grik!" she shouted over the growing clamor. "Not Grik!"

He blinked rapidly in surprise and stared back across the water. He'd been so preoccupied by the strange vessel, as had everyone, that he'd failed to notice there were people on it. Well, not *People*, of course, but not Grik.

"What are they?" Risa asked, barely heard.

"What the hell are they?" Matt said softly, barely aloud.

"They look like monkeys! Or cats! Or . . . hell, what are they?!" blurted Sandison.

"Quite like lemurs, I should think," said Bradford in an excited tone, "although they do have a strong feline aspect as well."

"I don't know what a lemur is, or a feline neither. They look like cat-monkeys to me," grumbled Scott.

"Silence on the bridge!" Matt said softly but forcefully. "Tend your helm, Mr. Scott."

Keje-Fris-Ar stepped to the rail, surrounded by his personal guards, and waited for Adar, the High Sky Priest, to join him. Keje was short, even by the standards of the People, and he tended toward a mild plumpness common among the Body of Home folk. His arms were massive, however, as they'd been since his youth, when he'd been the greatest lance hurler in living memory. In his fortieth season, he was still among the best. When the People hunted the great gri-kakka, or "lizard fish," for its flesh and the oil from its fat, he still often found a place in the boats. His short fur was reddish brown, now salted with white, but his eyes—a much darker reddish brown—sparkled with youthful curiosity, along with a natural concern. As he gazed at the amazing visitor, one of his clansmen-guards dressed him in his war tunic, made of gri-kakka skin and covered with highly polished and beautifully chased copper plates. At his side was his scota, a long, broad-bladed sword used primarily for hacking gri-kakka fat but also a formidable weapon in his practiced hand.

Adar arrived, shouldering gently but firmly through the gathered people. His long purple robe hung from his tall, thin frame and billowed as a gust of wind breathed softly across them. On each shoulder was an embroidered silver star, much the same color as his pelt, which was the badge of his office. He stared intently at the unbelievable ship, but more specifically at the creatures upon it in their outlandish white, blue, and light brown garments. Creatures doing nothing more threatening than staring back at them. They were bizarre, to be sure, and taller even than he. They had virtually no fur at all, just little tufts on their heads covered by strange hats. A few had fur on their faces, but not very many. The most shocking difference, however, at least at a glance, was that the beings had no tails. At all.

Most looked back with as much apparent astonishment as the People displayed. Others evidently communicated with one another in some animated, alien fashion. Generally, though, their reaction to the meeting seemed to mirror that of the People. There was no fear in his voice when he spoke to his leader and lifelong friend. "Tail-less mariners," he said quietly. "How very strange indeed. Could it possibly be?" He shook his head. "Demons from the East, most likely."

Keje glanced at him and blinked questioningly. "The Scrolls speak of demons from the East? Specifically? The People are harried sufficiently by demons from every other direction. These must be distinguished demons indeed."

Adar allowed the slightest smile to appear on his perpetually stoic face. "Not specifically. Not in the Scrolls. But there is wisdom passed down among the Sky Priests that is not always written, my Brother."

Keje huffed. He noticed that some had seen the exchange and several blinked with alarm. He heard the word "demons" whispered and saw the effect ripple down the rail, fore and aft. He huffed again, in annoyance. "Watch your tongue, my gloomy friend. No one doubts I rule the minds and bodies of all the People of Home, but your words carry weight in their hearts." He gestured at the thing that lingered with such unnerving precision and spoke louder.

"They're not Grik. They're very strange folk, but they haven't attacked. I doubt they can. I see no weapons. No swords, axes, or crossbows at all. Their Home is very fast. If our Home was as fast, we would not need weapons either!" He laughed.

He watched as his words quickly spread to counteract the unease that Adar's comment had inspired. Adar inclined his head and lowered his ears in respect.

"You are wise, Keje-Fris-Ar. That's why you are High Chief of all the clans of Home, and I am merely a humble servant of the Heavens." The sarcasm was thick, but those nearby recognized the customary banter between their two leaders, and the mood lightened still more.

"I wonder what we should do?" Adar whispered in his ear.

"If they do nothing," Keje whispered back, "I will continue to stare at them. It has worked very well so far."

Captain Reddy moved onto the bridgewing, closely followed by Sandra and Courtney Bradford. He saw Gray standing with the number one gun crew on the foredeck, his hands behind his back. He too was looking at the huge ship, but by the expression he wore, he might have been watching an empty San Miguel bottle bobbing alongside in Cavite. The gun crew traded nervous glances, but they had themselves under control. The Bosun's presence probably helped, and Matt was certain that Gray had stationed himself there to hearten or intimidate the crew—whichever was required—in case the gun was needed.

Cigarette smoke wafted back from the gun crew, however, and Matt was amused that Gray had, at least momentarily, relaxed the prohibition against smoking on duty. With a start, he saw a cigarette dangling from the Chief's lips as well. He looked aft and saw that the transgression was universal. Even the unflappable Dennis Silva struck a light to a smoke with slightly trembling hands. The big gunner's mate never smoked. He preferred chewing tobacco, because there were no sanctions for safety reasons—as long as he remembered to spit over the side. Sandra Tucker seemed in a state of shock. She said nothing, but her expression of amazement was even more profound than when they had

seen the creatures on land. He didn't recall exactly when
she'd come onto the bridge, but he realized he didn't object
to her presence. Courtney Bradford merely stood, beaming
with joy and mumbling to himself.

Matt didn't know how he felt. Shocked, amazed, even
terrified perhaps. Not surprised, strangely, that a new impossible thing had occurred, just that it manifested itself in
such a way. He felt a bizarre sense of relief, in fact, knowing
with complete certainty that nothing was certain anymore.
Nothing. At least now he could plan accordingly. He looked
once more at the creatures staring back. He knew what a
lemur was—Bradford wasn't far off the mark. Crude as it
was, neither was "monkey-cat." They had tails like monkeys, he could clearly see, and they were furred in a wide
variety of colors. Their faces did look very feline, though,
and just like cats, he couldn't tell what they were thinking.
All was silent, fore and aft, when he finally spoke.

"Any word from *Mahan*?" he asked over his shoulder.

"Nothing, sir."

"Very well. Mr. Scott, right full rudder. All ahead two-
thirds. Let's see if we can pick up her trail." Even over the
rising whine of the blowers, Matt heard the chattering exclamations of the creatures when *Walker* surged ahead. On
impulse, he raised his hand palm outward and waved at the
inscrutable faces.

"Upon my word!" Bradford exclaimed when the gesture
was hesitantly returned by a few of the creatures as *Walker*
peeled away.

"Unusual," commented Adar as the strange ship receded
with magical swiftness. "Not only did they not attack, but
that one gave the Sign of the Empty Hand. That's encouraging, at least." The Sign of the Empty Hand was a
common greeting among the People, to show they held
no weapons.

"Perhaps it was just shielding its tiny eyes from the sun."
The crowd began to disperse, chattering excitedly. "Despite
what I said, I don't think they were helpless. What was that
long thing on the front of their ship if not a weapon? And
there were three others just like it. I think they must be
weapons."

"That possibility did not escape me, lord," Adar whispered back. "But if they were weapons, they did not use them, did they? Never before have we met others than our own kind that did not attack. I, for one, find that encouraging."

Keje huffed noncommittally. "I find it encouraging when I do not encounter strange beings that move faster than any Home ever has—and do not even have wings—before I have eaten my morning meal. Join me while I do, and we will talk more of what we've seen."

Virtually every surviving officer had gravitated to the crowded pilothouse. The petty officers, warrants, and division chiefs were there too, or gathered aft by the ladder behind the bridge. None abandoned their posts without proper relief, and all stations were manned, but nearly everyone who was responsible for other men had come. They hadn't discussed it, hadn't planned it in any way. It was as though they instinctively knew it was time to go to the captain and hear what he had to say. Matt wasn't surprised. He wasn't worried about mutiny, but he knew a threshold had been reached. The men had been through hell even before everything became so strange. When it had, they took it in stride, determined to carry on to the end. Only there was no end. Somehow, for some unknowable reason, nothing was the same anymore—and if Matt had learned anything about his destroyermen, it was that they didn't welcome change.

As he looked at them standing respectfully but expectantly nearby, he reflected that this might actually be harder on some because they were Asiatic Fleet. Many had been on the same ship, on the same station, and with the same shipmates for years. One of the fundamental characteristics of the Asiatic Fleet had been that nothing ever changed. Some would call it ossified; the ancient ships and obsolete equipment certainly supported that, but an all-pervading, decades-long routine had been established and until the War, there'd been no reason to disrupt it. The men with Filipino wives had expected to serve their time and retire in the Philippines, where they'd grown accustomed to the routine of life. The War destroyed that life, but they'd fallen back on the routine of the Navy and their duty. Many hoped that by doing their duty, they could restore everything to the way it had been before. Now even that hope was gone. All that remained was their ship, their duty, and each other. That would have to be enough. For now, that was all they had.

They'd gathered to hear what he had to say. To draw strength and purpose from one that they hoped—since the Navy thought he was smart enough to lead them—would be smart enough to figure out what to do. Matt didn't know what to do, as far as the "bigger picture" was concerned, and it was no use pretending he did. Inwardly, he was at least as scared as they were. But he had faith in these rough men, and to cross this threshold and move beyond it he knew he must appeal to their strengths—their independence and their industry. More than anyone else in the Navy, they were accustomed to surviving on the fringe. If anyone could do it, they could—if they stuck together. Only then could they protect their most immediate, most comforting routine of all: their life on USS *Walker*. With that as a foundation, they could meet the bigger challenge together.

"Shipwide," he said, wondering what he would say.

"Now hear this!" he began, repeating the preparatory phrase that would have been used for any ordinary general announcement. He turned with the microphone in his hand and stared out the windows forward, past the fo'c'sle, into the far distance where the hazy sky met the sea.

"A few of you may have noticed some strange goings-on." He smiled wryly and waited for the nervous laughter to die, then continued in a serious tone. "I don't know more than any of you about what's happened. When I find out, I'll tell you. That's a promise. I won't lie to you, though. The situation's grim. We're a beat-up tin can that's been through a hell of a fight. We have limited stores, ammunition, and fuel." He paused for emphasis, then hammered it home. "And I can't tell you where, or from whom, we can resupply. My immediate plan is to collect *Mahan* and then begin searching for a source to fill our needs. Once we do, we can worry about the big picture and decide what to do next. That's the bad news."

He sensed a flicker of humor over the profound understatement. "The good news is, nobody's shooting at us. The charts are correct, and we know where *we* are; it's just everyone else who has disappeared. Fortunately, that seems to include the Japs. We'll secure from general quarters."

He started to hand the microphone to the talker, but changed his mind. "One more thing," he said, looking now at the faces of his crew. "Whatever happened to us, you can look at it a couple of ways. You can say it's strange, and I sure can't argue. Weird? I'm with you. Bad? We'll see. You might also look at it as salvation, because we were dead, people. Whatever else it was, it was that." He watched the thoughtful expressions and saw a few nods.

"Wherever we go, whatever we do, no matter what's happened—whether we're still part of Des-Ron 29 or all by ourselves, we're *Walkers*! We're destroyermen! And we represent the United States Navy!" The nods became more vigorous and he sensed . . . approval. He hoped it would be enough. He sighed and glanced at his watch. "Return to your duties. Damage control and repair has priority. Funeral services at 1300. That's all."

As always, encouragingly, were the muttered replies: "That's enough!"

Lieutenant Tamatsu Shinya sat on one of the chairs beside the table in the wardroom, his hands cuffed together in his lap. A chain extended down to a pair of leg irons encircling his ankles. The bandage around his black-haired head drooped and obscured his left eye. The compartment was filled with cigarette smoke, but occasional gusts of fresh air reached him through a large hole in the side of the ship. Sitting across from him, leaned back in evident repose and busily creating the smoke, was the American Marine who'd been watching him since he regained consciousness.

He wasn't fooled by the Marine's apparent ease. Nor did he think the bandage on his leg concealed a wound that would prevent him from using the .45 holstered at his side if given the least provocation. His attitude implied that he would welcome an excuse. Together, they'd listened to the captain's words from a speaker on the bulkhead, and although he pretended not to understand, Shinya honestly didn't know if he felt like laughing or if he wished the terrible fish had gotten him after all.

He wasn't a career naval officer, but a reservist, the son of a wealthy industrialist. He'd spent several years in the United States and attended UC–Berkeley. He entered the Japanese Imperial Navy because he was supposed to, not because he was in favor of his country's China policy— although his father glowed with the prospects of a Greater East Asia Co-Prosperity Sphere. He entered the Navy because he was a patriot, and that was what his family did. Besides, the war in China was an Army operation. In the Navy, he would be among cooler and more thoughtful heads.

When preparations for war with America began, he couldn't believe it. He'd been there! He'd seen! He knew as well as anyone how dangerous war with the United States would be, not to mention—according to his sense of honor—wrong. He admitted it was difficult to be objective. He liked Americans, and he'd enjoyed California. It was possible his perceptions had been influenced by people he'd known and, yes, friends he'd made, but only to the extent that he better understood the vast cultural chasm that separated the two peoples. Despite the rhetoric on both sides, he understood the root causes of the war and that nobody was blameless, but the chasm of misunderstanding prevented any reconciliation. The alliance with Germany and Italy might have made war inevitable—and maybe even winnable—but he couldn't ignore his sense that the way it started was wrong and sure to provoke American fury.

Without question, the war was going well so far. The relic he was imprisoned aboard was an example of American unpreparedness. But he'd been at Balikpapan and saw what they could manage, even with what little they had. He feared the outcome if the war dragged out and new and better weapons reached these determined men. Then came the lopsided fight when his destroyer screened *Amagi* against the two old American ships. He'd been amazed and even proud of their bold charge. They'd had no other choice, but it was stirring all the same.

Of course, when two torpedoes exploded against his ship and it vanished from under him, all considerations except staying afloat became secondary. He didn't remember what struck him on the head, and he didn't remember being fished from the water. He did remember a bizarre, stomach-wrenching sensation when the Squall engulfed him, but nothing else until he woke aboard the American destroyer. He'd heard things, though, whispered by men who didn't think he understood.

And then he saw it, through the shell hole, just a while ago. The enormous ship. In that moment he knew all the rumors were true.

He didn't know how or if it would affect him. He was a prisoner of war, he supposed, but what did that mean? How should he act? His situation wasn't often discussed in training. Surrender was not considered an option by his instructors, so how to behave in enemy hands was never mentioned. Despite his "Americanization," he felt vaguely guilty for having survived, although there was nothing he could have done. The man who saved and surrendered him was dead, and he would never know why he'd done it. In any event, whatever he'd expected to happen to him as a prisoner, being shuffled from compartment to compartment but otherwise ignored wasn't it. No one even asked him a question. They had no idea he spoke English, but at least one of them, the young aviation officer, knew Japanese. It seemed unnatural they wouldn't care what he knew of the Imperial Fleet's dispositions. He'd resolved to tell them nothing, but no one ever came and he grew nervous— and wary.

Possibly they'd been so preoccupied with repairs and flight that they'd forgotten they even had him. He hadn't seen the captain, even though he knew the wardroom was where the officers ate. As he overheard the rumors of the crew, however, he began to suspect it wasn't just neglect that kept them from questioning him. Perhaps the relevance of what he knew had diminished to insignificance. Then, not long ago, as he gazed through the hole in the side of the wardroom, it became blindingly clear that whatever information he might have no longer mattered to his captors at all. So they sat, each alone with his thoughts, listening to muted machinery noises.

There was movement behind the green curtain leading

to officers' country, and a head poked around it and looked at them, surprised. The curtain slashed back in place and a retreating voice reached his ears. "Shit. The Jap."

The Marine smirked slightly and rolled his eyes. Then he looked squarely at Tamatsu. "That's the new exec. Somebody finally remembered you. Maybe he'll remind the captain." He grinned darkly. "I hope he throws you to the fish."

Thirty minutes later the curtain moved again and two men entered the compartment. One was younger than the other but had a brisk, businesslike demeanor. He had brown hair, but unlike everyone else Shinya had seen, there was no trace of stubble on his cheeks. His dark green eyes betrayed fatigue, but they were alert and curious. The other man was older, shorter, with a noticeable paunch. He looked tired too, and disheveled, but his expression wasn't curious. It seethed with predatory hostility. The guard jumped to his feet as rapidly as his injured leg allowed.

"As you were, Sergeant—Alder, isn't it?" said the first man.

"Alden, sir," he replied. "Sergeant Pete Alden. Marine contingent, USS *Houston*." He said the last with a grim glance at his prisoner.

"Glad to have you aboard, Sergeant. I apologize for not speaking with you sooner, but"—he allowed a wry expression—"I've been preoccupied."

"No apology necessary, sir."

"Nevertheless, I appreciate your taking charge of the prisoner in spite of your injury. How's the leg?"

"Fine, sir."

The captain accepted the lie. The injury didn't affect Alden's current duty, and there were plenty of wounded at their posts. Matt gestured at the Japanese. "Has he behaved?"

"No trouble, sir. Mostly he just sits and looks around. He does what I tell him, and I keep the crew from beatin' him to death."

Gray snorted, but Matt just nodded. He pulled a chair out at the table across from Tamatsu and sat with his elbows on the green surface, fingers intertwined, looking at the prisoner. The man looked back, unblinking, expressionless. Matt took a deep breath and exhaled. "What am I going to do with you?" he asked himself aloud.

Tamatsu felt a surge of adrenaline. He knew he should keep his mouth shut and pretend not to understand, but suddenly he couldn't see the point. From what he'd seen and heard, the war he was part of was gone, as were—evidently—their respective navies and probably even countries as well. He was overwhelmed by that possibility, and when he'd first heard the rumors he suspected some ploy to get him to speak, if he could. Dinosaurs on Bali, indeed! Then he'd seen the ship and, through his shock, he realized that now was the time. If they later, inevitably, discovered he'd been listening to their conversations, they would never trust him—difficult as it might be anyway. No matter what he thought of the war, he was no traitor, but he wanted them to trust him. Whatever happened, wherever they were, they might be there a long, long time.

Hesitantly, he cleared his throat. To the astonishment of the man across from him, he spoke in excellent, lightly accented English. "Captain, I am Lieutenant Tamatsu Shinya. I am your prisoner. Japan did not ratify the Geneva Protocols, but I give my word of honor I will cooperate every way I possibly can, short of treachery to my people or government. Under the . . . unusual circumstances, I find it unlikely that the cooperation I offer will cause harm to my country. If you are willing to accept it, Captain, I offer my parole."

There were a variety of expressions in the room. Tamatsu's face remained impassive, but Gray's clouded with anger and the Marine's eyes widened in shock. Matt leaned back in his chair, shaken by yet another surprise, but he gathered himself quickly. If there was anything he'd learned about himself lately, it was that he had a growing ability to flow with assaults upon his preconceptions and adapt quickly. He only wished the assaults were less frequent.

"Lieutenant Shinya," he said, "that's . . . a generous offer. I'll take it under advisement. I suppose you heard what I said on the comm a while ago?" The prisoner nodded. "Then you understand we're in a tense situation for which there are no guidelines or regulations to refer to.

Technically, you're a prisoner of war, and somewhere, I assume, that war still rages. It's my duty to present you to my superiors. Since I have no idea when or if that will ever occur . . ." He spread his hands out on the table. "I'll consider it. I hope you won't find it inconvenient, at present, if you remain under the protection of Sergeant Alden?"

Matt heard Gray grumbling as they worked their way aft. He'd decided to take a quick walk around—and be seen doing it—and look at repairs while getting a feel for the mood of the crew. He also wanted to talk to Spanky. The engineer was the only department head who hadn't heard his comments in person. Gray continued to growl under his breath as they climbed into the open air on the main deck and stepped into the shade of the amidships deckhouse. Men formed a line leading to the open-air galley and snatched sandwiches from the counter as fast as the cooks put them down.

It was unbearably hot. That, at least, was the same. He changed direction and went back into the sun and stooped at the drinking fountain on the back of the big refrigerator next to the number one funnel. A stupid place for a refrigerator, he reflected again, but a great place for a drinking fountain. He pushed the button, and the cool stream rose to his lips. He drank, savoring the refrigerated water. Gray joined him.

"You seem annoyed, Boats," Matt observed without preamble.

"That Nip. You ain't gonna let him go, are you?"

"If he behaves, I might. Christ, we've got enough to worry about without guarding a Jap. He offered his parole."

"So? They were making all nice before they bombed Pearl too. We wouldn't *have* to guard him if—" Gray shifted uncomfortably and glanced around to make sure no one was within earshot. "We ought to just get rid of him. He's a Jap, for cryin' out loud!"

Matt looked at him. "Get rid of him? You mean kill him?" He shook his head and stared at his crew for a long time while they talked and ate their sandwiches. He sighed. "No. We won't. You know why? Because we're Americans and we don't do that." He was quiet a moment longer and then strode aft again. "Wherever we are, we're still Americans," Gray heard him mutter.

The sun had just touched the sea when Spanky McFarlane stepped toward the rail near the number two torpedo mount. For the first time since their run from Surabaya, the deck was almost deserted. It had been a hard day in more ways than one, and with the most critical repairs complete, it was as though the crew had breathed a collective sigh of relief and then just collapsed. The only men he saw nearby were Dennis Silva and some of his hoodlum friends in the ordnance division, talking on the amidships deckhouse. Spanky ignored them. It was a moral imperative. If he paid too much attention to what those jerks were up to, he'd probably have to put them on report.

He took a dingy rag from his pocket to wipe sweat and grunge from his eyes. They burned like hell. He pitched it into the churning wake that scoured the side of the ship. Was it just his imagination, or had something actually snapped at the rag as it fluttered to the surface? He sagged against the safety chain. *Starting to get jumpy*, he thought, and fumbled for his smokes. With the ease of a practiced hand, he lit one in spite of the breeze and inhaled deeply. Yeah, it had been a hell of a day.

They'd buried their dead in the time-honored fashion soon after the Skipper came to talk. All those men—nearly a quarter of the crew—slipping over the side as the captain gruffly read the prayer. Spanky shuddered, wondering how deep the shrouded corpses went before being shredded by the piranha-like fish that seemed to be everywhere. The Old Man was thinking ahead, though. Instead of the customary four-inch shell sewn into their fart-bags to carry them down, they'd been sent to their graves with whatever wreckage or heavy piece of debris Spanky thought they could spare.

That was what the captain came to talk about, to tell him to discard nothing that might have any conceivable use. So Spanky detailed some men to sort the scrap pile they'd started and find the most worthless junk. Then he checked it himself to make sure he couldn't think of any use for it either. Only then was it passed on—a piece of *Walker*—to accompany her dead sons. He snorted ironically. At least a few of the men went down with the customary projectile, even if they'd been Jap shells pried from *Walker*'s hull. He was glad the Skipper was starting to think about the long haul, though. He'd seemed kind of overwhelmed the night before—and that was before they saw the ship. His speech helped a lot, and it came at just the right time. Spanky suspected the Skipper needed to hear the words just as bad as the crew did.

The sun dipped below the horizon and it began to grow dark. At least the day hadn't been all bad, he reflected proudly. He didn't know what difference the strange creatures on the big ship might make, but after the shock wore off, the fascination and speculation among the crew had done much to take their minds off their troubles. Also, they'd managed to get the number two boiler back on line. There was no hope for number one. The concussion had broken most of the firebricks. Besides, the lines and seals were shot, and he'd cannibalized it to revive number two.

He heard Silva's booming laugh and couldn't help but smile. It took more than a funeral and a battle and being transported to another world to get the big gunner's mate down. He could find humor in anything. For a moment, Spanky listened to the conversation. He couldn't help himself.

"I say they was more like monkeys than cats. Did you see them tails?" argued Tom Felts. "We ought'a call 'em monkey-cats!"

"Cats have tails too, you idiot," countered Paul Stites. "And their faces looked more like cats. Besides, 'cat-monkeys' sounds better."

"What do you think, Marvaney?" asked Felts of their friend, who stood by the rail above Spanky. Mack Marvaney only shrugged and stared into their wake. Felts started to ask again, but Silva rapped him on the shoulder with his knuckles and shook his head. Mack had a Filipino wife in Cavite. It was bad enough when they'd left the place to the Japs, but now . . . he was taking it hard.

"I have decided," Silva announced in a lofty tone that

usually brooked no argument. "We'll call 'em monkey-cats!"

Stites, grateful that Silva had kept him from pestering their suffering friend, rounded. "Hell, Dennis, that's what the snipes are callin' 'em! We can't let that stand!"

"The snipes are callin' 'em monkey-cats?" asked Silva darkly. "Those bastards didn't even *see* 'em. They were all creepin' around belowdecks the whole time we were there. Hidin', I bet! Critters could'a looked like three-legged hippos for all they know." He brooded in silence for a while, then stepped next to Marvaney to spit over the rail. He glanced at him, then turned to face the others. "I have decided!" he repeated grandly. "From this point on, they're cat-monkeys! We discovered 'em. We'll call 'em what we want!"

Spanky shook his head, then sucked the rest of the cigarette to the tips of his fingers and flicked the butt into the sea. By tomorrow the whole crew would be locked in the "cat-monkey-cat" debate. Still smiling, he patted one of the empty torpedo tubes. Even with only three boilers, this tired, shot-up ship that he hated and loved so much was probably the fastest thing in the world, if all it had to offer was big lumbering tubs like they'd seen that morning. "There's humor for you."

For the next day and a half, *Walker* steamed east, searching for *Mahan*. The other destroyer hadn't had much head start and she wouldn't be making full steam. They should have caught her in a few hours, but so far there wasn't a trace. Everyone was worried, not only because of her damage but because she represented the only other thing in this very strange world that was familiar. That was as it should be. Besides, some of their own shipmates were aboard her.

Captain Reddy wearily climbed the ladder and returned to his chair. He waved the men back to their duties at the warning: "Captain on the bridge!" He hadn't been gone fifteen minutes. A rising tension knotted his chest, and though he thought he hid it well, his concern over *Mahan* was making him almost ill. He had a terrible choice to make.

The windows had been replaced, and once again he

could look at the sea ahead without the wind stinging his eyes. Larry Dowden had the watch, but Matt couldn't stay off the bridge. He knew it looked bad, like he didn't trust Larry, but he'd hardly left at all except to go to the head.

"Report?"

"No contact, Skipper."

Matt nodded and resumed his silent brooding. They should have seen her. The weather was fine, the sky clear. The northeast tip of Alor Island was sharp and defined ten miles off the starboard beam. They'd reached the rally point. It had been agreed that they would meet here, or if *Walker* didn't make it *Mahan* would cut northeast around Wetar and drive south between Timor and Moa Island. *Walker* had cruised at twenty knots, but Matt was certain Jim wouldn't have pushed *Mahan* so hard. Even if he somehow beat them here, he would have lingered, and should have been visible on such a clear day. That left only the inescapable conclusion that she hadn't come this far. They must have passed her somehow, maybe in the dark, but she must be behind them. Unless something had happened to her.

That thought haunted him. It was his order that sent her away and led to this wasteful chase. He couldn't have known separation was unnecessary, but that did little to console him. Now the specter that haunted all destroyer-men could no longer be avoided. *Walker*'s fuel bunkers were down by a third. He had no choice. He spoke with a heavy heart.

"Mr. Dowden, bring the ship about. Reduce speed to one-third."

Larry sighed. He knew how painful the order was. He wasn't sure he could have made it. Maybe the other ship really was behind them, but it felt too much like giving up.

"Aye, aye, sir. Helm, come left to a heading of two eight zero."

Matt stood and looked at his watch. "Pass the word, Mr. Dowden. All officers in the wardroom at 1630." He paused. "Better see that our 'guest' is moved elsewhere." He turned to leave the bridge but stopped. "I take that back. Have Sergeant Alden escort the enemy officer to the meeting."

Dowden's eyebrows rose. "Also, ask Mr. Bradford if he'd be kind enough to join us."

"Aye, sir."

Cigarette smoke swirled and eddied in the breeze from the open portholes. The shell holes had finally been patched. Captain Reddy sat in his chair at the "head" of the table, all his surviving officers ranged down either side. The table was crowded, with representatives from each division. Larry Dowden, Chief Gray, Rick Tolson, Bernard Sandison, and PO Riggs sat on his left. On his right were Sandra Tucker, Spanky, Mr. Bradford, Garrett, and Lieutenant (j.g.) Alan Letts, the supply officer. The chair at the far end of the table was unoccupied. When Sergeant Alden escorted the Japanese officer into the compartment and seated him there, a hushed silence fell on the group.

Tamatsu sat with dignity, eyes fixed upon the captain. Alden leaned against the bulkhead behind his prisoner until Juan brought him a chair. He thanked the little Filipino and sat, his leg out in front of him. The room was charged with an electric hostility, and all eyes were on the enemy officer.

"This is Lieutenant Tamatsu Shinya. He's offered his parole and I've decided to accept, conditionally. He'll be treated with courtesy and allowed freedom of the ship—within reason. For now, however, he'll be accompanied at all times by Sergeant Alden. Sergeant? Is that acceptable to you?"

"Aye, aye, sir. There's not many places I can go now, though."

Matt nodded expressionlessly. "Lieutenant Shinya, allow me to present my officers." He named the others at the table, and they each acknowledged him with a nod, but most were clearly displeased. The reaction wasn't lost on the captain. "Gentlemen . . . and lady, Lieutenant Shinya's country and ours may still be at war—wherever they are—but that can no longer affect us. That's what we have to talk about. We must make plans based on the assumption that we're completely on our own and the United States Navy can't support us. At the same time, we must remain conscious of the fact that, no matter what, we're still part of that Navy. No relaxation of discipline will be tolerated, and there'll be no change whatever in the way we run this ship. Lieutenant Shinya is here because he is, literally, in the same boat we are and he is subject to the same rules and regulations as anyone else. There'll be no special treatment"—he looked at his officers with a grim expression—"or abuse. Mr. Dowden?"

"Uh, yes, sir?"

"Acquaint yourself with Lieutenant Shinya and discover if he has useful talents or abilities. One way or the other, find something for him to do. Everybody pulls their weight." He looked at Tamatsu. "Is that understood, Lieutenant? Those are my terms."

Shinya bowed his head slightly and replied. "I understand perfectly, Captain Reddy." There were murmurs of surprise when he spoke English. Most still wore set, closed expressions, but a few looked thoughtful.

Matt plowed right on to divert attention from their visitor. "First, as I'm sure you're aware, we've turned around. We should have found *Mahan*, but we didn't, so either we passed her somehow or . . ." He cast a hard glance down both sides of the table. "Or she's lost. We'll search as we retrace our steps, but we don't have enough fuel to go all the way to Australia and back to Surabaya. Besides, I don't really think Perth's there anymore."

"You've considered the probability that Surabaya isn't there either?" questioned Bradford.

"Yes. In fact, I don't imagine it is. But we must have fuel. Whatever's happened to the world, the geography's the same—at least around here. Can you think of any better place to find oil within our range? To be more specific, since you're our expert on this point, where around here would we most likely find oil? Oil that we can easily extract?"

Bradford steepled his fingers and looked thoughtful. The pipe between his teeth wasn't lit, but he sucked it speculatively. "I'll have to consider that. There's oil in this entire region, but I'm not sure where best to look. Surabaya, perhaps. There were significant deposits there, in our world. Deposits have been discovered recently under Flores as well. Allow me to consult my manuals. Perhaps they will tell me where it was first found, and how. That might have a bearing on where to look."

"Very well," Matt replied. "See what you can find and let me know as soon as you can." He shifted his gaze to Lieutenant McFarlane. "What else can we burn in the boilers? Can we burn wood?"

Spanky returned his gaze with horror. "Jesus, Skipper! You can't put *wood* in my boilers! It would screw everything up!"

Matt looked at him sharply. "I know it's not our first choice, but can it physically be done?"

"Yes, sir . . ." answered the engineer reluctantly, "but it would be terrible. All that ash—it would be hell gettin' it all out and it would screw up the boilers. Besides, we'd have to carry tons of the stuff. We've got nowhere to stow it and if we load it on deck, we'll be top-heavy as hell—beggin' your pardon, sir."

"But it would work in an emergency? To get us from one island to the next?"

"It would," he answered miserably.

"Very well. Come up with a plan to stow enough wood to take us, say, five hundred miles, if the need should arise."

"Aye, sir."

The captain turned to Sandra Tucker, and involuntarily his expression softened. "Lieutenant Tucker. How are things in your department?"

Sandra smiled at the mention of "her department," which consisted of herself, Karen Theimer—the only other nurse who'd remained with *Walker*—and Jamie Miller, the pharmacist's mate. There was no question it was her department, though, and a critical one. "Improving, sir. I think Rodriguez might return to limited duty in a week or so. His leg is healing nicely." She looked down the table past Tamatsu and glowered at Sergeant Alden. "Speaking of legs, though, there are some people running around on them that shouldn't be." Alden pretended interest in something under the table. "The others should survive, but it'll take time. There're plenty of 'walking wounded' still on duty, but even if I tried to keep them in their bunks, I don't think I could." She looked straight into Matt's eyes and continued. "Right now, everyone's keyed up, with so much work just to keep the ship going. When the crisis is past, I expect a lot of casualties from exhaustion. The crew's burning itself up. Wearing out." Matt nodded back at her, realizing she was talking about him as much as anybody. She continued. "Actually, the only one I'm really worried about is Davis. He has a persistent fever, and no matter what I do, it just won't break."

"He was bitten by the lizard?"

Sandra nodded. "Mr. Bradford says they're septic but not poisonous. That may be, even though they weren't the same lizards he's familiar with. It looks like a really nasty bacterial infection, but there might be some kind of toxic venom as well." She shrugged.

"Keep me informed," Matt said solemnly, and she nodded. "Mr. Garrett. How about guns? Small arms too." Garrett frowned. "Is there a problem?" asked Matt. Garrett's cheeks turned red, and he shook his head quickly.

"No, sir, no problem. I—I was just surprised by the question about small arms. I don't have the exact numbers off the top of my head. No excuse, sir."

The captain allowed a genuine smile. "A general idea would suffice, Mr. Garrett. I understand you've been busy with the number three gun?"

"Yes, sir," Garrett replied, visibly relieved. "We got it working. The main problem was in the wiring, but there's damage to the traverse gear. I'd like to get it in the machine shop as soon as I can. It binds."

Matt looked at him thoughtfully, but shook his head. "Not right now. I don't want any of our weapons out of action. Besides"—he looked at Ensign Sandison—"the condemned torpedoes have priority in the machine shop, except for essential repairs. Until we know more about those people on the big ship, I'd like to be able to put holes in it if we have to."

Garrett glanced at Bernie and saw him write notes on a pad. He looked back at the captain. "Well, sir, other than that, the main battery's okay. Gunner's Mate Silva's overhauled the machine guns, as well as the three-incher on the fantail. The magazines could be better. We depleted over a third of our four-inch fifty, and three-inch twenty-three point five—for all the good it did!" The useless-

ness of the three-inch gun at the stern would have been
a running joke—if it were funny. "We picked up a lot of
machine gun ammo in Surabaya, but those trigger-happy
goons burned through nearly all the extra. We still have
a little more than our full allotment, but . . ." He took a
deep breath. "As for small arms, I don't have exact numbers," he repeated apologetically, "but we're in fairly
good shape. It's not unusual for Asiatic Fleet sailors to
act as Marines—particularly in China, and the armory's
got sixty Springfields, and probably two dozen 1911 pistols. We also have four Browning automatic rifles and half
a dozen Thompsons. The ammunition headstamps are
pretty old—1918—but the stuff looks okay. There's even a
few thousand rounds of the old thirty U.S., which is good,
because there're several crates, down under everything,
that say they have Krag rifles in them. Maybe somebody
picked them up in the Philippines?"

Gray grunted. "I doubt it. *Walker* was commissioned in
1919, and a lot of Krags were still in the Navy. I bet they
came with the ship. Probably never been out of their
crates."

Matt nodded. "Look into it. Anything else?"

"Aye, aye, sir. No, sir."

"Very well. Sparks? Does the communications division
have anything new?" Matt knew it didn't. He'd asked Riggs
several times that day and left standing orders that if they
received anything at all, he was to be informed at once.

Riggs shook his head. "Nothing, Skipper. The equipment's operating perfectly. Everything checks out. There
just isn't anything to hear." Everyone already knew it, but
to hear him say it again only deepened the gloom.

Matt sensed the darkening mood and pushed quickly on.
As he often did, he turned to the Chief to boost morale.
"Any major holes left, Boats?"

"Nothing you'd call *major*," he replied with a hesitant
grin. "The old gal's always leaked like a sieve. No matter
how many holes we patch, she was riveted together, and
there's probably not a seam in her bottom that doesn't
seep, but damage control's done a hell of a job." He glanced
at McFarlane and grinned even bigger. "Apes and snipes
been working together so well, it ain't natural. We haven't

patched holes in the funnels and such, but everything that'll let water in has something welded over it."

McFarlane nodded. "She'll float, Skipper, and as long as we have power to the pumps I'll keep her pretty dry." He looked around the table. "She needs a yard, though." There were grim nods.

"We know, Spanky," said the captain quietly. "Anything else on your end?"

McFarlane shook his head, conscious that he'd lowered everyone's spirits again. "Uh . . . no, sir, not really. I was thinkin', though. As long as we're trying to conserve, we might want to figure out more ways to do it. Like, we might have the apes leave off chippin' and paintin' until we figure out what to use for paint when we're out. That sort of stuff."

Gray started to protest that if his holy deck wasn't maintained in these tropical waters, there'd soon be no deck to maintain. But you couldn't use what you didn't have. "Spanky's right," he admitted grudgingly. "I know how the apes'll moan if they can't perform their favorite pastime." He grinned encouragingly and there were scattered chuckles. "But we have only so much paint. I have to paint the welds, but maybe we can let the cosmetic stuff slide."

"That's a good point," said Matt. He turned at last to the supply officer, Alan Letts. Letts was a skinny kid from North Dakota with red hair and extremely fair skin, complete with freckles. He hated the sun, and even brief exposure left him resembling a radish. He was rarely seen above deck, and then only in the shadows, as if direct sunlight would melt him down to a puddle of wax. His sincere antics to avoid sunlight were vastly amusing to the crew, and he was very popular. He was a good sport too, and no matter how sensitive, his skin was also thick. Sometimes, in a spirit of fun, he allowed sailors to escort him around the ship with a Chinese parasol. Despite his efforts, even as he sat in the wardroom, great patches of chalky skin dangled from his face and arms and small specks had settled to the table. He was a good supply officer and knew all the bureaucratic angles, but those no longer applied. His greatest flaw, from Matt's perspective, was a complacent laziness. He suffered from the endemic Asiatic Fleet disease of "go with the flow." Matt hoped he could make the transition to the new imperative.

"How does it look for supplies?" the captain asked.

"We'll be okay for a while. We loaded up before we left Surabaya. Nobody wanted to leave anything for the Japs." Letts's eyes flicked toward their guest. "At present consumption, meaning normal, we've got three weeks, easy, before we feel any pinch on perishables. The refrigerator's stocked up. After that, we have canned stuff for about that long." He grimaced. "I'm not counting Vienna sausages. We better find something else before we're down to that, or there'll be mutiny in the chow line." He brightened. "Even if we don't cut back, we're in good shape food-wise for a month, month and a half."

"We can't cut rations," pronounced Matt decisively, "not as hard as the men are working. Besides, that'd really wreck morale. We'll just have to find food." He looked at Courtney Bradford, and his eyes twinkled. "I wonder what dinosaur steak tastes like?" There was general laughter at Bradford's incredulous expression.

"Eat dinosaurs? My God. The man's talking about eating dinosaurs!" the Australian muttered to himself.

Matt returned to Letts. "Fresh water?"

Walker's boilers were an open feed-water design, so they used seawater for steam, but the crew needed fresh water for cooking and drinking. The storage tanks were small and, even in normal times, bathing was a luxury. The men often lined up naked by the rail for a good spray-down with the fire hose. The salt water drove them nuts when it dried and caused rashes and other discomforts, but it was refreshing.

"Water's a problem," admitted Letts. "With the condensers in the shape they are, we have about a month's worth, at current usage."

"Okay. So we need fuel, ammo, food, water." The captain arched an eyebrow at Gray. "And paint." There were more chuckles despite the fact that no one knew where to find any of those things. "What else?"

"About a million things, Skipper," Letts replied, "but those are the most immediate. I'm sure Lieutenant McFarlane could add quite a list of spares, but—"

"Right. Make a list of everything we need, but more importantly, figure out how we're going to get it. Use anybody you need, but find answers." Matt swiveled in his chair to look at Courtney Bradford. "Would you mind being conscripted?"

The Australian took his pipe from his mouth and his eyes widened with pleasure. "Delighted, Captain! Delighted. How can I assist?"

"Work with Letts to sort this out. You'll be his special assistant. I know this isn't the same world you were such a student of, but you must have a better idea where we can find supplies than any of us do. Agreed?"

"Absolutely, Captain Reddy. I'll do my best!"

"Of course you will."

Matt glanced at Sandra when he said it, and saw the twinkle of amusement in her eyes. He smiled at her. He was pleased. All in all, the discussion had gone fairly well. His people were engaged, and actively working to solve problems. Morale was better than he would have expected, and the crushing terror of their situation was kept at bay—for now—by a veneer of normalcy. The tasks were unusual, but the familiarity of doing them within the extended family that was the crew of USS *Walker* was reassuring.

Throughout the conversation, Lieutenant Shinya was silent. After the initial hostility, he seemed to have been forgotten, and he just listened. He was amazed by the familiarity with which the Americans talked and worked together. No one was afraid to speak, not even the most junior person present. It seemed chaotic compared to his more-regimented experience, but it also appeared effective. There was no hiding the fact that they were in a predicament, but there was no hesitation to mention failings that might reflect poorly on any department. That made it easier for the captain to assess the situation. He doubted a similar meeting aboard his own ship would have progressed as well, and he felt strangely refreshed.

Just then, Juan entered the compartment with his carafe and began filling cups. He paused by Tamatsu. His face bore a look of anguished loathing, and Shinya was reminded that, no matter what, he was still considered an enemy. Juan took a deep breath and started to tilt the carafe. It began to shake. Suddenly he slammed it on the table as if the handle was too hot to hold. He looked at Matt in horror.

"I—I am sorry, Cap-tan Reddy," he whispered. "I cannot." He then drew himself up and strode through the curtain into the passageway. Everyone watched him go, except Tamatsu, who continued to stare straight ahead, but his gaze seemed somewhat lower. Matt sighed. Nothing was going to be easy.

Walker steamed leisurely in a west-northwesterly direction for the remainder of the day, back across the Flores Sea into the Java Sea once more. The sea picked up toward evening, and a gloomy overcast obscured the growing moon. Matt ordered the running lights lit—unthinkable just days before—and stationed men on the two searchlights. They were to sweep the horizon at ten-minute intervals, both to show the lights and to see what they could. The ship began to roll as the swell increased just enough to remind everyone that regardless of war, dinosaurs, sea monsters, or even strange beings on giant ships, ultimately, *Walker*'s greatest adversary was the very element for which she was made.

By 2200 that night, halfway through the first watch, she began to pitch as the sea ran higher. Matt was dead to the world, on the bunk in his small stateroom. *Walker*'s antics didn't disturb him in the least; he was used to them, and after everything else, the normal, unpleasant motion of the ship was even soothing in a way. When he finally surrendered completely to sleep, in his cabin for the first time in days, he found a depth of untroubled slumber that even the ghosts couldn't sound. So when they hit the fish and he was nearly thrown to the deck, it almost didn't wake him.

The small light over his desk was still vibrating when he looked at it, confused. The speaker above his pillow squawked in Lieutenant Garrett's urgent voice. "Captain! Captain to the bridge, sir. Please." He coughed and cleared his throat, then pushed the comm button. "On my way." He slung his legs over the side of the rack and yanked on his trousers and shoes. Pulling on his shirt and plopping his hat on his head, he hurried down the short corridor to the companionway and scrambled up the ladder. In the shelter by the radio shack, he finished buttoning his shirt and mounted the stairway to the pilothouse. The blowers had abated, and the way the ship rolled even more sickeningly told him the engines had stopped.

"Report!" he demanded. Garrett stood on the starboard bridgewing staring down at the water. The wind had picked up and he'd been drenched by spray. He turned. "Sorry to wake you, sir, but we hit a whale, or fish—or something. It looks like the one that ate the Japs. Down here, sir." He pointed and Matt peered over the rail. The searchlight above them couldn't depress far enough to directly illuminate the creature, but the diffused light was sufficient for him to see it clearly.

Walker broached to in the moderate swell when the engines stopped, and the giant "fish" wallowed and bumped against the hull in her lee. Garrett was right. It looked like the one they'd seen previously, although not as large. Every now and then, the waves caused its great head to rise, and the long, slack jaws were frighteningly clear. A large black eye the size of a trash-can lid stared sightlessly up at them. The cause of death was a huge gash behind its head, and the water was tinged black with blood as it washed from the wound. Sandra Tucker, her hair disheveled, appeared beside him, rubbing her eyes.

"It's horrible," she said. Excited voices came from the main deck below as destroyermen gathered to gawk. Bradford joined them and his voice rose above the others.

"Amazing! We simply must keep it! You there! Find something to tie onto it!" Matt heard one of his crew shout, "Bugger off, mate!" in a fair copy of the Australian's accent.

"Damage?" he asked.

"A lot of broken coffee cups," Garrett answered nervously. "That's all I know so far. The exec took Bosun's Mate Bashear to have a look. Lieutenant McFarlane and the Bosun said they'd meet them there."

The comm on the bulkhead whistled and Matt picked it up himself. "Bridge," he said. "Captain speaking."

"McFarlane here, Skipper. There's a little water coming in on the starboard side around frame number six. Nothing serious . . . just another seam." Spanky's voice was thick. He too had finally been asleep.

"Good. Can the current watch handle it?"

There was a pause before Spanky's voice returned. "Yes, sir. I think so."

"Then you and Boats hit the rack. That's an order."

"Aye, aye, Skipper," came the tired reply. Matt stepped to the rail with a soft sigh of relief. Sandra was still there. She'd overheard.

"Thank God," she murmured. "It may sound strange, but every time this ship gets the slightest scratch, I feel it in my own skin."

Matt grinned. "I know how you feel. When I first assumed command, I honestly didn't think much of her. But now, after all she's been through . . ." He shrugged, and gestured at the dead fish. It had floated off a dozen yards or so. "Of course, her thin old skin's the only thing between us and those things. That tends to focus your appreciation amazingly." He chuckled, and after a brief hesitation, she joined him. They felt a faint, shuddering vibration under their feet, and another huge fish, probably two-thirds as long as *Walker*, rose beside the ship. It must have scraped her bottom as it passed. Without hesitation, it lunged at its dead cousin and snatched an enormous swath of flesh. Bright bone and white blubber lay exposed and more blood clouded the water. Silvery flashes began to reflect the searchlight's beam. With a startled cry, Sandra clutched his arm.

"Mr. Garrett! Let's leave our dinner guest to his meal before he samples the side dish, if you please!"

The blower wound up. A flying packet of spray struck Matt and Sandra and soaked them both. The water had an unusual taste and Matt realized it must be blood. He spat, then looked at Sandra apologetically and cleared his throat.

"Excuse me, ma'am," he said in a wry tone. "Got a bad taste in my mouth."

He glanced down at the main deck, where Bradford was watching the huge fish devour the smaller one with rapt fascination. He seemed oblivious to the spray that inundated him and swirled around his feet. Another form stood near him at a respectful distance, and the captain recognized Shinya in the gloom. He was watching as well, but his expression was entirely different. Matt wondered vaguely where Sergeant Alden was, but decided it didn't matter. Any mischief the Jap could cause was dwarfed by the perils all around them, and judging by his expression, the last thing Shinya wanted was to wind up in the water again.

Matt looked at the woman at his side. Her teeth were beginning to chatter from the wind on her damp clothes. Her long brownish hair hung down in wet tangles, but her eyes were wide and bright. He couldn't decide if it was fear he saw or fascination akin to Bradford's. He felt a chill himself and shuddered involuntarily. "Why don't we go down to the wardroom and dry off?" he suggested.

Gunner's Mate Dennis Silva sat on one of the "seats of ease" in the aft crew's head smoking a cigarette. He still didn't like the damn things, but he had only so much chewing tobacco and a man had to have his nicotine. The seats were little more than boards across a trough through which sea water flowed. The compartment stank of waste and sweat, and with the sea getting up, dark, nasty water sloshed back and forth on deck. Every time the brackish wave threatened him, Dennis raised his feet until it passed.

The aft crew's head was generally considered snipe country, and that was the main reason he went there to relieve himself. Just to aggravate the snipes. No one made a real issue of it because, for one thing, it didn't *exactly* belong to the engineering division and, for another, Silva was a big, powerful man who in spite of an easygoing nature had a dangerous reputation. Proprietary claims to the heads were even more ridiculous, at least to the outside observer, because only a single bulkhead separated them and both were located in the aft deckhouse, behind the laundry and torpedo workshop. That didn't make trespass less serious in the eyes of the crew, however. So naturally, Dennis Silva sat and smoked while men came and went and attended to their business on the other seats nearby. No one spoke to him, but they gave him many dark looks indeed.

Stites, Felts, and a torpedoman named Brian Aubrey found him there. They clustered around the hatchway as if reluctant to cross the threshold and braced themselves against the motion of the ship. "There you are!" exclaimed

Stites. "You missed it. We ran smack into one of them big dinosaur fish, like ate the Japs, and killed it deader'n hell!"

"Good," muttered Silva. "It's time we killed somethin'."

"Yeah," added Tom, "and then a even bigger one took to eating the first one just like that!" He snapped his fingers. "It was something to see, and here you was all the time, in the snipes' crapper!"

Silva glanced disdainfully at the two snipes sharing the compartment. "This ain't the snipes' crapper," he said very slowly and distinctly. "It's Dennis Silva's crapper when Dennis Silva's takin' a crap!"

One of the "snipes" was Machinist's Mate Dean Laney, two seats down from Silva. He was nearly as tall as the big gunner's mate, and just as powerfully built. "You better watch your mouth," he growled. "You damn deck-apes don't belong here."

Silva sucked his cigarette and looked at him. "What are you gonna do, go whinin' to Spanky or Chief Donaghey and tell 'em I'm using your crapper?" He raised his voice to a high-pitched falsetto. "Lieutenant Spanky! Dennis Silva's in our crapper! And—he's takin' a crap! Do somethin'! Make him stop!"

Laney lunged to his feet with a curse and Dennis rose to meet him, both with their trousers around their ankles. Just then, the ship heaved unexpectedly and the combatants lost their balance and fell to the deck in a tangled, punching heap. They slid against the bulkhead in the disgusting ooze and just as quickly as the fight had begun, it ended as the men considered their battlefield. Dennis began to laugh. Laney didn't. He put his right hand on the seat nearest him and started to rise, but realized the seat was the red one—reserved for men with venereal disease. He snatched his hand away and splashed to the deck with a cry just as the ship pitched upward and the tide of muck flowed around him. Dennis laughed even harder and rose to his feet, pulling up his ruined trousers. He reached down to give Laney a hand, but suddenly stepped back.

"The hell with you, Laney! You want me catch it too?" He wiped his hands on his soiled trousers and, on second thought, rinsed them in the long sink across the compartment. He posed for a moment in front of the mirror, powerful muscles bulging across his chest and biceps. Then he relaxed and looked at his clothes. "Damn. Snipe shit all over me. I'll have to burn these duds and who knows when I'll get more?" He looked back at Laney, who was at least as filthy as he. The other snipe was still seated and had ignored the whole thing. "C'mon, Laney. Why don't you have a cup of coffee with some real live destroyermen? Someday you'll tell your grandkids."

"Go to hell," Laney said, but he rinsed himself as best he could and followed through the laundry where they replaced their T-shirts. They exited on the deck behind the number three torpedo mount. The sea was heavier now, and the deck twisted beneath their feet like a live thing as they lurched forward, leaning into the spray. Above their heads, on the searchlight tower, the beam swept slowly back and forth, a beacon for their absent sister. Finally, they reached the protection of the gun platform that served as a roof for the galley. There were several men standing in line with cups and the galley hatch was up. They were waiting while the cook and his mess attendant filled the big coffee urn with a new batch. They grabbed cups and took their place in line.

"Hey, Earl," Dennis said to the cook, shouting over the churning sea, "you got anything besides peanut butter sammiches and scum weenies?"

Earl Lanier shook his head mournfully. "Sorry, fellas. Can't cook with the sea kickin' up. Hard enough just to make coffee. Got some cold beans, though."

"Scum weenies in 'em?"

"Yep."

Silva grimaced. "No thanks. Say, you got any of them apples left?" Again Earl shook his head.

"Juan says the rest of them apples are for the officers," said Ray Mertz, the mess attendant.

"Well, who's in charge here, Earl? You or Juan?" demanded Dennis as it came his turn and he filled his cup.

"I am, damn you. But Juan got them apples hisself for the officers' mess. You're just lucky he shared some out."

"Officers," grunted Stites, as if the word was a self-explanatory curse. Silva nodded, as he was expected to, but without much conviction. He normally didn't have much use for officers either, but he figured they could've done worse under the circumstances. Their officers sure had their work cut out for them. All their lives were in the officers' hands and he didn't envy them the responsibility.

"Still got some pickles left," offered Mertz. Dennis started to refuse, but then reconsidered. If things were as bad as he suspected, there was no telling when he'd taste a pickle again. Much less an apple. There might come a day when he'd dream about that last pickle he'd turned down.

"Sure, Ray. Gimme one."

Felts jabbed Laney with his elbow and motioned around the corner of the galley at a figure by the starboard rail, staring at the heaving sea. "Hey, snipe, lookie there," he said in a grim tone. "That's that Nip officer! What the hell's he doin' on the loose?" Laney's eyes widened.

"I'll be damned! You 'apes sure ain't particular about the company you keep!" Angry faces turned to the machinist's mate, but they looked guiltily uncertain that he might be right.

"Yeah, what's up, Silva?" demanded Stites. "You're tight with the Chief. What's he think about lettin' Nips run all over the ship? I think we ought'a pitch the bastard over the side."

Silva munched his pickle and looked from one to the other. "Gray don't like it, and I don't either, but leave him be. Captain's orders. He's on parole, or somethin'." He shook his head. "Whatever the hell that means. I don't reckon them Jap bastards paroled them boys on Wake." They were silent a moment, watching the shape as it left the rail and disappeared down the companionway. "'Sides," Silva added gruffly, "he's prob'ly the only fella in the whole wide world lonesomer than we are right now."

Spanky sat hunched in his favorite chair near the throttle-control station, his second-favorite mug clutched tightly in both hands between his knees. It was a big ceramic mug that held twice as much coffee as was generally considered right. On one side was a stylized view of Oahu from the air, and on the other was a raised-relief sculpture of a virtually nude hula girl reclined provocatively on a Chevrolet emblem. His very favorite mug with the totally nude *pair* of hula girls had been destroyed, and he wasn't going to let anything happen to this one. He raised it carefully to his lips and took a sip as he listened to the sounds of the ship laboring in the moderate seas.

Over the years, he'd grown used to the noises she made and prided himself on his ability to diagnose problems just by sound or "feel." After all the damage and repairs she'd undergone, *Walker* moaned with all sorts of new sounds and resonated with many feels he wasn't accustomed to, and he felt disoriented as he tried to identify and categorize them all. He shuddered to think of the stopgaps and jury-rigged repairs he'd performed, and he was secretly amazed that the ship was still afloat, much less under way. He grimaced at the thought of how they might have to stay that way. Wood in the boilers! That would finish them off. The thing was, if they were down to burning wood, that meant they had nothing else, so with a bleak but philosophical grunt, he resigned himself to the possibility.

He was supposed to sleep. The captain had actually ordered him to, but he couldn't escape the premonition that something would come disastrously unwrapped as soon as he did. Besides, while he worked he didn't have to think about the dark, looming scope of their situation. It was finally starting to hit the crew. There were several guys hanging out near the throttle station now, talking about just that. He listened only halfway, but for the first time really, he noticed an edge of fear.

He rubbed his tired eyes and looked up to see two pale faces peering at him from the gloom. He was a little startled, since he hadn't known the Mice were there. As usual, they ignored the conversation flowing around them. He sighed.

"What are you doing up? This ain't your watch. Get some sleep."

Gilbert blinked at him and looked around the compartment. The other men were arguing about the creatures on the big ship again. His gaze returned to Spanky.

"We seen a dinosaur before," he said in a conspiratorial voice. "Me and Isak. We seen one in New York, in a big museum, on liberty a few years back."

McFarlane's eyebrows rose at the non sequitur. "That so?" he managed.

Isak nodded grimly. "God's truth. Course they was all bones. There was more than one, but one looked sorta like those we saw on Bali the other day, only the one in New York was bigger." They paused and looked at him expectantly, as if waiting for him to comment. He just stared, baffled by their train of thought. Gilbert got impatient and spoke again. "Oil's made out of dinosaurs, they say. A long time ago a bunch of dinosaurs died and took to festerin', just like a dead cow, and all that old black ooze seeped into the ground and turned into oil. 'Least, that's what they say."

"Stands to reason," said Isak. "If oil ain't made out'a dinosaurs, why would Sinclair have one on their sign?" He paused thoughtfully. "Which them little dinosaurs on Bali looked a lot like the one on the Sinclair sign, 'cept they weren't green."

McFarlane's eyebrows had risen as far as they could go. He was way too tired for this. "Boys," he began, but Gilbert actually interrupted him.

"Beggin' your pardon, sir, but that got us thinkin'. We was both wildcatters when we was kids. Oklahoma, Texas, Colorado, Wyoming . . . We brought in a lot of wells before we got in the Navy."

"We didn't like it, though, neither of us. Too much damn sun and dust—and heat too, but heat ain't all that bad. That's why we got in the Navy, though," put in Isak, and what passed for a tentative smile crossed his face. "We know a thing or two about heavy machinery, but we like burnin' oil better'n findin' it."

Gilbert looked at his partner with an air of bitter resignation, but nodded agreement. "We got to thinkin'. If things is like they say, then if we're gonna keep our boilers fed with oil, I guess we'll have to drill for it." Gilbert took a breath. "We know how, and if that's what it takes, well . . . we know how."

Spanky looked at them with surprise and then slowly nodded. "Thanks, boys. I'll remember that."

Matt and Sandra dried their hair with towels from the officers' head. Matt's hair took only an instant, short as it was, and he watched Sandra, drying and brushing her long, almost-brass-colored strands. He'd known she was attractive, but at that moment, arms over her head, wet blouse tout against her bosom, she was the prettiest woman he'd ever seen and he resisted an electric urge to take the brush himself. Suddenly he realized she'd caught him staring and his ears burned. The expression on her face was . . . what? Fortunately, just then Bradford swept into the wardroom. He was still excited about what they'd seen.

"Amazing! Such jaws! I'm certain you're thankful we didn't hit the larger one, Captain Reddy! Of course you are!"

"I think we should all be thankful for that, Mr. Bradford," Matt replied, both grateful and resentful of the intrusion.

Bradford looked quizzically from one to the other, for the first time sensing tension between them, and attempted to quell his enthusiasm. "Quite so. Forgive me. I do get carried away. I've not forgotten the seriousness of the situation. In fact, it's been foremost on my mind. I've done a bit of preliminary research—oh, for my office library!—and I may have a few helpful suggestions for your Mr. Letts tomorrow."

"I'm glad to hear it."

"Yes. Bear in mind, however, anything I suggest is qualified by the assumption that we are, well, where we were, for lack of any better way to phrase it."

"I think you may safely assume that, Mr. Bradford," said Matt. "Our charts of this area are pathetic. Some actually date from the eighteenth century. Depths were all wrong even before . . . Anyway, I don't think there's ever been a proper survey unless the Dutch did one. That being said, there's enough agreement over landmarks and positions that we know to be accurate that I don't think there's any question we are, as you put it, where we were."

Sandra set the brush on the table and ran her fingers through her still-damp hair. She spoke for the first time and her lip quivered slightly. "That still leaves the question we've all been avoiding." There was a trace of bitterness in her voice. "What happened? I wish someone would think of something, even if it's wrong. It's driving me nuts, and I'm coping well compared to some. Ensign

Theimer won't even come out of the cabin. Nobody wants to talk about it! I know everyone's afraid"—she looked at Matt with eyes reflecting a strange mix of accusation, respect . . . and something else—"even you, Captain. But everyone just keeps going as if nothing unusual's happened at all."

Matt smiled a sad, gentle smile. "Thank God they do, Lieutenant Tucker. You're right. We are scared. And between the three of us in this room," he confessed woodenly, "I'm more scared than anybody. But we'll continue to do our duty because we *have* to. It's all we've got to hang on to and it's our only hope to survive."

Bradford shifted uncomfortably and Sandra covered her face with her hands for a moment, but nodded. "Of course, Captain. I'm sorry. I'm just . . . tired." She looked up and her eyes were rimmed with red. "This crew—everyone—is exhausted, but I've just about emptied the dispensary of sleeping pills."

Matt's eyes narrowed, but she quickly dispelled his concern with a flick of her wrist, and the corner of her mouth quirked upward. "Oh, don't worry. There weren't many on board to start with and it's not an epidemic. I made it sound worse than it is. If the truth were known, half these guys would conk out if you gave them a chair to sit on in front of a firing squad." She shook her head with genuine admiration. "It beats me how most stay so calm." She frowned. "Not all have, though, and some you'd think have dealt with it really haven't." She sighed. "Like me, I guess. It's like a nightmare, or some H. G. Wells or Sir Arthur Conan Doyle novel."

"Well," said Matt, "since the charts are correct, that eliminates *The Time Machine*, according to you, Mr. Bradford. Also, there's the matter of furry people with tails on ships bigger than the *Hornet*. That leaves *The Lost World* our most likely scenario." Sandra looked at him, surprised that he'd read those works.

"Actually," said Courtney Bradford, "I think you're both wrong."

"So what do you think?" asked Matt with a half smile.

Bradford looked solemn. "I don't know yet. I expect an epiphany once we've done more than just sail about. The water looks quite the same as before, you know." There was a hint of accusation in his tone.

"Quite the same except for the fish," said Sandra dryly.

Bradford bowed his head to her, conceding the point. "Indeed." He paused and looked down at the table, then glanced at them both. "Have you ever considered how your life might have been if you'd done something different? What a monumental impact some choice or deed can have on the rest of your life? Captain, what if you hadn't joined the Navy? What would you be like today? Would you even be the same person? Some people think, if they think about it at all, that they'd be the same, just doing something different. I disagree. I believe it's our actions, as well as the context and environment in which those actions take place, that make us what we are. But what if? What if your mother had never met your father? Your grandmother, your grandfather? What if the United States had lost its revolutionary war? What if the Roman Empire had never fallen—or never existed? What would the world be like today? Would it be much the same, except for that one small thing?"

Neither Matt nor Sandra answered. Matt just looked at him with a tired, speculative expression. Sandra's face wore no expression at all, but the clenching muscles in her jaw betrayed a growing tension.

"I think the world would be entirely different," Bradford continued quietly, "and the more distance between the moment of change and the present, the more profound the differences would be."

"I've . . . studied history a little," Matt said self-consciously. "I've often wondered 'what if' about a lot of things. I suppose every historian does, whether they admit it or not. What if the South had won the Battle of Gettysburg, for example, or that Serb hadn't shot the archduke of Austria? Things might've been different. Maybe a lot different." He looked at the Australian. "What's that got to do with anything?"

"Maybe nothing," said Courtney Bradford in a cryptic, falsely cheerful tone. "Maybe everything."

The sun rose sharp and fierce in a cloudless sky. The storm, if it could be called that, was over, leaving only a slight chop as *Walker* eased back into the gap between Bali and Menjangan Island. All through the night they'd searched but found no sign of *Mahan,* and everyone harbored a forlorn hope they'd find her where they left her. Matt considered it possible, even likely, that if Jim couldn't nurse his ship all the way to their rendezvous, he'd bring her back here, thinking it the first place Matt would look. Unfortunately, when they cleared the shoals and nosed into their previous anchorage, they were disappointed.

Bali remained a clear reminder that they were lost to the world they knew, its shores still teeming with unlikely creatures and its unterraced coastline a vast, panoramic plain broken by copses of unfamiliar palmlike trees. Again the crew lined the rails to stare. Unlike the sea—normally a destroyerman's natural element, but now one that inspired dread—the land seemed populated by comparatively pastoral creatures. They all remembered the lizard that bit Leo Davis and made him so sick, but that was on Menjangan Island. Maybe they weren't on Bali. The pygmy "brontosauruses" and other apparent herbivores browsed, cowlike, in full view and in broad daylight, seemingly content and unafraid of predators.

They crept closer. The outdated charts showed plenty of water, but Matt figured two hundred yards was close enough, and they dropped the hook once more. He peered at the shore and Courtney Bradford already had his "own" binoculars up. Matt wasn't sure whose they'd originally been, but possession being what it was, he doubted the owner would get them back. He shook his head with a little grin.

"Lieutenant Dowden, you have the deck. We'll remain here for the day and hopefully *Mahan*'ll show up. Double lookouts at all times. I'm not really worried about Japs anymore, but anchored, we can't maneuver. I think we've had enough surprises for a while. In the meantime, you'll plot a course for Surabaya. If *Mahan* doesn't show by dusk, we'll proceed there." He looked at Bradford and saw the desolate expression. His grin returned. "Mr. Bradford, Mr. Letts, and a small party will accompany me ashore. Have Campeti break out Springfields, sidearms, and ammunition for a party of eight. Hmm, better make that ten pistols, and throw in a tommy gun and one of the BARs. We'll leave two men and the Thompson with the boat."

He studied the contrast between Bradford's excited happiness and Lieutenant Dowden's horror. He chuckled. "Don't worry, Larry, we won't wander off. In fact, I don't intend to leave sight of the ship. It's time we saw face-to-face what we're up against. But if we get in over our heads, be ready to blow the hell out of anything we can't handle. Understood?"

Dowden swallowed. "Yes, sir. Aye, aye, sir."

Silva hefted a BAR and a bandolier of ammunition. He flashed his friends a toothy grin. "I'm goin' a'huntin'!" he said as he took his place with the other members of the shore party, climbing down into the whaleboat. They were Carl Bashear, Mack Marvaney, Glen Carter, and Alfred Vernon. Tony Scott and Fred Reynolds would remain with the boat on the beach. They were in it now, waiting for the others. Silva watched Marvaney climb down ahead of him. His expression was wooden, almost vacant. "Cheer up, Mack!" he said. "It'll be a hoot!" Marvaney glanced up at him and smiled, but the expression never reached his eyes.

Reynolds stood in the bow with his Springfield at the ready, and Scott fiddled with the throttle, a Thompson slung on his shoulder. Blue smoke rose from the idling motor as one by one the party descended the rungs welded to the side of the ship. The captain went last and he paused before he did, looking briefly at the faces nearby. Lieutenant Garrett wore an anxious expression, and Matt winked.

"You and Larry take care of my ship, hear?" His eyes flicked toward number three. It was manned, and already trained to port. Stites was its captain and he met Matt's gaze with a confident nod. He nodded back and looked at Garrett. "Carry on, Lieutenant," he said and disappeared over the side. As soon as he stepped into the boat and found a seat, Scott advanced the throttle. With a gurgling rumble they left *Walker*'s comforting side and steered for the mysterious shore.

Immediately, they felt the bumping, and several men exchanged nervous glances. Even Silva gave a start when something hit the hull under his foot. They knew it must be the vicious silvery fish—or something like them—but fortunately nothing bigger saw fit to taste the boat. In spite of the heat, gooseflesh crept along Matt's arms at the very thought of falling overboard. The memory of the feeding frenzy for the shipwrecked Japanese was vivid.

There was a breeze out of the south-southwest and the sea was still choppy. Little packets of spray misted them as they neared land. The sky was almost painfully bright and clear, and its contrast with the shoaling water became less and less distinct. The greens of vegetation were more or less as they should have been and the sun was as bright and hot as always. Letts tried to keep his lotion-smeared skin under the shade of a wide straw hat. The normalcy of the scene only accentuated the striking abnormality of their situation and the impossible creatures grazing along on the coastal plain ahead.

There were no breakers, only a gentle surf washing onto a beach of gray-black volcanic gravel. The bumping subsided and then stopped completely a few dozen yards from shore. All the same, no one was anxious to step into the water, regardless how shallow. Scott skillfully nosed the whaleboat through the surf until they felt a crunchy resistance as it slid to a stop. For a moment everyone looked at the few yards of water between them and land. They could actually see the bottom, but there was nervous hesitation all the same. With a short bark of a laugh, Silva hitched up his gun belt and hopped over the side. The other men sheepishly did the same and Matt stepped up through the empty seats, jumped out into the shallow surf, and waded ashore with outward unconcern. Letts and Marvaney brought up the rear. Reynolds and Scott carried a line and began looking for something to tie it to.

"You men stay here," said the captain. "Keep a sharp lookout and don't goof around. We won't be far and if we hear you shoot, we'll come running. If you have to, cut your cable and clear off the beach, but hang close enough to come back for us. If you hear us shoot, stay here and prepare to shove off. Understood?"

"Aye, aye, sir," they answered in unison.

Bradford was already hurrying excitedly away from the

beach with a couple of hesitant men behind. Matt sighed and raised his voice. "We'll all stick together, if you please!"

They marched inland in a loose column of twos, watching their flanks with care. Matt had grown up around weapons and had hunted all his life, so the Springfield he carried was a familiar and welcome companion. Especially now. He and Bradford walked side by side at the front of the column, looking at their surroundings. The grass was deep, waist high in places, and the broad, spiny leaves reminded Matt of johnsongrass. There were no brambles or thorns or such, but the grass was distinctly uncomfortable to walk through. *Maybe more like South Texas cordgrass*, he thought. Ahead was the first herd of the animals that looked like brontosauruses. They fed on the leaves of strange-looking palms that stood in a large clump. The way they moved and the sounds they made seemed entirely appropriate and very elephantlike. Any similarity ended there. Their necks were as long as their bodies, and they stood stripping vegetation much higher than any elephant ever could have.

There were about a dozen of the animals of all sizes in the group, and as the men drew nearer, they paid them no heed. The shore party slowed their pace as they approached, but made no effort to conceal themselves. At seventy-five yards they were finally noticed, but only in passing, and without alarm. A few animals momentarily stopped their contented feeding to look in their direction. With slow, stupid, cowlike expressions, they regarded the invaders, then resumed their ceaseless meal.

"Not real concerned, are they?" Matt observed quietly.

"Perhaps they're unaccustomed to predators large enough to be a threat," theorized Bradford, "or they consider the size and strength of their herd sufficient to ward off danger. May we get still closer?" Matt looked around. There was nothing on their flanks, just knee-deep grass stretching for a distance in either direction. He could see the boat and the men they'd left with it, less than a quarter mile away. Beyond was *Walker*, framed by an achingly beautiful panorama, Menjangan in the background.

"A little closer, I suppose."

They crept slowly forward. Instinctively, nearly everyone stooped into a semi-crouch as they walked, their subconscious minds insisting that nothing as comparatively small as they should ever stalk anything as big as the creatures before them without making *some* effort to conceal themselves. All except Courtney Bradford. He remained entirely erect, with his binoculars glued to his face. "Oh, my," he repeated over and over.

At fifty yards Matt was about to call a halt when suddenly every animal in the herd stopped eating and their small heads pivoted on giraffe-like necks simultaneously. The motion reminded him absurdly of antelopes and the way whole herds often changed direction as if by pre-planned command.

"Uh-oh," said Letts from just behind. One of the biggest animals in the group appeared to gather itself and stretched its neck to full extension. Its sides heaved and a tremendous shrill bugling sound erupted. Other necks extended, and within seconds all the creatures were bugling and bellowing together.

"Okay, people, let's ease back a little."

Everywhere across the plain, groups of animals stared, and sounded off as well. Other creatures, the shape of rhinos, but with bony, spike-studded crests behind their heads, also began trumpeting, and one group tossed their heads and trotted to a more distant herd of brontosauruses and filled gaps in the defensive line they'd established. Together now, both groups raged thunderous defiance at the destroyermen. More interspecies alliances sprang up among the scattered herd groups. "Amazing!" Bradford gasped.

The big bull from the closest group stomped and pawed aggressively at the ground. A cloud of dust rose around him and saplings were cast aside.

"Back away," ordered the captain. He'd never seen anything like this, but whatever was going on, they were vastly outnumbered and ridiculously outmassed. *Walker*'s guns could break up a charge if the distant creatures made one, but the nearest herd was too close for that, and he had no illusions about how effective their small arms would be. A .30-06 could kill an Asian elephant if the shot was placed just right, but where do you "place" a shot in a brontosaurus? "Mr. Bradford, let's go."

Reluctantly, the Australian turned to face him. His gaze

froze, however, on something beyond Matt's shoulder and his face drained of color. Matt spun, and there, not twenty yards away, eight large lizards rose from the grass, poised as if to attack. They looked vaguely like the Menjangan lizards except they wore dun-colored fur, or possibly downy feathers, and standing upright was clearly their natural posture. They were formed in a loose semicircle that effectively blocked the men's retreat. Behind him, the bull still rioted and one of the "lizards"—the leader perhaps—opened its mouth in a silent snarl, baring a horrifying array of razor-sharp teeth. Wicked talons lengthened the four long fingers of each outstretched "hand." The creature shifted its weight like a cat about to pounce. At that instant, from the beach came the distinctive *bra-ba-ba-ba-ba-bap!* of a Thompson and the deeper *crack* of a Springfield. Matt discovered he had plenty of adrenaline left, after all.

"At the lizards, open fire!"

Just as he gave the command, the creatures struck with a piercing shriek. Three fell in the initial volley, but the things were *fast* and as big as a man. Silva waded forward with the BAR and Matt was deafened by the metronomic *bam-bam-bam* of the weapon. His rifle was too cumbersome for close quarters and he fumbled for the .45. He yanked it from the holster and flipped the safety off just as one of the nightmare creatures hurtled past a madly dodging Carl Bashear and sprang toward him. He fired four times and then leaped aside as the thing crashed to the ground right where he'd been standing. It gathered its feet and tried to lunge, even with blood pouring from its chest and its left eye blown out. He shot it twice more before it collapsed. He fired once at another as it ran past him, fixated on Glen Carter, and cursed when the slide locked back. Carter was chambering another round in his Springfield, and he glanced up in horror at the death rushing toward him. Alan Letts, hat lost in the grass, turned and fired twice into the creature, shattering its leg, and it sprawled on the ground at Carter's feet. With a quick glance of gratitude at the supply officer, Carter slammed his bolt forward and shot the lizard where it lay, still scrabbling to reach him.

A wrenching scream arose to his left and Matt spun with a fresh magazine in hand, poised in the well of his pistol. One of the monsters was hunched over in the tall grass, struggling with someone on the ground. Bashear, Silva, and Vernon poured in a fusillade of pistol fire until it finally lay still. Another was on the ground struggling to rise, bright-pink froth spraying from its nostrils with each gasping breath. Bradford stood just yards away, rifle still pointed in its general direction, staring with eager fascination. Bashear strode up, shouldered him aside, and shot it in the head. There was an incredulous snarl on his lips as he regarded the Australian.

Matt turned, scanning all directions. The herd of brontosauruses, alarmed by the battle, had ceased bugling and drawn off, leaving only the big bull standing his ground. One of the attackers was still alive, running away with a long-legged, upright lope, faster than any man could match. Not much like the Menjangan lizards at all, he reflected. With a strangled curse, Silva snatched the BAR from the ground and loaded another magazine. He racked the bolt and brought the weapon to his shoulder. A sustained burst spat at the fleeing creature and clouds of dirt, rocks and shredded vegetation erupted around it. Suddenly it jerked and fell. Legs and tail flailed above the grass as Silva calmly replaced the magazine again and hosed the area until all movement ceased.

With another glance at the brontosaurus, Matt hurried to where the other men were looking at the ground. Lying half under one of the dead monsters was Gunner's Mate Mack Marvaney, his head torn nearly completely off.

"Goddamn lizards, or whatever the hell they are!" bellowed Silva, savagely kicking the carcass even after it rolled off his friend. Matt was shocked and somewhat embarrassed to see tears streaking the dust on the big man's face. He looked down at Marvaney and felt a spinning maelstrom of rage and anguish. His pulse thundered in his ears. What in the hell were they going to do? What was *he* going to do? They'd been ashore less than an hour and already lost a man. What kind of world had they wound up in where everything in the water and on the land was trying to eat them? How in the *hell* could they cope with that?

He looked at the men standing nearby. They all wore mixed expressions of rage, shock, and fear. He knew they'd rather face ten *Amagi*s than spend another hour ashore. Well, that was fine, because they were leaving and he knew just how they felt. But they'd have to go ashore again—if not here, then somewhere—if they were going to survive.

"Bring Marvaney," he croaked savagely, then pointed at one of the dead creatures. He cleared his throat and tried to speak more normally. "Bring that too."

The shooting by the boat had stopped, but two men still stood on the beach beside it. Thank God. The herds were bugling and trumpeting again and the big bull was growing bolder. It was time to leave.

There was sadness and angry murmuring when they carried Marvaney on deck. He'd been a fun-loving, friendly sort before depression over leaving his wife had set in, and he had no enemies aboard. Many sympathized and even identified with his unhappiness, although he'd taken it harder than most. But besides the fact that he was well liked, his death seemed somehow more tragic than those in battle. He was the first to die since they came through the Squall, and they couldn't even blame the Japs. All he'd done was go ashore. It showed them how vulnerable they were. The Japanese Navy had been a juggernaut, seemingly dedicated to their personal destruction, a task it nearly accomplished. But at least that was a threat they could understand. The things happening now, ever since the Squall, were beyond their comprehension. If Mack had been killed by the Japanese, it would have been tough, but that was the breaks. That came with being a destroyerman. Being killed by a giant furry lizard wasn't part of the deal.

The murmuring dwindled into shocked silence when they hoisted the creature aboard. The shore party, including the captain, watched while others did the work. Tony Scott and Fred Reynolds had easily killed the two creatures that attacked them, and nobody but Marvaney got so much as a scratch, but Matt figured they'd been through enough. All were pensive and subdued, except the Australian, who hovered like an expectant father as they lowered the lizard beside the number two torpedo mount. Matt was repulsed by the creature and found Bradford's solicitude mildly offensive, but he couldn't really blame him. That was just the way he was; besides, it was important that they learn as much from it as they could and he was the best qualified to do that.

The carcass already stank and the heat would soon make it worse. On its feet the lizard was tall as a man, but it was considerably heavier, so they shifted it onto a torpedo dolly and Matt followed as they rolled it into the shade of the amidships deckhouse. Part of its weight advantage came from the massively muscled legs, which looked more like those of an ostrich or emu than those of the Komodo-like lizards on Menjangan. The feet had three ostrichlike toes with vicious, hawkish claws. Slightly offset on the inside of each foot was a large scimitar-shaped claw, twice as long as the others. More of the weight came from a stubby, powerful tail, tapered sharply from the hips but flared into a thick, almost birdlike plumage of darker, striated "feathers"—for lack of anything else to call them. The "fur" covering the rest of the animal was dun overall, but the striations were faintly evident over the length of the beast. The arms looked very human, with distinct forearms and biceps, even though the shoulders were more like those of birds, where wings would mount. Four clawed fingers were on each hand, and one was very much like a thumb. The longish neck supported a toothy head straight out of a horror movie. The gray eyes were glazed in death, but retained a measure of reptilian malevolence.

Courtney Bradford was happily lecturing the spectators like a group of medical students with a cadaver. "And look!" he said excitedly. "The eyes are quite far forward and unobstructed! There's no question about stereoscopic vision! A formidable predator, believe you me! And those jaws! Terrifying!"

They were. The head tapered to a sharp point and the lower jaw seemed almost delicate, but powerful muscles bulged where it attached to the head. Matt had never seen anything with so many densely packed, razor-sharp teeth. It was almost cartoonish, like a piranha, but there was nothing humorous about it. Those teeth were clearly designed to tear flesh and crunch large bones. They reminded him vaguely of a cross between a shark's teeth and a cat's canines, only there was virtually no gap between them.

He was surprised to see how the crowd had swelled. Half the crew was present. He also noted that the gloom and dread that had been so pervasive had begun to lift somewhat. Many of the men most affected by Marvaney's death now listened with careful attention. *Of course!* he thought, and wondered if the Australian did it on purpose. Show them the enemy, especially a dead one, and it might still be scary as hell, but it also became clear that it could be killed. He looked at Courtney Bradford with new respect as the man jabbered happily on about how fearsome the obviously vanquished creature was.

He felt a hand on his arm and turned to see Lieutenant Tucker's concerned face, her eyes locked searchingly on his. He forced a smile. "How long have you been here?" he asked.

"Ever since you came aboard. Are you all right?"

He stepped slightly back. "Swell. We had some excitement, but we're all okay except—" He stopped and shook his head. "Why?"

She just patted his arm with a fragile smile. She couldn't tell him that the expression he'd worn when he came aboard had frightened her with the intensity of its rage, and devastated her with the depth of its hopelessness. She doubted anyone else had really noticed—men could be so stupid about such things—and he now seemed himself again. But that quick peek beneath his so carefully controlled veneer of confident self-assurance wrenched her heart, not only with fear for her own survival but also with compassion for this man who carried such a heavy burden for them all.

"Nothing," she said, and smiled a little brighter. She heard Bradford's voice rise above his dissertation.

"Ah! Lieutenant Tucker! There you are, my dear! You're quite the surgeon, I understand. Would you be so good as to assist me"—he grinned—"while I slice this bugger up and show these lads where to aim next time?" There were growls of approval and a predatory jockeying for the best view. Bradford wiped his brow and smiled wryly. "I'm afraid if we wait too long, it will be a nasty task indeed."

*   *   *

Matt sat on his bunk, his face in his hands. His sweat-soaked hair and clothes felt clammy under the fan. He sighed and spoke into the comm. "Bridge, this is the captain."

"Bridge, aye."

"Inform Mr. Dowden I'm in my quarters. I'll be up shortly."

"Aye, aye, sir."

Matt paused awkwardly for a moment. "Thanks," he said at last, and dropped back on the rack to stare at the overhead.

Another one, he thought grimly. All those men lost in the running fight, then *Mahan* and now Marvaney. What next? There had to be something he could have done to stop all this. Marvaney was a good kid. Unlike Silva, or pretty much the entire ordnance division, he'd never been a discipline problem aboard or ashore. He just did his job. He raised a little hell, like the rest, but he never pushed it too far. Maybe the pretty Filipino girl had something to do with that. Matt only saw her twice, both times when they docked in Cavite after some maneuver. She was always waiting on the quay, to snatch Marvaney up before he could escape with his hooligan friends. He always went willingly, too, without the false bravado and showing off of others under similar circumstances. It was clear he loved her very much. He was distraught when they left Cavite after the Japanese bombed it to splinters. After the Squall, he just sort of . . . went away. Matt shouldn't have let him go ashore. He hadn't even thought about it. Now Mack was dead, and it was his fault.

Finally he grunted and sat up. Sulking wouldn't do anyone any good, least of all Marvaney. He'd just have to do better, somehow. It was his duty, and he'd never shrunk from responsibility, but this was . . . different, and so very, very hard. He wasn't just a junior destroyer captain anymore, who only had to follow orders. His job had changed profoundly. For a moment he envied men like Silva, men who did their jobs but were free to leave the care and responsibility to others at the end of the watch. Matt's watch never ended. He *was* the job. He only hoped no one else would have to die before he figured out what, exactly, it had become.

He replaced his shirt with a dry one, ran a comb through his greasy hair, and put his hat back on. He searched the mirror above his little desk for signs of the anxiety that threatened to overwhelm him, and with a wary snort, he shouldered through the curtain to become captain of DD-163 again.

Dennis Silva leaned against the vegetable locker between the number three and number four funnels while Stites, Campeti, and Jamie Miller worked. They were sewing Marvaney into his mattress cover, and blood glistened black against the white cloth where it soaked through from his gruesome wound and dried in the afternoon sun. Silva felt ... depressed, he guessed, and that was an emotion he'd never experienced before. He always said he had only four "feelings"—horny, hungry, happy, and mad—and he was less than half joking. Now he knew a fifth. Mad was part of it, sure. But it was deeper and less focused and had already lasted longer than the others ever did. He'd felt it since Marvaney was killed, and that had been what? Almost three hours ago? *Must be depression,* he told himself with a sigh. *No tellin' what I'll be pinin' over next.*

He would miss Marvaney. They'd been shipmates for four years and raised hell from Cavite to Singapore— until the dummy got married and reformed. But they had a lot of laughs and busted a lot of heads, and he'd always been a good man at your back. Now he was dead and Silva realized he'd lost one of the few people that his loose definition of "true friend" applied to. He wished he had a drink.

"Don't forget 'the object,'" he grumped, referring to the item that he'd chosen to carry his friend to the depths.

Campeti glared at him. "Can't you think of nothin' else? Christ, it ain't hardly fittin'! And besides, what are we gonna listen to?"

"The object" was a bundle of about fifty records, part of a large collection Marvaney had aboard and often played on a portable wind-up turntable. The 78s were plenty heavy, more than sufficient to carry him down.

"Relax, Sonny. I only picked the old stuff nobody else likes. He liked 'em, though, and he ought'a keep 'em."

Campeti shook his head. "All right, Dennis, but when they're gone, they're gone. We might never hear them songs again."

"Suits me. I like dancin' to livelier tunes. Them waltzes and shit is for grandmas."

"Dancin'!" snorted Campeti, a general, growing concern on his mind. "Who with?"

They were silent while "the object" was solemnly placed at Marvaney's feet and the last stitches finished. Finally, the young pharmacist's mate spoke tentatively. "Chief Bashear said he killed six lizards. How many did you get, Silva?"

Dennis snorted. "Six, huh? Where I was standin', I didn't see him kill any. Well, one, maybe. Give him an assist."

"How about you?" Miller prodded. Silva shrugged. "Two or three, I guess. Hell, everybody was shootin'. Who knows?"

Stites glanced at Campeti and then looked at Silva again. "How about the Skipper? Boy, he sure looked mad!"

Silva nodded. "Yeah, he got one or two. With his pistol. He just stood there and let one run right up to him and *bam*!" He clapped his hands. "Right in the eye! The Skipper's got guts, I'll say that." He looked thoughtful. "He was mad, though. I never seen him that mad. I don't know if he was madder that they got Mack or that we ran out'a lizards to kill. He wasn't even that mad that time in Subic when me and—" He stopped, and a huge grin slowly spread across his face. "Well, never mind, boys. I got that rocker back later anyway." The others laughed as they finished preparations to send their friend to his watery grave.

That evening, as the sun touched the horizon, there was a small, forlorn splash alongside the lonely, rust-streaked ship. For a while, it remained still as the gloom deepened and the running lights snapped on. It must have been a strange, alien image to any creature watching from shore. Puffs of smoke rose from the aft funnels and hung motionless in the calm evening air. Then, slowly, it began to move. Most of the creatures paid it no heed; their interests were wholly devoted to packing vegetation into their large, multiple stomachs. If they'd witnessed the strange events of the day, they'd already forgotten.

Not all had forgotten, however. Some watched intently

and continued to stare at the lights as they moved through the slot and into the strait beyond, long after the shape of the ship itself was lost to view.

Keje-Fris-Ar sat on a stool beside his breakfast table in the ornately decorated chamber that was the foundation for the central tower of Home. It was the largest chamber on the entire ship that wasn't given over to livestock or cargo, and it was tastefully adorned with colorful tapestries and finely carved figures. Puffy pillows clustered in the various discussion areas, and in the center of all towered a nearly mature Galla tree, growing from a basin of earth that extended down to the very keel. Ample sunlight for it to thrive flowed through colorfully decorated hatches that were usually, as now, flung wide. A gentle breeze circulated to rustle the long, green-gold leaves. The only thing marring the dignity and splendor of the chamber was the small, plain table, set to one side, where Keje-Fris-Ar, High Chief of all the clans of *Salissa* Home, and his companion, High Sky Priest Adar, enjoyed their morning meal. The splendid hall was Keje's personal office, throne room, and council chamber rolled into one, where matters of great importance to all the clans were discussed. On such occasions, the ceremony and dignity were solemn indeed. But for everyday use, when there were no great matters to attend in proper form, Keje preferred his little table. Besides, he knew it amused Adar to dine with him thus.

The High Chief was the absolute monarch of Home, but the three towers supporting the great wings were controlled by their various chiefs, who enjoyed a degree of autonomy. An autonomy that could grow tiresome. Sometimes, the Sky Priests acted as intermediaries between the clans, because they were of no clan and all must serve the Heavens. Because of this trust, and because the Sky Priests—at least on *Salissa*—weren't oppressively spiritual, they enjoyed a position of esteem and a reputation for impartiality when dealing with the everyday squabbles among the several chiefs. But their efforts in this regard were subordinate to their primary duty. Their charge was to read the Heavens and ponder the stars and interpret them to others, who saw only points of light. The Sky Priests told them where they were, where they were going, and how to get there. They relayed the truths of the Heavens, which were above all things.

It was the High Chief who had to cajole, inspire, or force the clan chiefs to cooperate to do what the Heavens decreed if the Sky Priests couldn't help them agree, with him or each other. That was one of the reasons he generally declined the pomp of his exalted office, at least in everyday life. He didn't demand the near deification some High Chiefs of other Homes enjoyed, through constant ritual and an untouchable attitude, but he enjoyed a higher, more genuine status than many of his peers through respect for his abilities and wisdom. There was always contention, but his Home suffered less from the incessant squabbling that sometimes plagued other Homes because he led by example and was followed by the willing.

That didn't mean he didn't enjoy his status. He believed he was a good High Chief, and the People of *Salissa* Home prospered under his rule. What it did mean was he felt more comfortable eating at a small table, with his Sky Priest, whenever important rituals didn't interfere.

"So tell me, my lord," spoke Adar, delicately dabbing at his whiskers with an intricately woven kerchief, "have you given more thought to our visitors on the quick, smoky vessel?"

"No," grunted Keje around a mouthful of baked akka egg. "None at all since we last discussed them before we parted last night, to sleep." He was mildly annoyed with his friend's preoccupation with the strange tail-less beings. Deep down, he was just as curious as Adar, but he had other things to concern him, and their meeting had been so brief that it was pointless to speculate and rehash questions for which they'd likely never have answers.

Adar blinked rapidly with constrained amusement. "Surely, lord, you have thought of them a little." He paused and grew more serious. "I certainly have." His lips moved into a full grin. "As you know." Keje's eyelids fluttered questioningly.

"My lord, consider again how momentous it was. We encountered an entirely different species, which, at the very least, possess knowledge of sea vessels far surpassing our own—or the Grik." Adar looked intently into Keje's eyes. "And I repeat: they did not attack us! When has that ever been? Only once before, by the Prophet, and they were tail-less beings as well! The Grik are our Ancient Enemy. That much is clear from the Scrolls. They drove us from our ancestral home—on *land!*—so long ago that the Scrolls cannot even tell us what that life was like. But it was the Grik who forced our people to build the great Homes to travel the world in safety, across the hostile sea. But the Grik have learned to travel the sea as well. Not as well, or as safely, thank the Heavens, but nothing has changed in all that time. Yet again they seek to drive us, whenever we meet. The war that began so many ages ago is not over for them." He stopped, and looking down, he shuddered. "I believe they are truly evil, just as it is written, and I fear for our people. Our race."

Keje blinked agreement, although he still couldn't divine the Sky Priest's point. What did the Tail-less Ones have to do with any of that—or was that his point?

"My lord, you know the sea and what manner of vessel best swims upon it, but something is changing. The Grik have found us, their ancient prey, but until recently they could do little about it." He held up a dark, furless palm. "They do invariably attack, and People are sometimes slain, but their vessels are as nothing compared to the walls of Home. Yet in our lifetimes we've seen the size of their vessels increase, as well as the number of attacks. When last I spoke to other High Sky Priests, at the Gathering of Homes, I heard the same from them. Their frail vessels cannot protect them all, and many are probably lost, yet they keep coming, senselessly. From what I can tell, there is no motive other than to attack us, and the Western Ocean is no longer the barrier it was."

Keje was silent as he contemplated the words. Beneath the stool, his tail swished. One of the youngling servants carried away their platters. When she was gone, Keje spoke.

"I know what you are saying. The Grik make advances and we do nothing but repel them when they strike. What else can we do?"

"They advance and we repel them," agreed Adar, "but what if they strike colonies, or trade lands, where people don't have the walls of Home to defend them? What if they attack in some new way that cannot be defended against? They already use fire, and that's bad enough. What will become of us? It would be like the exodus in the Scrolls once more, only this time with nowhere to flee."

"Well, but what *does* this have to do with the Tail-less Ones? We've discussed all this before!" questioned Keje. He was exasperated, but he felt a gnawing agreement with Adar's words. "Do you believe these new Tail-less Ones are somehow related to the old? Is that what you're saying?" Keje huffed. "It is coincidence, nothing more. Their ways are as different from the others as ours are from theirs."

"We cannot know, my lord, if they're the same or not. It may not even matter. I say only this: they did not attack us."

"Yes, yes, you've said that before!"

"They did not attack us, and they're clearly unafraid of the Grik. With such a speedy vessel, they would have no reason to fear."

With dawning comprehension, Keje regarded the Sky Priest. "You believe we have squandered an opportunity," he stated flatly.

"Yes, my lord, I do."

As if on cue, the sound of running feet and a rising tide of alarmed voices reached them through the open windows of the hall. The coincidence wasn't lost on either of them, and they stared at one another. Keje's personal Guard detachment raced in and stood before him. Some were adjusting their armor. Kas-Ra-Ar, Keje's cousin and captain of the Guard, bowed his dark-furred head. "My lord," he said simply, "the Grik come."

Keje blinked acknowledgment, and turning, he bellowed for his armor. "From which direction, cousin?" he asked.

"West-southwest, and south, my lord." Neither Kas's expression nor the tone of his voice changed when Keje's eyes pierced his. "Yes, lord, there are six. All larger than we've ever seen."

Keje paced the battlement spanning the great floating island that was Home. It was an open deck extending beam to beam and formed the ceiling to the forward part of the

Great Hall. Since the hall was so large, Keje's vantage point was several dozen tails above the main deck. On the other two towers, the level wasn't as prominent, and merely served as the foundation for the towers of apartments between the wing tripods. The platform on the central tower was larger so the High Chief could direct his people in storms—and battle.

The turnout of the Guard was more disciplined than just a few days before. Every male, female, and youngling on *Salissa* Home that was old enough, fit enough, or large enough to bear arms was technically a member of the Guard, but the "active" Guard consisted of the strongest and most fit from each clan. Its members spent time each week engaged in martial exercises. These consisted of athletic training and practice with weapons, but since they were so rarely called to fight, the training was geared more toward preparation for the frequent competitions between the various clans.

Rivalry was fierce and provided entertainment for the People. But the rivalries sometimes became bitter, so the active Guards of the various clans, even while preparing for the common defense, almost never practiced together. The combined active Guard of *Salissa* numbered nearly four hundred and, when the reserves swelled their ranks, Home could boast almost sixteen hundred defenders. But many had never fought, and fewer had fought together. Standing together clan by clan, they didn't even know how. And none of them—none of Keje's people in all the world—had ever faced more than one Grik ship at a time.

As he paced, Keje stared aft and to the left, toward the distant haze of land. He confirmed with his own eyes no fewer than six ships of the Ancient Enemy stalking his people. His insides twisted. He wasn't afraid to fight, and he didn't think he was afraid to die, but he'd fought the Grik before. One-sided and seemingly senseless as those fights had been, he'd seen a glimpse of what they were capable of. Their appalling savagery and apparent disdain for their own lives was so utterly alien that he'd always harbored a secret terror of what might happen if they ever attacked in sufficient force to gain the decks of Home. Now it seemed that the nightmare was upon them. He would see what it was like at last.

The Grik were closing fast, and their speed made it seem that *Salissa* really was an island, incapable of independent movement, even though the great wings were taut and straining against the freshening breeze. He watched as weapons were issued to females and younglings who'd never held them in their lives, other than to prepare food. His eyes blinked furiously in impotent realization. It was all his fault. He'd lived with the nightmare for many years and he should have prepared his people better.

The festive tarpaulins and awnings came down. Perhaps the most evil and insidious thing about the Grik was they seemed to delight in using fire as a weapon. The Homes of the People were built to last virtually forever, and his Home was barely a generation old. But it was made of wood, and the woods that served best were hardwoods steeped in resin. Resin that took fire with an obdurate flame. Barrels of sea water were always kept at hand, but now more barrels and buckets of water were hauled up by ropes as quickly as possible while they prepared for the unprecedented deluge of fire that they knew would come. Water droplets misted down as the fabric wings were doused. More water sloshed on the decks, making them slippery, but it couldn't be helped. He hoped they wouldn't soon be slick with blood.

He looked around. Adar was there, surrounded by his acolytes. All were armed, but they blinked nervously, since none had ever trained for war. The Sky Priests trained only in the mysteries of the Heavens. It never occurred to them to study the mysteries of one race intent on destroying another. They couldn't be risked on the walls, but if the enemy reached this place there would be no noncombatants. There would be only fight or die.

Keje's immediate family was with him on the battlement as well, but that was ancient tradition, not favoritism. In battle, the High Chief had enough to worry about without adding concern for his family. That family held no official power simply by familial association. In theory, their status was no higher than that of any fish cleaner or wing runner of the People. They often held status of their own, through merit, but the idea of a fixed aristocracy—at least for the High Chief—was repellent to the fiercely, if inconsistently, egalitarian People. In practice, it was more complicated. The office that Keje held was hereditary—subject to ratification by the Clan Assembly, of course—but no one remembered when a succession had been blocked. Therefore, a certain "royal family" atmosphere and collective protectiveness existed toward the heirs of any High Chief.

Unlike the wings, whose chiefs passed their position to the elder heirs, the elder, or "senior," of the High Chief's heirs were expected to move on in Homes of their own when the time came. When the final heirs came of age and the High Chief died or stepped down, they would succeed him. All could have Homes, if they chose, peopled by the younger heirs of the "parent" Home. This ensured continuity on the parent Home through the experience of the wing clans, as well as the Homes newly founded and led by the High Chief's elder heirs. "Wars of succession" did not occur, populations were controlled, and all the Homes of the People were distantly related to some degree. That more and more of the "elder heirs" were choosing to establish "Land Colonies" with the resources granted them concerned some, who feared dissolution of the old, traditional ways, but practically, the burgeoning Land Colonies provided support for the still-growing number of Homes. In any event, because of this arrangement, there really was no "crown prince."

In theory at least. In Keje's case, his only mate died young, leaving him a single heir, Selass. Keje wasn't old and would certainly mate again, perhaps many times, but for now, Selass was it. She therefore constituted the only "immediate" family to stand with him on the battlement that day.

Her new mate, Saak-Fas, was another matter. Keje didn't like him and his daughter knew it, but he couldn't describe his dislike beyond a general discomfort over a supremely self-centered attitude. His dislike intensified considerably today when Saak-Fas appeared on the battlement with Selass instead of on the wall where he belonged. The only fighters posted to the battlement were the High Chief's personal armsmen, and just a few of those. Everyone else, besides the Sky Priests, were bearers of commands, or runners, who would race down the catwalks and carry his orders where directed. Keje decided he would send Saak-Fas on such an errand when the time came, and he had no regard for what his daughter would think of that. He did notice that Selass appeared uncomfortable, and he wondered if it was shame, or simply the fact that death was so near.

He studied the Grik ships as they approached in three pairs. They looked identical to others he'd seen, but they did seem somewhat larger. Possibly sixty or eighty tails long. Even at a distance, he saw their decks teeming with the loathsome creatures, their mail and weapons glittering in the bright sunlight of the otherwise perfect day. Keje summoned the first of many runners he expected to send before the battle was done. One way or another.

"Instruct the lance throwers not to shoot beyond one hundred tails, and to shoot only where their hulls meet the water." The runner blinked acknowledgment and raced away. The lance throwers had the only standoff weapons *Salissa* Home possessed. They were like the crossbows of the Guard except they were much, much larger. Intended for defense against mountain fish, or to slay their smaller cousins, four of the lance throwers were mounted on pivots along each side. It took six people considerable effort to crank the wrist-thick bowstring into the firing position, but they could hurl a spade-headed lance three tails long and a hand-span in diameter a distance of three hundred tails with accuracy enough to hit a mountain fish in the eye. That was a target only slightly larger than Keje's breakfast table. Such accuracy was essential because the eye was the creature's only vulnerable spot.

That was Keje's only preparatory command. Maneuver was pointless; the far more agile Grik could easily counter anything he tried. All that remained was to wait and see how the blow would fall.

Chack nervously clutched one of the massive shrouds supporting the forward tripod and watched the enemy approach. His stomach was knotted with fear, and the reason his hands were clamped so firmly on the shroud was so none would see how badly they shook. He and half his clan were on the forward platform, near enough to the fighters below to act as a reserve but also free to race aloft and adjust or repair the wing. His weapon, a large, long-bladed axe, leaned against the railing nearby and he devoutly hoped he wouldn't have to wield it. He was strong and athletic, but his fighting skills were poor.

He'd never done well in the frequent competitions. His form was good, but his timing was sloppy. Risa was much better with weapons than he, and she often tried to coach him, but it did little good. He knew no amount of practice could force martial competence upon his fundamentally unaggressive character. He'd been in fights—everyone had. No matter that *Salissa* was very large—it was still too small to avoid conflict. He never won those fights, but he was rarely injured. He was very good at avoiding blows, through speed and deft responses, but he'd always had an abiding reluctance to deliver them. His fights ended inconclusively when his adversary tired of trying to hit him. It was clear that he was no coward, because he was willing to stand and take it if they could dish it out. He just didn't dish it out in return. Chack considered that a victory in itself, even if it never settled anything. The problem today, however, was that if he raised that axe, it meant all was lost unless the last wing runners fought. Simply avoiding blows wasn't an option. The only way to stop the Grik was to kill them.

In all previous encounters, the Grik had never attempted to talk. Whenever they sighted the People, there was only one response. Attack. No matter how small the ship or how ridiculous the odds, they *always* attacked. And when they fought, if they ever actually came to personal blows, there was only mindless, berserk savagery without any concept of giving or receiving quarter. They fought until they were killed, even if they'd lost limbs or been disarmed. Always. It was madness.

It wouldn't be long now, Chack thought. They were close. A pair of ships closed within two hundred tails on the left, abreast of the forewing tower. Another pair ranged up on the right. The final pair was closing aft, as if they meant to strike three, or perhaps six, places at once. It was strange, Chack thought absently, that they should attack thus. But then, they'd never seen more than one Grik ship at a time, and the way they fought—Chack shuddered—they seemed incapable of cooperation. Yet this attack would be coordinated.

The ships themselves were huge by Grik standards, half again larger than any ever seen. Every detail seemed the same, only on a larger scale. Probably to hold more warriors, he thought. Each had three of the ridiculously puny masts that the Grik favored, with three billowing sails instead of wings on the first two and a triangular sail on the aft. Another stubby mast protruded from the front of their ships, but there was no sail upon it. It seemed to serve more as a countersupport for the stays that held the others.

The hulls were low and sleek, except for separate elevated decks at the front and back. The sides were painted a uniform red, the bulwarks black—what could be seen of them. From front to back, over the bulwarks, were hundreds of garishly painted oval shields. Some were one color, others were many, and most bore some design, but each belonged to a Grik warrior, and those masses of warriors packed the decks and stared at the People with an unnatural, cold-blooded quiet. Wisps of smoke swirled from their midst and vanished to leeward, and Chack swallowed hard when he realized their fire weapons were ready for use.

There was almost no sound from those around him either, only low murmurs of soft conversation. Risa had been spinning a ribald tale, but now even she was silent. They were as ready as they'd ever be, and yet there was no way to be ready to face the death—and the kind of death!—that they all, deep down, knew had come. Risa was at his side and she put a hand on his arm and looked deeply into his eyes. She bared her teeth in a feral grin.

"I know you will fight well, my Brother," she said, guessing his concern. "It's not as if they are People, after all." Then her grin faded and she looked away from him, toward the approaching ships. Very calculatingly, she spoke again. "I do not want you to die, but this time if you won't fight, you won't be the only one they kill." He looked at her and blinked a quick flash of betrayal, but then just as quickly, he knew she was right. A vague sense of shame and a fierce determination welled within him and, leaning over, he picked up his axe and laid it heavily on the rail before them. She saw it and recognized the promise it represented, but said nothing. Together, they watched and waited.

Rising voices reached them and they turned to face the battlement. There, in the distance, Adar stood, arms outstretched, his long robe flowing around him. It was the stance of supplication. Quickly, most within Chack's view imitated the gesture and, almost as one, they turned to face the Sun. Risa poked him savagely in the ribs and he joined her in the pose. The warm rays swept across his face and he could see the mighty orb even through his closed eyelids. With the rest of his people he spoke the words: "Maker of All Things, I beg your protection, but if it is my time, light my Spirit's path to its Home in the Heavens!" He crossed his arms on his chest and knelt to the deck. There was an audible rumble of knees on wood as hundreds did the same. Clearly, not all participated because someone cried out in alarm and Chack looked up.

A crimson, snakelike pennant unfurled from the masthead of one of the ships, and even as it snapped taut and streamed over the sea, a great, harsh, hissing cry arose from all the ships at once. It came as a wave of sound like the wind and sea in a gale, but there was an unnatural malevolence that the sea had never meant. Shields were plucked from bulwarks and weapons clashed against them, adding a monstrous throbbing, metallic heartbeat to the sound. It was the loudest, most terrifying thing Chack had ever heard, as thousands of throats and weapons clamored at him across the water. Then, as the terrible din reached its peak, six Grik ships turned as one to destroy his Home, his family, his world.

The afternoon watch came on duty, and the normalcy of tradition-bound procedure left Matt heartened. For a moment the terrible, unreal events of the previous days seemed remote. The sea was mild, the sky was clear, and a firm, cool breeze washed across him from the open bridgewing. It seemed to cleanse him of the depression and trepidation that had settled upon him. It was one of those days that made destroyermen glory in the seemingly effortless speed and grace of their sharp-hulled ships instead of cursing them for their inconsiderate tendency to pitch and roll in

heavier seas. It was a heaven-sent respite for him, as well
as the rest of the crew, and whether they took their mood
from their captain or not, he saw more smiles and normal,
ordinary goofing around than he had in many days.

He sat in his chair and leafed through the pages of the
report. Davis's leg was still not improving, but more of the
invalids were ready for light duty. Spanky, Letts, and, of all
people, the Mice were designing a drilling rig and had convinced Bernie Sandison to endorse their scheme to use the
torpedo tubes on the inoperable number three mount for a
condensation tower to refine the oil once they found it. He
looked out at the fo'c'sle. Gray had the first deck division
repairing topside damage, although Matt knew how the
Bosun suffered over the dingy, reddening deck and the long
streaks of rust that had begun to take hold. One man with
a quart can of paint followed behind the welders as they
refitted and straightened twisted stanchions and worked
to repair the shell damage to the starboard hawse. The anchor on that side was gone forever, but they were winching
the spare into place while he watched. He was surprised to
see the Japanese officer helping, under the supervision of a
certain Marine, who sat on the capstan bollard and watched
like a chain gang overseer. The men working with Shinya
kept their distance and cast many resentful looks, but they
were letting him help. It was a start, Matt supposed. All in
all, it was a pretty good day.

The only things darkening his mood were the subconscious fuel gauge, creeping ever downward in his mind, and
the continuing dull ache over what might have happened
to *Mahan*.

He heard voices behind him and turned to see Courtney
Bradford and Sandra Tucker asking permission to come on
the bridge. Matt smiled broadly, waved them over beside
him, and stood up. "Good afternoon, Lieutenant Tucker,
Mr. Bradford. A fine day, is it not?"

"Indeed it is, Captain," replied the Australian, and Sandra smiled back at him. "I thought you'd like to know that
we've finished our 'science experiment' at last, and can
manage without its, uh, services any longer."

"Thank God," said Matt, and chuckled. "I take it . . .
I *hope* you mean you pitched the stinking thing over the

side?" Sandra and Bradford had worked through the night and into the morning dissecting the dead creature from Bali. Some of the crew watched throughout, duties permitting, and Bradford kept up a running lecture the entire time. The rest of the crew, however, were increasingly vocal about the overpowering stench. Now they both stood, tired but with satisfied smiles on their faces.

"Yes, um, it has gone on to the reward it so richly deserved," answered Bradford in a dry tone. Matt chuckled again, but was secretly amazed that Bradford had given up so easily. He'd half expected him to ask to keep it in the refrigerator—or his cabin, if necessary. But Matt saw now that Courtney Bradford had undergone a transformation. It may have been subtle, and possibly fleeting, but he'd been there when they were attacked and he saw what happened to Marvaney. Besides, fascinating as the creatures were, they had also, at the very least, kept him from studying anything else. The furry lizards of Bali had become his enemies as surely as the Japanese.

"Well, what did you find out?"

"Quite a lot, actually. We don't believe they were lizards at all. At least I don't," he said. "Miss Tucker is not quite so fully convinced of that." He nodded at her respectfully. "But I believe they are somewhat more like birds in many ways."

"Birds? With teeth like that? You must be joking."

"No, sir, he's not," said Sandra. "I know a good bit about human anatomy, and anatomy in general, I suppose, but I'm obviously no expert on these creatures. Nobody is. Mr. Bradford has more experience studying ... similar things than I do, and I can see his point. They're built like birds—or emus and ostriches, to be more precise—except for the upper arms, and their bones are hollow, but incredibly strong like a bird's. Our opinions diverge because of those upper arms, their tails, and well, their heads too, I guess. Their tails have feathers, but they're muscular like an alligator's. And their upper arms show no sign of being vestigial wings, but seem to have evolved as arms to *be* arms. And of course their heads." She shuddered slightly. "Or more specifically, their jaws. There's nothing birdlike about them at all."

"But my dear lieutenant," countered Bradford, evidently continuing an argument. "You're basing your opinions more upon what they *look* like and less on what they *are* like—"

Matt held up his hand, smiling still, to stop him. "Enough. While this is all very fascinating, my most pressing question involves their intelligence. Are they as smart as they seemed? I mean, there were ten of us and ten of them, and they displayed what to my mind could only be described as the *tactic* of hitting us and the men at the boat simultaneously—in a way that would keep us apart. As well armed as they are with teeth and claws, one on one, they had every reason to expect the advantage."

Sandra was silent, and Bradford shifted uncomfortably. "We don't really know, I'm afraid," he said at last. "Theoretically, yes. They certainly have the brain capacity, and in proportion to their body size, their brains are similar to our own. Then again . . ."

Matt nodded. The very idea of something that ferocious being smart was daunting indeed. There was no question that they would have to go ashore again. Maybe not on Bali, but the first time they had set a foot on land, something had tried to bite it off. They had to presume that other places wouldn't be any different. Somehow, they had to figure out how to go ashore—and work there—without being eaten.

The crow's nest comm whistled. "Bridge, lookout," came the tinny voice of Elden.

"Bridge, Riggs here," replied the petty officer.

"PO, I've got smoke on the horizon, bearing zero one five. A hell of a lot of smoke. There's so much I thought it was a cloud at first. It's pretty much the same color—not black like an oil fire. Whatever's burning is pretty big, though, and it's in the water. Not—repeat, *not*—on land."

"Excuse me, please," said Matt to his visitors, raising his binoculars.

"Can you see what it is yet?" Riggs asked the lookout. "Is it a ship, or what?"

"Negative, PO. All I see is smoke. Whatever it is, it's still . . . Wait! Damn! I'd about swear it was that big monkey-cat ship!" Matt lowered his binoculars with a strange mix of disappointment, relief, and curious concern. Disappointment that it wasn't *Mahan*, but relief that it wasn't *Mahan* on fire. The curious concern was for the monkey-cats, as Elden called them, if that's who it was. *Well*, he thought, *if it is, maybe it's time we met*. Besides, they appeared to be in trouble.

"All ahead full," he ordered. "Come right, fifteen degrees."

Walker's head came around and she quickly gathered speed. Water peeled back from her bow as she charged, the feather nearly reaching the fo'c'sle. The men on the foredeck stopped what they were doing and stood with fluttering clothes, their faces turned toward the rushing breeze and the towering column of smoke in the distance. Five minutes passed, then ten.

"Bridge?" came Elden's voice. The normally unflappable shipfitter sounded unusually strained.

"Bridge, aye."

"It's the monkey-cats all right, and there are several large three-masted ships around 'em. Most are lashed to her, and it looks like they're fighting! The monkey-cats are definitely burning—and maybe one of the other ships as well." There was a moment's pause. "I think there's a hell of a fight going on."

Matt turned to Reynolds. "Get the range from Mr. Barry," he ordered.

"Aye, aye, Captain," said Reynolds, wide-eyed. It was his first stint as talker, and it was just his luck something serious would happen. He spoke briefly into the microphone and listened for the response. His voice squeaked slightly when he reported. "Sir, Ensign Barry estimates the range at about fifteen thousand yards."

"Very well. Sound general quarters, if you please."

The deep gonging sound that was part horn, part buzzer resonated through the ship, and surprised men snatched helmets and life vests as they raced to their stations. Some rolled from their racks, disoriented for a moment, and hesitated like they would never have done before the Squall. Feet clanked metallically on the ladder as Lieutenant Garrett and the rest of the fire-control team gained the bridge and scampered to the platform above. Bernard Sandison appeared, tucking in his shirt, along with torpedomen Hale,

Carter, and Aubrey, who took their places at the torpedo directors.

Reynolds recited a litany of readiness reports, and after much longer than Matt approved, he made the announcement: "All stations manned and ready, Captain. Mr. Dowden has the auxiliary conn and reports . . . um . . . the chaos he viewed from his perspective looked like a shore-patrol raid on an Olongapo . . . whorehouse." His face turned pink.

Matt grunted and glanced at his watch. "Pathetic," he announced. "A Jap car salesman with a rowboat and a stick of dynamite could have sent us to the bottom by now. Sparks, inform the Bosun that the deck division was the last to report." Everyone cringed to think how the Chief would exact his vengeance for that humiliation, and he was heard even now, bellowing at the crew of the number one gun.

Much of the confusion was caused by the need to stow the "peacetime" awnings that now covered the deck spaces, but Matt knew most of the blame was his. He'd grown lax about daily drills since they no longer faced imminent annihilation by the Japanese. That didn't mean all threat of annihilation had passed, and despite their trauma—or maybe because of it—drill was now more important, not less. He resolved to make sure his destroyermen were never caught flat-footed again.

He sat back in his chair, Sandra and Bradford not entirely forgotten but relegated to that portion of his mind not preparing to fight his ship if need be. "Mr. Sandison. What's the current status of our torpedoes?"

"One, three and five are loaded, prepped, and ready in all respects."

"No news on the condemned torps?"

"No, sir. I still have them apart in the shop. One didn't even have a repair tag, so we're checking it out, piece by piece. The other's propulsion machinery works fine; it just needs recharging. But it's clearly a dud. The warhead housing is all crumpled in. The tag said one of our subs fired it into a Dutch freighter by mistake and it didn't go off, but it punched a hole in her side and got stuck. Yard-apes fished it out of the freighter when she got into port." Sandison smirked ironically. "Everyone was lucky on that deal."

There'd been far too many "duds" of every sort. In this one case it was fortunate, but Matt hated to think how many American ships and submarines might have been lost, and enemies spared, simply because of faulty ordnance. A lot of the antiaircraft shells on *Houston* had been duds, and they'd never even suspected it because they hadn't been allowed enough live-fire practice. The same was true for the torpedoes. The suspected causes ranged anywhere from faulty detonators to a tendency to run too deep. He knew they hadn't performed well at all during the night action at Balikpapan, and most of the success there was due to gunnery. Whatever the case, he prayed they weren't carrying around, carefully husbanding, and relying on useless weapons. "Keep working on it, Mr. Sandison," was all he said.

Facing forward, he peered through his binoculars again and focused at the base of the column of smoke. He now saw for himself that there was indeed a battle under way. But compared to anything he'd ever expected, the word "battle" was wholly insufficient to describe it.

"My God . . ."

The excellent optics and seven-power magnification of the MK1 M2 Bausch and Lomb binoculars transformed the distant, blurry shapes into a high-relief scene of unprecedented horror and desperation. The . . . medieval nature of the combat wasn't what shocked him, however. What left him speechless was the obvious total involvement of the defenders and the utter lack of regard for casualties and noncombatants by the attackers. And then there were the attackers themselves.

Courtney Bradford had his own binoculars in front of his eyes, and his hands began to shake. "My God," he finally echoed.

Snarling, Chack swung the axe with all his strength and entirely severed the tail of a Grik warrior, poised to finish Risa, who lay unconscious and bleeding on the catwalk. The Grik shrieked and toppled forward, robbed of its counterbalance, but it fell on Risa and the snout opened wide, revealing razor-sharp, densely packed teeth prepared to savage her throat. He swung again and buried the axe in the Grik's back, halfway to the breastbone. It collapsed instantly in a spray of hot blood and Chack heaved it aside. He grabbed his sister by the arm and slung her off the catwalk to a pair of ancient garden tenders below.

The garden tenders were the oldest and most frail people of Home and, so far, the only ones not actively committed to the fight. Their task was to help clear the wounded and try to tend their injuries. Chack feared his sister was dying. He hadn't seen the wound, or the blow that struck her down, but her fine fur was matted with blood and she felt lifeless in his arms. His own fur was matted with blood as well, some wet and some half dry. He didn't think any was his, however. He'd fought like a demon, like he'd never imagined he could, ever since the pompous Saak-Fas had arrived and imperiously sent their last reserves into the faltering defense. The last wing runners had seen the need already, but waited for Keje's command. Released at last, they charged down the shrouds, and Chack looked to see if Saak-Fas accompanied them, but he was nowhere in sight. Nor had he seen him in the long hours since.

Surely, the People had never known such a battle! In the beginning, the Grik used their fire weapons to disperse the defenders. Flaming spheres, twice the size of a person's head, arced across the water to explode against the side of Home. Fire ran like water into the sea, but some made it onto the catwalk and the flames rapidly spread. Some spread onto people too, and Chack raged at the memory of their screams and the stench of burning fur. While they fought the flames, the Grik closed. Lance hurlers fired with a crash, and the Grik ships were festooned with their shafts, but still they came. Finally they were alongside, directly below, and their hulls ground together. Crossbow bolts rained down and thumped into bodies, shields, and the enemy decks, but then the ladders came. Hundreds of grappling hooks and dozens of ladders from each ship rose and locked the combatants together. The Grik swarmed up. The Guard slashed ropes and pushed at the ladders, and attackers rained into the sea, to be crushed between the hulls or shredded by the incredible seething multitude of flasher-fish that churned the water into a glittering, silver-red cauldron of death. But still they came, as they always did, and there were so many.

Very quickly, the fighting became hand to hand when first a few, then many Grik gained the decks of Home. Scotas and axes rose and fell, as did the strange, curved short-swords and spears of the Grik. Spreading flames went unfought as defenders were forced to grapple with the attackers. Chack had stood with his sister, transfixed with horror as they watched the awful slaughter. A triumphant cheer began somewhere aft, and they turned to see a column of smoke and flames spew skyward from one of the Grik ships. Apparently their entire store of fire weapons was ignited on deck, and a keening, whistling, collective shriek rose from the burning warriors. Some, deliberately or in mindless panic, leaped into the sea and were torn apart. Gri-kakka had risen as well, and several cruised sedately through the turmoil, snapping at struggling figures. The Grik ship was rapidly consumed. Burning sails flapped, and crackling flames licked up the spindly masts until they withered and fell amid a huge cloud of steam and sparks. The hulk drifted slowly away, a roiling, lifeless inferno. But there were more.

Unaffected, the other Grik continued the attack. That was when the wing runners went into the fight and Chack became a warrior at last.

The first Grik he killed was an accident. He'd practically landed on it when he slid down the shrouds. Striking out instinctively with his axe, he clove through the leather helmet it wore and split its skull in two. He expected to be nauseated, to feel some remorse, but there was nothing. Nothing at first. Then a quickening surge of . . . exhilaration flowed through his heart and limbs. With a bellow, he waded forward, swinging the axe two-handed in the precise reaping motion he'd been taught. An astonishing, wondrous, visceral glee filled his soul as the murderers of his people fell before him. Through the long hours he hacked and slew, Risa by his side, shouting encouragement, and the pride in her voice was clear, even over the din of battle. Then she fell.

Now the sun was halfway to the horizon, above the mountainous shore to the west. He didn't know how many Grik he'd killed, satisfying as it was. He did know it wasn't enough. Their losses were terrible, but regardless how many were slain, still more waited on their ships to crowd onto the battlefield that *Salissa* had become. And those that still fought did so with a fresh abandon as shocking as their savagery. One ship had sunk alongside, pierced by lance-hurler shafts. So many lines held it fast that it hung, just below the surface, its masts crawling with Grik. The weight of the hulk caused *Salissa* to heel a few degrees.

Another Grik ship went up in flames, but only after it was lashed to *Salissa*. Its funeral pyre provided the fuel to ignite a fire on Home itself that threatened to consume it. Flames raged out of control on the right side of the first tower, and the forewing—the very symbol of Chack's clan—burned above. Flames roared hundreds of tails into the sky, while charred and smoldering pieces of fabric snowed down upon them. Ironically, the only thing saving the weary, dwindling defenders was that the heat on that side was too intense even for the Grik to bear. That left a front only fifteen tails wide to defend on the left side of the tower. Once, the Grik broke through into the very body of Home, and the slaughter among the garden tenders was terrible. A counterattack by Keje and his personal Guard managed to repulse the thrust. Keje had abandoned his position on the battlement and along with his personal Guard—and even Selass, Chack saw with surprise—he was everywhere. Whenever the enemy began to break through, he and his diminishing followers somehow stemmed the tide.

The battle aft was going well, but only one ship grappled there. Chack and his fellows were fighting the better part of three Grik crews, and one ship was still unengaged. It hadn't lashed on with the others when the one before it caught fire. For most of the day, it sailed around, looking for a good place to strike. The lance hurlers still in action flailed at it mercilessly, however, and it looked a little low in the water. At present, it actually seemed to be moving away, although Chack could barely see through the smoke, which stung his eyes and made each breath an effort. If he hadn't known better, he'd almost have thought it was leaving! That was absurd, of course. The Grik never ran. Always, they were either destroyed or left wallowing helpless in their intended victim's wake. It was probably positioning itself to take advantage of the wind so it could attack some uninvolved point. When it did, it would surely turn the tide. Of course, it made small difference. The fire that preserved them for the moment would destroy them in the end. If it wasn't extinguished soon, all of *Salissa* Home would burn.

Chack fell out of the battle line to catch his breath. Only so many fighters would fit in that limited space, and mercifully, it allowed them to rotate out briefly every now and then. He was panting with exhaustion, and his tongue lolled, but miraculously, his only wound was a shallow slash across his left shoulder. He trotted to a freshwater barrel and drank greedily. The water had a reddish tinge from bloody hands that had reached for the cup, but he didn't care. All that mattered was the soothing liquid wetting his parched throat. Dropping the cup back in the barrel, he looked about for a moment.

Younglings, garden tenders, and other old ones raced or crept back and forth, depending on their ability, carrying water to the fire. Their efforts, while noble, were in vain. Chack felt a growing dread that no matter how the battle went they were all going to burn. The entire forewing was gone, and the flaming debris had fallen on the tower, adding to the conflagration. It would all be for nothing. He hoped with a surge of grief that his sister was already dead—at least then she wouldn't die in the flames. In bitter resignation, he hefted his bloody axe with aching arms and turned back toward the fight—just in time to glimpse two large columns of water straddle the lurking Grik ship, and a mighty explosion of fire and smoke at its waterline that sent it rolling onto its side.

"My God, sir! How can we not take sides! Just *look* over there!" cried Bradford incredulously.

Matt stared at him, his face granite. "I didn't say we wouldn't help. I said I wish we didn't have to—because when we do, we take sides. We know nothing about what's going on. For all we know, those ... attackers are the good guys! Just because they look like the lizards on Bali doesn't mean they are the same. What if somebody judged our actions simply because we look like Germans? Also—and I'll only tell you this once, Mr. Bradford—you're on my bridge at my sufferance. One more outburst and I'll have you removed. Is that clear?"

"Will you remove me too?" demanded Sandra, her eyes flashing like pistol muzzles.

Matt sighed angrily. "Lieutenant, I wish you weren't here *now*. We may be about to go into battle. In case you've forgotten, you have a battle station!"

She stared at him, unrepentant and smoldering. The rest of the men in the pilothouse very studiously observed anything but the confrontation with their captain. Even so, it was plain that their sympathies rested with Bradford and Lieutenant Tucker.

"Look," said Matt, as reasonably as he could, "this isn't our fight . . ." He immediately raised a hand to ward off interruption. "Yet. I feel inclined to help the—what did you call them? Lemurians?" Bradford nodded determinedly. Personally, he had had quite enough of this monkey-cat or cat-monkey business. "I feel inclined to help them too," Matt repeated, "but *we are all alone out here*. If we do, we might get involved in an all-out war, and we have no idea what resources the enemy has. *We* damn sure don't have any. Besides, look at those ships! Unlike the . . . Lemurians . . . those lizard people have ships right out of the eighteenth century. *Our* eighteenth century! The similarity in design is too perfect to be coincidence! They must've had contact with other humans! Maybe other people came through a squall—or something like we did—before. Don't you see? If that's the case, maybe these lizards can tell us about them! Maybe they're still here!" He was silent for a moment as he let his point drift home. "If we shoot at them, I doubt they'll give us answers."

He swiveled in his chair, gazing through the windows at the battle, closer by the moment. "On the other hand . . ." he murmured darkly, and said no more. The Lemurians were certainly outnumbered, and given the obvious disparity in the ships' speeds, there was no question who started the fight. So far, none of the creatures seemed to have noticed their approach. With the smoke so thick and the fighting so intense, that was understandable. But sooner or later, they would be noticed. Maybe the sight of the destroyer would have the same effect as before, and everybody would just stop what they were doing and stare. That might provide an opening. It wasn't much of a plan, but it was all he could think of short of going in with guns blazing.

In spite of his argument, he knew, deep down, that was what he wanted to do. Marvaney's death was still fresh, and the creatures battling the Lemurians certainly resembled the ones that had killed him. Besides, from what he saw, they weren't any more civilized than their apparent cousins on Bali. He might lose the chance to gain vital information, but sometimes you had to do something just because it was right. "Let's see what happens," he said at last.

"Captain, Mr. Garrett says they must've seen us," said Reynolds. "One of the lizards is coming about. Range is now twenty-one double zero."

Matt saw the change in aspect as the ship tacked, head-sails filling and pulling it around. He'd walked the decks of the USS *Constitution* as a kid and was struck by her uncanny resemblance to the ship that was turning to meet them. The color was different—this ship was painted entirely red—and there were no gunports, but otherwise it looked just like an earlier version of the old frigate, even down to the number of masts and the sail plan. "Slow to two-thirds," he commanded as the range diminished.

"Twelve double zero," said Reynolds behind him, parroting Garrett's estimate as the range wound down. The lizard ship was wearing a lot of canvas and Matt estimated its speed at eight to ten knots. Respectable, but troubling. This bold, all-out approach was more like the behavior of the Bali creatures than he quite liked. They didn't seem overawed by the destroyer at all, or even carefully curious like the Lemurians had been. They acted more like they were trying to come to grips.

"Nine hundred yards, sir."

"Slow to one-third. Come left thirty degrees. Guns one, three, and four will track the target."

"Bridge," came the voice of Elden. "A lot of those lizard critters are gathering in the target's bows . . . They have swords and shields." The final words were incredulous.

"Pass the word for Chief Campeti. Have him issue rifles and sidearms to any deck personnel not part of the gun crews. Prepare to repel boarders." Matt was struck by the strangeness of the order even as he gave it. Probably not since the War of 1812 had the captain of a U.S. warship given the order to repel boarders on the high seas. He allowed himself an ironic smile. "At three hundred yards, the number three gun will put a shot across her bow if she doesn't ease off."

He glanced at Sandra and Courtney Bradford. They watched with mixed expressions, but at least Bradford's ire had faded. Matt raised an eyebrow with a look that seemed to say, "What were we arguing about?" and lifted his binoculars again. The sight that greeted him sent a chill down his spine. Elden was right. A large group of lizards stood in the bow of the oncoming ship, brandishing swords, spears, and garish shields. Their toothy mouths were open wide in an unheard shout or chant. Many clashed their weapons against their shields and seemed quite exercised. Even more ominous, many were holding what appeared to be grappling hooks, and as he watched, more and more joined those already poised on the fo'c'sle. There were hundreds of them, just on that one ship.

"Three hundred yards!" came Reynolds's breathless report.

In a calm voice, devoid of inflection, Captain Reddy uttered a single word. "Fire."

He never lowered his binoculars, but watched as the number three gun crashed and, a bare instant later, a geyser erupted between *Walker* and the approaching ship. A sheet of water cascaded down on the lizards and sent a few of them scrambling. But far from having the desired effect, the shot seemed to make those remaining in the bow redouble their clamoring and yelling. A moment passed, then another, and the ship showed no sign of turning or heaving to.

Suddenly, at two hundred yards, something roughly the size of a medicine ball arced lazily up, high in the air, from amid the gathered lizards. An instant later, a second object rose, and then a third. Everyone in the pilothouse saw them with unaided eyes. The objects reached apogee, tumbling end over end and trailing wisps of smoke. Down they came, closer and closer until two plummeted into the sea scarcely a dozen yards off *Walker*'s port beam. On impact with the water, they ruptured and a ball of fire rose skyward and burning fluid of some kind spread flames upon the waves. The third was closer, and when the projectile ruptured, burning fuel actually washed up *Walker*'s side, just below the number one gun.

Matt lowered his binoculars and looked at those standing nearby. When he spoke, his voice sounded vaguely surprised, but his eyes were suffused with fury.

"Did they just throw those balls of fire at *us*?"

For just the slightest moment, he reflected upon the consequences and ramifications of his next act, but the decision came without any apparent hesitation. He stepped briskly to Reynolds, took the headset from him, and spoke directly into the microphone. "Mr. Garrett, this is the captain. Commence firing."

Chack rubbed unbelieving eyes. Three more simultaneous explosions annihilated the stricken Grik ship. Debris and parts of bodies rained into the sea hundreds of tails in all directions. The shattered hulk was quickly awash. Shredded sails fluttered as the center mast teetered and crashed amid the struggling, dying Grik. The tumult of battle briefly ebbed as the People—and the Grik—tried in vain to pierce the haze and smoke with red, running eyes to see what had occurred. The ship sank quickly from sight, leaving only tangled flotsam and shrieking carrion for the insatiable fish. Beyond, Chack saw a strangely familiar shape.

The Tail-less Ones! he realized with a sense of wonder, then repeated his thought at the top of his lungs. "The Tail-less Ones! They have returned! The Tail-less Ones destroy the Grik!" With a gleeful bellow, echoed by many, and a surge of unexpected hope, he waded back into battle. The Grik fought just as fiercely as before and, if anything, with renewed frenzy. But the frenzy was different somehow. For the first time he sensed desperation and—could it be?—fear. Chack fed off that, real or imagined, as he swung his axe in great arcs that hewed heads and arms and chests. His own arms ached and the axe became difficult to grasp. Sometimes it slipped sideways and he struck a Grik or its shield with the flat of the blade and felt the blow jar his bones, but still he fought on. Others sensed the difference as well, and they pushed the Grik with renewed energy. The flames began to envelop the forward tower and, reluctantly, the Grik gave ground. It was that or burn.

Chack found a moment to cast a glance at their saviors. They approached closer, but after so decisively dealing with the unattached ship, they hesitated, as if unsure what to do. He understood. They'd clearly decided to help the People, but their magical weapons weren't selective enough to influence the battle for Home itself. At least he thought that at first.

"What now?" whispered Matt. They'd thrown away any hope of neutrality when they destroyed the lizard ship, and there was clearly no hope for survivors. That was a terrible aspect of naval war in this new world that he would have to bear in mind, he thought, watching the flashing shapes consume the last of the creatures in the water. They'd fired in self-defense, but he doubted the hundreds of lizards fighting the Lemurians would see it that way. Okay, so maybe two salvos were excessive, but they'd made him mad. Now, like it or not, he had chosen sides, and as precarious as the situation on the big ship looked, this wasn't the time for half measures. One side or the other would win this fight, and it didn't seem like a good idea to let it be the ones they'd shot at.

"Come left, to one three zero," he said coldly. "Gun crews stand by, but cease firing. Small arms will commence firing at one hundred yards. The targets are the lizards on the Lemurian ship. The machine guns may fire, but have them conserve ammunition and be careful of their targets. Concentrate where the enemy is massing, away from the 'friendlies.' Rig all fire hoses and have handlers standing by." He clasped his hands behind his back, listening to the responses, and stared straight ahead at the battle.

Sandra moved beside him, also looking at what they were getting themselves into. "I'm sorry, Captain," she said in a small, quiet voice.

He looked at her a moment, then nodded with a shrug. "Me too," he said. "I guess it's not in me to watch something like this without trying to help. But Lord above, we have enough problems without winding up in the middle of a war!" He spoke quietly, so she was the only one who knew, truly, what an agonizing decision it had been. They heard the crack of Springfields as riflemen on deck chose their targets, and the starboard .30-cal opened with short bursts of its own.

"These . . . Lemurians better be worth it," he said grimly. "Because every bullet we fire for them is one less we'll have to save our own asses with." With that, he stepped away from her and onto the starboard bridgewing to take *Walker* back to war.

"Hot damn!" growled Dennis Silva as he racked the bolt back on the starboard .50-cal. "We finally get to kill somebody!" Ordnance Striker Gil Olivera was beside him, poised to change the ammunition box when it was empty. He giggled nervously. Alfonso Reavis and Sandy Newman also stood nearby, Springfields over their shoulders, but their job was to gather spent shells before they rolled into the sea. Silva didn't know why; as far as he knew, they couldn't be reloaded. Even if they'd had more bullets—which they didn't—they didn't have powder or primers. Oh, well, he didn't care. He'd finally been ordered to kill the hell out of somebody, and he was ready. If Campeti wanted guys scurrying around picking up his empty brass, that wasn't his concern.

The sound of battle on the burning ship was awesome. The roaring flames could be heard over the blower, and the screams and shouts from alien throats lent the scene a surrealistic aspect. He couldn't see much through the smoke, though, and he squinted over his sights. There. There seemed to be a battle line of sorts formed just aft of the base of that big tower forward. It was burning like mad, and the heat and smoke must be hell. He pointed it out to Felts, who stood between him and the number three gun with one of the BARs. "Everything forward of there looks like nothin' but lizards!" he shouted. Felts squinted and nodded. If they got too much closer, they'd be shooting up. One of the lizard ships was sunk alongside, between them and the enemy horde, and men were shooting lizards from its rigging.

"I see it, Dennis. If we shoot in among that bunch, we ought to get half a dozen with each shot!"

"'Zactly!" said Silva, and grinned.

"Just be careful not to hit any of them monkey-cats!" warned Felts.

Silva rolled his eyes. "The hell you say, Tommy Felts! They're cat-monkeys, goddamn it! How many times have I got to tell you! Are you strikin' for snipe, or what?"

Before Felts could answer, Silva let out a whoop and pressed the butterfly trigger on the back of his gun. A stream of tracers arced across the short distance through the smoke and into the densely packed mass of lizard warriors.

"I'll teach you to kick *my* 'Cats, you unnatural sons-a-bitches!" Silva screamed.

Keje-Fris-Ar felt dazed as he sagged with his hands on his knees, panting. The world was upside down. He'd been wounded superficially in many places and was faint with fatigue and perhaps loss of blood. His tongue was swollen, his lips cracked and bleeding, and he'd lost his voice hours ago. He blinked thanks when Selass gave him a large copper mug, but his hands shook uncontrollably and he couldn't drink. From the gloom, Adar was beside him, helping to hold it still. Pridefully, he tried to shake off the Sky Priest's hands, but didn't have the strength even for that. Instead, he drank greedily with closed eyes as the tepid water soothed his throat. But even with eyes closed, his mind still saw the momentous things he'd witnessed.

He'd seen things that day that rivaled the epic power of the Scrolls themselves. Acts of courage and horror without compare—without precedence—as far as he knew. And he'd seen wonders beyond comprehension, such as the power of the Tail-less Ones who'd so unexpectedly come to their aid. Without whose aid they'd have surely perished. But beyond even that, he'd seen what that power did to the Grik. The People helped, of course, but it was the power of the Tail-less Ones that worked the miracle he could hardly believe, even now. The Grik had broken.

They hadn't been merely repulsed; he'd seen that before.

They'd utterly and completely *broken* and fled in absolute terror from the combined assault of the Tail-less Ones' magic and the vengeful ferocity of the People. There'd been confusion on both sides at first, when suddenly there raged a hammering sound like nothing ever heard and the Grik—but only the Grik—began dying by the score. Hundreds fell, horribly mangled, in the space of a few short breaths, and they couldn't fight—couldn't even see—whatever was killing them! The panic began in their rear, behind the fighting, and Keje first noticed it as a lessening pressure in front of his fighters. Wary glances of alarm became shrieks of rage and terror, as the Grik saw their comrades dying and fleeing behind them. Keje saw it too, and despite his own shock, grasped the opportunity. He led the charge that swept the enemy entirely from the decks of Home.

The killing had been wanton and the victory complete. He couldn't count how many Grik were cut down from behind, or hacked and clawed one another to death as they fled back to the ships still lashed to *Salissa*. Hundreds simply leaped into the sea, so total had their panic been. One Grik ship got clear, so the victory wasn't entirely complete, but the other tried to flee in full view of the Tail-less Ones' amazing ship, and two thunderous booms from their strange tubes left it a sinking wreck. The ship then surged forward, apparently to chase the other, but almost immediately slowed and came about, back to the side of Home. The strange beings rushed to and fro, dragging heavy ropelike things around their deck, and then, to the further amazement of all, water surged upon the fires raging in the forward part of *Salissa*.

A gentle, refreshing mist still descended on Keje as dusk slowly ended this momentous day and his People gleefully rolled Grik corpses over the side. With an effort, he disengaged from the supporting hands of his oldest friend and daughter and crept painfully to the rail. There below, he saw the same figure looking up he'd seen just days before. Fighting pain and weariness with nothing but will, he raised his right arm and gave the Sign of the Empty Hand. He hoped, somehow, the gesture would convey a fraction of his gratitude.

In the glare of the dwindling flames, he was sure the creature raised its hand as well, and he slumped into the arms of his friend and his daughter—and others. As they carried him away he realized that tomorrow the sun would rise on a different world. One in which the Grik were more bold and more numerous than their worst nightmares could have foretold, but also a world in which the Grik had been broken, and his People had powerful friends.

*T*he battle was over—at least the fighting part was. Like all battles, the aftermath looked as gruesome and painful as the strife. *Walker*'s searchlights illuminated the continuing toil on the deck of the huge ship that floated, still smoldering, less than a hundred yards away. The Lemurians tending their many wounded and throwing their enemies over the side appeared hesitant to enter the powerful beams at first, but they quickly recognized the friendly gesture, if not the power behind it. They now took full advantage of the unusual illumination. *Very practical creatures,* Matt observed. He'd hesitated to use the lights, concerned that they might perceive them as some sort of threat or an unwholesome act on *Walker*'s part. His concerns were quickly put to rest. Even if the Lemurians were uneasy, after what *Walker* had done for them, they were evidently prepared to accept her benevolence.

"Secure from general quarters," he said quietly, and joined Sandra, Bradford, and the torpedo-director crew on the bridgewing. The torpedomen were unplugging their headsets and securing their equipment. He glanced up and behind to see Garrett and several others leaning on the rail of the fire-control platform, watching the labors of their "allies." A tiny meteor arced over the side as Chief Gray, on the foredeck below the splashguard, guiltily flicked a cigarette away. "The smoking lamp's *lit*, Boats," Matt called down with amusement. The number one gun crew chuckled, and Gray turned on them in a vitriolic frenzy. Matt listened to the humorous tirade and shook his head.

"We should help them," said Sandra, referring to the scene on the wounded ship. She paused, remembering her meager resources. Their supplies were limited, and so were the personnel of her "division." Karen Theimer was increasingly withdrawn, and Jamie Miller was just a kid. Besides, they couldn't all go. Still . . .

"I should help them. I should go across immediately and offer assistance, Captain." She'd turned to face him, her words changing from an observation to a formal request.

He looked at her thoughtfully, but reluctantly shook his head. "That might be a good idea," he temporized. "It wouldn't hurt our résumé with our new friends either, as long as they recognize your efforts for what they are. But it's just not possible."

"I'm afraid I must insist, Captain. We had no casualties and I'm sure I can make my intentions known. Pain has no language. Even if I can't speak to them or know their physiology, I can help bandage. My God, they may not even know about germs!"

He nodded sympathetically and spoke very gently. "I admire your courage and compassion. But it really is impossible and you must not insist." He gestured over the side. The sea still churned with the silvery, tuna-sized fish. Whenever another lizard hit the water, it frothed and thrashed anew. Sandra followed his gaze and bit her lip. "There's no way I'm risking you or Nurse Theimer—not to mention a boat and crew—until things settle down. By morning the fish may have had their fill, and in daylight we might give it a try."

"There's no other way?" she asked, almost plaintively.

"No. In daylight, if those things are still down there, and we can get the Lemurians to understand, we might shoot a line across and rig a bosun's chair. But that'll take coordination and some very careful station-keeping. If one of those plesiosaurs shows up, we might have to maneuver . . ." He stopped. "That won't work either. Hopefully by then we can just use a boat."

He spoke no more and just stared across the water. His face was troubled, frowning. He was anxious to meet the

Lemurians for a number of reasons. First, he certainly agreed with Sandra: if they could render medical assistance, they should offer it. More important, they'd just waded into a war in a big way, and he had no idea where they stood or how big a war it was. Possibly the lizards were simply raiders, the local equivalent of Malay pirates. Maybe the Lemurians represented the greater power, and even if there was a general war going on, they'd just ingratiated themselves to that power and all their problems were solved. But it was equally possible that the reverse was true. One of the lizard ships had escaped, and however powerful they might be, there was no doubt about the role *Walker* played in the battle. What's more, they might not be so easily discouraged by modern weapons again. He wanted answers. And there lurked another problem: how in the world would they communicate? Perhaps Bradford would have suggestions.

After a while Sandra tentatively put her hand on his in the darkness. "I'm sorry again," she said.

He looked at her, genuinely surprised—by the words and the touch. "What for?"

"For . . . a lot of things. For pressuring you. Doubting you. I know how hard it was, how much you wanted to avoid this. But you did the right thing."

He looked at her very frankly and sighed. "I think so too, or I wouldn't have done it. I hope we're both right." He smiled. "I guess we'll find out."

With the dawn, the sea regained its deceptively mild appearance and Captain Reddy ordered the larger motor launch prepared instead of the whaleboat. It was safer, and he wanted as many observers as possible. Sandra, Bradford, Gray, McFarlane, and Letts would go with him, along with two carpenter's mates and an armed security detachment consisting of Silva, Felts, Reavis, and Newman. Tony Scott was coxswain. On a whim, more than for any other reason, Matt accepted Lieutenant Shinya's request to go, although he would be the only one without a sidearm. He wasn't really worried that Shinya would do anything untoward, but he believed—and even took time to explain to him—that the crew wouldn't approve.

Again, he left Larry Dowden in command. "I don't expect any trouble," he told him, "but that's what I thought last time. Remain at general quarters while we're away. They've got to be expecting to say howdy in some fashion, but I'd rather do it on their ship first. If we wait around too long, they might decide to visit us, and I don't want them roaming around my ship until we know more about them."

"Understood, Captain, but I still ought to be the one to go," Dowden said with a frown.

Matt grinned. "May be, but I'm the captain, so I get to do what I want. Seriously, though, I agree in principle, but—well, we've already been through this. You can be the first to meet the strange alien creatures next time, Larry. I promise."

He climbed into the launch, which was already level with the deck. That was another good thing about the launch, he thought: it could be lowered with them in it. Slipping and falling into the water was no longer just an embarrassing gaffe; it was a death sentence. The keel smacked the waves and, with a burbling roar, they started across. The sun was up, but it was still early and Matt hoped they wouldn't catch the Lemurians in a crabby mood before their version of morning coffee. More important, he didn't want to surprise them. He needn't have been concerned. Evidently, they'd been watching his ship very closely because, as soon as they approached, many of the creatures stopped what they were doing and scampered to the rail. Strange, excited cries alerted others.

"Hail the conquering heroes," the Bosun growled.

As they drew nearer, the ship's sheer size was even more impressive from their lower perspective. The rail was easily a hundred feet over their heads, and there was no question that the thing was as large as one of the new fleet carriers. Maybe bigger. That made the damage it had sustained even more amazing. The forward superstructure was completely destroyed, and the foremast tripod stood naked and charred. The pagoda-like tower had collapsed upon itself to become a mere heap of smoldering rubble. Clouds of ash billowed to leeward like gouts of steam. The forward part of the hull was scorched as well, though there didn't seem to be serious damage to its structural integrity. It was massive, and while it was clearly made of wood, there was no telling how thick it was. Matt was surprised to discover that the bottom was copper-clad, much like *Walker*'s sailing-navy ancestors. No doubt the copper extending several feet above the sea served the same purpose here—to protect the hull from wood-eating organisms.

They coasted alongside, approximately amidships, until the launch almost bumped. But Scott was an excellent coxswain even with the more unfamiliar launch, and he avoided actual contact by the thinnest margin. They saw no way up, however. There were no steps or ladders for them to climb, and for the moment they could only stare at the numerous heads, high above, peering back down at them. Suddenly, a very familiar-looking rope-and-rung arrangement unrolled down the side with a clatter and jerked to a stop almost upon them.

"Well," said Bradford, "not exactly a red carpet, after all, but certainly a warmer welcome than they gave their last visitors." There were several chuckles, and Matt took the ladder in his hands.

"Ordinarily, I always say 'ladies first,' but this time I'll break that rule." There were more chuckles and a few uneasy glances at Lieutenant Tucker. Her reputation and stature had reached an unprecedented level, for a non-destroyerman (and a woman). She possessed undoubted skill as a healer and was genuinely friendly to those in her care. But she'd flown signals of an equally unprecedented temper, and her sense of humor had yet to be tried. She didn't take offense at the captain's attempt to seem light-hearted about his protectiveness of her, however.

"Boats, you're next, then the security detail. Once they're up, everyone can follow as they see fit." He started up the ladder, but then stopped. "Everybody stay cool and friendly, and remember who you are and what you represent." With that, he resumed his climb. He tried to appear brisk and confident and hoped no one detected his nervousness. He wasn't afraid, exactly, but he had to admit to some anxious uncertainty. Never in his most bizarre dreams had he imagined that he would be doing what he was right now. Nothing he'd ever done had prepared him for this moment, and he didn't have the slightest idea what to do. The only thing he was sure of was that nobody else did either and he'd better not screw it up.

Finally, he reached the rail and paused for a moment before jumping to the deck. Many of the creatures had gathered around, and they drew back at the sight of him, their inscrutable faces staring with large, feline eyes. They were every conceivable color, like three generations of kittens from a wanton barn cat. Long, fluffy tails twitched behind them, seemingly independent of their owners' stoic immobility. And they were short. He hadn't realized it, watching them through binoculars, but they were much shorter than he'd expected. The tallest he saw came only to his chin, and it was considerably taller than the others. He? She? He assumed it was a he, though he had no basis, yet, to make that guess. The majority of the creatures were dressed haphazardly, in what appeared to be a mixture of daily garb and the occasional piece of leather and copper armor. All seemed weary and many were wounded, but most were still armed with an axe or a short scimitar-like sword. Significantly, none were brandishing those weapons at him.

What set the tall one apart, aside from his height, was that he was covered entirely in a dark purple robe with large stars sewn across the shoulders, and the long-tailed hood was pulled tight around his face so that only his piercing gray eyes could be seen. The creatures nearest him seemed more alert than the rest, more detached from the moment, and they had a protective, proprietary air about them. Because of this, and his dress, Matt took him for a leader, or at least an authority figure of some kind. Gray clambered over the rail to join him and as he did, he put his hand on one of the enormous backstays supporting the center tripod. He took it away and looked at it. The stay was coated with thick black tar. He arched an eyebrow at his captain and Matt nodded. He'd seen it too. He stepped forward and the two of them, the robed figure and the naval officer, quietly faced one another while the rest of the party boarded. All the while, there was silence. Matt couldn't even fall back on Navy custom and salute their flag, for there was none, at least at present, but maybe ... maybe that didn't matter. Tradition was tradition, and he expected even if they didn't understand it, they would recognize it as such. Maybe they would appreciate the respect that went with it.

Abruptly, he pivoted to his right, facing aft, and snapped a sharp salute. Then he turned to the robed figure and saluted him as well.

"Lieutenant Commander Matthew Reddy, United States Navy. I request permission to come aboard, sir."

The Lemurian blinked rapidly with what might have been surprise, and his lips stretched into what looked for all the world like a grin. Matt held the salute a moment longer, and then on impulse slowly lowered his hand until he held it, palm outward, toward the creature in the purple robe. Very deliberately, it pulled the hood from its face. It was still "grinning" broadly, although the expression didn't extend beyond its mouth. Matt suspected that, like cats, their faces weren't made to display emotions as humans did. The "grin," if that's what it was, spoke volumes, however, and now others nearby grinned too. To the amazement of the humans, the one in the robe carefully imitated Matt's salute and held up his hand as well. Matt heard a gasp behind him, as well as Gray's gravelly chuckle.

"Permission granted, Skipper," he said quietly.

The Lemurian clasped both his hands to his chest and spoke: "Adar."

Bradford pushed his way next to the captain. "Upon my word! Do you suppose he means *he* is Adar, or that's the name for his people?"

Matt sighed. "I was about to ... ask him that, Mr. Bradford. Please, let's have no more outbursts. It might confuse them and I'm confused enough for us all right now." He pointed at the creature. "Adar?" he asked.

The Lemurian blinked twice and, if anything, his grin grew broader. He spread his hands out from his sides and bowed.

Matt clasped his own hands to his chest and said, "Matthew Reddy."

The creature struggled to wrap his mouth around the unfamiliar sounds. Then he made an attempt.

"Maa-tyoo Riddy."

Matt grinned back at him. "Pretty good." He turned and proceeded to name those who accompanied him, and then pointed across the water where the destroyer kept station. She really was a sight, he reflected. Streaks of rust covered her sides and the patched battle damage was made conspicuous by the fresher paint. The lizard firebomb had scorched a large section of her hull just aft of her number, and the paint was bubbled and flaking. Most of the crew was on deck at the moment too, watching them. The tattered Stars and Stripes fluttered near the top of the short mast aft.

"USS *Walker,*" he said.

A respectful silence ensued that lasted while all the Lemurians gazed at his battered ship. Adar's grin went away and he somehow radiated solemnity when he spoke again.

"Waa-kur."

He blinked rapidly and gestured toward an opening in the large deckhouse behind him. He hesitated uncertainly, looking back, then strode purposefully through it. The other creatures cleared a lane. Apparently, he expected them to follow. Matt looked at the Bosun, who shrugged, and he glanced at the others and caught Sandra's eye. He shrugged too, and strode after the purple-robed figure, followed closely by his companions. Silva made a half-strangled, incredulous sound. Matt looked back.

"What . . . ?" Then he saw it too. Suddenly, there was no doubt Adar was male. For the first time—driving home how distracted they were—they realized many of the Lemurians staring with open curiosity were also openly, glaringly— very humanly—female. Except for bits of armor, none wore much more than a kind of skirt, or kilt. Supremely practical, since their tails made other types of clothing inconvenient, but few tunics were worn by anyone. Furry breasts of a shape and proportion entirely, fondly, familiar (except for the fur, of course) unself-consciously jutted at them from all directions. Not surprisingly, Silva was the first to notice.

"Oh, my God!" squeaked Newman.

"Fascinating!" breathed Bradford.

"Not unusual," said Sandra, a little sharply, Matt thought, and he saw her cheeks were pink. "Even 'back home' it's not unusual at all for primitive people to go around like . . . this."

"Way too 'unusual,' far as I'm concerned," whispered Felts, and Sandra's cheeks went darker.

"Silence!" growled Gray with less than normal vehe-mence. Clearing his throat, he went on, "Quit gawkin' at their dames! You want 'em to eat us? Pick up yer eyeballs. They're *critters*, for God's sake!"

Matt coughed. "Not 'critters,' and not too 'primitive' to take offense, so keep your eyes"—he looked straight at Silva—"and your hands to yourselves. That's an order!"

They stooped to enter the doorway, but inside was a much larger chamber than expected. It spanned the entire "ground" floor of the tower and the ceiling was as high as a college gym. Tapestries of coarse but ornately woven fib-ers decorated the walls, and large overstuffed pillows lay about the room in groups. It was a scene of considerable opulence compared to the scorched and bloodstained ex-terior. But even here, the scent of burnt wood and charred flesh and fur was all-pervading. Matt wondered how long that dreadful smell would linger like a shroud. In the center of the hall, the ceiling opened up to allow a strange-looking tree to rise, far above their heads. The only trees he knew were live oaks, cedars, and mesquite, so he couldn't tell if it was more like a palm tree or a pine. But whichever, the thick, strangely barked trunk rose ten or fifteen feet before it branched into stubby limbs with delicate, greenish-gold palmated leaves. He looked at it curiously, but was more intrigued by the shape of another Lemurian seated on a stool at a small table nearby.

The creature sat completely still except for his tail, which swished slowly back and forth. Others stood around him, but it was clear that the short, powerfully muscled one with reddish-brown fur was who they attended. Matt wasn't startled to recognize him as the one he'd waved to before. Without hesitation, he strode forward, closely followed by his companions, and held his hand up once again in what was evidently a universal sign of greeting, even here. Adar positioned himself next to the seated figure who, Matt saw upon closer inspection, had been wounded many times. Numerous cuts and slashes were evident across his power-ful frame, and they hadn't been bandaged. Instead, a clear, but slightly yellowish viscous fluid had been smeared into them. Matt wondered what it was, and he could almost feel

Sandra's anxious desire to go to him and help. He wasn't sure the Lemurian needed any assistance.

For one thing, the dark eyes that held his seemed clear and focused and devoid of any distraction that excessive pain or fever might cause. Very solemnly, the creature raised its own hand and held it up in greeting. It spoke a few gravelly syllables and its mouth spread into a grin. Again, the expression went no further, but Matt sensed sincerity reflected in the dark pools of the Lemurian's eyes. The one named Adar gestured with evident respect.

"Keje-Fris-Ar," he said and bowed his head slightly. All the other Lemurians did the same. "U-Amaki ay Mi-Anakka ay *Salissa*," Adar added, and the dignity with which he spoke implied a lofty title.

"I expect he's the big bull around here," whispered Gray, more to the others than to Matt. "Other one's probably a witch doctor or pope or somethin'."

In spite of himself and the situation, not to mention the tension he felt just then, Matt almost burst out laughing at the Bosun's inappropriate comparison. "Chief," he said through clenched teeth, "are you trying to get us killed? If you are, I bet one more comment like that will do the job." Matt hadn't looked at him when he spoke, but Gray's voice sounded sincerely flustered.

"Uh . . . sorry, Skipper. But, I mean, we could recite nursery rhymes and they wouldn't know the difference."

"No, but we would, and I doubt they'd react well if we all started laughing right when they're naming their gods or something. So put a lid on it!"

"Oh . . . *oh*!! Aye, aye, Skipper!"

"They are quite incredibly ugly," commented Jarrik-Fas, Keje's kinsman and head of *Salissa* Home's active Guard. He spoke quietly to Adar while the two groups regarded one another. "They have almost no fur and their skins look pale and sickly."

Adar replied from the corner of his mouth. "They looked beautiful enough yesterday when they helped drive off the Grik. Do you not agree?"

Jarrik grunted, but there was agreement in the sound.

"The gri-kakka were welcome, too, while they devoured our enemies. But we'd not have wanted them to linger overlong."

"True, but had they remained, there's no question the gri-kakka would have done so in hopes of devouring us as well. Here there is that question. If the Tail-less Ones desired to devour us, they could have done so already with the power they possess. Yet they come peacefully before us."

"Not un-armed, though," observed Jarrik. "I don't know what those things are that some of them carry, but they must be weapons. And yet they give the Sign of the Empty Hand while their hands are not empty."

Adar was silent, thinking. He knew Keje was listening to the words of his two most trusted advisors, even as he watched their visitors. "That's true," Adar said, "but perhaps among their kind, the sign is more a figurative thing than a literal one. Perhaps it means their hands are empty toward us but not toward all."

"And perhaps the sign means something else to them entirely," grumbled Keje, speaking for the first time. "But the one who seems to be their leader has an empty hand, and it's with him I must find some way to speak. Besides, would you have gone unarmed with me to their ship, Jarrik?"

Jarrik looked at the back of his leader's head. "No, lord, I would not," he admitted. "Not that it would matter in the face of their magic."

The Tail-less Ones muttered among themselves as well, and Adar wondered if their conversation ran along similar lines. The long weapons some carried had been placed on their shoulders, suspended by straps. That was encouraging at least. Nearly all of them were talking now, and a large one, with less fur than the others, talked the most. Their faces moved in a manner he had to conclude displayed emotion in some way, since they had no tails and they rarely blinked. Their strange little ears couldn't possibly convey any meaning.

Another spoke quite a lot as well, one that was smaller than the others and had very long fur on its head. The proportions of its anatomy indicated it was female, but it was difficult to tell with all the cloth they wore.

"The Scrolls make no mention of these creatures?" Keje asked, and shifted uncomfortably.

"I'm not sure, lord," Adar temporized. "Not specifically. There is the reference by Siska-Ta to the tail-less race that departed into the East long ago," he said grudgingly, "but their vessels were utterly different. They had sails, much like the Grik." He tilted his head back, remembering, and quoted a line copied from the First Scrolls taught to him as a youngling, which he now taught his apprentices. It was in the forgotten language of the ancient Scrolls themselves, and none save the Sky Priests bothered to learn it. They had to, since it was the language of the ancients in which the secrets of the stars themselves had passed to them.

"And upon the longest of the long days, when the Sun Brother was large and close in the sky, they freed their great ship from the bottom of the sea and sailed into the East, into the emptiness of the Eastern Sea." Adar smiled slightly with pride in the power of his memory. He read the Scrolls often, but he rarely spoke the words. He glanced at the Tail-less Ones and was surprised that they'd stopped speaking. All were looking at him with what he surmised to be very intent expressions. The one with so little fur stared with his mouth open wide. The one with the black fur and the darkest skin stepped near their leader and spoke into his small, misshapen ear. The leader, eyes wide, looked at the speaker with even more apparent amazement, but nodded, and the black-furred one turned to Adar.

"This said . . . speech . . . yours?" asked the creature in the ancient language of the Scrolls.

Keje lurched to his feet in shock, just as Adar hit the floor in a dead faint.

Matt stood in *Walker*'s pilothouse staring uneasily at the huge, wounded ship to starboard. They were creeping along in a generally north-northeasterly direction, at less than four knots. He reckoned that was as fast as the Lemurian ship could go in this wind, with all her damage. The Bosun stood beside him, as did McFarlane and Larry Dowden. The rest of the bridge watch went about their duties, but the usual banter was absent as the destroyermen strained to hear their words. He knew all the details would spread as fast as if he announced it on the shipwide circuit, but he felt no particular reason to keep the conversation secret. Everyone would know soon enough anyway.

"Latin," murmured Gray. "Who would've ever thought it?" Matt nodded.

"But how?" asked McFarlane wonderingly. "I mean, *how*?"

"How . . . any of this, Spanky?" Matt gestured vaguely around. "It should make it easier to communicate, though I doubt many of the men know more Latin than Lemurian. But I don't know how any more than you do. That's one of the things maybe Bradford or Lieutenant Shinya will find out."

Courtney Bradford, Lieutenant Shinya, Lieutenant Tucker, and the rest of the security detail had remained behind on the Lemurian ship and would stay for the rest of the day, with orders to learn as much as they could and render any possible aid. Once it was clear that his people had nothing to fear, Matt had decided to return to *Walker*. There was little he could add to the discussions, since he knew virtually no Latin, and with their now common enemy abroad in such unprecedented numbers—an enemy they now had a name for—he didn't want to be separated from his ship if the Grik returned.

"Finding out about the Grik was valuable, but frustrating. We still don't know very much. I don't think the Lemurians do either. They've never been attacked in such force before, though."

"They sure seemed appreciative for what we did for them," muttered Gray, and then he grinned. "Once that Adar fella came to, he jabbered up a storm."

"You understand some Latin, don't you, Bosun?" asked Dowden.

Gray smirked. "About enough to know that's what it is when I hear it. My mother was Catholic and she made me learn a little. Spanky should know more, though. Both his parents were Catholics." His eyes twinkled. "And he sure took up with enough good Catholic Filipino gals!"

"I'm Catholic," confirmed Spanky, narrowing his eyes at the Bosun, "but as far as understanding Latin, it might as well be Greek to me." He grinned sheepishly. "I never even tried to pick any up." He frowned. "Course, I never would have figured that little Jap could *speak* it!"

Gray turned to Matt. "Yeah, Skipper, what about that? I nearly joined Adar on the deck when he opened up. You think it's a good idea to leave him over there? I mean, he may have given his parole and all, but he's still a Jap. And how the hell does a Jap know Latin?" he grumped.

"Beats me," admitted Matt, "but Bradford knows it even better, and I guess he'll keep an eye on him. Besides, I think he's sincere about his parole," he added guardedly. "What possible advantage could he find in betraying us, anyway?"

"I don't know," said Gray darkly, "but he's a Jap. That's all the reason he needs to betray us."

Matt and the rest of his senior personnel were waiting for the launch when it drew alongside. He was anxious to hear what the rest of the boarding party had learned. As they came aboard, however, he quickly realized a few were missing. Bradford presented himself to the captain, although he didn't salute. He looked tired but excited.

"Where's Lieutenant Tucker?" Matt demanded immediately. "And Lieutenant Shinya and the two gunner's mates?"

Bradford made a shooing gesture. "They're perfectly fine, I assure you! Lieutenant Tucker has become engrossed in things medical and remained behind to assist with their wounded—as I'm sure you'll remember giving her permission to do." Bradford's face darkened. "They have quite a lot of wounded, I'm afraid. Perhaps half their people—and as many as a quarter killed—many of them children and the very old. The fighting must have been horrific, sir. Horrific!" He fumbled in his shirt pocket for a scribbled note. "Here's a list of supplies Miss Tucker would like sent over." Matt took the note and handed it wordlessly to Alan Letts. "In any event," continued Bradford, "the Jappo volunteered to remain and translate—extraordinary, that!" His eyes grew large. "Why ever in the world a young Jappo would want to learn Latin is quite beyond me, but I shall surely ask him! Yes, indeed! Oh, well, those two strapping lads—Silva, I believe, and . . . the other one—stayed behind to protect Miss

Tucker, and the Jappo, I suppose, although they're in no danger, goodness, no! The United States Navy represented by USS *Walker* and all her people are quite popular and appreciated just now!"

Matt wasn't happy that Sandra had remained behind, but he had to admit she was in good hands if trouble arose. He was less sanguine about Dennis Silva's ability to refrain from starting trouble, however. "Very well," he said grudgingly.

"Were you actually able to talk with them? I mean conversationally?" Dowden asked.

"Well, yes, after a fashion. My Latin is slightly rusty—not many people speak it now, you know—but I've kept it up fairly well. It's virtually a necessity for my less professional pursuits. Did you know nearly every plant and creature has a Latin name? Of course you did." He gratefully accepted one of the precious Cokes and took a sip. "Ahem. Well, there are some differences, mostly in pronunciation. Frankly, the way their mouths are shaped, I'm astonished they can make human sounds at all. I did discover they learn their Latin from a written source—which makes sense. Otherwise, it would probably have become incomprehensible over time, passed down word of mouth."

Matt started to ask what written source, but Lieutenant McFarlane spoke first. "How long do you think they've been speaking it?"

"I don't think one could say they speak it, per se, as a language at any rate. Only a small percentage understand it at all, and those seem confined to a certain caste, or sect. Their society is segregated into several such groups, based on labor distribution, similar to the differentiation between your deck-apes and engine room snipes, but to a much higher degree.

"As best I can tell, there are three major castes, or 'clans,' among them, although it's a bit more complicated even than that because—" Matt held up his hand and made a winding motion as if to say "get on with it." Bradford looked sheepish and nodded. "Well, first you have the . . . I think 'wing runners' might be the most accurate translation. They're the ones controlling the masts and sails, much like 'topmen' would have done in our own sailing past. Then they have the 'Body of Home' clan—which is what they call their ship, by the way—*Salissa* Home. I've no idea what a '*Salissa*' is. Perhaps it means 'Home of our People,' or something like that. It may be their tribe." He blinked and rubbed his nose. "The Body of Home clan is the most numerous, and would be roughly parallel to 'waisters' in days of old. They're the ones who perform all the chores and duties required for everyday life: fishing, gardening, hull repair, et cetera. It's usually from this clan that their leaders arise, by the way. The third caste is the navigators or, to be more precise, 'Sky Priests.' There are very few of them, but they have a unique status. Their religion is all wrapped up in the semi-deification of the sun, the moon, and the heavens inclusively—which is not all that surprising, I suppose. I didn't have time to delve too deeply into their theology, of course, but I get the impression it's somewhat vague."

He looked at them and smiled. "The heavens are certainly important, not least because of their reliance upon the sky for navigation! There's much more to it than that, I'm sure, but you see? That's why their Sky Priests are taught Latin!"

Matt shook his head and wondered if he'd missed something. He was becoming used to Bradford's stream-of-consciousness way of communicating, but sometimes he missed the thread and it could be tiresome. He cleared his throat. "And why was that again?"

"Well, I don't know what they use as a general written language, or even if they have one at all. But one thing that chap Adar made perfectly clear was how surprised they were that we could speak the Ancient Tongue of the Sacred Scrolls themselves!"

"And what exactly are these Scrolls?"

"Why, I suppose they're much like our Bible! Complete with an exodus myth and admonitions to behave! I gathered from his few references that it is very Old Testament in nature."

"I take it, then," Matt said, trying not to let his impatience show, "that somehow these Scrolls are written in Latin?"

Bradford looked at him as he might a dull pupil in a classroom. "Of course they are! That's the whole point, don't you see? Not only are they a Bible, of sorts, they're also charts and navigation aids as well! That's why the priests must learn to speak a language that's even more dead here than it ever was back home."

"Prob'ly why there's so few of 'em," Gray put in with a snort. Bradford glared at him.

"It also raises an intriguing question," said Letts. "The Latin makes it clear they've had contact with humans at some time in their past. We already suspected the, ah . . . Grik had. Judging from their ships, it was within the last few hundred years. The question for the Lemurians is when did it happen? I'm not sure it matters in the grand scheme of things, but my impression was that none had ever seen or heard of human beings and we were as big a surprise to them as they were to us. Did they get Latin from a Latin—like Romans or something? Or was it some guy, like Mr. Bradford here, just passing through who taught it to them for a hoot?"

"That's an interesting point. I'd like to have the answer to that question myself," Matt said. He shrugged. "Partly, I admit, because it *is* a fascinating question, but mainly because it may make more difference than you realize, Mr. Letts. When they learned it, that is. I agree it probably wasn't in their living memory, but if it wasn't too long ago, maybe, somewhere, there are still other people like us to be found. If so, finding them is going to be increasingly important." He cleared his throat. "You may have noticed the men's reaction to the Lemurian females?" There were thoughtful nods. "As time passes, certain . . . frustrations are going to become more acute. If it's possible there're other people in this world, we're going to need to find them—and not just because of that. If the Lemurian/human contact was thousands of years ago, though, that possibility seems more remote. Besides, if that's the case, it might create complications beyond the obvious."

"Indeed?" replied Bradford. "How so?"

"Look at it like this. Hundreds of years ago, maybe more, somebody wrote these Scrolls, or taught one of them Latin so they could write them down. They've based their spiritual beliefs on those writings. Out of the blue, strangers show up, deliver them from their enemies, and speak the sacred tongue. All this may not have sunk in yet, and if only a few of them speak Latin, it might take a while. But when it does, we might be faced with a decision." He looked at the faces around him, all staring intently back. He sighed. "They might think we're *gods*!" he said quietly. "What are we going to do then?"

The items on Sandra's list had been brought over—needles and catgut for stitching, mostly. There were many, many wounded, and most had deep slashes, although there were a few arrow wounds as well. Those were the ones that concerned her most. She could handle stitching slashed flesh and binding superficial cuts, but she was very afraid to go fishing around inside the unfamiliar creatures trying to dig something out when she didn't know their anatomy.

She knew she would have to, though. The only treatment the Lemurians seemed to know for battle injuries was to apply the same viscous paste she'd seen on their leader. She had no idea what it was, but it apparently had certain analgesic and antibacterial properties. It might even be better than sulfanilamide. Whatever it was and however well it worked, it couldn't stanch blood loss or repair muscles and sinews hacked in two. Learning to deal with so many casualties at once had apparently never occurred to them—just as fighting such a battle hadn't. She hoped, however, that if the paste worked as well as they assured her through Lieutenant Shinya it did, very few amputations would be required.

It was slight consolation, looking at the sea of bodies stretched before her in neatly organized, blood-soaked rows. She was just a nurse. She was a very good nurse, but up until recently, she'd been a peacetime nurse who'd never faced anything like this. She'd taken it upon herself to learn more about her profession than required and she felt competent to assist in most surgical procedures, but until just a few days before, she'd never dealt with actual battle casualties. Now this.

The severity and variety of the wounds left her appalled. She knew that modern warfare often inflicted even more ghastly wounds, but usually at a distance. The idea that enemies could stand face-to-face and hack each other apart to produce wounds like those she saw made her skin crawl like the sight of a bullet wound would never have done. She was in so far over her head that she felt her composure and her previously unshakable confidence beginning to slip. With sudden clarity, she thought she knew precisely how Matt must feel, caught up in events far beyond what his training and experience had prepared him for. He'd done a pretty good job, she reflected, even if he didn't know what he was doing. Somehow he always managed to act as though he did. That might work well in matters of leadership, but it wasn't the best approach when it came to medicine, she thought wryly. Or was it?

Adar and several apprentices hovered nearby, talking with Lieutenant Shinya as she sewed. Many other Lemurians, young and old alike, watched her work intently. Besides her efforts, however, there was virtually no other treatment under way. She finished suturing a long gash in a young Lemurian's leg while it stared at her unflinchingly with large, liquid eyes. She stood and tried to wipe hair from her eyes with her forearm. It was covered with sweat and she only managed to paste the loose hair to her face. Without a word, an uncustomarily attentive Dennis Silva poured alcohol on a rag and handed it to her. She began wiping blood off her hands and trying to get it out from under her fingernails. The harder she tried to get it all, the madder she got.

"Lieutenant Shinya? Would you be kind enough to signal the ship and ask Captain Reddy to send Pharmacist's Mate Miller and Ensign Theimer over to help? My God, there must be two hundred or more I haven't even seen yet!" She paused, considering. "Also, please ask Adar why none of his people are helping. They may be unaccustomed to this kind of medicine, but all I'm doing is sewing them up." She gestured around. "And I know they can sew!"

"Of course, Lieutenant." Tamatsu turned and began to speak. Adar answered and Shinya relayed his message. "He said he didn't know you wanted help. It's customary among his people for those with specialized skills to guard their methods. He said their healers—many of whom are watching you work even now—would like to try the methods they have seen, but are afraid you will be offended."

She shook her head and almost screamed with frustration. "The only thing that offends me is they'd be willing to let their people suffer over something that silly!"

"Then I will tell him you will freely share your expertise. I will not relay your last statement, though," he said just a little primly. "To them, I am sure it's not silly at all."

"Then tell them to bring boiling water! And find out if they have any alcohol or anything I can use for an antiseptic! I'm just about out!"

Shinya nodded curtly and spoke to the Lemurian official again. Sandra wasn't sure how fluently the two communicated because the Japanese officer punctuated his statements with hand gestures and repeated phrases, but Adar seemed to grasp what was said and soon barked commands. To Sandra's surprise, within moments a cauldron of boiling water appeared, as well as a dark earthen cask, or jug, that had a pungent aroma. *They must have had the stuff nearby,* she thought. *They'd have been using it already if I hadn't been here.* Chagrin surged through her. She realized she'd just naturally assumed she knew more about medicine than these "primitives" and dived right in. They may have even been as angry with her as she was with them! *It says something for the regard they must hold us in,* she thought. *Otherwise, they might've just killed me!* She shook her head and pointed at the cask. "What's that?"

"It's a fermented spirit they make from fruit, Lieutenant Tucker," Tamatsu replied. "They call it seep."

Silva leaned forward, suddenly interested. "Hey, Jap, ask him if it can be drank!"

Tamatsu looked at the big destroyerman a moment before he replied. "Gunner's Mate Silva," he said in an icy tone, "I have given my parole to your captain, as well as my word of honor. But I'm still an officer in the Japanese Imperial Navy. If you do not address me with the respect due my rank, or at least that due one man of honor from another, I won't ask him that, or anything else for the remainder of our visit today. I do not think Captain Reddy would be pleased if our communications broke down entirely because one of his men was rude."

Silva bristled. The words "mighty uppity for a stinking Jap" actually formed in his mouth, but somehow he caught them and clenched his teeth. At his full height, he towered above the other man, but Tamatsu merely looked at him, unconcerned. Silva visibly uncoiled, and after a moment a grin spread across his weathered, stubbly face. "Well, I'll be damned, but you've got guts, Jap . . . I mean *Lieutenant* Jap." He held up a hand with a wider grin. "No offense, but I don't know your name."

Tamatsu bowed slightly. "Lieutenant Tamatsu Shinya," he said.

Silva nodded back, but his face darkened. "I ain't gonna call you sir, no way in hell. You *are* a Jap. But I'll call you Lieutenant Shinya, if that makes you happy."

"That will suffice, Gunner's Mate Silva," he said, and a slight grin formed on his face as well. "And, yes, the Lemurians do drink seep, although there's no telling what it would do to you."

Silva arched an eyebrow. "Well! In the interests of science, and prob'ly diplomacy too, I reckon it's my duty to find out!"

Sandra, who'd managed a grin of her own by now, cleared her throat. "Your duty, Mr. Silva, is to assist me and stay out of trouble. That duty most emphatically does not include testing the local booze. Do I make myself clear?"

Silva glanced at the cask and licked his lips. With a force of will, his expression changed to a beatific smile. "Aye, aye, sir!" He blinked. "Uh . . . ma'am—hell, that's a mouthful!" His face lost all expression whatsoever as Sandra looked at him sternly. "Perfectly clear!" he managed at last.

Sandra straightened her back. There was a pain high in her hips that had grown more intense from leaning over to tend the wounded. For the first time in a while, she looked around. Already, Lemurian healers had swept into the "hospital area" on the open deck between the center and the shattered forward tower. They treated the injured in their own way. Some examined the stitches she had made, and jabbered in their quick, excited tones. Obviously, body language added a great deal of meaning to their speech, and she was growing convinced that their blinking eyes conveyed much as well. She walked into the almost-shade under the catwalk above. She couldn't venture farther because that was where a sort of orchard of large pear-shaped

fruit began. She'd heard it called polta fruit. The orchard
ran entirely around the ship for a width of about fifteen
feet. The wide catwalk was pierced at regular intervals by
gratings that allowed light to the plants. The fruit itself,
despite its familiar shape, had the color and shiny texture
of purple grapes and grew in bunches as well, nestled in a
mass of waxy, yellow-green leaves.

At the edge of the orchard was a Lemurian she knew was
tall by the standards of his people, and his upper body was
more muscular than most. He wore nothing but a bright
red kilt stained dark by the blood matting his brindled fur
and still seeping from a couple of cuts. He leaned on one
knee over the still form of a female of similar color, raising
her head so she could drink from a cup. One of the swords,
like a cross between a machete and a scimitar, lay beside a
blood-encrusted axe.

The female had clearly been in the fighting. Sandra had
treated others as well. The first time she removed a bloody
leather tunic from one of their "professional" warriors
and discovered furry breasts beneath, she was shocked.
Adar and his entourage were standing right there, though,
and made no sign that the discovery of a female in the
ranks was unusual. As she'd said earlier, the semi-nudity
didn't surprise her—although she'd finally rounded savagely on Silva and his buddies when she overheard their
comments about the "cat-monkey booby farm"—but she
hadn't been prepared to find females not only fighting for
their lives in a desperate situation but doing so as actual
warriors.

After a time she grew inured—if not accustomed—to the
apparent fact that among Lemurians there was total equal-
ity of the sexes. At least as far as warfare was concerned.
But in this instance there seemed a contrast between that
and the tender, very human concern she saw of a male for
an injured female. She moved toward them unobserved.
Adar was busy discussing something with Shinya and another Lemurian who'd approached. Silva, "distracted" again,
suddenly noticed she'd wandered off and hurried after
her, lugging his BAR. The big Lemurian straightened and
regarded them as they neared. The female tried to rise,
but Sandra made a lay-back motion with her hands and

crouched beside her. The male and Silva remained standing, facing each other.

A quick survey showed Sandra no obvious life-threatening wounds, but there was a nasty cut above the left eye, slick with the healing lotion that Lemurians seemed to use as liberally as Mercurochrome. A possible concussion, then, but the eyes were alert. She smiled and crossed her hands over her chest. "Sandra," she said. The female's eyes fluttered rapidly and she glanced at the male who was now staring intently at Sandra as well.

With a wince, the female raised her left arm and patted herself. "Risa." Then she pointed at the male and said, "Chack."

Shinya and Adar joined them. "Lieutenant Tucker, Adar tells me their leader, Keje-Fris-Ar, desires we attend him once more."

Sandra nodded, but reached out and gently patted Risa's hand before she stood. "Very well, but please ask him to tell this one I hope she feels better soon." She turned to Silva. "Stay here, and when Ensign Theimer and Pharmacist's Mate Miller arrive, tell them whatever they do, don't act like they're taking over—just assist any way they can. Understand?"

"Yes, Miss . . . Lieutenant Tucker. I'll tell Reavis and Newman that very thing, but me and Felts'll tag along with you."

"Really, Mr. Silva, that's not necessary."

He grinned. "Maybe not, ma'am, but I think we will anyway. Skipper'd have us thrown to the fishes if we let you out of our sight."

Sandra sighed. "Very well. If you feel you must loom menacingly in the background wherever I go, I'll not upset you by protesting further, but promise you'll do so as peacefully as possible?"

"Absolutely, ma'am," Silva said with an expression of purest innocence. "Everybody'll tell you I'm as peaceable a critter as there is."

Near dusk, the launch bumped into *Walker*'s side for the final time that day, and the passengers carefully climbed the metal rungs to the deck above. The nurses went first.

The one named Theimer seemed almost catatonic, and Lieutenant Tucker had to help her up. Tony Scott had noticed she wasn't quite with it when he took her across, but she looked even worse coming back, and she hadn't said a word either time—not that he paid much attention, or even really cared. He just wanted out of the boat. He'd been in the launch most of the day, with the terrible silvery fish—and occasionally larger things—bumping against it. He'd controlled the urge to fire the Thompson over the side in mounting terror, but he hadn't set it down all day. Now all he could think about was getting something more substantial than the wooden hull of a twenty-six-foot boat between him and whatever lurked below the surface of the water he'd always loved. He scrambled up last, urging Silva ahead of him.

"Calm down, Tony. What's your rush?" jibed Silva as he neared the top, over Scott's labored breathing below.

"Goddamn you, Silva! If you don't hurry, I guess you'll find out in a minute when I throw you in the water!"

Silva laughed as he clambered onto the deck and turned to offer the coxswain his hand. "Hell, they're just fish, Tony, just like sharks. Sharks ain't never spooked you before."

As soon as he gained the deck, Scott moved quickly to the center, as far from the water as possible. Silva and Felts followed. Miller, Reavis, Newman, and the two nurses went below while others hoisted the launch aboard. Scott took a cigarette from Felts and lit it with trembling hands. He took several deep drags, eyes flitting nervously from point to point but carefully avoiding faces. "I been on the water all my life," he said at last. "I grew up in Fort Lauderdale and had a sailboat, a fourteen-footer I'd take on the open ocean in the Gulf before my daddy figured I was old enough to drive." He drew in another lungful of smoke. "Had some scrapes, too. Bad weather. Sharks . . ." He glanced at Silva, searching the big man's face for ridicule. He shrugged. "From then to now, I ain't *ever* been afraid of the water." He shuddered. "Until today. It started creepin' up on me when I went across to *Mahan* right after the Squall, but I guess it finally got the better of me. Even those critters that got Marvaney didn't spook me like that constant bumpin' all day long. Knowin' . . ." He shook his head and looked back at Silva. "They ain't just fish, Dennis, and this ain't the Java Sea. Not anymore. I've known it from the start, but with everything going on, it just never sank in till today. I finally realized the water ain't even just the water anymore. The water's death, fellas, and if I had my druthers, I'd never go near it again."

He'd been speaking in quiet tones, but evidently louder than he thought. They heard a gruff laugh and turned to see Dean Laney by the rail, leaning on the safety chain by the number one torpedo mount. The big machinist's mate wore a sadistic grin.

"Don't that beat all? The *coxswain's* afraid of the water! Har! I bet you'll be strikin' for snipe now, so you don't have to look at it no more! Course, when I tell ever-body what a chickenshit deck-ape you are, Spanky won't even take you as a bilge coolie!"

Scott bristled, but Silva held him back. Then he grinned and sauntered over to the stanchion next to Laney. He peered over the side.

"Woo, Laney, you're so brave! I ain't never seen a snipe this close to the water before! I hope you're holdin' that safety chain tight. I wouldn't want you to fall!"

"Hell with you, Silva! Least I ain't scared of the wa . . . Aaah!"

He shrieked when Dennis pulled the pin on the stanchion that held the chain in place. He went over the side and the chain went taut with a clanking thud heard over Laney's high-pitched scream. Silva looked down and saw the machinist's mate bouncing against the hull, mere feet above the deadly sea, hands clenched tight on the chain, his upturned face contorted by a grimace of terror.

"SHIT! Help! *Help!* Goddamn you to *hell*, Silva! HELP ME!"

"But you ain't scared of the water, Dean," Silva called down mildly.

"I . . . I *am* scared, damn you! HELP ME!"

Silva heard running feet, and Felts and Scott grabbed the chain and started pulling.

"Shit!" exploded Scott. "You could'a killed him!" Other men arrived and between them they soon had Laney on deck, gasping and shaking, tears in his eyes.

"You could'a killed him!" Felts accused under his breath. Silva shrugged, then squatted and looked Laney in the eye.

"Damned ol' rusty pin must'a gave," he said. "No tellin' what might happen if a fella ain't careful what he does—or says." He stood and laughed. "Whoo-ee! Lucky you was holdin' that chain, Laney! Gives me the willies. The very idea of fallin' in the water scares the shit out'a me!"

Sandra scrubbed her hands in the tiny basin in the compartment that once belonged to Lieutenants Ellis and Rogers but that she now shared with Ensign Theimer. Karen sat expressionlessly on a small chair, knees together, staring at her hands on her lap. They were caked with dried blood, and black rings encircled her fingernails. There was more on her clothes and face, and it even streaked her hair where she'd been squirted by a pulsing artery.

"You did well today, Karen," Sandra complimented her. Which was true—to a point. She'd followed orders and done her job, stitching wounds in her professional, economical way. She'd done exactly what she was told to do—but no more. All the while her face was slack, her eyes dead, as if her body ran on autopilot but she wasn't really there. Sandra saw that the expression was still the same. She sighed.

"Get cleaned up and go to the forward berthing space with Jamie Miller to check on Seaman Davis. I have an idea I'd like to try." Ensign Theimer didn't respond. She didn't move. "Karen?" Worried, Sandra dried her hands and looked in the other nurse's eyes. For a moment she saw no recognition, no spark of human consciousness. "Karen!" she shouted and shook her roughly by the shoulders. "Karen, speak to me!"

Huge, shiny tears welled up in the empty eyes and when she blinked, they gushed down her face—and somehow she'd returned from wherever she'd been hiding. Her large, glistening, haunted eyes desperately searched Sandra's, but didn't see what they'd hoped. She closed them again, and a piteous moan escaped her lips.

"I want to go home!"

Sandra went to her knees, embracing the younger woman as tight as she could.

"Oh, God, me too, me too!"

The tears came then, like rivers, from both of them. For a long moment, Sandra held her while Karen sobbed and sobbed. Finally, when it seemed she'd exhausted herself, Sandra drew back and put her palm on Karen's face. "Me too," she whispered again, "but I don't think we can. For some reason, here we are and we've got to deal with that. I need you, girl. God, I can't do this alone! The ship needs you, and so do these men. We both have to be strong—to hold up."

"But it's so hard!"

"I know. Believe me, I know! I nearly lost it myself today. But don't you see? We can't! We don't have that . . . luxury. Too many people are counting on us, and we're all they've got. We can't let them down—we can't let ourselves down." She wiped the bloody hair from Karen's eyes with a gentle, tearful smile. "You okay?" Miserably, Karen nodded, and Sandra squeezed her filthy hands. "I'm glad you're back—don't leave me again. I'm the first woman chief surgeon on a United States warship. I'll mark you AWOL!"

Karen snorted a wet, almost hysterical laugh, but nodded.

"Good. Now get cleaned up and check on Seaman Davis. We don't want these goons to think we're weak sisters." She watched while Karen, still sniffling, washed her hands and then left the compartment. As soon as she was gone, Sandra felt the tension flow out of her and she put her face in her hands. "I want to go home too," she repeated, whispering, almost surrendering to sobs herself.

She still had to talk to Matt. It would probably be a long talk, and all she really wanted was to curl up in her bunk and fall into a dreamless sleep. She shook her head, wet one of the dingy washrags, and wiped the grime and tears from her face. Standing in front of the noisy little fan with her eyes closed, she let the tepid breeze dry her and tried to pretend it was refreshing. After a moment, she ruefully realized that she was fooling herself. She ran a brush through her sweat-tangled hair and stepped through the curtain.

Seated in the wardroom talking in quiet tones were the captain, Bradford, Gray, Dowden, Shinya, and Sergeant Alden, who seemed relieved that his charge had returned to his custody. The Marine was getting around better every day, but the idea of his climbing up and down ships, given the consequences of a fall, was ridiculous. He took his "escort" duty seriously, though, and he'd been disappointed when his request to accompany them to the Lemurian ship was denied.

They stood and greeted her with strained smiles, and Lieutenant Shinya nodded politely. They couldn't have avoided overhearing Karen's sobs, or indeed much of the women's conversation. Sandra realized with a start that Matt's "smile" seemed even more troubled than the others'. As soon as they resumed their seats, Juan appeared at her elbow and poured a cup of weak coffee (he'd begun to conserve) that she'd have mistaken for tea if not for the smell. Ordinarily, in meetings like these, Juan would have excused himself, but ever since the Squall, he often lingered, and Matt didn't send him away. He figured it was easier to inform the crew through the grapevine than make announcements every day. Besides, Juan would be careful what he passed on.

"I trust you're well?" asked Bradford. "Mr. Shinya told us your efforts were tireless."

Sandra smiled wanly. "Not tireless," she said. "It's been a tough"—she paused and looked reflective—"but interesting day. I think we were a help, once I figured out when to leave well enough alone, and we learned a lot."

The others nodded solemnly.

"True," said Matt, "but I wish you hadn't stayed behind."

"I wasn't alone. Lieutenant Shinya was there."

Matt glanced at the Japanese officer speculatively but nodded.

"As were several armed men," Tamatsu said. "She was in no danger. Your gunner's mate . . . Silva? He is a formidable man. If the lieutenant had been threatened in any way, I believe he would have contrived to destroy their ship around us, by himself."

Gray grunted. "Silva!" he muttered. "He's part of what I was worried about." Everyone, including Tamatsu, laughed at that.

"Well," said Matt, "you must be starving. Juan? Pass the

word for sandwiches, if you please." The Filipino bowed his head and whispered through the wardroom curtain. There was no telling who was on the other side, but he returned to his place against the hull with the expression of one who fully expected the task to be performed.

"While we're waiting, tell us what happened when you went to see this Keje again," Matt suggested. "Lieutenant Shinya said you should be the one to speak, but I'd like to hear what you both have to say."

Sandra nodded. "He was weak from his wounds, but not debilitated, I think. Their medicine's not nearly as primitive as I expected. They have no concept of germ theory, but their infection rate is low. They clean wounds with hot water for no other reason I could see than that it just makes sense to do so. They hold cleanliness in high regard." She glanced down at her uniform blouse and wrinkled her nose to the sound of sympathetic chuckles. "They also apply a kind of salve to wounds that must be antibacterial in some way, in addition to being a local analgesic. I asked for a sample and they gave me a whole jar. There's no telling if it'll be helpful to humans, and I don't know what it's made of yet, but I want to try some on Seaman Davis, with your permission. His fever just won't go away. He's still in danger of losing his leg, at least."

Bradford nodded enthusiastically, but Matt regarded her thoughtfully. Gray looked downright dubious. "I know they believe in the stuff—nearly everybody over there had some smeared on 'em, but do we know it actually works?"

Sandra held out her hands palm up. "The only evidence I have after so short a time is their absolute faith and certainty. Many of their wounds were bites, you know, and some who were bitten far worse than Davis were treated with the stuff and considered lightly injured."

Matt scratched his ear. "Does it have the same effect on the Grik? I mean, have they used any on the Grik wounded and if so, do they think it'll work?"

Sandra glanced down at her hands, clasped on the table. When she looked back up, her expression was hooded. "There were no Grik wounded, Captain."

"But . . . that's impossible!" interrupted the Australian. "They can't all have died! It's imperative I see one alive!"

"There were no Grik survivors on the Lemurian ship, Mr. Bradford," Sandra restated. "Many committed suicide after they were abandoned, mostly by jumping into the sea. The rest were . . . helped over the side by the Lemurians."

"No prisoners, then," Captain Reddy observed quietly.

"No, sir." Sandra shook her head. "Like everything else we've observed in this world, there's no compromise between total victory and total defeat. You win or you die. Warfare among the Lemurians themselves—at least 'Home against Home'—is so rare there's no memory of it. They have their problems, sure, but evidently they don't kill each other over them, beyond the rare duel. The Grik, however, are the 'Ancient Enemy'—that's how they're referred to. Their conflict literally extends beyond their history, although pitched battles like the one we intervened in are rare, if not unheard of. Mostly, they've only had to contend with what amount to harassing attacks or raids. But the frequency is increasing, and no one's ever heard of attacks by six Grik ships at once."

"Any idea why they do it?" Matt probed.

"Not really. In spite of the Grik being the Ancient Enemy, the Lemurians don't know a lot about them. They just know that when the Grik come, the Grik attack. It's the way of things. They fight like maniacs and they don't take prisoners, so neither do the Lemurians." She rubbed her tired eyes. "I'm not sure they even understand the concept of surrender." She glanced at Lieutenant Shinya and was struck by how similar to his culture, in that respect at least, the Lemurians had been forced to become. However, unlike Imperial Japan, the Lemurians were anything but militaristic and expansionist. She noticed the others looking speculatively at the Japanese officer as well, but Tamatsu endured their stares with stoic indifference. If he was troubled by their scrutiny, he didn't let it show.

"Well," said Matt, and sighed with slight relief. "Maybe we're not stuck in such a big war after all—just a really long one." There were chuckles. "The Lemurians fought well against a really scary enemy, but if they thought the Grik were a major problem, I think they'd be better prepared. Be more warlike themselves. With a few simple expedients, I don't think a dozen Grik ships could board something as big as their ship." There were nods, but Sandra wasn't sure. America hadn't been very prepared for Pearl Harbor.

"Anyway," said Matt, "we were talking about the salve." He let out a long breath. "Try it, if Davis is willing. I won't force him to take some alien cure." Sandra nodded acceptance. She knew Matt must have hoped she could experiment on a wounded Grik first, but if the stuff worked as advertised, it would save Davis's leg. She'd done all she could, but the bite had left an incredibly persistent infection. His immune system was fighting it, but she didn't expect it could do so indefinitely or totally. She was sure she could get him to try it.

Bradford leaned forward in his chair. "Did you get any indication why our first meeting with their leader was so short?" he asked. "He seemed alert, eager, and energetic at first, particularly after we established communications. Then, suddenly, he spoke a few words, and we were ushered out. Was that normal protocol?"

"I don't think so," answered Sandra. "Maybe we did take them by surprise. He was probably under medication of some sort, something to make him sleep—they also put great store in the healing power of sleep, by the way—but . . ." She lowered her voice and looked pointedly at the curtain.

Matt noticed the direction of her glance. "Sergeant Alden, clear the passageway. I'm sure if there's anybody in it they have duties elsewhere."

"I will go check the sandwiches," said Juan. "Do not stir, Sergeant. I will shoo them off."

When the steward left, they all looked back at Sandra expectantly.

"Thank you, Captain. All I really wanted to say, though, is that quite a lot of Lemurian medicine is evidently intoxicating. They brought out some stuff that nearly got me drunk just smelling it. Even the salve seems to make them a little dopey. I think when we arrived, their captain, or whatever he is, had just taken a dose of something, and when it started to hit him he sent us away." She grinned. "I don't think he wanted to be tipsy in front of the powerful strangers."

"Indeed?" Bradford said appreciatively. "I wish more of

our statesmen would refrain from conducting business in such condition."

There was a knock on the bulkhead beyond the curtain.

"Sandwiches, Cap-tan."

"Thanks, Juan. Come in, please." Juan stepped through the curtain and held it for Ray Mertz, the mess attendant, who carried a platter piled high with ham sandwiches. He set it on the table, then he and the steward ducked quickly back down the passageway. Everyone dug in immediately, and Sandra closed her eyes when she bit into the thick slice of ham nestled between two pieces of fresh-baked bread. With just a little mustard, it tasted heavenly. She was even hungrier than she'd thought. The Lemurians had offered them food, but it smelled strange and she wasn't ready to trust the local fare. Silva had eaten some of the purple fruit, and she wondered absently how he was feeling about now.

"So, what else did you talk about during your second meeting?" Matt asked.

Sandra sped her chewing and swallowed at last. "Well, pretty much the main point was that their leader, Keje-Fris-Ar, wants to come aboard us here. Tomorrow."

"Here they come!" Dowden said unnecessarily when the boat cast off and moved in their direction. Almost an hour earlier, they'd been surprised to see a large section of the Lemurian's hull, about twenty feet wide, open and swing outward, releasing a low, wide-beamed barge. The compartment, or whatever it was, had water in it, and the boat just floated out. There it stayed for a time, already crewed, until the more important passengers were lowered into it by means of a large platform that descended from the deck above.

"That's some trick," murmured McFarlane, scratching the young beard on his chin. He glanced apologetically at the captain. "Structurally, I mean. It's like they go around with a fully enclosed harbor. Makes sense, as far as they'd have to lower a boat, but the engineering problems and stresses involved must've been something else."

"The structural engineering capabilities of the Lemurians are quite formidable," said Bradford. "To construct such a colossal ship to begin with . . . well." He shrugged.

Captain Reddy, carefully groomed and resplendent in his whites—as were all his officers—glanced around the ship. They'd done their best to make her presentable, but the ravages she'd undergone were evident everywhere. Even a visiting admiral would understand, but he wanted to make a big impression. It would have to do. The crew was dressed as sharply as possible, but most had dyed their whites in coffee—as ordered—at the start of the war, and the result was an unsavory mottled khaki. Now, with the passage of time, most of the coffee had leached out in the wash and they only looked dirty. He grunted. The order had come down from somebody who thought the ships would be more difficult to spot from the air without a bunch of white uniforms running around on deck. It was one of the sillier of the panicky and often contradictory orders they'd been issued right after the attacks on Pearl Harbor and Cavite. There was nothing he could do about it other than group the men who still had whites separately from those who didn't, as if there were some great reason for it. It was all entirely symbolic, but he didn't know how important a part symbolism might ultimately play. He spoke to the Bosun.

"Assemble your side party, Chief. I'll join you shortly." He absently hitched the Sam Browne to distribute the un-accustomed weight of the holstered pistol and the other . . . object suspended from it. He grimaced. While running an inventory of their small-arms ammunition, Campeti discov-ered a crate of heavy long-bladed cutlasses, pattern of 1918, that had probably been commissioned with the ship. There were four dozen of the things in heavy blue-gray canvas-wrapped scabbards, and they looked absolutely new. Gray suggested that the officers wear them so the Lemurians would see weapons they recognized. He didn't intend it as a threatening gesture, or so he said, but to show the 'cats—even while they were surrounded by all sorts of incompre-hensible things—that they shared some basic similarities.

Matt resisted the idea as ridiculous. If they had to fight with swords, a dozen of the Lemurians could slaughter them all, judging by their skill against the Grik. But Court-ney Bradford weighed in on Gray's side, surprisingly, with the comment that it might be wise to remind their visi-tors that they were, after all, warriors. Matt grudgingly relented and ordered all the officers, POs—and especially the Bosun—to wear one of the damn things. He had it easier. Instead of the heavy cutlass, he had his ornate Naval Academy dress sword, which he'd worn precisely twice—once at graduation and once at a friend's wedding. He knew it was a fine blade, and it had certainly cost him enough, but even now he couldn't imagine any eventuality that would force him to draw it in anger. He looked down at the fat barge, pitching on the choppy swell as it came alongside. Hitching his belt up again, he stepped quickly down the pilothouse steps to the deck.

Heaved to, *Walker* wallowed sickeningly even in these light swells, her low freeboard giving them periodic glimpses of the approaching party as the ship rolled. It was going to be tricky—and a little undignified—gaining the deck of the destroyer after the genteel fashion in which the Lemurian leaders were lowered into their barge, but there was no help for it. Besides, the creatures looked better equipped to climb the treacherous rungs than humans were. Gray took his place with the side party, Carl Bashear with him, and raised the pipe to his lips.

"You want me to do it?" Bashear whispered as the first Lemurian hopped onto the rungs and quickly neared the top.

"No, damn it. If anybody's gonna pipe aliens aboard *Walker*, it's gonna be me."

The piercing wail of the Bosun's pipe startled the burly Lemurian with the reddish-brown coat, but then he cocked his head at the Chief with interested recognition. He seemed even more startled when all those present saluted. He wore the same copper-scaled tunic as the day before, but the bloodstains had been cleaned and the scales had been polished to a flashing glory. Beneath the armor, he wore a long blue shirt, finely embroidered with fanciful fishes and adorned with shimmering scales like sequins around the cuffs. A long mane covered his head and extended to the sides of his face like huge muttonchops and was gathered and tied at the nape of his neck with a bright ribbon. His very ape-like feet were bound in sandals with a crisscrossing mesh of copper-studded straps extending to his knees. From a baldric across his chest hung a short, fatbladed sword, securely tied into its scabbard with another bright ribbon formed into an elaborate bow. He looked around for a moment, as if taking everything in—the aft funnels with their wisps of smoke, the four-inch gun above, the torpedo tubes.

And, of course, the people. He looked from face to face until he recognized Matt. Then he grinned a very human grin and faced aft and saluted the flag that stood out from the short mast. He turned to Matt, still grinning, and saluted again. With evident difficulty, his mouth formed the unfamiliar words: "Meeshin ta caamaa-burd, zur?"

There were incredulous murmurs, and Matt realized his jaw had gone slack. Sandra, standing behind him, leaned forward and whispered in his ear. "We spent about an hour on that yesterday. He wanted to do it. He said he owed it to our people."

Soon the entire Lemurian party, numbering almost a dozen, was aboard. To the surprise and delight of the assembled destroyermen, all saluted the flag and the captain. It was an important and very moving moment, and the Lemurians couldn't have done anything that would have more thoroughly ingratiated themselves with *Walker*'s crew. Grimaces and glances of suspicion disappeared, and a mood of camaraderie prevailed as Matt led the delegation under the amidships deckhouse, where refreshments were laid out. It wasn't much, but Juan, Earl Lanier, and Ray Mertz had done their best with what they had. On the stainless-steel counter running the length of the galley, a variety of light dishes were arrayed, along with carafes of iced tea.

After a brief hesitation, Keje himself tasted the tea and a grin of delight crossed his face. Whether it was the tea, the sugar, or just the novelty of ice that did the trick, it was extremely well received. Soon all the Lemurians were standing in the shade, drinking tea and exclaiming loudly in their chittering, yowelly voices, much to everyone's delight. Gray grudgingly offered Adar a Coke. After a trusting gulp, the dignified Sky Priest spewed foam from his mouth and nose, and the crew roared with laughter. Gray patted him hesitantly as he coughed, and then took a quick gulp from the same bottle to show their visitors he hadn't meant to poison their priest.

Ignoring the spectacle, Keje stood with the captain, eying a Vienna sausage rolled up in a slice of cheese with a toothpick stabbed through it. Bradford stood nearby, as did Shinya, ready to interpret. The Japanese officer still wore the dark blue uniform he'd had on when he was rescued, although it had been cleaned and mended as much as possible. He was the only one dressed in blue, and he stood out. Matt had contemplated having more men wear blues, in spite of the heat, to avoid drawing too much attention to the fact that Shinya was different, but he decided the men might resent it and he didn't want to add any fuel to that fire.

"Mr. Bradford," Matt said, "why don't you remain here as interpreter for the crew to the Lemurian party while Lieutenant Shinya accompanies me?" They'd already decided the crew would have Mr. Bradford. "Perhaps Captain . . . uh . . . His Excellency . . ." Matt stopped, at a loss.

"He is correctly referred to as U-Amaki," Tamatsu supplied.

"Yes. Well. Perhaps Captain U-Amaki and some of his officers would like to see more of the ship?"

Shinya spoke to Adar, but Keje blinked assent even before the translation was complete. He couldn't speak the Ancient Tongue, but through his lifelong association with Adar, he'd learned to understand it well enough.

"He would be delighted," Shinya said. "But his name is Keje-Fris-Ar. U-Amaki is his title—like 'Captain.'"

"Oh."

Keje, Adar, Jarrik, and Chack followed the leader of the Tail-less Ones. They were accompanied by the fat one, the female, and the dark-skinned one—who seemed different, besides just the color of his clothes. The rest of the group was left carousing and drinking the wonderful cold drink in the shade with many other Tail-less Ones.

Chack was enjoying himself, and was happy that the strange beings seemed so friendly, but he was unsure why he was there. He was proud to be chosen, of course, but he didn't know why. He still ached from his many small wounds, just as the High Chief did, but he knew he'd fought well in the battle. Perhaps Keje honored him for that? If so, it was an honor indeed, for he'd done no more than many others. At least it was a sign that Keje harbored no ill will toward him over Selass. At the moment Selass was a subject he didn't care to dwell on.

As the Fat One raised a heavy lid of some kind on the deck and gestured inside, Adar translated: "The Fat One—Gray is his name—says the fires that move the ship burn in that hole."

Keje bent over and peered within, but he saw nothing except darkness. When they'd all looked, Gray fastened the lid with a spinning wheel, and they moved toward steps leading to the deck above.

Chack was conscious of constant motion as the small ship moved on the water. Up and down and side to side. It was enough to make him queasy, despite living on the water all his life. He wondered how the Tail-less Ones stood it all the time. He was unaccustomed to anything this small and cramped. He was a wing runner, and he rarely ventured forth on the barges or other small vessels, so it was disconcerting. He suppressed a shudder and tried to think of something else.

Inevitably then, his thoughts returned to Selass as they mounted the steps. Evidently she was again without a mate. Saak-Fas had disappeared in the fighting, and no one had seen him since he delivered the message sending Chack into battle. He wasn't among the slain, or anywhere else on Home. He must have gone over the side. Chack wouldn't mourn him, but his loss left Selass available. Strangely, he wasn't sure how that made him feel. He wasn't the same person she'd toyed with and rejected so short a time ago. Everything was changed. His home in the forward tower was gone. Risa, always the strong one, was weak with injury. His mother was well, but without a home for her clan. The Grik had come, but been destroyed and put to flight, and of course, they'd met these strange ... what was the word? Amer-i-caans. So much that he had known and expected to remain constant was suddenly different or gone—and he'd changed perhaps most of all.

Preoccupied, tramping up the noisy steps, he nearly bumped Jarrik-Fas, who'd inexplicably halted. Shaking off his reverie, he peered around the guardsman at

Keje, who'd paused at the top of the steps. Everyone else stopped, including the Amer-i-caans, to watch him. With one of his finger claws, he scraped at a reddish streak on the rail and raised it to his tongue. His eyes widened with astonishment.

"It is metal, as I suspected," he murmured to his companions, "but what it tastes like . . . cannot be."

"It is, my lord," confirmed Adar quietly. "Iron."

Chack's mind reeled and he looked around in shock. "But surely, lord," he stammered, "it cannot all be iron?"

Adar blinked sharp displeasure at Chack's outburst. "It's iron. All of it. It must be, for the red streaks are everywhere. Now speak no more unless you are given leave." He sniffed. "They will think us rude."

Keje muttered something that Chack didn't catch and joined the Amer-i-caans waiting above.

Gray was scandalized by the Lemurians' preoccupation with the rust. He took it as a personal affront that they should be so obvious about noticing the lack of maintenance. Shinya had spent more time among them, and he thought he understood. He spoke aside to Matt.

"Captain Reddy, they've just realized your ship is made of steel."

"I think you're right. Must be a shock too. They have iron weapons, so they know what it is, but the idea of making something this size . . ." He paused. "They had to know *Walker* was metal, ever since they set foot on her. I wonder what they thought it was?"

"Copper, most likely, Skipper," said Gray, simmering down. "Who knows? I sure as hell don't know how they made something the size of their ship out of wood!"

"Point." The captain stepped into the wheelhouse and beckoned their guests to follow. Once inside, with the self-conscious bridge watch going about their duties, Keje looked through the windows, at the wheel, at all the strange and mysterious devices and the maze of conduits overhead. His eyes swept everything, recognizing the utility, if not the function, of what was clearly the control area for the American ship. He was puzzled that the utilitarianism was so extreme as to preclude decoration of any kind, but everything seemed laid out with profound practicality. To his seaman's eye there was an aesthetic quality in that.

His gaze fell upon the chart table, and with quickening heart and mounting incredulity he recognized immediately what he saw. Adar saw it at the same instant and was staggered by the implications. With a cry, he rushed to the table and leaned protectively over the chart, his eyes sweeping back and forth, taking in the strangers' reactions. They showed no concern except perhaps for his inexplicable behavior. He tried to grasp the chart, but something was there—something clear—between his claws and the paper he sought. *What is this magic?* he thought desperately. *Why would they do this? Do they mock us with their power that even the Sacred Scrolls themselves are nothing but curiosities for all to gape upon without the training to understand?* He looked at Keje's stricken blinking, and the Amer-i-caans behind him, staring. They seemed bewildered. Adar sensed no hint of gloating or malice, only curiosity and concern. Even after his sudden outburst, none seized a weapon. Perhaps there was no mockery here. Perhaps there was something else? Perhaps they understood. Could it be?

Keje edged closer and peered at the chart Adar hovered over. "Their Scrolls are better than your Scrolls, Adar," he said dryly. "Really, you must control yourself. We are their guests. They will think us rude," he quoted.

"You go too far, Keje-Fris-Ar!" Adar retorted sharply. He glanced at the chart again. The detail was amazing! "The value is in the thing, not what is on it! You flirt with apostasy!"

"Wrong. I'm no Sky Priest, but wisdom is wisdom, regardless of the source. Is it apostasy to recognize the value of this Scroll, as they obviously do, and put it in an honored place where all may gain its wisdom? Or is it apostasy to suspect, like you do, that they might be as those Tail-less Ones of old who passed us this wisdom before?"

Matt and the others had gathered round and were watching the exchange. Clearly, the Malay Barrier chart had created a crisis of some sort, but they were at a loss to understand what it was. The 'cats plainly knew what the chart represented, but why should Adar throw such a fit?

"But to have them here, where all can see . . . " sputtered Adar. "It's not right!"

"Where is it written only the Priests of the Sky may know the mysteries of the Heavens?" Keje softly asked. "Among our people, only Sky Priests can interpret the drawings in the Scrolls because they alone have the Ancient Tongue, but anyone may strive to become a Sky Priest, not so? I've looked upon the Scrolls myself—you showed them to me! I can even read some of what is written. Does that make me a Sky Priest—or an apostate?"

Adar was quiet for a moment while he thought. Of course Keje was right; it just didn't *seem* right. He sighed.

"I apologize, my lord. It's just . . . " He'd been gazing at the chart while he spoke, his eyes taking in the shapes of the islands he knew so well, when he felt he'd been physically struck. "The words!" he managed to gasp. "The words are not in the Ancient Tongue!"

Keje saw it was true. Some of the island names were the same, but there was much more writing than he remembered and it was totally unfamiliar. "Their own language?" he speculated. Adar could only nod. It must be. The Ameri-caans still watched them, and he suspected they were becoming impatient. He would have been. "Ask them where they come from. Maybe they will even tell us."

Adar cleared his throat and spoke the ancient words. As soon as Shinya translated, Captain Reddy peered at the chart himself. Adar knew their home couldn't be anywhere on the scroll he saw. The Scrolls of the People were more comprehensive. Less than a third of the known world was laid out before him, and he had at least passing acquaintance with all the places shown. The meaning of his question was clear, however, because Matt put his finger on what Adar recognized as their current position and then paced away, far across the wheelhouse, to stand on the opposite side. He pointed at the deck, looking intently at Adar with his small green eyes.

"They are from the East! Beyond the world, beyond even the Great Empty Water, perhaps! The way no vessel can go!"

"In case you haven't noticed, Brother," Keje said with heavy sarcasm, "this vessel goes wherever it wants!"

*   *   *

The humans were intrigued but not overly concerned by Adar's behavior. They assumed that he'd recognized the chart, and an example of commonality had been found.

"Ask them where they're from," Matt instructed. There was muttered conversation in their own language, and finally Adar pointed over the water at their ship. Matt nodded. "Of course, we suspected as much. It certainly seems self-sufficient enough for long stretches away from land. But your people must have some place, on land, where such things are built?" He spoke directly to them, even though Lieutenant Shinya was obliged to translate everything he said. "Wood only grows on land and other things—copper, cordage, things like that—can only be found ashore. Your people must have settlements where you can make repairs?" All four Lemurians looked at him for a long time after Shinya finished speaking. They seemed hesitant to answer.

Matt understood that they might not want just anyone to know where their settlements were, but he and his crew had saved them from the Grik. If they wished them ill, that was not the simplest way to show it. This logic was apparently not lost on the Lemurians, because finally Keje leaned back over the chart. Adar said something, but the Lemurian leader shook his head and placed one of his clawed fingers on the map.

"Jesus Christ!" blurted Gray. "Borneo!"

Several crewmen on the bridge muttered in surprise. Matt looked over the shorter Lemurian, where his claw touched the chart. "Well," he said, "I believe we've been there once before." He straightened and looked meaningfully at the Bosun. "Balikpapan."

He turned back to Keje. "You have damage," he said, and then gestured around him. "We have damage too, and need supplies. Besides, the Grik may return. We'll help you get there, if you have no objection."

Matt led the Lemurians on a quick tour of the rest of the ship. The only attractions he avoided were the engines and the main armaments. They passed the guns and torpedo tubes several times and, plainly, the Lemurians were interested, but despite Bradford's advice, Matt thought they shouldn't focus too intently on the fact that *Walker* was a warship. And besides, what they didn't know about her capabilities, they couldn't tell to others. The same was true regarding the engines. It seemed to him that the Lemurians were sophisticated enough not to attribute everything they didn't understand to magic. But it wouldn't hurt to let some things remain mysterious. Particularly when that mystery protected the only two advantages *Walker* had in this strange, screwed-up world: her speed and her weapons.

Inevitably, not all the Lemurians were content to let *Walker*'s secrets unfold with time and trust.

Jarrik-Fas insisted that they ask the Amer-i-caans about their amazing weapons that could destroy the Grik from afar with such speed and efficiency. Keje was reluctant, since he could tell their hosts were less than willing to discuss it now. Ever since he'd seen the chart, however, Adar had assumed Keje's pragmatic skepticism. The reverse was true for Keje. That the Amer-i-caans had Scrolls of their own meant they almost certainly had some understanding of the Heavens. To him, that was reassuring. As different as they were, it was a sign that they were perhaps not all that different after all. Adar was in a mood to find fault, though, it seemed.

"I dislike secrets. If they would avoid speaking of their weapons, what else might they conceal?" he asked as they neared the amidships deckhouse again, with its squat four-inch guns, trained fore and aft.

Keje blinked exasperation. "A short time ago you were displeased that they display their Scrolls for all to see, and now you accuse them of being overly secretive? Brother, you contradict yourself."

Adar grunted and showed his teeth with a youngling's chastened grin. "I suppose you're right, my lord. Perhaps I was dismayed by the way they display their Scrolls as if just anyone can understand them. What struck me hardest, in all honesty, was that perhaps among them anyone can. Particularly if they're written in their own tongue. No one likes to think their life's work is un-needed, even by another species."

"Perhaps not all understand their Scrolls. Any one of them may be your counterpart, for all we know," Keje speculated. "But your knowledge and value are not limited to the Scrolls. You're a Sky Priest, after all. I doubt they could all be as conversant with the Heavens as you. It's one thing to read a Scroll. It's another to *know* the meaning. Yet another fascinating thing to learn about these creatures, in time. Besides, if they are as the ones who came before . . . of course they have Scrolls of their own!"

"Does that mean they are . . . gods?" Chack almost squeaked.

"Of course not!" snapped Adar. "There is but one God, silly creature! Even the 'others' were merely beings, as ourselves, who brought the wisdom of Heaven. They are to be exalted, but not worshiped. They admonished as much themselves. These creatures are wise as well. As wise as the others? Who is to say, but still merely beings."

"Whatever they are, I'm glad they like us." Keje grinned.

"I still want to know more about their weapons," Jarrik insisted.

"Oh, very well." Keje relented. "Ask if you must, Adar, but be discreet. I am usually the worrier, but after yesterday I'm inclined to trust these 'Amer-i-caans.' For now, I'm content to let them keep their weapons' secrets, as long as they use them on our behalf." His warning spoken, he had to admit he was as anxious to learn about the amazing weapons as they. He listened intently while the translations took place.

"They've asked about the guns, Captain Reddy. They want to know how they work. How they destroy things far away with only a puff of smoke and loud noise."

Matt sighed. "They were bound to ask. I'm surprised they waited this long. Hmm. Tell them the purpose is much like their big crossbow batteries—to throw a large bolt very far. Only we propel the bolt with an explosion, uh, expanding gas—smoke, instead of spring tension. The smoke throws the bolt very far, faster than the eye can see." He didn't want to get into a ballistics lecture then and there, so he temporized. "A lot of the destructive force of the bolt is caused by the speed alone. Tell them it's very involved and I'll be happy to tell them more when we can converse more easily. Oh, also tell them how fascinated we are with their weapons, and look forward to learning more ourselves." The creatures stared at the number two gun as they stopped almost beneath it. The four-inch hole with its spiraling lands and grooves gaped wide at the muzzle.

They rejoined the rest of the Lemurian party, who were still being fed and studied by the crew. The fraternization remained good-natured, and Matt was relieved to see everyone getting along so well. The camaraderie of their shared victory probably helped, but he suspected his destroyermen were happy to find anyone who wasn't hostile after all they'd been through.

"If you need any assistance, we have carpenters and shipfitters aboard," said Captain Reddy. He looked at Sandra before continuing. "Our medical division also remains at your disposal." Sandra nodded in agreement.

Keje blinked assent when Shinya told Adar what the captain had said, and he replied, "I would like to leave one with you so we can better learn your speech. I believe, with better understanding, the friendship between us will grow and become . . ." He grinned. "Less inconvenient." He gestured Chack forward, and the young Lemurian stepped up with some hesitation. "This one I will leave. Chack-Sab-At. He is not only a worthy person, but I've just recently discovered he's a brave and skillful warrior."

The statement was made without irony, and Chack couldn't decide if he was more surprised by the honor or the words of praise. Or was it just an excuse to get him away from Selass? For some reason, as likely as he'd have considered it a few days before, he was no longer sure. He was uncertain about too many things lately. "I won't fail you, my lord," he murmured.

"He'll be welcome," Matt said through Tamatsu.

"Excellent. Now, noble as young Chack is, he is small recompense for your generosity. Is there nothing we can do for you? You mentioned supplies? And repairs?"

"Our supplies are fine for now, although if you can spare some of your fruit, we'd like to try it." Matt gestured around and shrugged. "As you can see, we don't have space for gardens. The only other thing that might ease my mind is if you can tell me where to find the black substance you use to coat your stays and shrouds and seal your seams. Is it available where we're going? At your settlement?"

Keje was silent as Tamatsu interpreted, but then looked about with surprise. "You have leaks? I was not aware you had a use for gish. Of course. We carry much, just for that purpose. And yes, it is abundant where we go." He made a chittering sound that Matt now recognized as a chuckle. "At the trading land, it bubbles from the ground!"

When Tamatsu finally interpreted Keje's words, via Adar, for the first time he could remember, he saw the captain's lips spread into a genuine grin.

"Well! In that case, why don't we all have another glass of tea?"

The next week involved backbreaking activity for some, as work parties constantly plied between *Walker* and the Lemurian ship, and abject boredom for others, as the destroyer described slow, fuel-efficient circles around the plodding behemoth. Only the number four boiler was lit, but it provided more than enough steam for the monotonous six-knot circuits. With only two wings *Salissa*—or *Big Sal*, as almost everyone called her now—could average only three or four knots herself. If *Walker* went that slow, in the long swells of the Java Sea, she'd barely have steerageway and would roll her guts out.

To Matt, it seemed that Chack was constantly nearby, always out of the way but always there. Watching. In reality, he spent more time with Sandra, Garrett, and Sergeant Alden. Matt had no time to teach him English, and certainly none to learn Lemurian, but Chack was learning fast from his other acquaintances, and Matt understood him better each day.

Some of the men spent a lot of time on the 'Cat ship as well. Bradford practically lived there, and the English lessons were well under way. A lot of the men came back using Lemurian words for things—which drove the Bosun nuts. He never complained about Chinese or Filipino words, but for some reason he took offense to the "jabbering away like a damn cat-monkey." Only after Matt quietly explained that he wanted the men to learn the language did he relent.

Chack slept in the forward berthing compartment with the crew and ate what they ate and generally got along quite well. They'd adopted him, like a pet or mascot at first, but as he learned to speak English they began to realize he wasn't a pet, and that although he was small, he was probably as strong as Silva. His status was blurred. Not a pet and not a destroyerman—but he was becoming a shipmate.

In contrast to Chack's treatment, Shinya still faced open hostility, although his presence—and continued existence—had gained a meager level of acceptance. Strangely, that probably had as much to do with Silva and Alden as anyone. The two men didn't like the Jap, but a growing respect was evident. Matt hoped the men would lighten up eventually. Lieutenant Shinya was proving valuable, and not only as a translator. When not engaged as such, he often toiled with Sandison in the workshop on the condemned torpedoes. He wasn't a torpedoman, but he loved machines. Bernie actually *did* seem to like him. He certainly appreciated his help. If anyone could ever crack the ice between Shinya and the crew, the engaging torpedo officer from Idaho would be the one.

On the bridge, Matt glanced at his watch and looked at Lieutenant Garrett. "Sound general quarters, if you please."

"Aye, aye, sir. General quarters! General quarters!" the gunnery officer repeated in a raised voice. Electrician's Mate 3rd Class Mike Raymond activated the alarm and put on the headset at the talker's station, plunking a helmet on his head while the alarm reverberated through the ship. Chack, standing nearby, snatched a helmet and put it on as well. He looked slightly comical since it was much too large and covered his catlike ears. He grinned happily and blinked in excitement. Matt learned in one of his evening sessions with Bradford that Lemurians conveyed much the same meanings by blinking that humans did with eyebrow/facial expressions. It was like emotional Morse code. He wondered if they were born with the ability or had to learn it. At least it made more sense than Gray's theory that they all had a nervous tick, but he had no idea what the blinks meant, and except for their grins, Lemurian faces remained opaque and stony to his perception.

Chack cinched the chin strap and exuberantly scampered up the ladder to the fire-control platform and his "reserve lookout" post. There was no mistaking his body language—he was clearly enjoying himself. Seconds later, reports filtered in while Matt gazed at his watch. Finally, the last department reported and he smiled to himself. *Better*, he thought. *Not great, but shorthanded as they were ...* He shrugged. Ever since the battle with the Grik he'd run twice-daily drills. Not only did it break the monotony and keep the crew on their toes, but it reminded them that USS *Walker* was still a United States Navy ship—wherever the rest of that Navy happened to be.

"Well done, Mr. Garrett. Pass the word; all departments have improved over their last time. You may secure from general quarters."

Spanky tapped a pressure gauge on number four and grunted noncommittally. Chief Harvey Donaghey, the assistant engineer, had reported for the division while he inspected the cantankerous boiler during the exercise. So far, it was operating perfectly. Number two was in reserve, and number three was cold for the first time since they'd made their dash from Surabaya. When he peeked inside, he wasn't at all happy about the condition of the firebricks. A near miss must've shaken stuff loose, he decided. He glanced up and saw that, as usual, the Mice were watching from the gloom. He sighed.

"Nothin' wrong with number four," Isak said. "Don't know why you don't like her. We gonna be somewhere we can tear down number three anytime soon?"

"We could do it now, but it wouldn't be easy." Gilbert glowered. "Would've been nice to put into Surabaya."

"Surabaya ain't there, boys," Spanky said—again. The Mice blinked at him.

"All he said was it would have been nice," Isak muttered.

They nearly had put in, the day after their first visit from the 'Cats. Not because they expected it to be there, but just to *see*. Captain Reddy finally decided against it, for several reasons. First, of course, was fuel. There was no use wasting it for a sightseeing trip. Second, Surabaya was inhabited, according to what Bradford had learned, but the people there weren't "of the sea," whatever that meant, and weren't necessarily friendly. It was strongly implied that if *Walker* steamed into the harbor unannounced, the consequences might be awkward. After all, even *Big Sal*'s people had thought *Walker* was some new Grik ship at first. Finally, there was the potential damage to morale to consider. Seeing someplace like Surabaya—or someplace where Surabaya should be—was yet another trauma that the captain would sooner put off.

Java was over there, though. Spanky had seen it receding on the horizon to the south. But even at a distance, he could tell it wasn't the Java he'd known. There were no picket ships or minelayers, no freighters loaded with weapons and supplies. No cranes and docks and filthy, oily water. No PBYs occasionally flying patrol and no haze from the industry—or smoke from fires caused by Japanese bombs. Of course, there weren't any Japs either.

As always, the Mice flustered him by jumping from one subject to another. For once, it was just as well.

"How come we ain't got a monkey-cat? Damn deck-apes have one. Why can't we?" Isak complained.

"'Apes don't have one either. They're not pets. They're allies."

"What? Like Limeys?"

"Yeah, sort of like that. Besides, it's too hot. I expect if one came down here, he'd die. They have fur, you know."

The Mice looked at each other. "Fur?"

Spanky eyed them more closely. "Haven't you seen one? Haven't you even seen the one that lives aboard?" The two firemen shook their heads. "Damn, boys! You've *got* to get out of here once in a while!"

At dusk, Keje stood with Adar, Jarrik, and Kas-Ra-Ar on the battlement, now cleaned of all evidence of battle. They couldn't forget the fighting, however, because of the charred, gaping wound that had once been the forward tower, tripod, and wing. There was also the constant smoke from the furnaces that carried the souls of their lost ones to the Heavens. Ordinarily, there would have been a single pyre for all, and the funeral would have been somber but festive. The dead had gone to a better place, after all. But there were so many, and their loss was so keenly felt, that Adar could speak the words, but none could summon the customary gladness. Also, since only the furnaces could be used, the "Rising" went on and on, and the smoke was a constant reminder of all they'd lost. Even so, repairs continued, and the sounds of mauls, saws, and axes reached them over the breeze from aft. Some Amer-i-caans still worked too, even though their last boat of the day had left hours ago. The Tail-less Ones didn't seem to do anything by half measures, even when it came to friendship.

Keje was thankful. So many of *Salissa*'s strong young people had been taken that without the Amer-i-caan methods for moving heavy objects and debris, he doubted they'd have managed so well. He watched with admiration while cranes made from the charred lower portions of the tripod easily lifted huge pieces from where they'd fallen when the tower collapsed into the lower parts of the ship. The tower's survivors now lived with the other wing clans, but so great were their losses in battle that the other two wings were still understrength. He'd hoped this would be the season for the people of *Salissa* to branch out—for the Home to have a daughter—but that wouldn't happen now. They didn't have the people, and they'd be lucky to find the resources to repair *Salissa*—much less build a new Home.

He noticed a figure leaning against the rail, staring at the iron ship. It was Selass. She'd spoken little since her mate disappeared, and he wondered if she mourned him. Saak-Fas had been disagreeable, but he was young and powerful and possibly even attractive. He could see how his daughter might grieve even though their joining was so brief. He shrugged. She would recover and, in time, mate again. Perhaps even to the young wing runner of the Sab-At clan? There was much more to Chack than Keje had once thought. He'd been misguided to discourage that match.

"My lord?"

Keje realized that Jarrik had been speaking. "I'm sorry, cousin. My mind roamed. Forgive my rudeness and repeat yourself." Adar blinked mild reproof.

"We were discussing the Amer-i-caan ship, lord."

"Ah. It does dominate most of our conversations of late. By all means, continue."

Jarrik shrugged aside his chagrin. "But if their ship, this 'Waa-kur,' is indeed iron, how could it possibly float? Our swords and those of the Grik do not float, nor does anything else made of iron that I know."

"Copper can be made to float, and it's even heavier than iron," Adar said smugly. "Cast a drinking cup into a barrel. Does it not float? Home is sheathed in copper, yet we float as well. I do not marvel at the possibility of an iron ship, but the fact of it. That is perhaps their greatest mystery and their most significant advantage. The skill to work so much iron!"

"What about their weapons?" challenged Jarrik bluntly. "Their weapons are iron too. From the big weapons on their ship to the small ones they carry. The principle is the same for all, I think, and the pertinent parts are all of iron."

"I marvel at their weapons, but I confess greater envy for their speed," Keje said.

"What need we of speed?" Jarrik asked. "We live on the sea and by the sea. If we flew to and fro with such speed as theirs, we couldn't hunt the gri-kakka or even launch the boats."

"They do not always fly, and they slow to launch their smaller craft—which also move without wings or oars," Keje pointed out. "But if we had such speed, we would never have lost so many people. The Grik could not have caught us."

"True," agreed Adar, "but I've been wondering something, and Jarrik's thoughts about the fish hunt reinforce my—I hesitate to call them concerns, but . . ."

Keje frowned at him and blinked impatience. Since the incident with the Scrolls, Adar had become the skeptic. "What troubles you about our new friends now, besides their impious treatment of Scrolls?"

Adar looked uncertain. "I'm not sure, and I'm less concerned about the Scroll issue than I was, although other Sky Priests may be less understanding. I've yet to form an opinion regarding their piety, but it's clear that they have more Scrolls than we. I greedily learn their tongue so I can make sense of them. Bradford has explained much, and although it's impossible, I'm sure he actually believes they have Scrolls mapping the entire world! Even the bottom!" Adar chuckled. "For such a learned creature, he harbors some unusual notions!"

Keje looked at his friend, amused. "What, do Amer-i-caans believe the world is flat?"

Adar blinked a negative, but couldn't conceal a gentle grin. "No, lord, but he—and perhaps others—does not understand the most basic Laws of Things. That sweet water falls from the sky as a gift from the Heavens but, as it sours and turns to salt, it gets heavier and slowly slides off to the side of the world until it falls off." He grinned wider and quoted an old cliché. "No one can stand on the bottom of the world." The others laughed.

"Do their silly notions concern you, Brother?" Keje asked.

Adar's grin quickly faded. "No, lord. Two things brought the question to mind, and before you ask me what question, let me proceed. First, as far as we know, the Amer-i-caans do not hunt gri-kakka, or any fish at all. Nor do they grow crops. As amazing as their ship is, it's very small— which I must say became quite evident after a very short time—and dependent upon gish for fuel. That's the smoke from their pipes. Surely you recognize the stink? It's burning gish. I don't know how it works, but they must have gish, and quite a lot of it."

Keje blinked. "So? That's no problem. We know where there is much gish and they are welcome to it for helping us."

"Of course, but my point is, the Amer-i-caans are tied to the land by necessity. They eat only things of the land, as does their ship. They cannot be a true, self-sufficient, sea-faring race such as we. I also know they don't spring from any land I've seen, and together we've seen it all." He held up his hand. "Second, and perhaps most striking, they have only two females. Not only is that obviously far too few, but they are not even mated."

"Most unusual," agreed Keje, "and perhaps unnatural. But I had the impression that the first healer—their 'high' healer, I suppose—was mated to their leader. The times we have seen them together, she seems to argue with him enough! Perhaps among them, only leaders may mate?"

"Not so, lord. She and the other female healer are not mated."

They were all silent a moment, pondering.

"Well. I can certainly understand your perplexity, but what about this is sinister?"

"I never suggested it was sinister, lord. Merely strange—and in keeping with my question. When their healer came to help our wounded, she was obviously shocked to learn that many of our warriors are female, that we make no distinction regarding them when it comes to fighting. I asked Bradford about this, and he confirmed that among them, females do not fight."

"Go on," Keje prompted.

"Their ship bristles with weapons and has no obvious means of support. There are no females aboard, except two healers who do not fight because they're not supposed to." Adar looked at the others and paused to convey significance. The sun had almost vanished, but they still saw the destroyer cruising lazily, effortlessly, ahead. The reflected glare from the last rays of light hid her rust streaks and other imperfections. A single wisp of smoke floated from the aftermost pipe, and heat shimmered at the top. The curious piece of cloth they called a "flag" flapped tautly from the small mast that could have little other purpose than to fly it. "With this evidence, the only conclusion I can draw is that the Amer-i-caan ship has only one purpose: it's a ship meant entirely for war." He sighed. "What manner of people, besides the Grik, would build such a ship, and why so formidable? Did you see that many of the holes they patched were larger than the holes in their weapons? It strikes me that they have been shot at by something with bigger 'guns' than theirs. The Grik have nothing that would do that, or they would have used it on us. Besides, they claim to know even less about the Grik than we." Adar frowned and his eyes rested speculatively on the dark shape as the sun sank from view.

"So what is this question of yours, after all?" Keje asked.

"Only this: have we befriended a flasher-fish, only to find a gri-kakka on its tail?"

Reveille blared in the forward berthing space at 0400 to signal the morning watch. Sleepy men groused and cursed, rolling from their three-tiered racks. Chack, however, practically vaulted from his—one of the uppermost—and quickly donned the white T-shirt that Alan Letts had given him to make him look more Navy-like than the red kilt alone—his only other garment. "Good morning, good morning!" he chanted cheerfully, weaving through the dressing men and scampering up the companionway.

"Ain't natural," grumped Rodriguez, who'd finally been restored to full duty. "Even monkey-cats can't be that happy to wake up every day. He's settin' a bad example. It'll ruin morale, I tell you."

Elden grinned. "Sleep on deck and you won't have to watch him in the morning."

"Hell, I would! But every time, I get woke up drenched by a squall."

"You'd rather get woke up drenched by sweat?"

Rodriguez shrugged. "This close to the equator, don't much matter where you sleep, you're gonna do that. Sometimes I actually pity those damn snipes. I bet it hits a hundred and forty in the fireroom today."

"Hey, man, God didn't make 'em snipes. If we were in the North Atlantic they'd be toasty warm and wouldn't feel sorry for us, out on the icy deck."

"Icy deck!" moaned Leo Davis dreamily from his rack. Ever since Lieutenant Tucker had applied the Lemurian salve to his leg, he'd rapidly improved. So much, in fact, that some began to suspect him of malingering. He stretched and smiled. "Is it morning already? Which one of you fellas'll bring me breakfast in bed?"

Elden pitched a rancid sock on his chest, and Davis yelped and squirmed, trying to get out from under it without touching it. "Damn you! I'm an invalid!"

Chief Gray poked his head down the companionway. "Move it, you apes! Skipper's lookin' at his watch! If you ain't at your GQ stations in one minute he's gonna throw a fit!"

"I wonder why we're still doin' that?" Elden pondered aloud after Gray disappeared. Every morning watch, *Walker*'s crew manned their general quarters posts until two hours after dawn so they'd be prepared while the ship was most vulnerable—when an enemy might see her silhouette before her lookouts saw the enemy. After that, she steamed under condition III alert, with half her weapons manned all day. "Ain't no Jap subs out there," Elden continued. "Ain't no Jap ships or planes. Ain't no Jap Navy. Hell, there ain't no Japs, 'cept ours!"

"I don't know why, but the Skipper does, and he's the only one that has to," Rodriguez said, tying his shoe and hurrying for the ladder. "C'mon, or the snipes'll clean out the galley!"

Chack happily munched the strange yellowish-white substance rolled in a slice of bread. He'd heard them call it "eggs," but Mertz made it from powder, so they must have been joking. He liked the way Amer-i-caans joked, and they did it all the time. Sometimes he wasn't sure if they were joking or not, however. After it was cooked, the stuff did taste a little like eggs, and he particularly liked it with salt and "caatch-up."

Finished eating, he climbed to the fire-control platform, then up the little ladder to his new battle station on the searchlight platform above it. It was still dark, but just a trace of red tinged the eastern sky. A stiff breeze cooled him, and he felt a sense of exhilaration and speed, even at only six knots. That was still about as fast as he'd ever gone before, and *Walker*'s relatively small size magnified the sensation wonderfully. He knew it was only a fraction of what she was capable of, and he yearned to be aboard when she "stretched her legs," as his Amer-i-caan friends described it.

Lieutenant Garrett appeared on the platform below and smiled up at Chack.

"Good morning, Loo-ten-aant Gaar-ret! Morning-day good!"

"Indeed it is. Good morning to you as well. Why don't you light along to the crow's nest and take the first watch? Sing out if those keen eyes of yours spot anything. Understand?" Chack blinked with pleasure and looked at the tiny bucket far above. He'd spent most of his life much higher, but it was the highest point on the ship and he was thrilled by the novelty and—in his mind—the prestige of the post.

"Crow's nest? Me?"

"That's right, Chack. Crow's nest. You. Up you go."

"You want I go higher? I go top of pole?"

Garrett chuckled. "No, the crow's nest is high enough." He pantomimed putting on the headset. "You have to be able to talk and hear. But don't talk unless you see something!"

"Ay, ay!" Chack said, and shot up the ladder. Garrett shook his head, still smiling, as he watched the Lemurian climb. The long, swishing tail did make him look like a cat, or for that matter, a monkey. Whatever he looked like, he was becoming a pretty good hand, and nobody came close to matching his enthusiasm or agility. He was wondering with amusement if they could recruit more like him, when all weapons reported "manned and ready" and he reported for his division.

The sky went from red to yellow-gray and visibility began to improve. The other lookouts scanned for any menace with their binoculars, and a quarter mile off their port quarter, *Big Sal* began to take shape. The gray became suffused with gold that flared against the bottoms of fleecy clouds and cast a new coastline into stark relief off the port bow. Ahead lay the Makassar Strait and, beyond that, Celebes. But right now all eyes were glued to the landfall. Matt paced onto the port bridgewing and joined the lookout there.

"Borneo, Skipper," said the man in a tone of mixed excitement and apprehension. They had almost exactly the same view as when they'd last seen it, astern, after the Battle of Makassar Strait—just a few months before. Then they were running as fast as they could, with the enemy nipping at their heels. They'd been scared to death but flushed with elation after the only real "victory" the Asiatic Fleet had achieved: against the Japanese invasion force at Balikpapan. They sank several transports and a destroyer—just *Walker* and four other four-stackers—but it hadn't been nearly enough, and they were lucky to escape with their skins. They should have had a larger haul, but a lot of their torpedoes either never hit their targets or failed to explode when they did hit. That was when they first suspected something was wrong with them. Now they were returning, but not like they'd imagined they would.

"It looks the same," said the lookout, then added with a grin, "only there's no smoke from burning Nips."

"There was plenty of smoke," Matt agreed, "but we wouldn't have seen it from here. Balikpapan's still a hundred and fifty miles away."

They heard a whoop over the crow's nest comm. "Surfuss taagit! Surfuss taagit!"

After a shocked delay, the frustrated talker responded. "Where? Where?! What bearing? Who the hell's up there foolin' around? Maintain proper procedures!" There was no response. Matt looked up at the crow's nest, and there was Chack, not in it but on top of it, standing as high as he could and waving both arms over his head. He uttered a low-pitched, but astonishingly loud ululating cry. He was signaling something or someone ahead, and Matt turned and stared as hard as he could, scanning back and forth. It was that tough time of morning when submarines were so dangerous. The sky was growing brighter, but the sea was almost black. Unless something was silhouetted, it was practically invisible.

"There, sir!" cried the lookout. "Not three hundred yards away, dead ahead! A boat!"

Matt shifted his gaze and sure enough, a boat appeared in his binoculars. It was about forty feet long, with two tripod masts and junklike sails. It was also ridiculously close. There was no silhouette since the masts were short and Borneo provided a backdrop. He was amazed that even Chack had seen it. "Helm, right ten degrees. All engines stop!"

"Right ten degrees, all stop, aye," came the reply. Matt studied the boat and saw figures now, scampering excitedly about.

"More 'Cats," he said. "I'll be damned."

"Skipper," said Rick Tolson, "look a little to the left." Matt did so, and to his surprise he saw another boat. And another! "They're fishermen!" Tolson exclaimed with complete certainty. "Coastal fishermen! Look!" Each small ship had one end of a net hooked to its side, while the other was supported by a long boom. As they watched, the boom on the farthest boat began to rise. The end of the net drew closed as the boom rose higher, and a multitude of flopping, thumping, silvery shapes poured onto the deck. Nimble Lemurians waded among them with clubs that rose and fell. At a shouted warning, a few club wielders stopped and looked in shock at the destroyer coasting toward them. Chack silenced his booming cry, but jabbered excitedly at the fishermen as they drew near.

"Mr. Tolson, relieve the crow's nest lookout and send him to the fo'c'sle to talk more easily with the fishing boats. Use the engines to maintain position to windward of them, if you please."

Moments later, Chack was on the fo'c'sle, leaning forward and conversing with the nearest boat. Its crew hadn't raised their net and they all stood, amazed, looking up at him.

"He sure got there quick enough," Tolsen observed. "My God, I think he slid down the forestay!"

Matt chuckled. "Well, thanks to his keen eyes, we didn't ram anybody. But do have a word with him about procedures. The last thing we need is other guys trying a stunt like that—which they will—just to prove that if he can do it, they can too." He looked back at the fishing boats, their crews now shouting excitedly back at Chack. Beyond them in the distance, clearer now, was Borneo. Lush and green and familiar. And yet ... It was almost like seeing a photograph of a place he'd been. It looked like it, but it wasn't *it*. He remembered what Bradford had said about the "wild" Grik they'd dissected: judge it by what it *is* like, not what it *looks* like. There was a profound difference. He wondered how different Borneo would be.

They saw many more boats that day. Most were fishermen, like the first they met, and Chack explained that land People fished only mornings and evenings when the smaller fish came to the shallows where the gri-kakka felt confined. The big plesiosaurs could go shallow, but were usually content to linger in deeper water and wait for food to come to them. Most of the boats they saw weren't designed or equipped to hunt the brutes, although their fat was a valuable commodity. That was a job for a Home. Like all Homes, *Big Sal*'s People did hunt the big fish, and the result was her primary trade asset—gri-kakka oil. Much of her store was lost in the fire, but hopefully enough remained to finance her repairs.

Some boats ran away as soon as they sighted them, and some went on ahead after a short conference with Chack. A few stayed and took station on *Big Sal* as they made their way north-northeast. Occasionally, curious crews ventured to gawk at *Walker* and her outlandish folk, but generally they avoided the destroyer.

Late the next afternoon, as the sun neared the horizon and set the low clouds aglow, they entered Balikpapan Bay. For the first time since they'd seen her, *Big Sal*'s massive sails descended and scores of great sweeps extended from her sides like the legs of a giant centipede and she propelled herself against the ebbing tide right into the mouth of the bay. Matt wasn't sure what he'd expected. A small settlement perhaps. Chack and the others often referred to Balikpapan as the "land colony," and he guessed that made him think in diminutive terms. But the civilization they beheld was a virtual metropolis. Two more Homes, similar to *Big Sal*, were moored in the broad harbor, and hundreds of smaller vessels plied back and forth. A long pier jutted from a point of land almost exactly where they'd last seen Japanese troopships burning. The sensation was surreal. Lemurian fishing boats were tied to it now, and beyond the pier was a city.

That was the only word to describe it, even if the architecture was . . . unusual. Wooden warehouses lined the waterfront, but beyond were high pagoda-like structures much like *Big Sal*'s towers. Most were just a few stories tall, though broader than those on the ship, but a few reached quite stunning heights. These were multitiered, and each "story" was slightly smaller than that directly beneath it, which gave them the appearance of extremely tall and skinny Aztec temples. Otherwise, the pervasive "pagodas" continued to make a generally Eastern impression.

The most unusual architectural feature, however, was that every building in view—except the warehouses—was built

on massive stilts, or pilings, that supported the structures at
least a dozen feet above the ground. In the open space beneath them was an enormous market, or bazaar, that had no
apparent organization at all. As far as they could see from
Walker's bridge, it occupied and constituted the entire "lower
level" of the city. The market was teeming with thousands of
Lemurians, coming and going, engaging in commerce, and
deporting themselves more like the denizens of Shanghai
than the 'Cats they'd come to know. Color was everywhere.
Most of the buildings were painted, and large tapestries and
awnings were hung beneath and, in many cases, stretched
between them. The dominant colors were reds and blues,
but gold was prevalent as well, and the whole thing starkly
contrasted with the dark green jungle beyond and the dirty,
gray-blue bay.

"Looks like Chefoo," Gray murmured, mirroring Matt's
thoughts.

The arrival of the destroyer and the battle-damaged
Home hadn't gone unnoticed. Hundreds of spectators
lined the quay and watched as the two ships approached.
Small boats sailed back and forth, jockeying for a view, and
twice Matt ordered full astern to avoid running over the
more intrepid or foolhardy sightseers. The smell of the city
reached them on the gentle breeze, and although it wasn't
unpleasant, it too was somewhat alien. Riotous, unknown
spices on cooking meat and fish predominated, although
there was a hint of exotic flowers and strange vegetation.
All competed with the normal harbor smells of salt water,
dead fish, and rotting wood. There was even a tantalizing
undertone of creosote.

Big Sal continued past the wharf, the long sweeps dip-
ping, until she reached a point opposite a large, empty dock
with more warehouses and a tall wooden crane. There she
backed water and ever so slowly began to inch her massive
bulk closer to the dock. Lemurians scampered about in a
very recognizable way, and huge mooring lines were passed
to the ship.

"We'll anchor two hundred yards outboard of *Big Sal*,
Boats," Matt said. "Let's keep a little water between us and
shore until we find out what's what."

"Aye, aye, Skipper," Gray responded and clattered down

the ladder. Dowden conned the ship to the point Matt instructed, and with a great booming rattle, the new starboard anchor dropped to the silty bottom of Balikpapan Bay.

"Maintain condition three, Mr. Dowden," Matt ordered as he turned to leave the bridge. "I'm heading over to *Big Sal*. Mr. Garrett, Chack, Lieutenant Tucker, and two armed men will accompany me. Pass the word, if you please: dress whites and crackerjacks."

They motored across to *Big Sal* and made the long climb to its deck. Matt had been aboard several times now, but he was only just becoming accustomed to the sheer size of the ship. Courtney Bradford and the destroyermen who'd been helping aboard greeted them. Matt sent Bradford back to *Walker* to make himself presentable and told him to return in thirty minutes.

As usual, they went through the boarding ritual, but as soon as they had, the Lemurian who'd given permission raced off. When he returned, he was accompanied by Adar and High Chief Keje himself. Both were dressed in garments representative of their status. Adar wore the same cape or "Sky Priest suit" he'd worn every time Matt had seen him. Keje wore his polished copper armor over an even finer tunic than the one he'd first worn aboard *Walker*. Gold-wire embroidery graced every cuff, and his polished and engraved copper helmet now boasted the striated plumage from the tail of a Grik warrior. A sweeping red and gold cape was clasped at his throat by a chain of polished Grik hind claws. *He won't let anyone forget that* Big Sal *broke the Grik for the first time,* Matt thought.

Matt and the rest of his party, including Chack, saluted him. Matt still thought it appropriate, since Keje wasn't just the captain of a ship, but was, in effect, a head of state. Bradford was trying to sort out all the nuances of Lemurian society, but so far it seemed rather confusing. The closest analogy he'd come up with was that of the ancient Greek city-states, or possibly even the United States under the Articles of Confederation. Each Lemurian ship was considered a country unto itself, with its own laws and sometimes very distinctive culture. The Trade Lands or Land Colonies had the same status, but as they grew in size, they also grew in economic influence. So, although still theoretically equal, some of the more tradition-minded Homes resented the upstart "mud-treaders."

"Greetings, U-Amaki, Keje-Fris-Ar," he said, and Keje grinned widely, returning the salute.

"Greeting you, Cap-i-taan Riddy. Bad-furd teech I speek you words. Good, eh?"

Matt grinned back. "Very good, Your Excellency. I regret I haven't done nearly as well learning your language." Keje was still grinning, but clearly he hadn't caught everything Matt said. Chack elaborated in his own language.

"Ah. Good! Chack speek for we! He learn good!" Matt nodded at Keje's understatement. Chack really had made remarkable progress. He'd seen people pick up enough of a new language to get by with in a week, through total immersion, but he'd never seen anyone learn one as well as Chack in so short a time.

"He has indeed."

They waited companionably until Bradford returned. All the while, locals came aboard and talked excitedly with Keje's people. Many were shipwrights, looking at damage they expected to be commissioned to repair. But most were just visitors who wanted to hear the story of how it happened, and wanted most of all to stare at the strange people with no tails who came from the ship without wings. The decks of Home had taken on a decidedly festive, holiday-like atmosphere.

"What'll happen now?" Matt asked when their party was complete. The answer ultimately translated that they would soon pay their respects to "U-Amaki Ay Baalkpan," Nakja-Mur, where they would eat and drink and tell their tale. In addition to the fact that they had a wondrous tale to tell, it had been more than two years since they'd been here, and the local potentate was somehow related to Keje. There would be much to celebrate.

At the mention of "drink" and "celebrate" Matt considered sending the ratings back to the ship, but finally decided against it. They didn't seem the least inclined to go haring off on their own, and at least Silva wasn't among them. He doubted Lemurian society was quite prepared for the likes of Dennis Silva on the loose. God knew his men deserved liberty after their ordeal, but he wanted to learn a bit more about this place before he granted it.

A procession was forming in the waist and nearly every 'Cat on *Big Sal* was part of it. Bright kilts and garish costumes were the uniform of the day, and the tumult and chaos of the happy, grinning throng was almost as loud as the battle against the Grik. There'd be liberty for them, at least, and they were prepared to make the most of it.

"All Amer-i-caans not come land?" Keje asked in his stilted English.

"No, Your Excellency, not yet. My ship is very tired and has many needs. This is the first time she has stopped among friends where it's safe to make repairs. There's much to do."

"Work tomorrow! Tonight is glory-party. Friends meet friends!"

"Perhaps later," Matt demurred. With a polite but brittle smile he excused himself and stepped to the rail, where he looked out to his anchored ship in the dwindling light. Even to his prejudiced eye she looked physically exhausted. When he had first assumed command of DD-163, she'd seemed old-fashioned and undergunned, but in spite of that she'd given the impression that she tugged at her leash like a nostalgic thoroughbred—past her prime but not yet out to pasture. Now she just looked worn-out. Rust streaked her sides from stem to stern, and the hasty repairs stood out like running sores. A continuous jet of water gushed from her bilge as the overworked pumps labored to keep her leaky hull afloat. The anchor chain hung slack, and instead of straining against it she looked burdened by the weight. He was surprised by a stabbing sense of sadness and concern.

Sandra had joined him, unnoticed in the hubbub. "A coat of paint and she'll be good as new," she said brightly, guessing his thoughts. He looked at her pretty, cheerful face, but saw the concern in her eyes. His brittle smile shattered like an egg dropped on the deck, and he saw her expression turn to anguish. For an instant her compassion was more than he could bear. He forced a grin that was probably closer to a grimace, but as she continued to look at him, her hand suddenly on his arm, his face slowly softened into a wistful smile. How did she do that? In a single, sharp, wrenching moment, she'd stripped his veneer and bared his inner torment, but with only the slightest touch, she'd buried it again. Deeper than before.

"It'll take more than a coat of paint, I'm afraid," he whispered. He saw Keje beyond her, motioning at the spot beside him. "Looks like they're ready to go." Unwilling to break the contact, he crooked his elbow and held his arm out for her. "Care to join me?"

Keje and Adar, along with Matt and Sandra, threaded their way through the throng and took places at the head of the procession. Bradford was several paces back, behind the wing clan chiefs and Keje's other officers. Chack and Garrett were with him, as were the two other destroyermen. They weren't carrying rifles, but they had sidearms and the ridiculous cutlasses. Bradford wasn't wearing one, even though they were as much his idea as Gray's. The one time he did, he'd somehow managed to cut himself without even drawing it completely from its scabbard. He wasn't wearing a pistol either, but only because he'd forgotten it when he changed his clothes. Captain Reddy wore his Academy sword. With many hoots and jubilant cries from the ship as well as the dock, the procession began to move and they marched down the gangway, into the teeming city.

The festivities were heard across the water, beyond *Big Sal*, where *Walker* rested at last. Spanky McFarlane wiped greasy hands on a rag tucked into his pocket. His sooty face was streaked with sweat. "Sounds like a hell of a party," he said, staring at the shore.

"Yup," said Silva, and he spat a stream of tobacco juice over the side. Stites leaned on the rail by the number two gun, a cigarette between his lips. Spanky fished a battered pack out of his shirt pocket and shook one out. Silva handed him a Zippo. "Think we're gonna get fuel here?" he asked.

"Dunno. Hope so. We're down to seven thousand gallons, so we ain't looking for it anywhere else."

"Not without burning wood, I hear," Stites put in. Spanky glowered at him. "I reckon if anybody can squeeze oil out of the monkey-cats, the Skipper will. He's done okay."

"No arguments there," Silva grunted. "I just wish I knew what we're gonna have to do to get it—and what we're gonna do then."

Spanky looked at him curiously. "What difference would it make if you did?"

Silva grinned. "None, I guess." He walked to the rail and leaned on it beside Stites. "Might be fun to go ashore. Kick up my heels." His face darkened. "Ain't no women, though. That's gonna get tough, fast."

"All them other nurses gone on *Mahan*," Stites grumped, "and the only two dames in the whole wide world is officers. Where's the justice in that?"

"Maybe there're women somewhere," encouraged Spanky. "The Skipper thinks so. Those lizard ships were human enough, and the monkey-cats speak Latin, of all things. We can't be the only people who ever wound up here."

"Then we better find fuel quick so we can start lookin' for 'em," Stites muttered emphatically.

"Oh, I don't know," Silva reflected. "Some of them cat-monkey gals are kinda cute, if you don't mind that furry, European style."

Stites looked at him with wide eyes. "Shit, Dennis, you're one sick bastard!" After a moment, though, he scratched his cheek. "Course, after a while, who knows?"

Spanky cleared his throat. He knew—well, suspected—the men were joking and that was fine. But the joke was barbed and reflected a very real concern. Best keep it a joke for now. "I wouldn't worry about it. Strikes me they have higher standards, and I doubt you'd measure up. A goat wouldn't be satisfied with a deck-ape."

Silva affected offense. "Now, sir, that's no way for an officer to talk. Downright uncharitable. Keepin' all the goats to yourselves might dee-stroy the perfect harmony between the apes and snipes!"

Spanky laughed out loud. "I'll bear that in mind."

Of course, if the rumors he'd overheard about Silva trying to "murder" Laney were true, there was little harmony left to destroy. Officially, a rusted pin broke. With nobody, even Laney, saying otherwise, that's all there was to it. But tensions were high. So far, everyone was too busy working together to keep the ship afloat for things to get out of hand—except the "joke" on Laney. Spanky was sure that was all it was. Silva played rough and maybe Laney had it coming. He could be a real jerk. It was even kind of funny—since nobody died—and Laney sure wasn't as puffed up as usual. But once the ship was out of danger, they better find one of two things pretty quick: dames or a fight. If they ever added boredom to their fear and frustration, the "jokes" would stop being funny at all.

The procession wound through the heart of the open-air market that was the city of "Baalkpan." It was somehow reassuring that the name of the place was derived from the ancient charts the Lemurians considered sacred. If nothing else, it proved that whoever transcribed or inspired the Scrolls didn't speak Latin as a first language. Matt wasn't positive; his historical interests were focused elsewhere, but he was pretty sure the place-names in the region had been given or recorded by the Dutch within the last two or three hundred years. That also meant that whatever religious importance the Lemurians placed on the Scrolls was a relatively new addition to their dogma. Not its sole foundation. Other than that fleeting thought, however, at the moment he and his companions were far more interested in their surroundings.

They were again struck by the vivid colors all around. Nothing went unpainted, and the tapestries and awnings were remarkably fine. Printing technology was apparently unknown, because the delicate and elaborate designs decorating virtually everything they saw were woven right into the cloth. Accomplished as they were at weaving, however, the Lemurians wore very little—enough for the sake of modesty, but only just. Kilts were the norm, although some, like Adar—and Keje tonight—might don a cape as well. Other than kilts, clothing seemed to be worn only for occupational protection. Occasionally they saw someone dressed in armor of sorts, but even then it appeared more decorative than practical. Matt knew Keje's armor was real—even though it was carefully cleaned and polished, it was scarred with many dents and cuts that proved it wasn't just for show. The people of Baalkpan seemed happy and prosperous, if just a bit garish. But unlike Keje and the crew of *Big Sal*, they didn't look like fighters.

What they lacked in martial manner, they made up for with their enthusiastic greeting of Keje's people and the destroyermen. Matt saw plenty of naked curiosity, but no hostility at all. Little apparent surprise either, and it dawned on him suddenly that of course they'd known *Walker* was coming. They'd dawdled along with *Big Sal* for days after being seen, and word could have reached Balikpapan on the slowest fishing boat. There'd also been plenty of time for them to learn what happened with the Grik. Indeed, that seemed to have a lot to do with the enthusiastic greeting. They were "hailing the heroes home from the war." They saw the battle as a great victory and were rejoicing.

"It's just amazing!" Sandra shouted in his ear, over the tumult. He nodded. Large feline eyes of all colors gazed intently at them from the crowd. Here and there, Lemurian children scampered on all fours, their tails in the air, dodging between the legs of their elders. Others openly suckled their mothers. Ahead, a smallish brontosaurus was hitched to a cart loaded with something pungent. It balked at a command from its driver, apparently startled by the commotion, and bellowed in protest. The procession paused while the driver regained control of the beast and then continued on.

"Amazing!" shouted Courtney Bradford, suddenly just behind them, oblivious to protocol. "They use dinosaurs like oxen, or mules! I wouldn't have thought they were intelligent enough to domesticate! The dinosaurs, I mean."

"You'd be surprised," Matt replied. "I knew a guy who rode a Longhorn steer around like a horse, and a Longhorn can't be any smarter than a dinosaur."

"Indeed?"

They passed fishmongers hawking their wares who stopped to gawk at the procession. Mostly, they sold the familiar "flasher-fish" they'd all seen quite enough of, but Matt was surprised to see other types of fish as well. He'd almost imagined that the flasher-fish, vicious and prolific as they were, must have virtually wiped out every other species in the sea. Now he saw that wasn't the case, although the other fishes, by their size and formidable appearance, didn't look any more pleasant to meet. There was a large crustacean resembling a giant armored scorpion with a lobster tail that looked able to propel it forward as well as back. He was intrigued by a small version of the plesiosaur they'd rammed, and a very ordinary-looking shark. He'd thought sharks wouldn't stand a chance in these far more lethal waters, and he suspected they weren't the dominant predators he'd always known them to be.

He glanced behind and saw that the procession was growing more boisterous, but it wasn't as large anymore. Many of *Big Sal*'s crew had been tempted away by diversions or acquaintances. There was still quite a throng, and city dwellers caroused along with them as they made their way toward a massive edifice, squat in comparison to others but much broader and more imposing. It rested on considerably higher stilts than the buildings nearby, and growing up through the center and out through the top was a truly stupendous tree.

At its base, the procession finally halted and the crowd noises diminished. Keje stepped forward and raised his hands, palms forward. When he spoke, Chack quietly translated as best he could.

"Greetings, Nakja-Mur, High Chief of Baalkpan!" Keje's voice seemed unnaturally loud now that everyone nearby was silent. "I am Keje-Fris-Ar, High Chief of *Salissa* Home, come from the Southern Sea with mighty friends, trade, and tales to tell. May we come aboard for counsel?"

There was a moment of silence, then a powerful voice from an unseen source boomed at them from above.

"Come aboard, and welcome, Brother. It is long since *Salissa* Home visited these waters, and some of your tale has arrived before you. Come, eat and drink and tell me your tale. Bring these mighty friends of yours. I would meet them!"

Adar glanced back at them and suddenly spoke urgently to Keje. Keje looked at them and seemed to hesitate, but then clapped Adar on the back and scampered up the rope ladder that was, apparently, the only way up. Adar looked at them again with what might have been uncertainty, but then followed his leader. Matt motioned for Sandra to make the twenty-foot climb and with a smile she grasped the ropes and started up. Matt would have sworn he hadn't consciously considered it when he suggested she go first, but he caught himself watching the shapely nurse ascending the ladder above and for a moment he was almost mesmerized. The white stockings didn't hide her athletic legs, and the way her hips swished from side to side at the bottom of her wasp-thin waist ... He shook his head and looked away, vaguely ashamed, and saw all the other men watching as well. He coughed loudly and meaningfully and gestured Chack closer.

"How come these people build everything so high off the ground?"

Chack looked at him blankly, then his eyelids fluttered with amusement and he grinned. "Is, ah, tradition? Yes. Remind us of old ways. Also, keep dry when high water. Bad land lizards not climb good, too."

Matt grinned back at him. "Makes sense to me!" With that, he made his own way up.

Large as it was, Captain Reddy never imagined that the enormous hall he entered would possibly hold all who came along, but it did—as well as an equal number of locals. The size and shape reminded him of an oversized basketball court, dimly lit by oil lamps that exuded a pleasant, if somewhat fishy smell. Huge beams supported the vaulted ceiling and great gaudy tapestries lined the walls, stirring gently with the soft breeze from banks of open shutters. Dominating the center of the hall, the trunk of the massive Galla tree disappeared into the gloom above. Except for the size of the tree and the height of the ceiling, it looked like the Great Hall on *Big Sal*. Matt guessed there were close to five hundred occupants, talking animatedly, and for the moment, no one paid them any heed.

Along one wall, a long bar was laid with colorful dishes heaped with food. Every ten feet or so was a cluster of copper pitchers containing a dark amber liquid that smelled like honey and bread. Matt saw others grab pitchers and begin to drink, so he seized one each for himself and Sandra. Bradford took one too, but when the other destroyermen moved in that direction, Lieutenant Garrett scowled and shook his head. Matt peered into his pitcher and sipped experimentally. He looked at Bradford, surprised.

"Tastes . . . sort of like beer," he said. "Not bad, either." Sandra took a tentative sip and Bradford raised his mug. A moment later, he lowered it and smacked his lips.

"Ahhh! Beer! We've more in common with these Lemurians than we ever dreamed! I'd think the alcohol content is rather high as well."

Matt glanced at Garrett and the security detachment and felt a pang of remorse. They looked at him like dogs watching him eat. "Go ahead, men, but just one mug apiece. Mr. Garrett? See to it. All we need now is drunken sailors!" He and Sandra politely moved along the bar with the crowd, sampling small dishes here and there. The spices were different and some were quite brutal. Many of *Big Sal* 's 'Cats proudly pointed out this or that and made suggestions, but most of the locals just watched, wide-eyed.

"Cap-i-taan Riddy!"

Matt turned toward the somewhat familiar voice and faced Kas-Ra-Ar, Keje's cousin, and captain of his personal guard.

"Com plees."

Bradford had obviously been as busy teaching English on *Big Sal* as Chack had been learning it on *Walker.*

"By all means," Matt replied. "Mr. Garrett? Please supervise our protectors. Lieutenant Tucker, Mr. Bradford, would you accompany me?"

They followed Kas through the boisterous throng, threading their way down the far side, away from the buffet. At the other end of the hall, they came to a less-packed space, where Keje and Adar stood near a seated figure dressed in flowing robes of red and gold. The figure was easily the fattest Lemurian they'd seen, but he gave no impression of sedentary weakness. His dark fur was sleek and shiny with just a hint of silver, and he radiated an aura of strength and power despite the massive stomach his hands laid upon. He regarded them with keen, intelligent eyes as they approached and raised his hand palm outward and thundered a greeting in his own tongue.

Matt returned the gesture, and the Lemurian's eyes flicked to the sword at his side. Keje spoke quickly in Nakja-Mur's ear. While the Lemurian chief watched them, unblinking, Adar translated to Courtney Bradford.

"Never has he seen someone make the Sign of the Empty Hand when that person's hand wasn't empty. I believe he's referring to your sword, old boy."

Matt glanced with surprise at the sheathed ceremonial weapon. They'd worn the swords—as before—to seem less exotic. It hadn't occurred to him that it might cause trouble. Keje would have warned them if they were committing some terrible breach of convention. Wouldn't he? He thought quickly. "Tell him my hand *is* empty. Among our people, only the unsheathed weapon is a threat because it shows intent. The sign is given as a token of friendship and reflects more the intent than the actual fact."

"It is a lie, then?" came the question. Keje seemed uncomfortable and Adar radiated an air of vindication. Matt felt a surge of anger and wondered if they'd been set up. Sandra unobtrusively squeezed his arm.

"Tell him it's not a lie. We came here as friends, as we came to the aid of *Salissa* Home. We'd like to be the friends of all the People. Since our intentions are friendly, *not* making the sign would have been a lie. Among our people, friends may go among one another armed and still remain friends. Is that not the case among his?"

After the translation, Nakja-Mur just stared for a moment, but then slowly, his lips parted into a grin. Matt looked at Keje and saw he was already smiling. "I tell Nakja-Mur you people always armed because you always . . . warriors. Always. You ship made for fighting only. Not so?"

Finally, they'd come to the point. He'd never lied about it, but he had downplayed it. Now, Matt knew, there was only one possible answer. The truth.

"USS *Walker* is a ship of war," he admitted quietly.

"Who you fight?" Adar asked. "Who you fight all the time you need ship only for war?"

Matt realized it was the first time he'd heard the Sky Priest speak English. "We fight the enemies of our people . . . and the enemies of our friends."

"You fight Grik?" Adar translated for Nakja-Mur.

"We've already fought the Grik."

"You fight again?"

Matt glanced at Sandra and Bradford. They were both

looking at him, realizing that what he said in the next few moments might have grave consequences for them all.

"If the Grik come and you can't fight them alone, we'll help. That's what friends do. But friends don't ask friends to do all their fighting for them."

Nakja-Mur spoke to Adar, all the while watching Matt's face as if curious how to interpret human expressions. Adar repeated his words as carefully as he could. "After battle tale of U-Amaki Ay *Salissa*"—he paused and looked at Matt—"Keje tell fight. Grik fight bad, but hard. Fight new way, bigger ship. More Grik than see before." He took a quick gulp from his tankard. "New thing," he said. "Different thing. Maybe Grik come . . . bigger, like long ago."

Matt was concerned about the Grik, of course, but he wasn't too worried about *Walker*'s ability to handle several of their ships at once, if need be. They were the "Ancient Enemy," that much he understood, and he knew the 'Cats held them in almost superstitious dread—with good reason. But he guessed he'd begun to think of them more along the lines of his "Malay pirate" model than as an actual expansionist menace. They'd been "out there" for thousands of years, after all. His assessment was based on his limited conversations, as well as the lack of any evident preparations to meet a serious threat. Especially here. He'd shifted his primary concern to establishing good enough relations with the Lemurians that they would help with fuel and repairs. If a limited alliance, in which *Walker* chased off a few Grik now and then, was the only way to meet those needs, then he was prepared to agree to one, but he wanted to avoid an "entangling" alliance that left either too dependent on the other.

Now, though, it seemed they were actually afraid the Grik might attack here. That didn't fit the "pirate" model. He was dismayed how vulnerable the people of Baalkpan were, even compared to their seagoing cousins. They'd always referred to it as an "outpost" or "colony," and he supposed that description had left him thinking Baalkpan was small and possibly even transient. Certainly easily evacuated. Now, of course, he knew that the land colony of Baalkpan would be about as easy to evacuate as . . . Surabaya. But even against six Grik ships, Baalkpan had enough people—complacent as they were—to repel an assault with ease. Something had been lost in translation—or had they been "downplaying" too?

Adar continued. "If Grik come bigger, like long ago, there be ... plenty? Plenty fight for all." Matt looked at Nakja-Mur and then at Keje who stood by his side, watching him. Then he glanced at Sandra and sighed.

"Tell me more about the Grik."

The party proceeded around them, loud with happy cries and chittering laughter. A troupe of dancers found enough space near the trunk of the great tree to perform feats of astonishing agility and admirable grace. They were accompanied by haunting but festive music produced by drums and a woodwind/horn that sounded like a muted trumpet. All the while, a space was left surrounding the thronelike chair of Nakja-Mur and his guests while they discussed the peril they faced.

Nakja-Mur touched a chime. At the signal, a truly ancient Lemurian emerged—as if he'd been waiting—from a chamber behind his chief, dressed in the robes and stars of the Sky Priests. Around his neck was a simple brass pendant, tarnished with age but suspended by an ornate chain of gold. He clutched it when he suddenly spoke the same, but more polished, Latin that Adar had first used to communicate with them.

"You understand the Ancient Tongue," he grated.

"Yes! I mean, uh, that's true, Your ... Eminence."

The old Lemurian gave a start when Bradford replied, but continued in his raspy voice. "I'm disquieted by that, but it's clearly true. I would learn how this can be. But that will wait." He seemed contemplative for a moment, but then visibly gathered himself to speak again.

"I'm Naga, High Sky Priest of Baalkpan. I will tell you of the Grik and of the People. The Scrolls are our ancient history, our guide, our way, our very life, but they are incomplete and there are gaps—great gaps—between their beginning and the now. Hundreds of generations passed between the beginning times and when we learned the Ancient Tongue. The Truth was passed by word of mouth all that time before it was recorded." He blinked several times in a sequence that Bradford thought signified regret. "Perhaps, much was lost," he continued, "but the Scrolls clearly tell of a time when all the people lived together in happiness and peace on a land in the west. A land vast and beautiful, safe from the capricious sea. A land lush and green and covered with trees and protected by water. And the Maker of All Things, the Greatest of all the Stars above, filled the waters around the Ancient Home with wicked fishes that kept our people safe from the monsters across the water on the western land.

"And thus it was, for age upon age. The People lived and died, but were prosperous and happy and needed only the trees for their homes." He shook his head in lament and blinked again, rapidly. "But for some, it wasn't enough. The fragile perfection of the People's existence was somehow lacking, it seemed. Some built boats, to range upon the sea and take fishes there. They wandered and explored, and finally it came to be that one of the boats was cast upon the western land of monsters. The Grik," he added darkly. "The Grik slew them and ate them, but then wondered from where did they come, this new prey?"

Bradford translated as quickly as he could, but began to fall behind. The old priest waited while he caught up, and then continued.

"The Grik built boats for themselves. They copied the very boats delivered unto them. They were poor sailors, and many perished and the flasher-fish and gri-kakka grew fat on their bodies, but there were always more. Finally, they reached the ancient paradise of our People. Only a few came at first, like now." He stopped and looked at Nakja-Mur. "And they were killed and cast into the sea. The People were not warriors and many died, but they were able, for a time, to slay all that came." He paused for effect. "But there were always more."

The party went on, unabated, but a circle of silent listeners had formed around them. The old Sky Priest lifted a copper mug to his shriveled lips and drank.

Bradford turned to Matt. "My God, Captain! Do you know what this means? Madagascar! This 'ancient paradise' simply must be Madagascar! These people are quite clearly related to lemurs—as I've believed from the start! I admit the relation has become somewhat distant . . ."

"Distant!" snorted Sandra. "Most lemurs are no bigger than a cat. None I know of are bigger than a chimp!"

"That's where you're mistaken, my dear. A species of giant lemur once dwelt on Madagascar, a species almost as large as our friends. I've seen their very bones!" His brow furrowed. "But they were not nearly so . . . humanlike in form. Nevertheless! This gives me almost enough information to advance my theory regarding—" He was unable to finish because the wizened priest spoke once more.

"The war for paradise must have lasted generations. We know not, because the Scrolls do not say. But during that time, the People learned to build great ships—the Homes of the Sea—and so were prepared when the Grik became too many and the People were finally cast out, forced to wander the vast oceans, never to return to our sacred home." Naga paused to catch his breath and allow Bradford time to translate. While he waited, he looked wistfully at the great tree in the center of the hall. "At first, we wandered blindly. We had not yet learned the Heavens—to follow the paths they laid before us. We knew the Great Star, the Maker of All Things who lights the world and brings brightness to the void of night, and we knew his little brother, who washes the night with a cool, sleepy light, but we did not know that the smaller stars yearned to show us things. Many perished when their Homes were cast on unknown shores, and it's said the bones of those ancient wrecks bleach there even still. But enough survived to carry on. Lost and scattered by storm and darkness, our people did survive. Over time, they saw the light in the darkness and learned the wisdom of the Heavens. It was then that they knew the stars for what they are—the bright essence of those who have gone before and watch over us from the sky."

He looked at the humans for a moment and Bradford could have sworn that he blinked in speculation. He continued. "Some settled in the northlands, and others in the south. Some eked out an existence on tiny islands in the middle of the Western Sea, but always, where there was land, eventually there were Grik. The only ones to gain a shadow of freedom from war and fear were those who lived on the sea. Only the sea was safe, for the Grik do not love it and did not know how to build the great floating Homes.

With the deep waters between us, where the mountain fish dwell, for a time there was peace and it seemed the Grik had forgotten the prey that escaped them. We found these lands where the Grik did not thrive and those that did were weak and primitive and we made colonies, or land Homes, for the first time in age upon age. A hundred generations passed. More. The people lived well and in peace. Baalkpan and other colonies rose to thrive and prosper and the great Homes of the sea plied the oceans and slew the gri-kakka for his sweet oil and restored contact between the scattered ones so we could become one People again. Different, diverse, and far-flung, but still one People even if languages and beliefs had changed.

"The Grik became no more than a myth, a terrible legend to frighten younglings into doing their chores, but no longer did they haunt our dreams. The terrible enemy that stole our home and nearly destroyed us had become less than a fable. The backward Grik here were hunted and slain, and those on the islands nearby did not know tools and weapons. On a few islands, some live still and no one ever goes there to stay."

"Bali," Matt said aloud, and the old priest blinked a curious affirmative.

"Then, like a gift from the Heavens themselves, the first Tail-less Ones came in three ships, suffering from storm and loss. They were tired and weak and poor in food, but friendly and rich in wisdom of the Heavens. We fed them and nursed them and helped them repair their ships and, in return, they taught us that the stars did indeed show the way, but one could *see* the way only through the Sun, since the Sun alone was the child, and as one with the Maker of All Things. From the Sun we take direction, and with direction, the stars in the Heavens would show us the way from place to place. They told us the names of the stars and the names of places as well, like Baalkpan and Borno and Baali. But the greatest gift they bestowed upon us was the Ancient Tongue by which the Scrolls were drawn and written at long last, and in which we now converse."

"My God," whispered Matt. "The stars are 'ancestor spirits,' the son of the sun is the sun . . . Father, Son, and Holy Ghost."

Sandra nodded. "Whoever came before left behind more than they thought."

"Yeah, I'd hoped the 'Scrolls' weren't so deeply incorporated—"

Naga interrupted. He'd watched their varied reactions, but he didn't pause for long. "At last there was a way for all the People to understand one another again, and to go from place to place without ever having been there, and in safety!"

"What happened to them? What did they look like?" Bradford asked quietly. His face remained impassive, but when he glanced at Captain Reddy, his eyes were intent.

"As far as what they looked like, all that is recorded is they had no tails, as you do not, which is strange and disturbing enough. The circumstance of their arrival is also somewhat similar . . ." He hesitated. "As far as where they went, that's a tragic story in itself, and one that, I fear, has finally returned to task us. A learned one among them, a scholar of great wisdom with the name Salig-Maa-Stir, taught our fathers the Ancient Tongue and drew the lands and waters and placed names upon them. It's said his leaders did not approve, and when they found out he'd done this thing, they forbade him to teach us their everyday tongue or the magic they guarded. Nevertheless, he loved the People and told us what he could through a tongue ancient even among his kind. Eventually, even this wasn't allowed, and Salig-Maa-Stir was kept away except to barter for goods. His greatest pupil, however, a female named Siska-Ta, picked up the narrative of the visitors. It was she who told the tale of the leaving of the Tail-less Ones.

"They claimed their home was far to the west, beyond even the Land of the Grik. But in spite of their wisdom, their Scrolls, and their tools, they were lost and alone and all their people were gone. Salig-Maa-Stir claimed that their land had ceased to be. Siska-Ta and our fathers assumed their people were slain by the Grik, and the horrors of old legends resurfaced. But before he was taken away, Salig-Maa-Stir said his people were not conquered, they had simply ceased to be."

Matt and Sandra looked at one another.

"This was a horror even worse than the Grik, but they

never gave explanation. However, it came to pass that one of the ships wanted to go to their home and see what had become of it. Our fathers told them the legends, and warned them of the danger, but they knew. They *knew*! They'd met the Grik already! This was terrible news for the People, for it confirmed the legends and meant that the Grik truly did exist, as the priests had been saying all along. But what worried them most was that if the Tail-less Ones returned to that evil land, the Grik might learn their ways and soon find us as well! The leaders of the other ships shared this concern, but they had not the will or right to stop the one from trying.

"Finally, it was decided the one would go west, bearing only those who desired to go, with only the most rudimentary weapons and the scantiest of Scrolls. It was hoped that if they were taken, the Grik would learn nothing about where they'd been, where they were going, and most important to the other two ships, where we were and where they would go. On a blustery spring day, the one sailed west—we expect now to its doom—and the other two sailed east, and disappeared into the vast, empty Eastern Sea, beyond the known world. That was almost three hundred seasons ago."

The old priest took another long swallow from his tankard and smacked his lips over eroded, yellow teeth. It was evidently a story he'd often told and now that it was done, the somber theater of the telling passed and his mood once more reflected that of the party that continued to thrive.

"Did this Siska-Ta ever write any more?" Bradford asked.

"Oh, yes indeed! She became the first true Sky Priest and not only finished the early Scrolls but traveled the world and taught the Scrolls and the Ancient Tongue to all the People. It is from her we know the shape of the world, from this side of the great Western Sea all the way to the Eastern Ocean, where the waters fall away and the world ends. She also compiled histories of the many people she met and went among. She was a Prophet. A great Prophet."

"Do the Scrolls show where the Ancient Home of your People lies?" Bradford questioned eagerly, certain that he'd solved his riddle.

The old priest closed his eyes in a long, mournful blink. "Alas, they do not. We know it is beyond the Western Sea, where none dare go. The waters are without bottom, as are those of the Eastern Ocean, and great monsters dwell there. And of course, beyond the Western Sea are the Grik."

"Did the Tail-less Ones leave nothing of themselves at all? Nothing you could point to and say, 'This was theirs'?" Sandra asked.

"Some ornaments and cloth, some of which still exist," the priest said dismissively. Then he glanced at Nakja-Mur before speaking again. "Other than that, only this."

He raised the pendant resting against his chest and held it forth. Matt, Sandra, and Bradford all leaned forward and peered at the tarnished brass disk. It was about the size and shape of a hockey puck, or a can of snuff. Reverently, the priest undid a clasp and raised the lid of the device.

"Is it not wondrous?" he asked.

Before them was a very old pocket compass. A tiny folding sundial lay retracted to one side, and beneath the crystallized, almost opaque glass, a small needle quivered and slowly swung to point dutifully in a northerly direction.

"My God," murmured Captain Reddy. The compass itself was a fascinating discovery, but what caught his attention, and took Sandra's breath, was the inscription under the lid.

Jas. S. McClain
Sailing Master
H.E I.C. Ship
HERMIONE

"My God," Matt said again.

"What's it mean? H.E.I.C.?" Sandra asked, almost a whisper.

"It means we were right, my dear," Courtney Bradford said. "We're not the first ones here. H.E.I.C. stands for the Honorable East India Company."

"As in the *British* East India Company?" she asked, astonished.

"So it would seem," Matt answered dryly. "I think we know now where the Grik got the design for their ships."

"You believe the Grik captured the ship that went west?"

"They must have. Indiamen at the time were built like warships, and the Grik ships we fought sure looked like seventeenth- or eighteenth-century warships—or Indiamen, I guess, come to think of it. I mentioned it at the time, and I also mentioned I didn't think it was a coincidence. Somehow I doubt the crew of that westbound Indiaman survived the technology exchange with the Grik. I wonder what happened to the other two?"

"But if they were British," interrupted Sandra, "why teach the Lemurians Latin?"

"They'd probably already figured out how messed up everything was, just like we did. According to Naga, they'd already run into the Grik too. They didn't want anybody knowing too much about them and, ultimately, where they went. But they had to communicate, just like us, and it probably seemed safe to teach the Lemurians a language no one knew. That would still leave them, or anyone else, unable to read their charts or get much information from the crew at large."

"That makes sense, I suppose," said Bradford, nodding. He glanced at Keje, who looked a little annoyed they were talking so long among themselves, but the other Lemurians just stared. "Thank God they didn't take cannon with them," he said fervently.

"That seems clear," Matt confirmed, "just like their Scrolls say. No weapons, or at least no extraordinary weapons, are mentioned to have been encountered since. I think it's safe to assume they must've removed the guns from the westbound ship. If they hadn't, the Grik would be using them and the Lemurians would damn sure know about them. Ask their old priest how long they've been fighting the Grik this round, and how long the Grik have been using this type of ship."

"The Grik have pushed us this time for only the last generation," Naga answered. "Until then, they were content to remain upon the land to the west. They'd still been mostly creatures of legend. But now they come again. It's just like the ancient times. The Grik come slowly at first, just a few at a time—but there are always more."

Keje spoke and Adar translated, since his English still wasn't up to the task. "During fight you help us, was first time we see such ships. Before, they look same, but ... smaller."

"It seems a stretch that their naval architecture hasn't changed in three hundred years, except to enlarge an existing design."

"The Grik are not innovators," Keje said savagely. "They only take. If they've taken nothing better since they learned the three-masted ships, they would see no reason to change. Now they know where we are, though, they will keep coming. We will fight, and we will kill them, but they will keep coming until we are all dead or forced to flee these waters just as we fled our Ancient Home."

So much for the "Malay pirate" model. They'd need another one. The "slow creep" that Naga described left too much to chance—like "when." They *must* get more information about the enemy. A familiar feeling crept into his chest. It was like the days after Pearl Harbor all over again, when he knew they stood almost alone, in the face of ... what? Something Big was all they knew, and they didn't know when or where. They'd been expendable then, an insignificant cog, and he was just following orders. He remembered how helpless and frustrated he felt that their fate was so arbitrarily sealed by unknown policies and strategic plans that seemed to make no sense. Now he was the one who had to make policies that might kill all his men—or save them. The crash transition from the tactical to the strategic left him overwhelmed. Sandra must have seen the inner desperation reflected on his face, because he again felt her reassuring hand on his arm. Finally, he looked at Keje.

"If they come, we'll help. I said that already. But we can help you now, better, before they come. Baalkpan's vulnerable, and no one seems ready to fight. If you prepare to fight now, you'll be better able when the time comes. Believe me"—he forced a half smile—"my people learned the hard way about being unprepared. Maybe this time it'll be different."

"I have not seen your amazing ship up close," said Nakja-Mur, "but Keje and Adar tell me of its wonders. Still, what can one ship do in the face of the Grik multitudes?" The word "multitudes" sounded bad, Matt thought with a sinking feeling.

"Not enough probably, by herself," he said flatly, "but a lot. The main thing *Walker* and her crew can do right now is help *you* prepare. And the first thing we need for that is fuel."

Walker swung at her anchor as the tide dragged her around until the busy, festive city of Baalkpan was off the port beam. It was totally dark and the lights cast an eerie, almost Oriental glow that reflected off the restless wave tops. Occasionally, sounds from shore reached Alan Letts as he leaned against the rail beside the number three gun. A party of men quietly worked on it, preparing to dismount it if they were allowed, so they could get at the balky traverse gear. Larry Dowden stopped by and spoke to Campeti, who supervised. ". . . in the morning . . ." was all Alan heard.

Screeching metal on metal and a string of obscenities came from the torpedo workshop. Letts was surprised to hear a hoarse Japanese shout respond to Sandison's tirade, followed by a crash of tools on the deck. When there was no further sound or cry of alarm, he chuckled. "That Jap's either going to make the best torpedoman Bernie has, or get fed to the fish." It still struck him strange having a Jap help with any sort of weapon, but Jap torpedoes worked just fine. Maybe Shinya knew something about them. He knew about machines; that was why Letts had suggested the appointment in the first place. If he had to work—and everybody did—that was as good a place as any. He stretched. It was nice to be on deck, breathing real air without the sun blasting the skin right off him. He scratched his forearm, rolling a ball of parched skin under his fingernails. *I'm starting to get just like the Mice*, he thought. *I can only come out after dark. God, I wish I was home.*

Off to the west, lightning rippled through dark clouds. *It'll probably rain*, he thought dejectedly, *and then I'll start to rot*. There'd been several days of uninterrupted sunshine—hot, as usual—but it normally rained once or twice a day. He didn't know which he hated worse, the hot sun that burned his skin or the hot, miserable rain that caused his skin and everything else to rot and mildew. All things considered, he'd *really* rather be in Idaho.

He lit a cigarette and let it dangle between his lips like he'd seen others do. It was an affectation he imagined they got from movies, but it looked cool, so he did it. Wouldn't be long before there weren't any smokes, he reflected. That wouldn't bother him as much as others. But some of the things they were running low on were important to their very survival, and he didn't have the slightest idea where to get more. He was the officer in charge of supply, but unless the lemur monkeys, or whatever they were, came through, there was no supply for supplies. He was a whiz at organizing and allocating and sending requisition forms through proper channels. In the past, if the stuff came, it came. But if it didn't, they always managed to make do or get by because there was always something to make do with. If the snipes needed a new feed-water pump, he would pick one up at the yard in Cavite or from one of the destroyer tenders like *Black Hawk*. If it was "the only one left" and they were saving it for *Peary* or *Stewart* because their supply officers did them a favor, then he could roll up his sleeves and swap and bid with the best. But when it came to getting something that wasn't there and never had been, and the only choice was to produce it themselves, he didn't have a clue what to do. He hoped the captain did.

He glanced to his left when someone leaned against the rail a few feet away. It was that nurse, the other one, with the auburn hair, the one that never said much. Karen something. Karen Theimer.

"Hi," he said. She glanced at him, but then looked back at shore. She put a cigarette to her lips and drew in a lungful.

"What do you think's going on?" She gestured at the city.

Alan shrugged. "Big Chief Powwow," he answered with a grin. "How should I know? I'm a meager lieutenant jay gee. Mine's not to reason why. I hope they come up with some supplies, though. Me being the supply officer, I always like to have supplies to be in charge of and, right now, there ain't much." She didn't grin or laugh, or say anything at all. She just took another puff. Standing so close, with the moon overhead and the flashes of lightning in the western sky, Alan was struck for the first time that she was really kind of cute. Of course, she and Lieutenant Tucker might be the only human females in the world—talk about a supply problem! He guessed it wouldn't be long before she started to look good if she had a face like a moose.

"I haven't been much help," she said matter-of-factly. "I've been having . . . a tough time adjusting to what's happened. I always led a sheltered life and thought becoming a Navy nurse would be a huge adventure." She looked at him for the first time, and her lips formed a small, desolate smile. "I guess I was right. I have to try harder, though. Lieutenant Tucker's right. If any of us are going to survive we're all going to have to pitch in, and in ways we might not expect. Everything's changed, and I have to figure out a different way of looking at things. Going across to the Lemurian ship scared me to death." She shuddered. "I mean, they're like . . . aliens from another planet! Like Martians. Add in all the carnage of the aftermath of battle and I guess I didn't handle it very well. But I did learn that being a Navy nurse doesn't mean just being a Navy nurse anymore. Do you know what I mean?" She suddenly pulled her hair. "God, why am I even telling you this? You're just some guy."

He looked at her and sighed, chagrined. "Yeah. I'm just 'some guy.' Maybe that's been *my* problem all along. I think I do know what you mean, and I'm ashamed of myself. I've been wallowing in my 'meager supply officer' status so long it never occurred to me that might mean something different now too. It took me longer than you to figure that out, though. Thanks."

She smiled at him, and this time he saw her dimples in the light of the city. "My name's Karen Theimer. What's yours, Lieutenant?"

CHAPTER
6

*L*ieutenant Benjamin Mallory and Lieutenant (j.g.) Perry Brister sat on chairs in Jim Ellis's cramped quarters on USS *Mahan* waiting for him to wake. Ellis's fever had finally broken the night before, and Pam Cross assured them he'd be fine—he just had to sleep it off. And so they waited, playing hand after hand of acey-deucey on the tiny table between them. Eventually, a groggy groan escaped the patient and he slowly came awake. His eyes seemed confused when he saw them, but he smacked his lips and croaked: "Thirsty."

In seconds the nurse appeared with a cup of water. "Here," she said in her brusque Brooklyn way. "Drink." Jim drank. When he spoke again, his voice was more normal.

"How long?" he asked simply.

"Almost two weeks since the fever hit. How much do you remember?" Brister asked.

"Not much," Jim admitted and tried to rise, but his expression contorted with pain and he settled back. "But I do remember that crazy bastard Kaufman shot me!"

It all came flooding back: the dinosaurs on Bali, the mysterious contact in the strait, the urgent signal for him to take *Mahan* east—which he did, but not for long. What was the point? There were *dinosaurs* on Bali! He didn't know what was going on, but there'd been no Japanese ships or planes since they came through the Squall, and he had a hunch there wouldn't be. He decided to turn around, to go back and rejoin *Walker*.

Kaufman argued with him, right there on the bridge. At first he remained reasonable, advocating that they continue to the rendezvous point off Alor. But when Jim gave the order to come about, Kaufman began to insist. He said Jim was risking all their lives and they'd die if they turned around. Jim ordered him off the bridge and that's when he just . . . lost it. He had a pistol and he took it out. Immediately, Jim and a couple of others jumped him and in the ensuing struggle, the gun went off. It probably wasn't even deliberate. Regardless, the bullet entered Jim's left leg, just below the knee, and exited the other side of his calf, right above the ankle. The men would have thrown Kaufman over the side right then, but he had the gun and time to talk. He said turning back was suicide; they'd done everything they could. The ship was a wreck and the men were exhausted. They deserved to live. Then Mr. Monroe, the only other officer besides Brister—in engineering at the time—took his side. He said they should listen to Kaufman, who was a captain, after all, and it was nuts to go back after all they'd been through. The crew began to go for it. They were angry about Jim being shot, but it wasn't like he was their captain or anything. He was just a strange officer who'd been put in charge. Kaufman only wanted to do what they'd been *told* to do, so that's how it was. Before Brister or Mallory even knew what happened, Captain Kaufman had the ship.

What he did next was inexplicable. Instead of heading for Alor, which had been his original purpose, he didn't make for Perth at all. He was convinced that there were carriers between them and Australia, so that left only Ceylon. They steamed east for the day, hugging the coast, and that night they shot the Lombok Strait. They'd still seen no sign of the enemy, but that made no difference to Kaufman. He'd become obsessed with reaching Ceylon and—Jim guessed—terrified of meeting *Walker*. He wasn't about to go anywhere the other ship might be. Jim was in the wardroom the entire time, undergoing treatment. Not under arrest, but more or less in exile. He kept up with events as best he could, mostly through Mallory and Brister. Much of the rest of the crew seemed hesitant to look him in the eye. There were exceptions, like Bosun's Mate Frankie Steele and Torpedoman Russ Chapelle, but not nearly enough to recapture the ship. Then, in spite of the best the surgeon and nurses could do, he lapsed into a fever. His last conscious recollection was they were nearing Tjilatjap, hoping to find some fuel. He cleared his throat.

"What happened at Tjilatjap?" His voice grew soft. "Was it even there?"

Brister and Mallory looked at each other, and finally Ben shook his head.

"No, sir. You don't remember any of that? We told you about it after we came aboard."

Jim just shook his head. "Pretend I wasn't there," he said, attempting to grin. "Start over. What did you find?"

"Nothing, sir. At least nothing that looked like Tjilatjap," said Brister. Like others who'd been there before, he pronounced it "Chilachap."

"What did you see?"

"Some strange, huge village—almost a city. I don't really know how to describe it. It was pretty big. Multistory structures, built on some kind of bamboo pilings. It was deserted, and most had been burned to the ground."

"Deserted?"

"Yes, sir. Well, sort of deserted. It wasn't abandoned willingly; it looked like there'd been a fight. Bones, sir. Bones everywhere, and a few mostly scavenged bodies off in the jungle. They were furry and had tails and . . . they weren't human."

"Sir," said Mallory stiffly, "there was nothing left alive out of a city of hundreds, easily, and it looked like whatever got them ate them. Not just scavengers either. Most of the bones were . . . piled up."

Pam Cross had left and reentered with a thermometer during the conversation. Her face was hard.

"Did you see it too?" Ellis asked.

"I did," she said simply and poked the device in his mouth.

Brister cleared his throat. "Well, sir, we got the hell out. Kaufman became even more unhinged. He insisted our only hope was Ceylon and had us pour it on. He wouldn't listen to reason. By then, almost everyone wanted to look for *Walker*, in spite of the consequences, but he said the next man who suggested it would be left in the whaleboat to look on his own." He wiped at the sweat beading his brow, and the nurse removed the thermometer from Jim's lips. She made a noncommittal sound. "Anyway, a storm kicked up and we shipped a lot of water. It wasn't much of a storm, but shot up like we are, we were lucky to survive. Things settled down by morning, but we had to pump out and make repairs, so we ducked into this little bay on Panaitan Island—"

"That's how we found the plane!" interrupted Mallory, a grin splitting his face.

"Plane?"

"Yes, sir. A PBY Catalina! If you can look out that porthole beside you, you might be able to see her!" Ellis struggled to rise, but he was very weak. Mallory immediately regretted the suggestion, but with a heavy sigh and rolling eyes, Nurse Cross helped him up. His head swam and his vision was blurred, but through the porthole, sure as the world, a familiar, battered seaplane was half beached on the island.

"You weren't kidding!" he exclaimed. "Where'd it come from?"

The two men shrugged. "Same place we did, I guess," said Mallory. "We steamed into the bay and there it was on the beach, its crew nowhere in sight. The place is crawling with lizards like bit your man on Menjangan . . ." He didn't need to speculate on the air crew's likely fate. "There were bullet holes all in it and it was full of water, but otherwise it seemed in pretty good shape—just out of gas. The radio's crapped out—we checked that right off. Salt water corroded all the connections was Signalman Palmer's guess. He's been working with us. Anyway, we figure the same thing happened to it that happened to us, and it made it as far as the Sunda Strait before it ran out of fuel."

"Maybe it was one of the PBYs that broke up the air attack on our ships when *Houston* took that bomb hit," speculated Jim. "Bravest thing I ever saw, three flying boats diving among fighters and bombers, trying to throw 'em off their aim." He shook his head. "Crazy."

"Could be," said Brister, "but that was a while before whatever happened to us . . . happened. Anyway, the good news is *Mahan* has high-octane gas in drums, aft, just like

Walker—ironically, in case they ever need to refuel a sea-plane. We put some in her and ran up the engines; no problem there, at least. The three of us've been working on her while everyone else works on the ship. My place is really here, I guess, but I don't think Kaufman trusts me."

"How long have we been here, and how long have you been working on it? Will it fly?" Everyone saw the hope kindle in his eyes.

"A week or so, and"—he lowered his voice—"another couple days'll have her in the air."

The general alarm sounded and they all jumped. "Battle stations, battle stations! Make all preparations for getting under way!" They looked at each other, perplexed by the commands. Suddenly Frankie Steele skidded to a stop outside the compartment.

"There're ships in the strait!"

"Ships?" demanded Jim.

"Aye, sir... Glad to see you better! But big sailing ships, like in the movies—only these are real—and they're headed this way!"

Jim looked at Brister and Mallory. "Go!" he said. "Save that plane! Don't let Kaufman leave it!" Without another word, the men charged out of the compartment. On the weather deck they met Ed Palmer, rushing down to meet them.

"Go!" said Brister. "Get what you can. Food, water, whatever you can think of, and meet us at the whaleboat!"

"What are you going to do?"

"Make a deal with the devil!" he snarled and mounted the steps to the bridge. Kaufman was staring at the distant ships through binoculars, and his hands were shaking. "Captain Kaufman! What about the plane? We can't just leave it here! Hell, we can have it flying by the end of the day! What are we running from?" Kaufman looked at him, and his bloodshot eyes were wide and glassy. He hadn't shaved or even combed his hair in days. There was nothing left of the cocky aviator Brister had first met when he came aboard off Menjangan. His face had the look of a hunted, panicked animal, and his condition had infected much of the crew.

"Here!" Kaufman said, handing him the binoculars. His

voice was shrill. In the distance, three red-hulled sailing ships struggled to beat up toward them. He focused a little more, and a chill swept down his back. "Those aren't people," he said lamely. They were monsters.

"Now you see why we have to go?" Kaufman insisted with manic sarcasm. "Hoist that boat aboard!"

"Wait," said Brister, licking his lips. "The current and wind are both against them. It'll be hours before they reach us. Let us try to finish the plane." He paused and tried a different tack. "If we do, we'll fly to Ceylon. Get help! Maybe they'll send an escort." That got through.

"Will you stake your life you can take off before they get here?"

Brister nodded.

"Good, because we won't wait. Mr. Monroe!" he said, raising his voice. "Take Mr. Brister and his assistants ashore, then return as quick as you can!"

"You won't even leave us a boat?" Brister asked, incredulous.

"No. You can go ashore, destroy the plane, and come back with Mr. Monroe, or you can try to fly it out. The choice is yours."

Perry shook his head. "Captain Kaufman, you are a coward, sir."

Without another word, he turned and dashed down the ladder. On the way to shore, he told the others what had happened.

"The hell with him. I'd rather take my chances with the plane," Mallory exclaimed. Palmer said nothing, but his face was grim.

"You didn't see what I saw," Brister said. "I think our visitors are the same ones that wiped out . . . whatever they were at Chilachap. It's either fly or die."

The coxswain with Monroe giggled.

They reached the shore and tossed their gear on the beach beside the plane. "At least give us a hand bailing!" shouted Perry as the whaleboat pulled away.

"*Mahan*'s already pullin' the hook!" shouted Monroe. "I'm not going to be left behind." He threw a mocking salute. "It's your funeral!"

"Bastard!" Palmer was seething.

They turned to look at the plane. Brister hoped he could make good on his vow. He didn't know what was coming, but that one look had scared the hell out of him. "Well, what are we waiting for?"

They dove into their task with frantic abandon. They were too busy even to notice when *Mahan* steamed away, but when they did pause for a quick look, it seemed that one of the strange ships was trying to follow her. It was no use, of course, and it quickly turned back toward the bay. They'd seen the Catalina, and either the tide was making or the wind shifted just enough, because they were getting closer.

"Bail, damn it!" Brister yelled, and buckets of water flew from the observation blisters. The tide *was* making, because suddenly they were floating, but they were still too heavy to fly. Mallory leaned on his bucket, gasping, and watched the closing ships.

"No way," he said. "We have to get off this beach before they box us in."

"She's still too heavy!"

"Yeah, but not too heavy to move." He scrambled up to the flight deck. "Palmer, throw off the mooring line!"

Ed hesitated. "But the fish might get me!"

"Those things'll get us all if you don't! You can reach it through the nose turret! Can you operate the gun?" A .30-caliber machine gun was enclosed in a Plexiglas turret in the nose of the plane.

"Yeah . . ." he said, a little uncertainly, but he dodged his way forward. The plane was floating almost freely now. A few nerve-racking moments passed.

"Got it!" came Palmer's muffled shout, and the nose immediately swung away from the beach.

"C'mon, babies!" Mallory said, and then whooped when both engines coughed to life. With throttles and rudder, he pointed the nose at the bay. The ships were much closer, and now he could see the creatures upon them with unaided eyes. "Oh, boy!" he shouted. "Here they come! I'm gonna try to motor around them, so keep bailing till I tell you, but be ready to get on a gun as quick as you can!" There was also a .50-caliber machine gun in each observation blister, but that was the extent of the PBY's armaments.

"Jeez, they're scary-lookin'," breathed Palmer, glancing forward.

"Yeah," panted Brister. "Bail!" Mallory advanced the throttles, and the big plane began to move.

"They're almost making a lane for us, like they want at us from both sides!" he shouted. "I'll make for it. Be ready on those fifties, in case they try to close the gap!"

Closer and closer the roaring engines took them. Soon they edged between the two ships, and the details they beheld were nightmarish.

"Shit!" Palmer screamed when something "thunked" into the thick aluminum beside him. It was an arrow! As quick as that, the plane drummed with impacts. "Shit!" he repeated. "They're shootin' at us!"

"Let 'em have it!" Brister yelled, and they opened fire on both of the terrible ships. Clouds of splinters flew where the tracers pointed, and bodies fell from the rails. A keening shriek reached them even over the guns, the engines, and the clattering, heavy brass cases that fell around them. "Pour it in!" he shouted as the incoming barrage began to slack off. A big greasy ball of flame erupted right behind the starboard wing and actually singed his hair. "What the *hell* was that? Step on it, Ben!"

Mallory needed no encouragement. He'd watched the "bomb" all the way in. He pushed the throttles to their stops. Sluggishly, the waterlogged plane picked up speed. The roar of the engines and hammering guns made it too loud to think. Another explosion washed the sea, but it missed them safely aft. The faster target must have spoiled their aim. Then, as quickly as the battle had begun, they sped clear of the monsters' ships and Brister shouted to hold their fire. The other ship was closing still, but at their current heading, it would never reach them in time to cut them off. Water from the massive wake they made splashed in through the blisters and hissed on the barrels of the superheated guns.

Brister turned to Palmer, eyes wide. "Wow!"

There was still a lot of water in the plane, but they plowed upwind as far as they could before they powered down. Mallory left the motors idling, props feathered, and helped them bail some more.

"Talk about your floating freak shows!" he gasped, throwing water past the gun. "Damn plane looks like a pincushion! Goddamn *arrows*!"

"Just be glad they weren't muskets or cannons," said Brister. "We wouldn't have had a chance! Arrows and firebombs were bad enough!"

"I'll say! What now?" Palmer asked.

"Keep bailing," Ben replied. "A few hundred more pounds and we'll get her in the air. Then we can dump what's left." He grinned. "Once we do that, start looking for holes!"

Less than an hour later, the battered seaplane clawed into the air and followed after *Mahan*. Mallory didn't know if the monsters saw them or not, now they were stuck in the bay. If they did, he wondered what they thought. The plane quickly overtook *Mahan* and landed at her side. Brister seethed with rage at the man who'd left them to their fate, but to his surprise Kaufman met them himself in the whaleboat with smiles and waves.

"Keep hold of yourself," Mallory said. "Remember, we're going to fly to Ceylon and save the day. Stick to the plan!" Brister simmered down, but all he wanted to do was kill the Army captain with his bare hands.

"Let's just shoot him with the thirty in the nose," Palmer said through a clenched-teeth grin.

"Won't work. Like Mr. Ellis said before he got sick, he's got too many on his side. Even if we got him, there might be a bloodbath. Some of 'em are crazy as he is, and they have all the guns."

"Okay," said Mallory, adjusting the throttles so he wouldn't smack the boat as it came alongside. "I'll stay with the plane—I have to. Get all the fuel and anything else you can think of. Maps, more food, whatever. Maybe even more people, but don't be too obvious. We know he won't let Mr. Ellis come."

"Right." Together, Perry and Ed jumped in the whaleboat.

"You really did it!" Kaufman gushed. "Did you have much trouble?"

"No," lied Brister cheerfully. "Piece of cake. Let's hurry up and get the fuel on board. The quicker we're back in the air, the quicker we'll be in Ceylon!"

Kaufman refused to allow anyone to accompany them. Three was enough, he said, to risk on such a dangerous flight. Perry did manage to slip away to "get some gear," and he went to see Jim Ellis before he left the ship. Jim was trying to climb the companionway stairs when he found him, supported by crutches and Pam Cross and Kathy McCoy. Beth Grizzel wasn't there.

"You made it," he said. "Thank God."

"Yes, sir. Thank God. No thanks to that bastard Kaufman. He left us to die."

"I know. Listen, you *must* find *Walker*! Kaufman's nuts; half the crew's nuts. It's just a matter of time before he kills us all. You know as well as I do, Ceylon's not there. There's no telling what is. Find *Walker*, find Captain Reddy . . ." He gasped from the effort of his words and exertions.

"We will."

"Tell him I'm sorry I failed him. I'm sorry I let the men down."

"It's not your fault, sir!"

"Isn't it?" Jim sighed. "Maybe not, but it's my responsibility."

"He shot you!"

Jim laughed bitterly. "A good commander would have shot him first! Now get your ass out of here before Kaufman starts nosing around!"

Perry looked at the two nurses. He hated to leave them behind, but Kaufman wouldn't part with them. The surgeon was acting funny, and the nurses were it. There were still a lot of wounded on the ship. Besides, their errand might be doomed from the start. They had only so much fuel and they had no idea where *Walker* was.

"Aye, aye, sir," Perry Brister said, and shook Jim Ellis's hand. Pam stepped quickly forward and planted a kiss lightly on his cheek.

"For luck!" she said, then punched his shoulder. Hard. "Tell Lieutenant Tucker we're keeping the faith." She glanced at Kathy and grimaced. "Two out of three anyway. Beth's as crazy as Kaufman." She shrugged and kissed him again, on the mouth this time. "Double luck! Now git out'a heah!" Blushing, Perry saluted Lieutenant Ellis and raced for the boat.

Later, when they thundered into the darkening sky and circled the lonely, misguided ship for the last time, Brister thought he caught a glimpse of Lieutenant Ellis leaning on his crutches by the rail, a small group gathered around him.

The two and a half weeks since *Walker*'s arrival had been a whirlwind of frantic activity. Despite acknowledging the danger they faced, Matt suspected the 'Cats weren't quite prepared for the pace the destroyermen set. The trauma of getting their economy and society on a war footing was causing a stir, but Matt and his crew knew what had happened at Pearl Harbor and Clark Field. They'd *seen* what happened at Cavite. They'd learned a hard lesson in preparedness, and as long as their fortunes were tied to those of their new friends, they wouldn't let them waste time they might later regret. *Big Sal*'s crew was equally motivated, and repairs to the big ship moved apace. The very day after the "party," *Walker* was moved to the pier and as extensive an overhaul as possible began. The number three gun was repaired, and all the circuits coordinating the main battery were checked and spliced. Steaming on only the number four boiler to maintain electrical power, they checked the other boilers and repaired firebrick. There was nothing to be done for number one so it was stripped and prepared for disassembly and removal. Spanky wanted the space for more fuel bunkerage—once they got fuel.

The Baalkpan Lemurians were just as amazed as *Big Sal*'s that *Walker* was made of steel. Whenever the welders went to work, the pier lined with spectators watching the sparks and eye-burning torches with as much enthusiasm as if it had been a fireworks display. Iron wasn't unknown to the People, but it was so hard to smelt that it was little used. Dave Elden had spent two years in a steel mill in Pittsburgh. He'd already talked to the proprietors of the foundry on the northeast of town, where he'd gone to have brass fittings cast. He reported they used the sand-cast method almost exclusively but were very good at it and there would be almost nothing they couldn't cast with a larger furnace and a little guidance. He even figured he could get them started on iron if a source for ore could be found.

Half the snipes set out into the jungle with Courtney Bradford and about a hundred natives in search of oil. The procession had looked like a nineteenth-century safari. They hadn't searched long before they found a likely place. Bradford's charts and journals were helpful, and he had most of the Dutch surveys. As long as everything was the same geographically, there was every reason to believe that oil could be found in the same places it had been back "home." He hadn't yet shared his theory, but they'd all been very busy. Matt already suspected what the gist of it was and looked forward to the discussion, but for now there was too much to do.

Materials were rafted upriver to the site, where, under the direction of the Mice, the men were constructing something called a Fort Worth Spudder. Captain Reddy had heard of the device but never seen one. His interview with the strange firemen was ... an experience. He'd seen them many times, of course, but he didn't remember ever speaking with them. Their conversation about the rig was what he imagined it would be like to talk to an opossum with a parrot on its shoulder. But they convinced him they knew what to do and how to do it. He just hoped they could explain it to others in a coherent fashion.

At the same time, men worked hard converting the tubes of the number three torpedo mount into a condensation tower. A place was being prepared near the drill site for their little refinery. A fueling pier with water deep enough for *Walker* to clear the silty riverbed was already under construction. The torpedo tubes were just a temporary expedient. Eventually they would build larger towers with greater capacity. But for now the empty tubes would have to do.

Lemurians scampered all over the ship, helping as best they could. Often they got in the way, but shorthanded as the crew was, the benefit of their curious, good-natured assistance outweighed the aggravation. Chack became like a Lemurian bosun's mate, and his coordination of the native labor was indispensable.

One morning, a large cart pulled by a "brontosarry" and driven by Alan Letts arrived, much to the delight of those aboard. The sight of the fair-skinned supply officer sitting on a seat under a colorful parasol—behind a dinosaur's rump—even brought a smile to the Chief's face. The crew's amusement quickly waned when they discovered what the cart was so heavily laden with. Somewhere the suddenly surprisingly resourceful supply officer had discovered keg after keg of white paint. Gray was guardedly ecstatic. He insisted on testing it, since nobody knew what was in it, or whether it would stick to steel. He wasn't about to let them smear a "bunch of whitewash" all over his topsides. When it proved satisfactory, he immediately began pestering Letts to find something they could mix it with to make a proper gray.

"Hell, Bosun," Letts replied, "this bucket's spent more of her life white than gray. It's not like we're hiding from airplanes anymore."

"Yah, but there's a war on, Mr. Letts. White's for peacetime."

The torpedo repairs were put aside. They still had the three that hadn't fired during their escape from Surabaya, but the others would have to wait. Under the supervision of Chief Donaghey and Bernard Sandison—who'd become quite a machinist in his own right—the machine shop was constantly in use making parts for the ship. They had little scrap steel, though, and wherever it would serve, they used copper or brass—both of which were readily available from local sources. Shinya had been reassigned as Alden's assistant—training the militia—but he still liked to help in the shop when he could.

It was in this maelstrom of apparent chaos, of flying sparks and paint chips, a fog of red rust dust, mazes of hoses and wires and a dozen different projects all over the ship, that they had their first visit by the High Chief of Baalkpan, Nakja-Mur.

Matt had seen him many times since their first meeting, and someone, usually Garrett or Dowden, went ashore to talk with him every day. But until now, the closest Nakja-Mur had come to *Walker* was to pace her length on the pier alongside, the morning after she tied up. He was fascinated by the ship, and Keje said he never tired of hearing about *Walker*'s role in the battle, but he'd never made an "official" visit and many were curious why. Now, with no warning whatsoever—a shocking impropriety among the People—the crowd of watchers and helpers on the dock parted and Nakja-Mur appeared at the gangway.

Keje and Adar, Naga, and a dozen guardsmen accompanied him. Despite the wonder that nearly forced a grin when he gained the deck, and the pleased curiosity he displayed when piped aboard by Gray's hastily assembled side party, Nakja-Mur wasn't happy.

"You are breaking me!" he growled when the captain met him with a salute. Matt blinked questioningly like Chack had taught him to do.

"Breaking you, my lord? I thought here, just as on the great sea Homes, the High Chief was the steward of the people's surplus—to be spent for the safety and benefit of all." Chack had quickly trotted up to join them and he translated the captain's words. Keje and Adar's subtle blinks of amusement indicated they no longer needed Chack's help.

"Of course you're breaking me! It's my duty to be a good steward, as you say, but it's also my duty to see the surplus wisely spent!" He looked about, speechless, and seized upon the sight of the paint kegs lining the pier. "There, do you see? Do you realize that's half a season's production of paint base? Do you have any idea what that costs?"

Matt shook his head. "You agreed that *Walker* should have anything Baalkpan could offer in the way of provisions and supplies if we would help you prepare for the Grik."

"Yes, but . . . paint?!" Adar leaned over and spoke into his ear. "Yes, of course I know iron rusts, but . . ." He stopped, and looking around again, he shook his head. "I apologize. They said your ship was iron, but I only now truly realized it. But, come, what difference does a little rust make?"

"My Brother," interrupted Keje, "once rust takes hold of iron it is not easily discouraged. That's one reason it's rarely used at sea. By us, at any rate."

"Well, but what of the scores of workers toiling northeast of the city, pounding a hole into the earth! What's the meaning of that?"

"Fuel, my lord. As we discussed. *Walker* must have . . . I believe you call it 'gish,' for fuel. Without it she can't move. She can't fight."

"But gish is plentiful in the north, in the coastal marshes. It bubbles from the ground, it pools, it reeks! It's of little use to any but seam sealers and makers of rope. New holes need not be made to take it up!"

"I'm afraid so. *Walker* needs more gish than can easily be imagined, and there must be a ready source close by."

"The People use wind to good effect," Nakja-Mur grumped.

"No doubt. So do the Grik. But *Walker*'s much faster than either—that's one reason she fights so well. To do that she needs gish, and lots of it. I told you all this," Matt said with some frustration.

"He doesn't know, my friend. He hasn't seen," soothed Keje. "He looks out for his people." He grinned. "And your ship is costing far more than the Grik yet have."

"He can pay now, with treasure, or later with blood," Matt snapped.

"He knows. He just doesn't like it. Believe me, on the whole, he's pleased. He's had many complaints, however, not least about the training your Marine person started. These land folk don't have strong bodies and are not used to the exertion required of warriors."

"Sergeant Alden knows the best warrior skills of our people, at least as far as land tactics are concerned. Lieutenant Shinya knows swordsmanship, and his methods are quicker and more lethal than yours." Gray suppressed a snort. He still thought Shinya belonged in the chain locker.

"True, but since Nakja-Mur decreed that all should learn rudimentary warrior skills, some ask why they must learn to fight when their treasure is paying you to do it for them."

Matt shook his head. "That wasn't the deal. I said we'd train them and help them fight. We won't fight the Grik alone."

"He knows."

Nakja-Mur spoke and Chack translated once again. "Two flasher-fishers arrived this morning with news of three Grik ships, nosing about in the strait. They didn't believe they were seen, but the Grik have never been so close. We're not ready to fight and I fear we will never be. All these preparations you make—the paint!—do not seem to make us more ready to fight!"

"We'll fight them first, if we must, until your people are ready. That was the plan from the start. But to fight, my ship must be ready!"

Off in the distance, they heard the low rumble of thunder.

"What will you do about the Grik in the strait?"

"If they enter the bay, we'll destroy them. If they linger nearby until we have fuel, we'll hunt them down and destroy them. You have my word. But you must talk sense to these complainers!"

Nakja-Mur looked steadily at him for a moment, then jerked his head downward in a Lemurian nod. The distant thunder continued to build, but it was drowned out by the number four boiler blowing tubes. They all looked aft and skyward as the soot settled on the deck and those working there.

"God*damn* snipes!" bellowed Gray, striding purposefully toward the aft fireroom hatch. "There's wet paint up here!" Captain Reddy stifled a grin. The thunderous drone rose a little higher in his consciousness.

"Maybe the High Chief of Baalkpan would like to tour the ship?" he said, but tilted his head, listening. With a start, his eyes widened in recognition and he glanced at the crow's nest. Empty, of course. Garrett was on the fire-control platform, however, and he'd heard it too. Their eyes met as realization dawned. The general alarm began to sound.

"General quarters! General quarters! This is no drill!" came Larry Dowden's voice over the speaker. "Captain to the bridge!"

Matt darted from the midst of the Lemurian delegation, ran through the chaos of the weather deck, and clattered up the ladder to the bridge. With no one to tell them different, the Lemurians followed after him. Men and 'Cats scampered everywhere, some purposefully, others less so, and Nakja-Mur was nearly sent sprawling by an ordnance striker carrying ammunition belts as he rocketed up from the companionway.

"What's happening?!" he angrily demanded.

"Something interesting, certainly," Adar replied.

Matt was gasping by the time he reached the fire-control

platform. He snatched the binoculars someone offered and began scanning the sky.

"There, sir. Aft, bearing one two oh! Coming right up the bay from the strait! It's ... it's an aircraft!"

"Agreed!" Matt snapped. "But what's it doing here and whose is it? Stand by all machine guns, Mr. Garrett, but hold your fire!"

They waited tensely, the men exchanging nervous glances while the clattery radial engine drone slowly grew more pronounced. Chack and Keje had joined them.

"What is that flying thing?" Keje's voice held an edge.

"Airplane," Matt murmured absently.

Keje glanced at the defensive preparations under way. "And I thought the Grik were a strange menace," he muttered. "You will fight this aar-plane? It will attack?" Keje cast a quick glance at *Big Sal*, moored helplessly to the pier. He'd never heard of a flying creature large enough to threaten people, but he'd seen coast raptors snatch fish from the water, and he suspected how vulnerable they would be to something as big as what he saw now. Obviously, by their actions, the destroyermen believed it might be dangerous. "Will it attack?" he asked again, more insistently.

Matt lowered the binoculars and a small, wondering smile played across his features. "I don't think so," he said, and added as an aside to Lieutenant Garrett, "PBY."

The plane grew larger, and the sun glinted dully off the dingy blue paint as it banked over the bay. The wings waggled a little, as if the pilot was unfamiliar with the controls—or maybe not. Only one engine was running. The big seaplane thundered low over the water, just a little higher than the small boats' masts. Sheets went flying, and there were many near-collisions as the unearthly monstrosity lumbered by. Matt couldn't help but grin at the startled antics of the fishermen. All the Lemurians on the pier or the destroyer stopped what they were doing and clustered uncertainly together.

The pilot plainly saw them now; he banked the plane harder and then steadied up, aiming for a clear patch of water off *Walker*'s starboard side. The big rudder kicked rapidly back and forth to compensate for the uneven thrust of the single engine. Wing-tip floats came down and the bull-nose with the Plexiglas turret seemed to sniff tentatively at the water. The blue roundels with the white star and red dot stood out against the salt streaks and the stained, off-color paint. It was the most beautiful thing Matt had ever seen. With a great splashing *thump,* the flying boat struck the water, and its forward progress was almost immediately arrested by the unskilled or underpowered arrival. It wallowed to a stop as the pilot cut power, then increased it. The noise of the port engine was tremendous as the plane gathered speed in their direction.

Nakja-Mur had joined them. "What is that dreadful thing?" he demanded in a shrill voice.

"I suspect it's a friend of ours," Matt replied when Chack translated. The pilot cut the engine about fifty yards away, and the noise abruptly lessened as the propeller wound down. Matt felt the relief around him. "Prepare to fend off!" he shouted as the plane drifted closer. "Launch the whaleboat!" In less than a minute, the boat slid down the falls and slapped into the water. As they watched, a windscreen on the side of the pitching aircraft's cockpit slid back and a grinning, bearded face emerged.

"Another Amer-i-caan!" Nakja-Mur exclaimed. "One that flies! *Flies!*" He was silent for a moment of sheer amazement, then turned to Matt and grinned. "I suppose I will have to feed that thing as well?"

"How many more . . . unusual friends are you expecting, Cap-i-taan Reddy?" Keje quietly asked. *Big Sal*'s "captain" was staring at the PBY with open wonder, but it was a serious question.

"I wasn't expecting this one. C'mon, let's meet our mystery aviator."

Lieutenant Benjamin Mallory's entire lower body felt numb and tingly from the long hours in the thinly padded metal seat of the shuddering aircraft. He had difficulty with his feet on the rungs as he ascended to the deck. He couldn't stop grinning, though. An hour before, he'd shut down the starboard engine and feathered its prop to stretch their fuel enough to reach this very bay. It was their final hope. They'd checked Menjangan, and pushed all the way to Alor before turning back. If *Walker* hadn't been at Balikpapan, he, Perry, and Ed would have been doomed, at best, to a lingering, miserable existence of solitude and privation without hope of rescue. More likely, some unfamiliar denizen would have quickly saved them the trouble. The sight of the old four-stacker nestled snugly against the pier amid the bustle of native people and shipping brought tears to Mallory's eyes. The smoke curling lazily from her aft funnel and the proud flag over her deck convinced him that, whatever the situation, *Walker* was here voluntarily and therefore they were safe.

He made it to the deck with the help of eager hands and threw a shaky salute at the flag, and another at Captain Reddy. He was startled by the sight of the ... natives, but not like he would have been a few weeks before.

"Lieutenant Benjamin Mallory, United States Army Air Corps. I request permission to come aboard, sir." He took a wobbly step to make room for those behind him as they also gained the deck.

"Ed Palmer, Signalman, glad to be back aboard, sir," said the second man, his voice hoarse with emotion. The blond-headed signalman from Oklahoma had expected to remain on *Mahan* only until they reached Perth. His inclusion in the unlucky destroyer's odyssey had taken a toll.

The third was a dark-haired man in ragged khakis who looked vaguely familiar. "Lieutenant jay-gee Perry Brister, request perm—"

"Brister! You're engineering officer on *Mahan*—you all came from *Mahan*! Where is she?" Matt demanded.

"We don't know, sir," Mallory replied. "The last we saw, she was off the west coast of Sumatra."

"Sumatra? My God. What was Jim Ellis thinking?"

All three men shook their heads together. "Not Mr. Ellis, sir," Brister said.

"Right," confirmed Mallory. The aviator's grin was gone. "Captain Reddy, it's a long story and you need to hear it now." He gestured at himself and the others. "Could we have some cold water? Or ... maybe even a Coke?"

"Certainly. Let's carry this conversation to the wardroom and you can tell me all about it after some refreshment." He turned to Dowden as the exec approached. "Is

Mr. McFarlane back aboard? No? Then pass the word for Mr. Bradford—he returned from the well site this morning, did he not?" Dowden nodded. "Very well. Ask him, Mr. Letts, Mr. Tolsen, and Mr. Garrett to join us in the wardroom. Better ask Lieutenant Tucker and Lieutenant Shinya as well."

"Sir, Lieutenant Shinya and Sergeant Alden are drilling the militia."

Matt nodded. "Of course." He glanced at the Lemurians. He'd practically forgotten they were there. For a moment he contemplated excusing himself, but realized that if he did, they might suspect he was keeping secrets. That might not be best. They knew something important was going on; after all, it wasn't every day a PBY flew into Baalkpan and landed in the bay. "Our guests may accompany us, if they please, but space in the wardroom's limited. They'll have to leave their escorts behind." He spoke to Dowden, but his words were for Keje. They implied that this needed to remain an upper-level meeting. Keje understood, and spoke to Nakja-Mur.

Carafes of iced tea were on the wardroom table when they filed in. Like Keje and Adar had been, Nakja-Mur and Naga were unfamiliar with human chairs, but watching Keje's more experienced motions, they managed to make themselves relatively comfortable. Of more interest to them was the egalitarian way the Americans gathered around the same table and drank from the same carafes. Lemurians prided themselves on their social tolerance, and they knew the Americans operated within a system of strict official stratification. For the first time, Nakja-Mur and Naga saw that the American hierarchy had more to do with tradition and institutional discipline than with a concept that anyone, even their captain, was intrinsically superior. Somehow, in spite of their surprise, they were strangely comforted.

They sat for a long moment, drinking, while an oscillating fan stirred the tepid air. The Lemurians drained their tea with relish and then waited patiently while the haggard newcomers rehydrated themselves. Finally, Mallory wiped his mouth and cleared his throat.

"My God, sir, that was welcome. We only carried a little

water, to save on weight. Enough to last a few more days, but ... Anyway, thanks, sir. Your ship was a sight for sore eyes!"

"Thank you, Lieutenant. Seeing that plane was pretty exciting for us. But what about *Mahan*? Where the hell is she and what happened?"

The three men glanced at each other, then haltingly, together, told how Kaufman took over the ship. Matt and the other humans listened in stunned amazement. They just couldn't believe it. Not only was it blatant mutiny, but under the circumstances it was insane. Brister told how Jim tried to take Kaufman's gun away, and he saw the rage on Matt's face when he told him Jim had been shot.

"He didn't kill him, sir," he hastened to add. "In fact, I think it was more an accident than anything." He almost smiled. "I heard Mr. Ellis was beating the shit out of him, if you'll pardon the expression. But Kaufman did shoot him. In the leg." There was a pause while the lieutenant's words sank in around the table.

"Go on," Matt ordered harshly.

They told how the mutiny had proceeded, and of Kaufman's obsession with Ceylon. Jim Ellis lapsed into fever and they put into Tjilatjap for fuel—only Tjilatjap wasn't there, and they told of the horrors they saw.

Keje stiffened in his seat. "Chill-chaap? This Amer-i-caan speaks of Chill-chaap?" Larry Dowden had excused himself, and now he hurried back in with a chart that showed South Java and the waters nearby. Nakja-Mur and the Sky Priest fairly bristled at the way he spread the chart across the table, condensation rings and all, but Keje and Adar had prepared them somewhat, so they didn't cry out in protest. Brister was looking at Keje when he put his finger on the South Java port of Tjilatjap. "Here, sir," he said.

"Gone," muttered Keje. "Chill-chaap is gone." He spoke to the other Lemurians in his own tongue. Nakja-Mur rose to his feet and shouted something at Keje, then continued shouting at everyone in the compartment. "He is ... excited," explained Keje in a subdued tone, barely audible over Nakja-Mur's rant.

"Well, tell ... ask him to control himself! We must hear what else these men have to say!"

"I will try, Cap-i-taan. But forgive him . . . us. Chill-chaap is nearly as large as Baalkpan. It was one of the oldest colonies, and the only one on Jaa-va that remained friendly to us. Many thousands of people—our people—lived there." Keje turned to Nakja-Mur and spoke in soothing tones. Slowly, the High Chief of Baalkpan eased into his seat. But his rage had only been contained, not extinguished. A moody, uncomfortable silence filled the compartment, and the quiet, after Nakja-Mur's outburst, was particularly profound.

"Lieutenant Brister," Matt prompted.

"Sir," continued Brister after a last look at their guests. "Tjilatchap, or Chill-chaap, is gone. Nothing left alive. And it looked like the people there were eaten, and not just by scavengers."

"My God," gasped Sandra.

"Yes," Keje growled. "Did I not tell you? We are mere prey to them." He looked at the nurse. "You asked once why we threw them into the sea." He shook his head.

Brister cleared his throat and resumed his tale. With Mallory's help he brought them through the storm and the discovery of the plane. Then he spoke of the monsters.

"Grik," Keje snarled.

"How many ships?" Matt asked.

"Three, sir."

Matt looked at Keje. "They can't have been the same ones we tangled with. It was at least two weeks later and hundreds of miles apart!" He turned back to Mallory. "What happened then?"

Ben described the hair-raising effort to get the plane off the beach. Between the three of them again, they told how they ultimately fought clear of the "monsters" and finally flew back to *Mahan*.

"They just left you?" Bradford asked incredulously. "Without a boat?"

"Yeah. Even if we'd changed our minds, it wouldn't have done any good. We had plenty of motivation. Those creatures—I've never seen anything like 'em, sir. They were . . . pretty scary."

Matt nodded. "We've seen them too, and they *are* pretty scary. I congratulate you all on your escape."

"Thank you, sir," they chorused.

"Did the lizards see you fly?"

"Maybe," answered Mallory. "We could still see them when we took off. Why?"

Matt smiled at him. "Nothing, Lieutenant. Don't worry about it. It might've been a handy surprise for later, that's all."

Mallory looked at his hands. "Sorry, Captain. I didn't think of that. Not till later. We saw half a dozen more of their ships while we were looking for you, but we were pretty high and far. If they heard us, I doubt they saw us."

"My God," murmured Bradford. "As many as nine ships, then. Perhaps a dozen, if the ones seen in the strait are still others." He looked at Keje, who seemed stricken. "Your enemy *is* here at last, and in force. We've not a moment to lose!"

Matt held up his hand. "I'm afraid we must lose a few more moments, Mr. Bradford. Lieutenant Mallory? What happened next?"

"Kaufman wanted us to fly to Ceylon, and we didn't say squat, but 'Yes, sir, will do.' We took on all the fuel we could and then came looking for you."

"I saw Mr. Ellis before we left," Brister said. "The nurses were all fine and were taking good care of him." He looked at Sandra. "Nurse Cross said they were keeping the faith. We talked a couple of minutes, and Mr. Ellis said . . ." He turned to Matt. "He said to tell you he's sorry—but, Captain, it wasn't his fault!" Perry's gaze was emphatic. "Anyway, they probably all know we went looking for you by now. At least the ones that aren't crazy will have some hope."

Keje cleared his throat. "Excuse me," he said. "These flying men bring momentous news. We learn Chill-chaap has been sacked and the Grik are indeed rampant, worse than we'd even feared. The dark time we've dreaded seems at hand. Now is when we will learn if all we've worked for, for generations—our colonies, our culture, our very way of life—will survive, or be cast to the winds once more. This . . . is important to us." The irony of his understatement wasn't lost. "I would think it would be important to you, our allies, as well. Yet you seem more concerned with this ship, this *Mahan*. What is *Mahan*, and what, or where, is Say-lon?"

Matt took off his hat in the awkward silence. He wiped sweat from his forehead with a handkerchief and slicked back his greasy hair. "Forgive me, my friend. I am concerned, and this news means our preparations are even more urgent. The significance of *Mahan,* however, is this." He looked around at all of them, but rested his gaze on Keje and Nakja-Mur. "*Mahan* and *Walker* are the same. They're just alike, and she has the same capabilities we have. What's more, her people are my people, and I'm responsible for them. I'm obligated to help them any way I can, just as I'm obligated, now, to help your people to the best of my ability. The reason *Mahan* should concern you, however, besides—like you said, we're allies—is there's another ship just like this one, apparently steaming as fast as she can directly toward the Grik. What if they take her? You say they're mimics; they copy the works of others. How long to copy *Mahan*? A while, surely. Maybe a generation or two. But what of the meantime? How will they use her? At the very least, they might figure out ways to counteract our superiority." He stopped and looked around. "We've got to get her back." He paused. "Or destroy her."

Nakja-Mur rose to his feet and, after regarding them all with a steady gaze, he began to speak. Keje translated as he did so. "You Amer-i-caans, you know us now. You may not know us well, but we've kept no secrets from you and our desperation is clear. Yet we know almost nothing about you. At long last, tell us where you come from. If you have two smoking ships, why not summon more? The flying boat outside is clearly made of metal, and yet it floats! It flies! With but three Amer-i-caans on board, it is a match for three Grik ships! We've never seen such wonders! Surely you can do anything! You can save us from the Grik! Please, summon more of your people. Together, we could destroy the Grik menace completely, and our two peoples could live in peace for all time!"

Matt looked at Nakja-Mur when Keje completed the translation. Conflicting emotions swirled through him, but he knew, in spite of his desire to pass as little information as he could—the same desire he suspected the first "Tail-less Ones" had—the Lemurians who'd taken them in and now depended on them so heavily had a right to know. He glanced at Sandra and caught a nod of encouragement.

"We can't send for help," he said, "because there's no one to send to." He looked at Sandra and smiled resignedly. Then he held the gaze of each American for a moment before returning his attention to the Lemurians. "Remember how the first Tail-less Ones said their home was gone? Ours is too. Whether that makes us like them or not, I'll leave up to you to decide. But I think it's time you heard a story about a war that was bigger than anything you can possibly imagine. A war so big, the entire world was engulfed in fire and millions had already died . . . and it was only starting. This ship that seems so impressive and full of wonders to you was only the smallest, most insignificant part of that war, in the grand scheme of things." He took a deep breath. "And it was a war we were losing. Then something happened and somehow, we were . . . here."

Keje managed an expression of confusion. "But you've told us you come from near the Edge of the World, from a land so distant we've no . . . ah, charts that show its position."

"That's true. We do. But the war we fought—the part we were fighting, that is—was here. Right here."

There was no sound but the voices on deck and the paint chippers plying their tools on a scaffold rigged alongside.

Courtney Bradford leaned forward in his chair. "My dear friends, Mi-Anakka and Americans, there's no question we all spring from the same world. There's no other explanation." He laid his hand on the chart before him. "These are the same, for the most part, as the Scrolls the People revere. The land shapes are mostly the same, although we've noticed a few slight differences. But the water is water and the air is the air and the heavens are no different. But in the world Captain Reddy described, where all upon it were at war—the 'world,' if you will, we come from—all this"—he gestured at the charts—"was the same except for one thing: the people and creatures that inhabit it. Where we come from—evidently an entirely other 'here'—there are no Grik, no mountain fish, and . . . no People." He leaned back in his chair and it creaked beneath him.

"Personally, I don't come from 'the Edge of the World,' like my American friends. I come from . . ." He glanced at the chart and put his finger on the small piece of coastline southeast of the Sunda Islands, right on the edge of the paper. "I think your Scrolls call this place 'New Holland' or something like that, although I assure you there were few Dutchmen when I left."

Keje was looking at him like he'd just crawled out of a gri-kakka's mouth with its stomach in his teeth. "I've been to that land," he said quietly. "There are colonies there, and in the south, they build some sea homes as well. I've never seen an Amer-i-caan."

Bradford sighed. "I'm not a bloody American, but that's beside the point. By your charts, everything's the same, but there aren't any of *us*. By our charts, everything's the same, but there aren't any of *you*. The only explanation is that, somehow, there are two worlds . . . parallel worlds . . ." He stopped and looked around. "Two worlds side by side, perhaps even occupying the same space at the same time, only on which life has developed, for some reason, in two entirely different directions."

"But—but—" Keje stammered, "that cannot be."

Bradford sniffed and leaned back again. "Perhaps not, but it's all I've been able to come up with. Captain?"

"No, Mr. Bradford, that's a better explanation than I'd have managed, but the idea's essentially the same."

Nakja-Mur said something and Keje spoke for him. "If that is true, then how did you get here?"

Matt spread his hands. "We have no idea. All we know is *Mahan* and *Walker* were together, fighting a battle against a powerful enemy ship. We entered a strange squall, and the next thing we knew . . . No—" He looked thoughtful. "We didn't really know for a while. But somehow we were here. In your world." Abruptly, his expression hardened, and he leaned forward, placing his hands on the chart. "Which means, since we've no idea how we got here, we haven't got a clue how to get back. However it happened, we're stuck with each other. Unlike the old 'Tail-less Ones,' we're not going to run off and leave you. Even if we wanted to, we can't. Our fates are intertwined. The survival of our people, yours and mine, depends on defeating the Grik. So you better explain to your complainers, Nakja-Mur, U-Amaki Ay Baalkpan, they have not yet begun to be inconvenienced! After the information we've received today, we're going to have to kick into high gear."

"High Gear. It means, All Out? Sink or Swim? Same?" Keje asked.

"That's right."

Keje blinked solemn assent. "Your man, Silva? He told me these, and I agree. He also told me another." He looked around the table with quiet dignity and determination, then looked directly at Nakja-Mur. "However the Amer-i-caans came to us, it's clear only the Maker of All Things could have arranged it as they say. If that is so, then surely we must all either Shit, or Get Off the Pot."

For once, it was a beautiful day on Baalkpan Bay. The humidity was low and it couldn't have been much over eighty degrees. There was a cooling breeze out of the south-south-west, and the launch's motor droned pleasantly with the sound of good health and proper maintenance. The water had a slight chop, stirred by the wind, and the occasional packet of spray spritzed Matt, Letts, Bradford, and Shinya in the cockpit of the launch. To them, it was refreshing. But to Tony Scott, at the wheel, each drop that struck him made him shudder as if he'd been sprayed with caustic acid.

Matt knew something had come over his once fearless coxswain, who'd acquired a deep and abiding terror of the water. All he could do was hope he got over it. They were too shorthanded to put him on the beach, at least until their Lemurian "cadets" were fully trained, and the man stoically refused to be relieved from his primary duty. He clearly hated the water now and he constantly cast worried looks over the side as if expecting to see some huge, ravenous fish pacing the boat. But he was, after all, the coxswain, and he wouldn't shirk his duty.

For Matt's part, he was enjoying the outing. *Walker* had been laid up for more than a month, and he'd grown anxious and irritable over her immobility. Her refit had gone as well as conditions allowed, and he expected she was in better shape now than when they'd left Surabaya ahead of the Japanese. But his anxiety over *Mahan* and the growing

Grik menace left him feeling frustrated and impotent. It was good to be moving over water again.

He looked back across the bay, toward his ship, but he couldn't see her. Seven of the huge Lemurian Homes lay at anchor off Baalkpan now, crowding the area near the shipyard. More were expected within the next few days. Nakja-Mur had sent word as far as his fishing fleet could reach, for a "Great Gathering," or in essence, a council of war, to be held. Many of the Homes were intercepted already on their way. The threat was apparent to all by now. There'd been other fights like *Big Sal*'s, although none against so many Grik, but at least one Home was overrun. Its smoldering, half-sunken carcass was seen aground on the northeast coast of Java, near where Batavia would have been. That news threw Keje into a frenzy, and he'd been willing, at last, to perform the modifications to *Big Sal* that Alan Letts had suggested. Even now, as the launch nosed into the estuary of the river the locals called the Sungaa, Alan was discussing his plan with Bradford. Captain Reddy was deeply interested in whatever scheme the recently hypermotivated supply officer came up with, but for the moment he couldn't help but be overcome by the primordial landscape surrounding them.

The Sungaa wasn't long and was navigable for only a short distance before it choked into a narrow, swampy stream. But the waters that fled into the bay from the Lohr Mountains to the north provided a quicker, more convenient passage to the site where they'd sunk their first well. Except for his brief, tragic foray on Bali, Matt had stepped on land only for frequent trips into the city to see Nakja-Mur. Now, after passing the last hardy outposts of fishing huts and "frontier" hunters—only a few miles from town—he beheld Lemurian Borneo in all its savage beauty.

Amid raucous cries, dozens of species of colorful birdlike creatures whirled and darted with the erratic grace of flying insects. Their short, furry feathers covered streamlined and exotically lethal leathery bodies. They incessantly chased small fish, insects, and any "bird" smaller than they were. Vicious aerial combat flared when one of the creatures caught something another wanted or thought it could

take. Unlike similar battles that Matt had seen among birds
back home, the losers here rarely survived. The bodies of
the slain never even made it to the water.

The deadly flasher-fish weren't nearly as numerous in the
fresher water of the bay, and they didn't venture upriver at
all. Matt's party passed a herd of large animals marching
solemnly through the shallows near shore. They were the
size of hippos, but looked like spiky armadillos with longer
necks and forelegs. Here and there, ordinary crocodiles
lounged on the muddy banks. For all Matt knew, the trees
hanging over the water were quite normal as well, but he
knew little about trees of any sort, so their wide, palmated
leaves looked exotic to him regardless. Bradford said they
were as unusual as the fauna and Matt took his word for it.
The whole scene was simultaneously shockingly beautiful
and horrifying in a deep, secret, instinctual way.

He tore himself from his reverie and saw that Shinya was
equally absorbed by their surroundings, but Letts, and even
Bradford, seemed unaffected. Of course, they'd both been
to the wellhead several times. Letts must have asked him a
question, because he and the Australian both looked at him
expectantly. "I'm sorry, Mr. Letts. Could you repeat that,
please?"

Alan grinned. "Sure, Skipper. What I asked is, should
we concentrate all the guns on one side of *Big Sal*, like a
floating battery, and just counterweight the other, or mount
guns on both sides? We may not have time or materials to
make enough for both."

Matt shook his head. "I'm not convinced there're going
to be any guns." Letts assumed a wounded expression.

"Sure there will, Skipper, if we have enough time. I've
been working with the guys at the foundry"—the "guys at
the foundry" were two Lemurian brothers who owned and
ran it—"and they say it's no problem. They cast anchors for
ships like *Big Sal* all the time, so they're used to throwing
lots of metal. You could cast five or six guns from the metal
that goes into one of those babies. Labor's not an issue. The
latest news has everybody fired up, and Nakja-Mur had kittens over the prospect of cannons of his very own. The only
two stumbling blocks, well, three, really, were getting somebody to let us cut gunports in the side of their ship, finding

enough metal to make the guns—a truly hellacious amount of copper and tin—and, of course, ammunition.

"Gunpowder's not a problem. All the components are readily available and sulfur's all over these volcanic islands. The real pain's building a powder mill. That's taking time. We can't use water power, since there're no swift rivers. Maybe we can try what the Mice came up with? Anyway, we'll get it sorted out. We can use copper for cannonballs—that's a cinch—but training gunners to hit something with them might be a little harder."

"What about boring true?" Matt asked, and Letts shrugged a little hesitantly.

"I have a few ideas along that line."

Matt shook his head. He didn't know what had cracked Alan Letts out of his amiable go-with-the-flow shell, but whatever it was, he'd become a dynamo. Maybe it was just that he, like the rest of them, had finally come to grips with the situation. "I bet Keje wasn't happy about chopping holes in the side of *Big Sal*," he mused. "How many guns are you planning to put on her, anyway?"

"I'm hoping on twenty per side, eventually. That may not seem like many, given her size, compared to the ships of the line back in the seventeen hundreds, but . . ." He shrugged.

Matt looked at him and blinked with surprise. It was a habit he'd picked up from their new friends. "Twenty! I thought you were ambitious thinking about two or three! How big are you planning to make them?"

"Well, that depends on what size we ultimately bore them out. I'm meeting with Mr. McFarlane and Bernie Sandison this evening and we'll kick that around."

Matt chuckled. "Very well, Mr. Letts. Keep me informed, but be sure you don't use anything the ship needs to make your tools!" A wry grin spread across Letts's face, as if he'd been about to ask permission to do that very thing. "As to what to do with them if you get the cannons made?" Matt paused. "Keje'll have to decide. It's his ship. A floating battery in the bay would be tough to get around, but if anything ever did, the whole defense might collapse. I've never been a big believer in static defenses, and I doubt Keje would be either."

Bradford nodded vigorously. "Yes! Yes! Look how much

good the Maginot Line did the French! And I'm not even going to start on Singapore! As for Keje's opinion, I assure you you're right. With some quite obvious exceptions, the Lemurians are seagoing nomads. The very idea of being semi-permanently moored in any defensive position would be utterly alien, and perhaps hateful to them. I imagine they'd do it as an expedient during battle, but to actively prepare for such a thing? You might lose all credibility if you made the suggestion. So far, they're willing to take your advice on matters of defense, but that's all any of us really are. Advisors. We have no official status in the chain of command. I'm not sure there really is one. Nakja-Mur is the overall leader of the People of Balik—I mean Baalkpan—but Keje and any other ship captain who comes ashore, I suppose, all seem to be equals. They command their own People, but are subject to the laws and customs of the territory or ship they set foot on. It's all so very chaotic! It would be far more convenient if they had a king, and all the various ships and places were part of some grand commonwealth!"

"Like the British Empire?" Letts goaded.

"Well . . . yes! Precisely! This current arrangement is far too much like your own various states. Always squabbling, and never agreeing to work together toward a common goal!"

Matt smiled tolerantly at the Australian. "The United States usually manages to pull together over the important things."

"Yes, but it takes wars to make it happen, I might remind you!"

"That may be," Matt confessed, "but it looks like the Lemurians have their war too."

No one spoke for a while as the launch crept farther upriver. Once, Scott almost lost control when a crocodile bumped the boat and he flailed madly for the Thompson submachine gun he always carried slung over his shoulder. "Hold your fire, Mr. Scott," Matt said, just loud enough to be heard. The croc was swimming disinterestedly away, and Tony gave him a sheepish glance as he regained control of the boat.

"How are things going ashore, Lieutenant?" Matt asked

Shinya. He'd been shaken from his trancelike study of the wildlife by the launch's capering.

"If you mean the preparation of the militia, Captain Reddy, I must report progress is poor, but improving." Nakja-Mur had decreed that all able-bodied People, male and female, should take training with Sergeant Alden and Lieutenant Shinya, as well as some of their own few warriors every other day. Attendance was mandatory, but from the beginning, participation was somewhat sparse. Many of the younger, more adventurous townsfolk turned out with a will, and some had achieved a level of training that let them perform as NCOs for the less-proficient attendees. Alden had even begun training an "elite" force of a hundred of the sharpest and toughest, which would, of course, become his "Marines."

The vast majority managed to avoid service at first, however, due to exemptions granted almost as a matter of course whenever they complained to the High Chief's secretaries that their occupations should be protected as "vital to the defense of the People." Some even had a point, and to be fair, many of the young, able-bodied Lemurians had been conscripted into the projects being undertaken for or by the Americans. All those were subject to military discipline, however, and put through a daily regimen of close-order drill and basic weapons training. As the Grik threat became more real, particularly over the last couple of weeks, Shinya had noticed an increasing number of faces at drill that he'd never seen before.

"What kind of numbers are we looking at?" Matt asked.

"It's difficult to say. Sergeant Alden and I drill them each day, but with a few exceptions, we only see them every other day." Drill took place on a large "common" at the foot of Nakja-Mur's Great Hall, and the High Chief often watched the proceedings. The place had once been, for lack of a better term, a "park" near the center of town. But the ground had now been so churned by marching feet and maneuvering troops that they'd taken to calling it the parade ground. It wasn't big enough for everybody, however, so roughly half the militia drilled one day, and the other half the next. It was dreadfully inefficient, but with the dearth of open ground in Baalkpan, it was the only answer. Shinya gazed thoughtfully at the water and turned back to the captain. "I think it's not impossible, right now, to field nearly fifteen hundred Baalkpan troops, reasonably well trained for the type of fighting we saw upon *Big Sal*. In two weeks, we can perhaps double that number. In six months, we could put ten thousand in the field, but that would include virtually the entire adult population of the city. To assemble such a force, however, will take an even greater sense of ... urgency than they now have."

"You mean we'd have to be literally under attack, here, to expect that level of participation?" Matt muttered in resignation.

Shinya nodded. "I fear so. Of course, by then it would be much too late to organize them properly. A few of Sergeant Alden's 'Marines' have gone aboard the Lemurian ships to get them to learn our drill so coordination would be possible at need. They've received ... a mixed welcome. As for the tactics we're teaching them, without the benefit of firearms, the only real options are those you suggested. A 'Roman' shield wall, backed by spearmen, backed in turn by archers." He shook his head. "One of the most difficult things was to get them to abandon their crossbows. These people are made for shooting bows, and a longbow has a greater range and rate of fire than a crossbow, but they didn't understand why we, a people with such technology, should advocate such simple weapons." He grinned. "Once they saw the superiority of longbows, it wasn't difficult to convince them." Shinya's expression became grim. "Of course, they want firearms."

Matt nodded. "I wish they had them, but without steel ..." He sighed. "Once we drag them out of the Bronze Age, we can have a look at flintlock muskets or something, but for now?" He held his hands out at his sides. "I know Alden's training some of his 'Marines' to use our weapons. How's he doing?"

"Yes, he's training fifty of them, but they only get to fire a few rounds each. Mr. Sandison has solved the projectile problem—I think he called it swaging? But the difficulty remains making new cartridge cases if the empty ones are damaged or lost. And, of course, the primers. No one seems to think gunpowder will be a problem"—he bowed toward Letts—"but it won't be smokeless at first, so the automatic weapons won't function well." He shook his head. "Of course, all these logistics matters are not my concern, particularly since I know nothing about them. But I understand that one of Mr. Sandison's concerns is replacing *Walker*'s depleted ammunition stores for her main battery. His experiments with the small arms are the 'test bed' for the four-inch guns."

"Lieutenant Shinya, I don't know how it worked in your navy, but logistics is the concern of any officer, infantry officers included—which is what you've become. I'm glad you're keeping up with it." Matt's gaze drifted forward, and he saw massive wooden pilings set in the riverbed some distance out from shore. As they neared, he saw that a framework connected them and a party of 'Cats was working to lay down a plank deck. They'd arrived at the fueling pier.

They secured the launch and trooped ashore. All were armed in spite of the small army of laborers nearby. Bradford had insisted, explaining that unlike in their own world, the large number of workers going about their business here wouldn't frighten predators away; they would only alert them to a smorgasbord. A fair percentage of the Lemurians present were, in fact, dedicated to security. They were armed primarily with oversized crossbows that threw a bolt two feet long and an inch in diameter. Matt remembered Bradford telling him there were some truly astonishing predators lurking in the jungles of this new Borneo, but he'd paid only passing attention at the time, preoccupied with the refit of his ship. Now he tried to remember some of the creatures Bradford had described. *They must be pretty big,* he mused, *if it took a handheld ballista to bring one down.*

At the edge of the clearing, three large cylinders stood atop adobe furnaces with a maze of heavy, local copper pipe twisting among them. Matt recognized the cylinders as the ill-fated torpedo tubes of the number three mount. He hoped they would prove more useful here than they had aboard the ship. Furry, kilted workers scampered around the apparatus that they hoped would become a functioning refinery—if they found anything to refine. Chief Donaghey and *Mahan*'s Perry Brister were supervising the project, and by their filthy appearance, they'd done more than that. Matt waved at them to carry on as the party continued past the high tower set in the center of the clearing. In it was a now fully recovered Leo Davis and one of their precious BARs. He looked like a prison guard overseeing a chain gang, but the obvious distinction was that he was there to protect the workers, not to prevent escape. More Lemurians stood guard at intervals along the trail leading from the fueling pier into the dense jungle surrounding it.

The wellhead lay almost a mile inland. The trail was wide, and down the center was a pipeline constructed from the curious oversized bamboo that seemed, in every respect except for its massive size, just like bamboo "back home." They'd seen it used extensively in local construction and for masts, of course, and it was a natural choice for those applications, being generally the diameter and length of a telephone pole. Matt hadn't known they were going to use it to transport the crude. Bradford and Letts noticed him appraising the arrangement as they walked alongside.

"Bound to leak like a sieve, Skipper," said Letts resignedly. "The couplings are short pieces of tin pipe pounded into the ends and sealed with pitch. I guess we can build something better once we have the time."

"No, Mr. Letts. It's ingenious. I hadn't even thought how we'd move the oil from the well to the refinery. Well done."

Letts looked embarrassed. "Well, it was really Spanky's idea," he demurred.

"A good idea, no matter whose it was." Matt paused, looking at the pipeline with a thoughtful expression. "I can't help but wonder, though. A fueling pier, a pipeline, even a refinery—all situated where they are just because of the wellhead. Are you sure we're not taking one small detail a little too much for granted?"

Bradford blinked at him and wiped the ever-present sweat from his brow with a handkerchief that might once have been white. Then he grinned mischievously. "Never fear, my dear captain. As you Americans would so quaintly say, the fix is in." He stopped and glanced at the sky. It was visible above the quadruple-canopy jungle only because of the pipeline cut. As so often happened at this time of day, the bright blue they'd basked beneath much of the morning had been replaced by a sodden gray.

"Oh, dear."

Isak Reuben took a final, long drag off his cigarette, and it burned fiercely, almost to his lips. He flipped the tiny butt off the platform, where it hissed and drowned in a puddle. The deluge had become a gentle drizzle, but it fell long and hard enough to soak him completely. Not that it mattered. He was always soaked, with sweat, and his filthy T-shirt clung to his skinny torso like a slimy, splotched, translucent leech. His fireroom pallor was gone, as was Gilbert's, replaced by the harsh reddish brown he remembered so well from his life in the oil fields. It was a color he'd hoped never to see on his own body again.

"Goddamn," he exclaimed matter-of-factly, "ain't White Mice now." He grabbed the cable that dropped down from one end of the walking beam and disappeared into the hole at his feet. The slack felt about right. "Wind 'er up, Gilbert," he croaked at his companion, who made a rotating motion with his hand.

A short distance away, a pair of young 'Cats sat on a brontosarry's back, and one made a trilling sound and whacked its flank with a stout bamboo shoot. With a guttural groan of protest, the beast began to move. It was harnessed to a giant windlass, and as it trudged through a slurry of mud, round and round, a belt running from a large-diameter central shaft transferred its meager rotation to a smaller, faster wheel. Another belt ran to yet another wheel, between the two in diameter. This one turned a crank that raised and lowered a pitman, causing the walking beam to go up and down. As it did so, it raised the cable-tool bit far down in the hole and then dropped it with a resounding "thud." The bit drove a few inches deeper every time.

Isak looked at the sky, beyond the eighty-foot bamboo derrick that still struck him as just . . . wrong somehow, and saw patches of blue struggling to disperse the clouds. He shook his head unhappily. Every time a squall blew up, he hoped subconsciously that it, like the one that had brought them here, would take them home. Home to the real world, where he could bask in the honest warmth and isolation of his beloved boilers, where steam was magically made. Steam that turned honest turbines. He frowned. Anywhere but here, where steam rose from the ground because the sun cooked it out, and where stinkin' dinosaurs pretended to be motors! He groped for another cigarette and frowned even deeper, staring at the massive animal trudging slowly around. "RPMs ain't much, but the torque's pretty respectable."

Gilbert touched the cable himself at the bottom of its stroke, as he walked over to join him. "What?" he asked.

"Nothin'."

Gilbert nodded. "Quiet rig." Both were used to loud engines doing the work of the dinosaur.

"Too quiet," complained Isak. "Ain't natural."

Gilbert nodded again, in solemn agreement. "Gimme a smoke, will ya?" His customary monotone was as close to a wheedle as it ever got.

"No."

"Why not? I shared mine with you."

"Yeah, and now yer out, ain't ya? Stupid."

Gilbert stared down at the well as the cable went slack, pondering. No question about it, Isak was the smart one.

The other fireman sighed heavily, shook a soggy cigarette out of the pack, and handed it over. Then he peered inside. "Now I'm as dumb as you. Only one left."

The well was situated in another artificial clearing, and one of their Lemurian security guards trilled a call from his watchtower near the pipeline cut.

"What's he jabberin' about?" Isak asked, irritably reaching for one of the old Krag rifles they always kept nearby. "I hope it ain't another one of them Big Ones. We really need bigger guns for huntin' around here."

The "Big Ones" he referred to were forty-foot monsters Bradford insisted were allosaurs. Unlike most of the other dinosaur species they'd encountered, Bradford's modern allosaurs were not stunted. They'd hardly changed at all from those in the fossil record—the only difference he could see, if anything, was they were bigger than their prehistoric ancestors. There weren't many of them, though, and even if they looked built for speed, they preferred to lurk along well-used trails in the dense jungle and let their prey come to them. The destroyermen called them "super lizards" in spite of Bradford's protests. Isak only knew they were hard as hell to kill and they scared the shit out of him.

"Hold on, Isak," Gilbert said. "They all sound like monkeys to me, but that don't sound like a lawsey-me-there's-a-Big-One-a'comin' yell."

They both stared toward the cut for a few moments more, then relaxed a little when they saw humans emerge into the clearing.

"It was too," Isak said. "That's the Skipper."

Matt waved at the Lemurian peering down from the tower. It was one of Alden's Marines, armed with a Krag. This was arguably one of the most important parts of the "fuel project," but aside from the sentry, there were fewer than a dozen people, including the Mice, working the site. Most of the labor currently involved cleaning and stacking the "bamboo" pipes they were using to case the well. At this stage, few hands were really needed to operate the rig and most were needed only when it was time to bail, or pull the bits for sharpening.

A pair of bits lay across hefty sawhorses now, and two workers held them down while another vigorously worked them over with a file. The bits were Spanky's idea. He'd used a heavy I beam meant for shoring up buckled hull plates. He cut the twelve-foot beam into three segments and cast heavy copper slugs on the ends to give them more weight. By all accounts, they worked well, but they didn't hold an edge and had to be sharpened a lot.

Matt stared, fascinated, at the bamboo derrick and the ingenious contraption operating it. He'd seen oil wells, but he didn't know much about them. All he could say about this one was . . . it resembled an oil well. That the derrick was a strange greenish yellow did a lot to undermine the impression, however. His gaze swept to the platform and he saw the two firemen staring back. *That's probably another reason there's not more workers here,* he conceded. It took special people to voluntarily spend much time with the irascible Mice. Even if those people had tails. Together, he and his party slogged through the swampy ooze surrounding the rig until they reached the platform and clambered up.

"Good afternoon, men," Matt began amiably. "Thought I'd see for myself how things are going." Isak just shrugged and looked around as if to say, "Well, here it is."

Bradford stifled a cough. "Yes, well, I think you can see they've done a marvelous job. Marvelous!" He beamed at the two men. "How deep are we now?"

Gilbert had retreated a few feet and stood next to the sampson post that supported the walking beam. Neither he nor Isak had been spoken to by officers more than a dozen times in their lives—not counting Spanky—and it always unnerved them a little. For the most part, throughout their Navy careers they'd lived in the fireroom, and officers lived . . . someplace else.

"Three hundred and sixty-nine feet, when the cable goes tight this time," Isak said, and he glanced furtively between the visitors. He suddenly yanked the filthy hat off of his head. "If you please."

"Excellent, excellent!" Bradford exclaimed. "Can't be far now!" He turned to face Matt. "As I said, the fix is in! I happen to know oil was found on this very spot in 1938! A respectable deposit, too. Quite adequate for our needs!"

Matt smiled at him. "But what makes you so sure it's here . . . *here*?"

Bradford blinked. "Why, you did, of course! As you said, the geography is the same. As we've all discussed at some length now," he smiled patiently, "this is our very same earth. Only a few inhabitants have been changed about. The very same oil found here in 1938 should still be down there, since no one's ever drilled for it!"

"I sure hope you're right, Mr. Bradford. I'm not certain it's the same thing. Just because Borneo's here, does that mean the same oil's under it?" A trace of sadness touched Matt's smile. "I'm morally certain the North American continent exists . . . here. Its shores and distinctive landmarks are probably like those we remember. The Paluxy River may still run where my folks' ranch should be. Do the same catfish I used to catch still swim that river, Mr. Bradford? I doubt it. If they do, they'd probably eat you." He held up his hand before Bradford could protest. "I'm just saying if we don't find oil here, we need to keep an open mind about where to look next. Above all, we mustn't get everyone's hopes up that finding it here's a sure thing." Matt's smile twisted into a grin. "Always remember, gentlemen, oil is where you find it—but it may not be where you left it!"

Gilbert nodded solemn agreement with the captain's words. What was that damned Aussie trying to do? Jinx them? He reached over and felt the cable. "Tight," he announced. Isak nodded. He addressed the Lemurians on the draft beast.

"Hey, you monkeys!" he shouted. "Stop-o el dinosauro now-o! Time to bail! Chop, chop!" The two young 'cats gave very human nods and hopped down.

"Been picking up the local lingo, I see," Letts commented dryly.

Isak shrugged. "Yep. Got to, I guess."

In the launch, Captain Reddy was thoughtful. He was encouraged by how far along the "fuel project" seemed, and if Bradford was right, it was just a matter of finding the right depth at the rig before *Walker*'s bunkers were full to bursting. The thought felt good, even though he couldn't shake his nagging concern. Contrary to what everybody seemed to take for granted, there actually were subtle differences in geography. Nothing pronounced, but enough to make him worry. For example, the land around Baalkpan Bay was higher than he remembered "back home." Less erosion? Lower sea level? Or something else? If everything in the world was different now, why not oil deposits?

Bradford said it didn't work that way. He said the ground under the well was geologically predisposed to form a reservoir for crude. Matt hoped he was right. In any event, now that he'd been there, he was confident that if there was any oil, it would be found. The strange firemen had everything well in hand. He sighed. Of course, then the refinery had to work. It was one thing to find oil and something else to turn it into fuel they could burn.

He listened to the others chatting about the wildlife they'd seen as the launch left the river behind and reentered the bay. A few colorful flying reptiles paced the boat and shrieked and swooped at the small fish churned up in its wake. Matt tuned out the conversation and, as he often did of late, found himself thinking about Sandra Tucker as he stared at the feathery whitecaps. He couldn't deny that he was attracted to her. Who wouldn't be? For that matter, with so few women and a ship full of men, who, in fact, *wasn't* attracted to her? In spite of the situation, he really liked her a lot and believed he wasn't unduly influenced by the scarcity of females. He was sure that under normal circumstances he'd have already made a move. But these weren't normal circumstances.

So far, in spite of everything, the crew had stuck together. There was friction aboard—there always was—but not much more than normal . . . yet. He couldn't imagine how everything fell apart so fast on *Mahan*. Jim was a good leader and he should have sorted it out. Probably would have if he hadn't been shot. Brister thought the breakdown was due to Kaufman's hysteria and the stress of their ordeal. At all costs, he had to prevent that kind of stress from taking root here. Right now the biggest stress to *Walker*'s crew was a lack of "dames." He honestly believed they'd eventually find more humans, and the two Indiamen that had sailed east so long ago were a solid lead. But in the meantime it was hard to dispel the sense that they were all alone. All alone, with only two women. He'd always believed in leading by example, and regardless of his feelings, he thought it wouldn't be fair to the men if he pressed his suit now. How could he expect them to show restraint if he didn't set the example? At the very least, it would undermine his moral authority—and that was really the only authority he had left. The men sure weren't getting paid. The situation was far too tense to risk jealousy and resentment by chasing one of the only two eligible females.

He glanced at Alan Letts. Maybe the only eligible female. Letts and Karen Theimer were seeing a lot of each other. Maybe that was why he'd been so industrious of late. Letts had better watch out, though. Matt knew Bernie and Greg were both sweet on the young nurse too. That was probably why his young officers were so formal to each other lately. There'd be trouble down the line, and the more he thought about it, the more disquieted he became. The "dame famine," as the crew referred to the situation, was likely to be more explosive in the long term than any shortage of fuel or ammunition.

He wished, for the thousandth time, that he hadn't sent the other nurses off in *Mahan*. Not just because of the dame famine, of course, but their presence might have taken a little pressure off. What it boiled down to was that somehow they had to find more people, and the sooner the better. He owed it to his men. He took a deep breath. But that would have to wait, and in regard to Sandra, he would have to wait as well. And so would *Mahan*, wherever she'd gone— at least until they had fuel to search for her—or other humans. Right now they had a war to prepare for and to fight. That was a kind of stress his men were accustomed to and one he knew they could handle.

"Some kind of regatta or somethin' goin' on today?" shouted Tony Scott over the engine and the spray they were making. Captain Reddy grunted and looked where the coxswain indicated. Across the bay, fishing boats pelted toward town as fast as they could. The growing mass of boats seemed to gather in all they came across, and sheets flew as more fishermen came about or set a new tack toward the wharves. On instinct, Matt glanced at his ship. He saw her now; the off-white experimental gray that the Chief had mixed was clear against the riotous color of the city and jungle beyond. Perplexed, he looked back toward the mouth of the bay and the Makassar Strait.

Standing in toward them under a fair press of sail was one of the red-hulled Indiamen of the Grik. All over the bay, the large conch-like shells the People used to sound the alarm began to blow, and the men in the boat heard the dull bass hum even over the exhaust of the engine.

"Step on it, Scott! To the ship, as fast as you can!"

Sandra peered over the top of her book as her next patient entered the wardroom. She was reading a battered copy of Henry Thomas's *Wonder Book of History, Science, Nature, Literature, Art, Religion, Philosophy,* which was making the rounds. It reminded her a little of Courtney Bradford: engagingly pompous and full of a little information on quite a lot. The old book came from the large, eccentric library of the dead surgeon, Stevens. She closed it and regarded her visitor with raised eyebrows.

"Dennis Silva, as I live and breathe."

Silva merely stood, staring stoically straight ahead and she looked at him more closely. The refit had exacted a toll on the destroyermen and their Lemurian helpers, mostly minor injuries and torch burns, but there were occasional serious hurts—crushed fingers and lacerations requiring stitches, for example. The complaints constituted a steady enough stream that she and Karen stood alternating watches in the wardroom, tending the wounded as they presented themselves. They usually shooed them back to their duties. The big gunner's mate had no obvious injury, however.

"Well?" she demanded impatiently. "What's the matter with you?"

Silva's face reddened even beneath his short, dense beard and savage tan. "'M sick, ma'am."

She looked at him incredulously. "Sick! You?" Silva's constitution was legendary. His record showed his only previous appearances before the ship's surgeon had been of the type to be expected of a rambunctiously male Asiatic Fleet destroyerman. She doubted that was his problem today, although with Silva . . . There *had* been rumors some of the men were experimenting with local females. Both species were certainly adventurous enough to try. She shuddered involuntarily and shook her head to clear the thought.

"Sick how?" she asked. Then she felt a chill. So far they'd been lucky, but she lived in perpetual dread of some unidentifiable plague sweeping the ship, something they had no immunity to.

Silva actually looked at his feet. "Got the screamers," he muttered.

"The screamers?"

He nodded. "Been in the head since yesterday afternoon, and I . . . kinda need to go now." Her eyes flicked down the passageway behind her, and he looked at her as if she were nuts. That was the officers' head! "I, ah, can hold it."

"What seems to be the cause of your discomfort? Something you ate?"

"Well, you see, tobacco's worth its weight in gold, and that damn Chack—"

Sandra slapped her forehead and felt a smile of relief cross her face. Silva's expression became more wooden at her sudden lack of compassion. "Has had you running around chewing on every dead leaf he can convince you to stick in your mouth!" she finished for him and laughed out loud. "Oh, that's rich! I heard about that! You should watch out for that boy! He's not the 'simpleminded wog' some of you guys think he is!" She giggled, then looked thoughtful. "It seems our Mr. Chack has a wicked sense of humor!" She made a mental note to tell Chack that some things that didn't bother Lemurians at all might be poisonous to humans—and that he'd better grow eyes in the back of his head and expect retaliation.

"I'm sure you'll be all right eventually, Mr. Silva. I know your ... experiments have been solely in the interests of science and the benefit of your fellow man, but why not take this opportunity to liberate yourself from your disgusting habit?"

Silva's expression could have been described as plaintive in a lesser mortal. "But what are we supposed to do? No tobacco, almost no coffee, no ... um." He paused, but quickly recovered himself. "It was bad enough fightin' the Nips, and now this? It's more than a fella can stand without a chew!"

Sandra nodded slowly. He had a point. Almost everyone aboard used tobacco. She knew that wasn't the only ... frustration, but she'd noticed tempers flaring more easily, and there'd even been some fights. Despite her feelings on the subject, there was morale to consider. She sighed. "Very well, Mr. Silva. I'll look into it. But I warn you, there may not be anything to replace tobacco."

He nodded gratefully. "Just as long as somebody's lookin'. Hell, these 'Cats don't even have betel nuts!"

Secretly, Sandra expected they probably did use some kind of stimulant besides the fermented polta fruit. Seep was already well known and much used when the men went ashore on the limited liberties Matt allowed, but it had some undesirable aftereffects. She still wasn't satisfied that it was even safe for humans, given the severity and duration of the hangovers, but Captain Reddy was right. Never give an order you know will be disobeyed. The only way to keep them from drinking the stuff was to confine everyone to the ship, which was unfair and would be worse for morale than the lack of tobacco.

As a replacement for the noxious weed . . . She again determined to speak to Chack. She was willing to bet that he, and many other young Lemurians, were enjoying their joke too much to share the knowledge if there was one. She would ask, she promised herself. And warn. If the rumors were true, Silva's pranks were not funny.

"Now, as to your complaint—" She held out her hands in resignation. "I don't even have anything left to relieve the symptoms. You'll just have to let it run its course. Be sure to stay properly hydrated, though."

"Hydrated? What's that?" he inquired darkly.

"Water. Drink plenty of water!" She paused. "But only ship's water. I don't even want to think about what the local water will do to you yet. Talk about the screamers!" She made another mental note to see McFarlane again. As long as they were burning the number four boiler, the condensers would manufacture fresh water in small quantities. Barely enough to drink, but nothing else. Everyone was constantly reminded not to drink anything that even *might* have local water in it. If they ever ran entirely out of fuel, they'd have to figure out something else. Boil local water, she supposed. At least there *was* local water and they could use it for cooking—and bathing—thank God!

Silva's expression became pinched. "I might, ah, better visit the officers' head after all, ma'am. Don't think I'll make it aft."

Sandra nodded and smiled. "By all means."

The general alarm began to sound.

The launch's occupants scurried onto the pier and raced for the gangway. They were nearly trampled by Lemurians scampering everywhere on the docks. The huge draft beasts bawled as their drivers whipped their flanks in panic. One of the elephantine brontosauruses bugled in fear at the commotion and reared up on its hind legs, upsetting the cart it was hitched to and then crushing it under its haunches. The driver barely jumped clear. Somehow, they managed to weave through the terrified crowd and run up the gangway. No side party waited and they hastily saluted the colors.

Chief Gray met them, puffing. "I have the deck, sir, I suppose," he said. "Mr. Dowden left about an hour ago with Spanky to talk to the yard-apes. Should be back any time."

"Never mind. Single up all lines and make all preparations for getting under way."

Gray glanced about helplessly at the chaos around them for just an instant, then saluted. "Aye, aye, Captain."

Matt turned to Shinya. "Marines are on parade today?" Shinya nodded. "How long to fetch Alden and a company of Marines?" Shinya scanned the mob choking the wharf and the pathways into the city. He shook his head. One Grik ship had appeared in the bay and the population acted like the enemy was loose among them.

"Sergeant Alden may already be trying to make his way here, but to go get him now? Impossible."

"I concur. Try to make it to *Big Sal*. Ask Keje for a hundred of his best warriors and get them here as fast as you can!" Matt didn't even ponder the irony of the Japanese officer's salute as he returned it and watched Shinya race back down the gangway. He turned and ran to the bridge.

"Captain on deck!" shouted Lieutenant Garrett. Matt nodded and stepped quickly on the bridgewing with his binoculars in hand. The Grik ship's dash toward the city had slowed, and it was practically hove to about four miles away. As if studying them. This ran contrary to everything he'd heard about their tactics. He'd expected them to charge right in.

"All stations report manned and ready, Captain," Garrett announced.

"Very well. Prepare to get under way."

Garrett seemed surprised. "But Captain . . . the fuel? We can sink him from here."

"I know, Mr. Garrett, but he's acting like he knows it too." He barked a dry laugh. "I think our reputation has preceded us. Besides, I don't think he's by himself." As he watched, brightly colored signal flags raced up the Grik's mast. "Yep," he said. "I bet there's at least one more hanging outside the mouth of the bay. Have engineering light number three and honk the horn. We'll give anyone close enough five more minutes to make it back on board."

"Light number three, sir?" Garrett cringed. Now he knew their fuel wouldn't outlast the day.

Matt sighed. "I'm afraid so. We also have to stop whoever that one signaled to. We can only make about ten knots on one boiler, but with this breeze picking up, maybe more out in the strait, I bet those Grik can make twelve." They'd taken on firewood for just such an emergency. He hoped they wouldn't have to use it.

"Aye, aye, Captain. Sound the horn, light number three, and cast off all lines in five minutes."

Two minutes later, Shinya and Keje asked permission to come on the bridge. Matt felt a surge of warmth at the sight of his Lemurian friend. Keje was dressed as Matt had first seen him, with his copper-scaled armor and a broad-bladed scota at his side. Shinya had found the time to buckle on his longer, thinner version that Sandison made from one of the cutlasses. It wasn't exactly a katana, but he could use it like one now that the guard had been cut down and the handle extended. Shinya still mourned his own ceremonial sword—lost when his destroyer went down—and the cutlass was a crude replacement. But he'd been moved by Bernie's gift.

Larry Dowden raced onto the bridge, breathing hard. In the background Matt heard the commotion of Lemurian warriors thundering aboard amid bellowed commands from the Bosun. "Sorry, Skipper," Larry apologized. "We nearly didn't make it. Spanky's aboard too—headed for the fireroom. He said with his two best guys ashore, he better bat the burners himself."

"Very well. Cast off the stern line. Left full rudder! Port engine ahead one-third!"

With a vibrating moan, *Walker* came to life beneath his feet once more. Ever so slowly, amid a churning froth of dark, musty-smelling seawater that sloshed up around the port propeller guard, the destroyer's stern eased away from the dock. "All stop. Rudder amidships. Cast off bow line!" Matt paused until he saw his last command obeyed. "All back one-third!" With a distinct, juddering groan, *Walker* backed away from the pier and *Big Sal*, tied up just ahead. When they'd made a suitable gap, Matt spoke again. "Right full rudder, all ahead two-thirds."

Throughout the maneuver Keje was silent. Now he just shook his head. "Amazing," he said aloud. He turned his inscrutable gaze upon the captain. "I've brought you one hundred of my finest warriors, Cap-i-taan Reddy." He grinned. "All were anxious to fight, of course, but I had the most trouble limiting their numbers when they learned they would go to battle on your magnificent ship!"

Matt clapped him on the shoulder. "They may be less enthusiastic if we have to paddle home. We really don't have the fuel for this!"

"Ah!" Keje sniffed and blinked. "A nothing! Once again we'll kill Grik together!"

Greasy black smoke belched briefly from the number three funnel and *Walker* gathered way. Matt looked through his binoculars. "Oh, boy, that's done it! He's going about. Piling on more sail."

Keje stood beside him, binoculars raised to his eyes as well. Unobtrusively, Larry Dowden helped him fold them to fit his face and showed him how to focus. Keje exclaimed in delight but continued to stare at the enemy. "Yes. He's running. I see the signal flags myself." He looked at Matt. "Twice now I have seen the enemy flee, and both times because of your ship. The one that escaped after the great fight must have passed word to others, or perhaps that's the very ship that eluded us. Regardless, there's clearly another in the strait, and beyond that, perhaps another. They must all be destroyed! If they carry news of Baalkpan to the place where they assemble fleets, they will return in force. We are not ready for that." Keje's ears and tail twitched with annoyance. "I am sure you must agree after witnessing that disgraceful display on the waterfront."

"They'll be ready, Keje," Matt assured him. "What I saw on the dock was the natural reaction of people who've suddenly been confronted with their worst nightmare. Remember, for a lot of people in Baalkpan, the Grik weren't real until today. They were creatures of myth—boogeymen. They've never faced them. They've never seen with their own eyes the terrible way they make war. Now they know the enemy *is* real and we haven't been training them for hoots." Matt gestured out the windows at the distant Grik. "In a way, this might be just what we needed to make the land folk take things seriously."

"I hope you're right," Keje grumbled. "It looked to me that all it did was turn their bowels to water."

Matt arched an eyebrow. "You should've seen us when the Japs bombed Cavite."

Walker steadied on course and gradually increased speed. Spanky was fully aware of the state of their bunkers and there was no pell-mell acceleration. Matt glanced about, trying to find something to use as a gauge for wind direction and speed. He settled on one of the fishing feluccas that pelted by in the opposite direction. The small, beamy ship sailed admirably close to the wind. Keje saw him studying it.

"Yes. The enemy has a favorable wind with their ... I think you call it 'square rig'? It's much the same principle as our 'wings,' and it serves best running with the wind on a quarter from behind, ah, quartering? Astern?" He shook his head. "I learn your language good, I think, but some words don't work yet."

Matt grinned at him. "They work fine, as far as I can tell."

Keje bowed in thanks. "Still, I think you could catch him before he makes it into the strait." Matt glanced at Garrett, who cast a quick look at the Lemurian. Matt nodded.

"He's in easy range, Skipper," Garrett confirmed. The Grik ship was less than two miles away, gaining speed. But the course reversal had cost him. Keje grunted as if to say, "I thought so."

"Very well. Let's let him get some more water under his keel, though. I don't want to sink him in the channel. Tell Spanky he can ease off the juice. Make him think he's keeping the distance." Matt smiled ruefully. "By the way, Mr. Garrett, my apologies. I have the deck. Please take your post on the fire-control platform. If there's another one, we might have some fancy shooting to do."

"Aye, aye, sir. Captain has the deck," he announced. After

he was gone, Matt shook his head. *Got excited*, he chided himself. *Not too good for the image of the stoic, all-knowing captain.*

"What about me, sir?" asked Dowden. "You want me aft?"

"Not yet. This'll probably be as close to shooting fish in a barrel as we'll ever get. But I may have a chore for you. Helm," he said to Tolson, "keep us dead astern of the enemy, if you please. Adjust speed as needed."

"Dead astern and as needed, aye."

The Grik ship was leaning on her wide beam, the pyramid of white canvas contrasting sharply with the dark red hull and the blue, white-capped waves. A long, foaming trail spread astern. "You can say what you like about those damn lizards," he said, "but they make pretty ships."

The mouth of the bay widened. Beyond the Grik, the open ocean of the Makassar Strait looked vast and empty. A few high clouds moved with deliberation across the otherwise clear blue sky. A touch of gray brooded over Celebes, but the local visibility was near perfect. Where was the other ship?

"Lookout reports a sail beyond the headland, bearing two two five," proclaimed the talker. Matt shifted his glass, but saw nothing because of the dense jungle that grew right down to the shoreline off the starboard bow. The lookout had a better vantage point, and the high masts of the Grik allowed them to see and signal at an even greater distance.

"Well, two for sure," Matt said speculatively. "Question now is whether the one we're chasing will turn to join her consort or continue on, leading us away. It might tell us a lot about them."

"Will it make a difference?" Keje asked anxiously.

"It shouldn't, in the short term." Matt was silent for a moment. "Say you had two or three fast ships and had just found the home of the Grik. They pursue. There's no way you can win a fight, but it's vitally important that someone get away with the information. What would you do?"

Theoretical speculation wasn't always a Lemurian strong point, Matt had noticed, but now Keje stared at the stern of the Grik ship while his mind sorted possibilities.

"I'd flee in a direction different than my consorts and

hope they might chase me or one of the others. Perhaps one might escape. Much like the original Leaving. If the herd splinters, the hunters cannot get them all."

Matt nodded. "Or the hunters might get them all one at a time. But what else might you try? If it looked like none would escape?"

"I might fight them, to delay them. Or ask one of the others to do so."

"Yeah." He paced to the helmsman and glanced at the compass pelorus in front of the wheel. Then he returned and looked at the sky, gauging the wind again. The Grik ship was in the strait. They also saw the other enemy ship, crowding more sail and hugging the coastline, sailing south-southwest. If the closer ship intended to follow, now was the time to turn. "The question is," Matt continued, "would you have ever thought the Grik might do such a thing?"

Keje was flabbergasted by the thought. He found it difficult enough to believe they were running away at all. The idea of any strategic or self-sacrificing thought entering a Grik head was so foreign and horrifying that it left him momentarily speechless. And yet he'd been watching the wind. Unlike the destroyerman, who relied so much on his engines, Keje was always conscious of the wind. He didn't need a compass to tell him the Grik should have already turned.

"If they think information about Baalkpan is more important than their lives, it would imply a more sophisticated enemy than the 'rear up and run at 'em' sort we thought we faced." Matt was watching the lizard ship as he spoke, and then he suddenly peered through the binoculars again. "Damn," he muttered as sails shivered and the enemy's hull changed aspect. "I sure hoped I was wrong. They can't get away, but they're not changing course to follow their friend—a heading that would give them more speed, by the way. Anyway"—he looked at Keje—"they want to fight. To 'delay' us." He shook his head. "Not happy about that at all." To the talker: "Have Mr. Garrett commence firing. Helm? Let's go after the other one. We don't have the fuel to screw around."

The salvo buzzer screeched. While *Walker* described a leisurely turn to starboard, three rounds from the number two gun left the large, once beautiful ship a shattered, smoking wreck, sinking in their wake. A four-inch projectile isn't very large in the grand scheme of naval riflery, but high-explosive against a wooden hull is no contest. Two rounds should have been enough, but Silva was pointer and his crewmates had noticed he wasn't quite himself. Good-natured ribbing followed his first inexplicable miss, but the 'Cats on board were suitably impressed by the effect of the second and third shells. Now *Walker* loped after the other red ship . . . and Silva glared at Chack. A moment later he grinned.

Keje stood beside Matt, sitting in his sacred chair on the starboard side of the pilothouse. Far ahead, but slowly growing, was their next quarry. Matt was impressed by its speed. There was a fine breeze and it must have been making close to thirteen knots. A short while before, they'd passed half-submerged casks and other objects and it was clear the Grik were lightening ship. He gauged the distance.

"Keje," he said, "I'd like to take that ship. They came snooping around to find out about us, and I want to return the favor. There's just too much about them we don't know, like where they come from, what they're doing and what they want. Do they really have a dozen ships in the Java Sea? More? I'm *sick* of never knowing what my people have to face!" He paused. "After we take out her masts, I'll have the machine guns and rifles kill as many as they can. Then we'll board. My question to you is do you think we can do it with a minimal . . . loss of life? My guess is they'll mass in the open, to receive us, and we'll be able to whittle them down considerably. But I have to rely on your people to do the bulk of the fighting. I can't spare many men for the boarding party and still operate the ship. Besides"—he gestured at the scota at Keje's side—"few of us are skilled in this type of fighting. Most who are were at the parade ground when we left." He took a deep breath and saw the gleam of anticipation in Keje's eyes. No one had boarded a Grik ship! The glory for *Salissa* would be beyond compare. The deed would be recorded in the very Scrolls!

Matt held up a hand. "I said I'd *like* to take it. One thing I've got to check first." He got up, stepped to the aft bulkhead, and activated the engine room comm. "Engineering, this is the captain. Let me speak to Mr. McFarlane."

"Aye, aye, sir." A moment later the engineer's gruff voice said, "McFarlane here."

"Fuel, Spanky."

There was a momentary pause, then a sigh. "Captain, if we reduce speed, secure number three and turn back right now, we *might* make it in without a tow."

"What about the wood?"

There was silence on the other end.

"We can burn the wood, Spanky."

Lieutenant McFarlane responded resignedly. "Aye, sir, we can burn the wood, but then the boiler'll be down for however long it takes to clean out all the ash, and I can't answer for whether or not it'll screw anything up." His voice was almost pleading. "Captain, by some miracle we've managed to keep three boilers operational. But there're no major repair parts in the entire frigging *world*."

Matt's shoulders slumped and he nodded at the intercom as if Spanky was standing before him. "Very well. Prepare to secure number three." He turned to the expectant faces in the pilothouse, then glanced out the windows at the Grik ship little more than a mile ahead. "Damn." He saw disappointment on Keje's face, in spite of the feline lack of expression. "We'll get another chance. It's time we learned something about your 'Ancient Enemy.' We must!" He strode back to his chair and looked at the ship ahead.

"Sink it."

It was dusk when they crept back into the bay. The fuel bunkers were entirely empty and the steam pressure had dropped to the point that maneuvering alongside the dock was out of the question. They dropped anchor close to where they had when they first arrived, and Matt wearily rubbed his eyes. None of the locals came out to see what was happening in the strait in case they needed assistance, and he'd been afraid they'd have to burn the wood anyway. The PBY was floating in its usual spot by the pier and he wondered how much longer it would have been before Lieutenant Mallory squandered some of the precious fuel they'd topped it off with to come and look for them. He saw several figures standing on the wing in the gloom, staring at them even now.

"We'll start ferrying Keje's people ashore immediately," he said. "We'll warp the ship over in the morning."

"Do not be discouraged!" Keje admonished him. He'd gotten over his own disappointment and was now almost giddy with their easy success. "You've won a great victory, and for my own sake, I'm glad *Salissa* was with you!"

"He's right," said Sandra. She'd been with them on the bridge ever since it became clear that there'd be no battle casualties. She gestured at the city, the lights even now beginning to burn. The dock was again lined with a chaotic throng, only this time instead of panic there was jubilation. "Those people saw their enemy for the first time today, many of them, and now they know that enemy isn't invincible. It'll mean a lot."

"It would have meant more if we could've gotten some information, and we still don't know about that third ship." In the last moments before *Walker* destroyed it, the Grik hoisted the same signal the first one had. Nothing was seen by the lookout, so even if there had been another Grik nearby, it probably wasn't close enough to see the flags. Still . . .

"As you told me earlier," Keje reminded Matt, "there will be another time."

Matt turned to Bernie Sandison. "You have the watch. I'll escort Captain Keje ashore, or to his ship, if he pleases." He shifted his gaze to Sandra. "Would you care to accompany us, Lieutenant?"

Sandra smiled. "Of course, Captain. Just let me change." She took a step away from him and held her arms out. She was still dressed in the surgical smock she'd put on when the ship went to quarters.

"I don't think—" he began, but Keje put his clawed hand on his shoulder.

"Yes, she should. And so should you, my friend." Keje looked at him appraisingly. "Wear your fine sword and your finest hat. You . . ." He grinned. "*We* have just won a great victory! We must look the part!"

*   *   *

Isak Reuben and Gilbert Yager sat on the huge wooden cleat the Catalina was tied to and smoked. They were indifferent to the bustle as well as the repeated calls by Lieutenant Mallory out on the plane to put out their cigarettes. Occasionally, a reveling Lemurian coughed in surprise as it passed through the blue cloud surrounding them. The Mice paid no heed. Finally, Mallory squatted near the wingtip of the flying boat, almost at eye level and just a few yards away. He decided to try reason.

"Look, fellas," he said, almost shouting over the throng, "if you don't give a damn about yourselves, think of the plane. Nobody smokes around airplanes!"

Another boatload of *Big Sal*'s warriors arrived on the dock to be received with cheering calls and stamping feet. Isak took another puff and looked at him. "Don't care about your damn plane, Army Man," he said. "All it did was sit there and ... float, while our *home* was out there by itself!"

"Typical," snorted Gilbert.

Mallory was in no mood to be harsh with the men—especially now. He did wonder where they'd gotten all the smokes, though. For the last hour, all they'd done was sit there and chain-smoke the damn things. Must've been Alden. The big Marine always had cigarettes. Some said when he came aboard in Surabaya, his duffel was stuffed with them. He must have loaded them down. And no wonder. Both the men were covered from head to foot with thick, sticky crude. It was matted in their hair and saturated their clothes. All that showed through the slimy black ooze was the whites of their eyes and, of course, the cherries on the ends of their cigarettes. He tried a different approach.

"But, fellas. This is a *Navy* plane!"

The next time the launch maneuvered to the pier it unloaded to a renewed crescendo of acclaim, which reached a furious peak when Matt, Sandra, and Keje climbed onto the dock. The triumphant crowd immediately mobbed them. Nobody really knew yet what had happened in the strait, but *Walker* was back and the enemy was gone. For now, that was enough. Sergeant Alden forced his way through the press and spoke briefly in the captain's ear. Matt stood at least a head taller than most of those around, and he looked about for a moment, his gaze finally settling on the Mice. Isak sucked down a last lungful of smoke.

"Crap. I bet he *makes* us put 'em out." Both men stood, leaving sticky blotches of tar on the cleat where they'd been. The captain was moving toward them. Finally, he stopped a few yards away, as if afraid to come any closer with his high-collar white uniform on. The contrast between them couldn't have been more profound. A strange, instinctual awareness blossomed in the back of Isak's mind, and his right hand moved upward in an unfamiliar, half-forgotten fashion, gluing his index finger to his forehead.

"We found oil, Skipper, if you please. Not an hour after you left this morning. Right where that Aussie said it'd be." He paused suddenly, at a loss. He didn't think he had ever spoken to an officer before he'd been spoken to. The smile that spread across the captain's face emboldened him, however. "Good thing you weren't there, sir. 'Specially dressed like that."

Gilbert nodded in solemn agreement. "Can we come home now?"

The din of celebration ashore had died down to some degree. Earl Lanier didn't know whether that meant the party was winding down or just moving farther away. He shrugged and wiped sweat from his eyebrows with his furry forearm. The small galley situated beneath the amidships gun platform was his private domain, but sometimes he wondered about the old saying that it was better to rule in hell than serve in heaven. Next to the boiler rooms, the galley was the hottest place on the ship. He might rule there, but he also served, and so as far as he was concerned, it was just hell without any perks at all. Groaning a little, because his stomach always made it inconvenient to stoop, he peered at the loaves baking in the big oven that traversed the aft bulkhead. They were ready. The smell of the bread made with what passed among the locals for flour was strange but not unpleasant, and the taste hinted of pumpkin. The crew complained, of course. Anything different was always the subject of complaint—which struck him as particularly ridiculous under the present circumstances. Lanier didn't care. As long as it made bread, of a sort, that filled the bellies of the men as they filed by, he was content. They'd have complained if it didn't taste weird. It was their duty to complain, he supposed, and it didn't bother him anymore. He knew they'd complain more if there wasn't anything to eat.

He opened the oven and removed the loaves and set them aside to cool. Then he went to his big copper cauldron and lifted the lid. A rush of wet steam flooded the galley and he grimaced. Inside the cauldron roiled a stew made from one of the local land creatures. He didn't know what it was, but it looked like a turkey with a tail. A short, stubby tail, to be sure, but a tail by any definition. It also didn't smell anything like a turkey. He plunged a ladle into the stew and stirred. Dark, unrecognizable chunks of meat pursued one another in the vortex. He raised the ladle to his lips, blew, and sampled the broth. His eyes went wide. "They won't complain about that," he muttered. "They won't even say a word. They'll just hang me."

He wiped his greasy hands on his apron and opened the spice cupboard. Not much left, he lamented. Plenty of salt, some curry, but almost no black pepper. Better save that, he judged. He pulled out a large tray heaped with little dried peppers he'd acquired in Java before the Squall and looked at them speculatively. He'd never tried one, but Juan said they were hot as hell. He picked one out and sniffed. Nothing. He touched it with the tip of his tongue. There was a little tingling sensation, but that was all. He grunted.

"What the hell?"

He grabbed a double handful of the peppers and pitched them in the stew. "Sure can't make it worse," he said to himself. He also shoveled in another cup of salt. "Fellas need salt," he muttered piously. "They sweat it out fast enough."

He stirred the cauldron's contents and replaced the lid with a metallic *clunk*. Then he wiped his hands on his apron again and checked the heat. Satisfied, he stepped to the other side of the galley and retrieved his fishing pole. It was a relatively short, stout rod made of a shoot from the curious Baalkpan bamboo. The line was rolled around it with about two feet of woven wire for a leader at the end. The hook was stuck in the handle. He took a stringy piece of the "turkey" innards and impaled it on the hook. The

mess attendant, Ray Mertz, slept in a chair near the hatch.
He was leaning against the bulkhead with the front legs off
the deck. Lanier was tempted to knock the others out from
under him, but settled for kicking his foot. The younger
man nearly fell anyway when his eyes fluttered open.

"Watch the fires," said Earl. "Time to get *my* breakfast."
Ignoring tradition, he whistled "The Krawdad Song" happily but quietly off-key as he strode from under the gun
platform. "Bad enough I have to cook the shit," he told
himself. "They can't expect me to eat it." Eat it he rarely
did. He, almost alone among the crew, liked the silvery
flasher-fish. Fried, mostly. The men were just squeamish, he
decided. Sure, they'd eat anything that went over the side,
from people to turds, but a catfish would too. Fried fish was
his favorite food in the world and had been since he was a
kid, near Pinedale, Wyoming. There the trout could be had
with little effort, and they fulfilled their purpose in life only
when they simmered in his skillet.

He stepped to the rail on the starboard side, next to
the number one torpedo mount. Not far away, the lights
of the city cast their ceaselessly shifting reflection on the
small waves around the darkened ship. It was almost eerily quiet. The boilers were cold, and for the first time he
could remember, the blowers were silent as well. The only
sounds besides water lapping against *Walker*'s plates were
the snores. Most of the crew was ashore on liberty, cel-
ebrating the victory, and there was still an hour or more
before the first wave of drunken revelers returned to the
ship. Many who hadn't been so fortunate, or who simply
decided to forgo the festivities—including some Lemurian
"cadets"—were scattered about, sleeping on deck, away
from the stifling confines of the berthing spaces. But they
were exhausted, and Lanier's quiet whistling disturbed no
one. He rotated the pole in his hand and the "turkey" innards began their slow descent to the water.

"Fishin'?" inquired a quiet voice from behind.

"No," Lanier sneered, "I'm rootin' up taters."

Tom Felts eased up beside him in the gloom. *The scrawny
gunner's mate must have the watch*, Lanier thought.

"Did you hear them Mice found oil after all?" Felts
asked.

The cook nodded. He felt genuine relief over that. "I wonder how long it'll be before we have any to burn?"

"Not too long, they say. Something about it being 'sweet,' or something. 'Cats already have storage tanks built. All they have to do is ship 'em over there and set 'em up. Few days, maybe." Felts sighed. "Sure hope so. I only thought I felt helpless before the fires went out."

Lanier nodded in the darkness. He cooked over charcoal, but with the lights out, it was hard to see in the galley. All he had were a couple of little lamps fired by the stinky oil of those big fish the 'cats hunted.

"Yup," he said, wishing Felts would go away. Suddenly, his pole jerked downward. There was no need to set the hook. Whatever had it, *had* it. He held on tight as the line whipped back and forth and the end of the pole jerked erratically. He didn't have a reel, so all he could do was keep tension while the fish tired and when it was spent, he'd drag it aboard. With the leader in the fish's jaws, the braided line would hold as long as the fish wasn't much over forty or fifty pounds. He grunted under the strain as it tried to go deep, under the hull.

"Whatcha got?" Felts whispered excitedly.

Lanier risked a quick, incredulous glance. "A fish, you idiot."

"No, I mean what kind?"

"Christ, Felts," the cook rasped, still trying to control his voice, "I don't know what *kind* any I've already caught are! It might be another one of them or it might not. Lay off!"

The fight went on a while longer, Lanier puffing with exertion and the gunner's mate peering expectantly over the side.

"I think he's runnin' out of steam," offered Felts encouragingly.

Lanier jerked a nod and blew sweat off his upper lip. He glanced behind to make sure the coast was clear. He didn't want to trample anybody. "Here we go," he wheezed. He turned and grasped the pole more firmly with his hands and under his arm and lumbered to port.

"Hey!" Felts exclaimed as something thrashed at the surface of the water and thumped and thudded up the side of the ship. Right next to him, less than a yard from his feet, some . . . *thing* right out of Felts's most fevered nightmare squirmed out of the darkness and onto the deck. It was six feet long, with the body of a flat snake except for a feathery "fin" that ran its length, top and bottom. Very much like an eel—except for the head. Its head looked sort of like a normal fish, but its eyes were huge and dark and full of malice and its mouth was stuffed with what seemed like hundreds of ridiculously long, needle-sharp teeth, flashing in jaws that opened impossibly wide. The lights from shore showed a rainbow color that shimmered as it flailed in spastic rage, snapping at the line, the deck . . . and Felts as it slithered past.

"Goddamn!" he squeaked and jerked back against the rail. Fumbling at his side for the pistol strapped there, he pulled it out, thumbing the safety off. An earsplitting roar shattered the night as he fired at the thing, again and again. Bullets spanged off the deck plates and whined over the water. Pieces of fish and flakes of paint rained down on the men who'd been sleeping nearby. The automatic's slide locked back, empty, and still Felts pointed it at the fish, jerking the trigger in convulsive panic.

Lanier flung down his pole. "You stupid son of a bitch!" he shrieked. Heads were coming up slowly off the deck as men raised them with understandable caution, and voices called out to one another. The sound of shoes running on steel approached and Chief Campeti arrived with a battle lantern in one hand and a pistol in the other. The Bosun wasn't far behind, dressed only in T-shirt and skivvies.

"What the hell's goin' on here?" Campeti bellowed. "Who fired a weapon?" He shined the lantern around. Eyes, human and Lemurian, squinted in the glare. Finally the beam fell on Felts's terrified face and the smoking pistol, still outstretched. Campeti redirected the light and involuntarily stepped back. Gray saw the fish too. It was shot to pieces, but its terrible jaws still snapped spasmodically. A hook gleamed brightly, piercing the lower lip, and the line trailed to port.

"Who brought that thing on my deck?" Gray demanded.

"I did!" Lanier snarled, stepping up. "I work my ass off feeding these goons and I try to catch a little fish for myself and what happens? One of 'em *destroys* it!" The cook had his filleting knife in his hand and Gray wondered if he meant to use it on Felts. Instead, he knelt beside the twitching fish as if by a dying loved one. The knife moved over the corpse in benediction. "Destroyed," he lamented. Quite a gathering of half-naked men and entirely naked Lemurians had assembled by now.

"Anybody hurt?" Campeti asked. There were murmured voices, but no replies.

"No eat!" came a voice from the group.

"What?"

"No eat!" One of the cadets edged forward and stared down at the fish. He looked up at Gray. "Bad fish. No eat. Make very ... dead sick. Chops? Chopping? Chopper! Chopper fish not food. Eat ... dead!"

Gray prodded Lanier with his foot. "You hear that? Felts just saved your worthless life."

Campeti shined his light at Felts, who'd finally lowered the gun. He was shaking. "You okay?"

Felts gulped. "Snakes, Chief. Ever since I was a kid. Then that thing came whoopin' up over the side ..." He shook his head.

Campeti took the pistol from his hand and nodded. "Me too." He shook out one of his last cigarettes and handed it over, then lit it for him when the gunner's mate's hands shook too much to do it himself.

Lieutenant Garrett had arrived. He wasn't wearing any more than Gray, but he'd put on his hat. "What's up, Chief?" he asked, and Gray told him what had happened.

While he was talking, Lanier stood up. "I demand that man be put on report!" he growled. "Shooting a pistol while everyone's sleepin', hell, he could'a shot somebody! Not to mention wreckin' my fish! He's in your division, Mr. Garrett. What are you gonna do?"

Garrett sighed and looked at Felts. They'd had a tough day and nerves were raw enough. Discipline was essential, but looking at that fish, *he* probably would have shot at it. "Ahhh ..."

"Yeah, and you're in *my* division, Lanier," said Alan Letts, stepping forward. He, like Campeti, was fully dressed, although he hadn't been on watch. "What am I going to do with you? Creeping around in the middle of the night, releasing dangerous, *poisonous* creatures to run loose on deck . . ." There were loud guffaws while Letts shook his head. "I hate to think what the captain would say about that." More laughter, and Lanier's chubby face blanched. Letts turned to Gray. "Bosun? Since the deck division seems most affected . . ." He paused until the laughter died down. "What with the damaged paintwork and the mess . . ." Even Felts was grinning now. "I suggest if Lieutenant Garrett agrees, you make the call."

Gray scratched his head and looked at Felts, whose grin immediately faded. Then he glared at Lanier, who wilted about as much as his abrasive personality allowed. When he spoke, his tone was very formal. "Mr. Lanier wouldn't knowingly allow anything more poisonous than the chow he feeds us aboard the ship"—hoots of glee—"so I hold him blameless so long as he cleans that nasty, slimy thing off my deck." His glare settled on Felts, who shriveled beneath its intensity. "On the other hand, I think the log should show Gunner's Mate Felts single-handedly defended the ship and her sleepin' crew from the sneak attack of a dangerous sea monster—provided I see him hard at work with a chippin' hammer and a can of paint first thing in the mornin', erasing all evidence of his heroic deed." He looked at Garrett. "Lieutenant?"

"If that suits you, Bosun, I guarantee he'll be here."

"Mr. Letts?"

"Fine by me. Chief Campeti has the deck, though."

Campeti shrugged. "Bravest thing I ever saw. Blood everywhere and every shot hit. Boy ought'a get a medal."

Gray called out to Lanier, shuffling away in disgust. "Let's see that thing over the side right now, Earl. I don't want to see it again on my plate."

As the drama ebbed and the snores resumed, Campeti stayed with Felts. He still had the duty, and he wanted to make sure he was all right.

"That was somethin'," Felts whispered. "Mr. Letts sure came through. I thought he was ashore. He's turnin' into a pretty good guy, for an officer."

"Yeah," Campeti muttered. "He was in a mighty good mood." Sonny Campeti was a man with many faults, and he was honest enough to know it. Spreading rumors wasn't one of them. Lieutenant Letts had stepped up to the plate beyond anyone's expectations. He'd gone from a comical, if popular, character to an essential member of the cadre that might get them through this alive. If the lipstick Campeti had seen smeared across his jaw in the light of the battle lantern was responsible for that, he wasn't going to make a peep. But damn!

Matt and Sandra remained at the celebration long enough to be polite, but the seep and other intoxicants flowed freely enough that they doubted their early departure was even noticed. It was the first time Matt had allowed the crew to really cut loose, and he was a little nervous about that. They'd been told to have a good time (they'd earned it), and there was much to celebrate. He just hoped they wouldn't celebrate too hard. They'd destroyed two Grik ships and they were beginning to hate the Grik almost as much as the Japanese. The Mice found oil right where Bradford said they would and the Australian's prestige soared. He was last seen sprawled, insensible, on a pillow with Nakja-Mur. The Mice had disappeared. Matt suspected they'd crept back aboard the ship, and he hated to tell them they were still needed at the well. Again he felt a thrill at the prospect of full bunkers. These long weeks he'd felt so helpless, unable to *do* anything, and he was haunted by the fact that, somewhere out there, was *Mahan*. With fuel, they might still save her. What haunted him more, however, was his battle with priorities, and his growing uncertainty over whether *Mahan* topped the list.

Intensely aware of each other's presence, Matt and Sandra strolled quietly and companionably in the direction of the pier. When they reached it, the dock was empty, but it hadn't been for long. A launch burbled slowly to the ship, filled with destroyermen in various states of animation. They were required to report aboard by 0100, and none were to remain ashore overnight. Dowden had gathered a few sober men and formed a "flying" shore patrol and was already sending those who'd become too rowdy back to the ship. He'd make sure they were all rounded up.

They stopped near the cleat where the Mice had been

sitting, and Matt remembered to keep his distance. He still wore his sole surviving "dress" uniform. Some men in the launch began a song, and because of Sandra's presence, he cringed when he recognized it. The words carried over the water even above the boat's loud motor—it was plain the men were far more interested in volume than quality. The loudest voice sounded suspiciously like Lieutenant McFarlane:

> The boys out in the trenches
> Have got a lot to say
> Of the hardships and the sorrows
> That come the soldier's way.
> But we destroyer sailors
> Would like their company
> On a couple of trips in our skinny ships
> When we put out to sea!

"Nice night," Matt said, lamely trying to distract Sandra from the chorus, but it was no use. It was the men's favorite part and they always belted it out.

> Oh, it's roll and toss
> And pound and pitch
> And creak and groan, you son of a bitch!
> Oh, boy, it's a hell of a life on a destroyer!

Matt glanced at Sandra, expecting to see her cover her mouth with her hand in shock or something, but instead she grinned.

> Oh, Holy Mike, you ought to see
> How it feels to roll through each degree.
> The goddamn ships were never meant for sea!
> You carry guns, torpedoes, and ash-cans in a bunch,
> But the only time you're sure to fire
> *Is when you shoot your lunch!*
> Your food it is the Navy bean,
> You hunt the slimy submarine.
> It's a son-of-a-bitch of a life on a destroy—*er*!

Sandra did cover her mouth now, giggling. The boat was nearing the ship. There was no moon and in spite of her new, lighter shade, they only vaguely made out *Walker*'s form in the darkness. She seemed forlorn out there with no lights, and moored away from the dock like an outcast. The song's last verse reached them with less vigor, as if the singers sensed the mood of loneliness as they came alongside. Or maybe now, after all they'd been through with the old four-stacker, they were less inclined to hurt her feelings. The last verse was more somber anyway.

> We've heard of muddy dug-outs,
> Of shell holes filled with slime,
> Of cootie hunts and other things
> That fill a soldier's time.
> But believe me, boys, that's nothing,
> To what it's like at sea,
> When the barometer drops
> And the clinometer hops
> And the wind blows dismally.

"They're fine men, Captain Reddy. Your crew," Sandra said softly.

"Yes, they are." He sighed. "And that makes it even harder."

"What? Using them up?"

He looked at her, surprised, but nodded. "Yeah, and that's what I'm doing. I've gotten them into a war I know nothing about." He shook his head. "Oh, don't worry, I'm not feeling sorry for myself. I know there wasn't a choice. We haven't had a choice since we went through the Squall. I'm not even complaining about that. However inconvenient it's made our lives, it saved us. It's just . . ." He couldn't tell her how he felt. Especially couldn't tell her about the doubts and nightmares and guilt he felt over *Mahan*. He'd made so many mistakes! And he definitely couldn't tell her how he felt about her. He changed the subject.

"You came out on the old *Langley*, right?" She nodded. The *Langley* was America's first real aircraft carrier. She'd been built on a merchant's hull and had a goofy flight deck

erected above the superstructure, earning her the nickname *Covered Wagon.* By modern standards, she looked
very strange and was too small and slow to be considered a
real carrier anymore, even before the war. She'd been trans-
porting P-40s to Java when Japanese planes hammered her.
She was helpless under the assault, and it was the most terrified Sandra had ever been—up to that time.

"We'd been on sweeps off Bawean Island, looking for
the Jap invasion fleet for Java when we heard about *Langley,*" he said. "We were heading to Surabaya to refuel when
Doorman turned us around." Matt's voice became a quiet
monotone as he stared across the water at *Walker's* silhouette. "The Japs *were* off Bawean. We'd just missed them.
We took off so fast, *Pope* couldn't catch us." He grimaced.
"Not that it made any difference. As soon as we cleared the
mines, we came under air attack again and there was nothing we could do but take it. We had a total of eight fighters left, and the Dutch were saving them to use against the
invasion as it landed." He snorted. "Eight planes weren't
going to stop the invasion force, but they might've helped
us find it, and kept the Jap planes off our backs." He was
silent for several moments before he continued. Sandra
waited patiently, quietly.

"The Jap screen for the invasion convoy wasn't much
heavier than us, for once, but we had no air cover at all. The
Japs corrected their fire with spotting planes throughout
the battle. It was a hell of a thing to see, though. Cruisers
aren't battleships, but even cruisers look damned impressive steaming parallel, blasting away at each other. Of
course all we could do was watch." He took a deep, bitter breath. "*Exeter* got hit, and a few minutes later, *Korte-
naer* took one of those big Jap torpedoes. She just blew up.
Edwards was right on her tail and had to swerve. By the
time we went past, she was upside down, folded in half. We
didn't see anybody in the water.

"*Electra*, one of the Brit destroyers, made a torpedo attack alone, to distract the Japs from finishing *Exeter*. She
was flying the biggest flag I ever saw . . ." Taking off his hat,
he passed his hand over his head and stared at the lights
on the water, remembering. "I guess every Jap ship in the
line concentrated on her. All we saw was waterspouts,

then steam and smoke ... then nothing." He shook his head with sad amazement. "It was getting dark and I guess Doorman'd had enough. We charged in and launched torpedoes while the cruisers turned away, but nobody got a single hit."

He shrugged. "We did break the Jap formation, though, and Doorman got away. You got to give him credit for guts. As soon as we gave them the slip, Doorman went looking for the transports again. We didn't. We were out of torpedoes and nearly out of fuel, and our engines were finished after running thirty knots all through the fight. Binford ordered us back to Surabaya."

The launch's engine could be heard again as it shoved off to return to the dock and await another load.

"Doorman wasn't an idiot. I didn't like the way they put him in charge, but his biggest problem was he never knew what he was up against, never knew what he was facing or even where the enemy was. Now I know how he must've felt. We don't *know* what we're facing either, and like I said when we first helped *Big Sal* ..." He stopped and looked at her. "Don't get me wrong, I'm glad we did! These people, Keje, Adar, Chack, even Nakja-Mur, they're good people. They've helped us and deserve our help in return. I just didn't feel right getting the men involved in a war we know nothing about. The Grik are bad news, maybe even worse than the Japs. They need to be defeated and, however it happened, we're here now, and we'll never be safe until they are. We've had it pretty easy so far, but there has to be more to the Grik than these little two- or three-ship task forces. Somehow, we've got to find out!"

"How?"

He grinned at her. "I don't know, but I'm working on it. Any ideas?"

Sandra smiled. She suddenly knew he would never have shown such vulnerability with anyone else on the ship. He wouldn't have spoken of any of this. What did that mean? "What happened to Doorman?" she asked. Matt's grin vanished.

"He ran into the Japs again that night. *DeRuyter* and *Java* were sunk. *Exeter* and *Encounter* made it back to Surabaya—where you came on the stage. *Houston* and

Perth got slaughtered trying to make it through the Sunda Strait."

"All because they didn't know what they were up against." She looked speculatively at the PBY floating nearby. "But now we have air cover and the enemy doesn't."

He followed her gaze. "Well, yeah, but unless we can make more fuel for it, it won't be much help. That's not out of the question, and we're going to try. Mallory says it'll burn gasoline, which we should be able to do, but it needs high-octane stuff. I don't know squat about that, but Bradford does and as soon as we have a decent reserve for the ship, he's going to try to sort it out." He shrugged and looked at the Catalina like one might a worn-out horse, wondering if it had the stamina for a few more miles or not. "Of course, parts to keep it in the air are even more impossible than the things we need for the ship."

"How much fuel does it have?" Sandra asked. "Enough to look for *Mahan*?"

When Matt answered, his voice was without inflection. It was a habit she'd noticed he used when he'd agonized over a decision and come to one he didn't like. "Maybe. But fuel's not really the issue. We tanked her up, and we have enough in drums on the ship to fill her again. But even if we had all the fuel in the world, I can't send anyone up in that thing unless *Walker*'s close behind. Not unless I have to. Riggs thinks he can fix its radio, and that might make a difference. Until then, I won't chance stranding somebody. It might also be different if we had some idea where *Mahan* is, but we don't. 'West of Sumatra' a few weeks ago is too damn vague to risk men's lives. For all we know, she's sunk . . . or the Grik have her already." He sighed. "My conscience tells me to chase her as soon as we have the fuel; she's my responsibility. But *Walker*'s my responsibility too, and I won't risk her on another wild-goose chase until we know the other team's lineup. *Mahan* and our friends'll have to wait—they'd understand."

"Do Mr. Mallory and Mr. Brister understand?" she asked. "I know they're pretty hot to look."

He set his jaw. "It doesn't matter if they understand. It's my responsibility."

"It does matter. They feel like they left them too. I think

you should talk to them. Explain." She hesitated, and bit her lip before she spoke again. "Weren't you just criticizing the Dutch for being too timid with their planes?"

Matt smiled, acknowledging the hit, but shook his head. "It's not the same. That plane is precious, beat up as it is. But I *will* risk it if I have to, and I'm pretty sure I will. But only in coordination with the ship. If I learned anything from Admiral Doorman—or the whole experience of the Asiatic Fleet—it was to never ride a tricycle in front of a steamroller with your eyes closed. Are the Grik a steamroller?" He shrugged. "The 'cats make 'em sound scary enough—and they are scary—but if all they have in the Java Sea is a dozen ships—" He grinned. "Ten now—maybe they're the tricycle and we don't have anything to worry about." He held his fingers apart. "We were *that* close to maybe finding out today. Just a few gallons of fuel might have set our minds at ease. Now . . ." He paused. "Unlike Admiral Doorman, I don't intend to chase shadows or hang ourselves out in the breeze until—" He stopped, and a strange expression crossed his face. "Until they come to us . . ." He grinned. "Or maybe I will!"

"What?"

"Just an idea. I'll tell you later." He gestured at the arriving launch, and one of the men clambered onto the dock. He seemed surprised to see the captain. "Are you ready to go back to the ship, Skipper?"

Matt glanced at Sandra. She shook her head.

"Not just yet."

Another man climbed from the boat, cursing. It was Tony Scott, trying to get farther from the water—at least until the next load forced him to cross it again. The two destroyermen stayed discreetly out of earshot.

"You're not using them up," Sandra said in a quiet voice. "The men, I mean. The world—this world, the one we left—it doesn't matter. The world uses them up despite anything you do. If you're not careful, you *can* use yourself up. You love your men. They know it and so do I." She looked up at him and, for a moment, he saw the lights of the city shining in her eyes. "And we all love you for it. That and other things." He swallowed, trying to remain impassive. What did she mean by that?

"We love you because we know you'll do whatever you can to keep us safe. But we also know we're at war. No matter what else has changed, that hasn't, and sometimes you have to risk the thing you love to keep it safe." She nodded toward the ship. "They know that, and they know because you're the man you are, you'll risk them if you have to." She sighed. "When we have fuel, we could just leave. We could go to the Philippines, or Australia. Maybe find fuel there. Eventually get to Hawaii, or even the West Coast. Maybe there aren't any Grik there. Maybe there's something just as bad, but what if there's not? We'd be 'safe,' but what then? We *need* friends if we're going to survive, and we've been lucky and made some. They happen to be in a fight for their lives. Besides being the best way to keep us safe, in the long run, helping them is the right thing to do. Your men understand that, Captain Reddy, and I bet if you put it to a vote, most would choose to stay. They know they might die. Life on a destroyer's dangerous work. They could have died 'back home' any day of the week, a thousand different ways, before the war even started. So the best way you can ensure that most won't die is to continue doing your job the best you know how. And when the time comes, fight your ship! Don't worry about what you can't control—just fight to win!" She grinned then, her small teeth flashing. "And quit feeling guilty for getting us into this mess! It was an accomplishment, not a failure!"

"I, ah, how . . . ?"

Her grin became a gentle smile. "I live only two doors down, 'doors' being thin green curtains, and you talk in your sleep."

He cleared his throat and looked in the direction of the sailors near the launch.

"No, not bad," she assured him. "But I know you blame yourself for everything from Marvaney's death to losing *Mahan*." Her smile faded. "That has to stop. If you don't start getting some *rest* while you sleep, you will start making mistakes."

He nodded at her. "I'll try. And thanks, Lieutenant."

She gave him a stern look. "You call the other officers by their first names in informal situations, why not me?"

"Well, because . . ."

"Because I'm a woman? I'm also your friend. At least I hope so. I think Keje even still thinks I'm your *wife*! Don't you think we could use first names, at least when no one's watching?"

Matt felt his cheeks burn, but nodded. He wondered how slippery a slope that would prove to be. "Okay . . . Sandra. But only when nobody's watching." His voice was quite serious as he spoke. "I'm sure you must know why."

Of course she knew why, and as she suspected, it was duty that kept him distant. Duty to his men. She felt a thrill to realize he really was interested in her, but also a deep sadness that the situation prevented them from acknowledging it. She forced a smile.

"Yes, Matthew. I understand."

Right then, the look on her face, the tone of her voice—he might have kissed her in spite of everything, to hell with the consequences. If Silva hadn't intervened. More precisely, if the growing calamity of the spectacle that Silva was generating hadn't done so.

A rampaging super lizard would have seemed sedate compared to his arrival. He was literally *wearing* half of Dowden's "flying" shore patrol. Even as they watched, one of Dowden's men—Fred Reynolds—went "flying" dangerously close to the edge of the pier. On second glance, he wouldn't have fallen, since he was chained to Silva's wrist.

"Lemme go!" he roared. "Where'd you take my girl? I'm in the mood for luuuve!"

"Oh, my God."

Not to be outdone by his predecessors, Dennis began singing as the men wrestled him closer to the captain: "I joined the Nay-vee to see the world! And what did I see? I saw the *sea*! I'm not . . . I won't? . . . I *don't* get seasick, but I'm awful sick of *seeeaa*!" He vomited on Reynolds, who was lying at his feet. "Archg! Sorry, boy . . ." He looked wildly around. "Where's my girl? My lady love! I ain't through dancin' yet!" He proceeded into an astonishingly graceful waltz—for a drunk with two men hanging on him and another chained to his arm. He stopped suddenly, as though surprised at himself, and hooted: "I'm a Gram-

maw!" Then he saw the captain. He came to swaying, exaggerated attention and saluted, dragging poor Reynolds
to his feet. "Eav-nin', Skipper! *Lootenit* Tucker!"

"Mr. Silva." Matt nodded. "You seem . . . true to form."

"Aye, aye, sir! Cheap seep! Hell, it's free!" He belched
loudly.

"Are you ready to return to the ship? Peacefully?"

Silva blinked, looking around. "Hell, no! These bastards
has . . . adducted . . . obstructed . . . *swiped* me from my
wife!"

"What? *What?* Mr. Dowden, what's the meaning of this?"
Before Larry could even begin to explain, there came a
shriek from the darkness.

"Si-vaa!" Two brindled shapes ran toward them, one
ahead of the other. The first, obviously female, leaped on
the gunner's mate and, combined with his other passengers,
nearly knocked him down at last. Matt thought she was at-
tacking him until she wrapped her arms around his neck
and started licking his face.

"There's my darlin' angel!" he cooed.

The other brindled shape caught up and slammed to attention, but even in the dark, it was clear that Chack-Sab-
At was quivering with rage.

"What the hell's going on here!" Matt bellowed. "Silva,
what have you *done*?"

"Cap-i-taan!" said Chack, "that's my sister, Risa. She is
unwell. That giant . . . creature has intoxicated her and . . ."

"He mate? He *marry* me!" Risa squealed happily. "He
Sab-At clan now!"

"*Never!*" seethed Chack. Sandra's hand now covered her
mouth in earnest, but Matt couldn't tell if she was hiding
shock or laughter.

"My God, Silva, I swear! If you've done anything to damage our relationship with these people, or if you forced . . .
God! Are you *insane*? I'll *hang* you!"

"Skipper, I'll swear on a Bible or Marvaney's record
stack—whatever you say—"

"You *lie*!" shouted Chack.

"He no lie!" Risa purred. "Nobody mad but silly Chack.
People no mad. People no . . . embarrassed? By mate! Si-
vaa *love* Risa!"

The shore party, those that could, eased away. Chack's ears were back and his tail swished like a cobra. He looked about to strike. Matt was preparing another volcanic response when Sandra tugged his sleeve and whispered in his ear. He looked sharply at her and was incredulous when he saw her nod.

"We'll get to the bottom of this," he promised darkly. "Mr. Chack, please escort your sister to her Home. At the very least, she seems ... indisposed."

"But ... Aye, aye, Cap-i-taan."

"What about my weddin' night?" Silva moaned, and Matt turned to him.

"My orders were that all personnel be back aboard by 0100. Since you had no special permission, you may not stay ashore to ... consummate your 'marriage,' nor may you do so on my ship! USS *Walker* is not a honeymoon barge!" He paused. There was one way to find out if Sandra was right. "Tomorrow I'll speak to Keje and Nakja-Mur and discover what further process, if any, is required to finalize your and Risa's ... nuptials. Perhaps a joint ceremony?"

He was rewarded by a marked widening of Silva's surprisingly sober eyes. Getting even with Chack was one thing, but he wouldn't enjoy the consequences of including his captain in the joke.

"Nighty night, sugar-lips!" Silva said, and gave Risa a kiss, which she returned with evident relish.

God, I hope it is a joke! Matt thought with a shudder.

After Chack stiffly led his sister away and a suddenly docile Silva was carried to the ship, Matt removed his hat and rubbed his eyes. "Jesus!"

Sandra laughed. "Is this the way it always was with these guys, back in the Philippines?"

"No! Well, yeah, but ... yeah." He smiled.

"I told Chack to watch his back." Sandra chuckled. "I wonder when he'll figure it out?"

"I wonder if it's over!"

"You don't think he really ... ?" Sandra gasped.

"If we're not surrounded by angry 'cats with torches in the morning, I'm going to pretend it never happened. But I guarantee Silva won't have the last laugh!" For a moment, the pier was empty again, but the electric tension between them was damped. Just as well.

Sandra cleared her throat. "Earlier, you said you had an idea. What was it?"

"What? Oh. Well, let me see if I can put my thoughts back together!"

What, then, would you have us do? How do we defeat them if the Ancient Ones could not?" The speaker was the High Chief of one of the great Homes. Seven of the huge vessels now floated in Baalkpan Bay, and all their chiefs, as well as a large number of senior "officers," were present in Nakja-Mur's Great Hall for this long-awaited council. There were even representatives from several smaller "land colonies." Gatherings on such a scale were rare, usually happening no more than once or twice a decade, and there was no official mechanism for summoning one. As far as Matt could tell, it might be as simple as shouted words from passing fishermen: "Big meeting at Baalkpan. Come if you want." Without better communications, that was probably exactly how it happened.

Great Gatherings were usually occasions for festivities, games, trade, and socialization. They were also times for crowded, prosperous Homes to branch off. To build new Homes and form new clans. It was a time that the People on their solitary wandering Homes looked forward to with pleasure and anticipation, wondering where and when the next would be held. But this one was different. All were aware of the seriousness of the growing threat, and those present, at least, seemed willing and even eager to discuss their next move. Few agreed what that move should be, however.

The Lemurian who'd spoken was Anai-Sa, High Chief

of *Fristar*, one of the Homes that had been in Baalkpan
Bay since before *Walker* arrived. He seemed young for his
rank, with a jet-black pelt and a spray of white whiskers
surrounding his face. His green eyes were intent. Besides
his heavily embroidered kilt, he wore only a multitude of
shimmering golden hoops around his neck and upper arms.
His people were "far rangers" who rarely entered these waters. Their "territory" was most often the South China Sea,
but Grik pressure had pushed them south. He was also the
most outspoken of the "why don't we just sail off where
there are no Grik" crowd.

Keje spoke in reply. "I would have you hear the words of
Cap-i-taan Reddy of the Amer-i-caans, and High Chief of
Waa-kur. He is High Chief of an independent clan and has
as much right to speak as anyone here. More, to my thinking, since he saved my Home from the Grik. The Amer-i-
caans have helped us prepare for this time with no concern
for personal gain." Keje stood before the silent group, looking out among them. He said nothing about *Walker*'s brief
sortie two weeks before that destroyed two more Grik
ships. All were aware of it, even if they hadn't been there
yet, and boasting sometimes detracts from self-evident
truth. Besides, the last thing Matt wanted was everyone
thinking *Walker* would save them all. As Keje suspected,
there were murmurs of protest. Not because the humans
weren't People, but because their ship was so small and
sparsely populated. Would they grant "Home" status to
fishing boats too?

Keje squared his shoulders and placed his hand upon the
scota at his side. "I declare Cap-i-taan Reddy is my Brother
as surely as any High Chief, and I offer combat to anyone
saying he does not deserve to speak." These last words
came in a growl.

There was some very unusual body language in response
to this threat, and some glanced to see Nakja-Mur's reaction. He merely stared at Keje's back across steepled claws
with his elbows on his knees.

"These Amer-i-caans come from far away, and know
more about war than we. Before they came to help us, they
were engaged in a struggle that defies belief. Their wondrous ship was just one of perhaps hundreds, and they

modestly tell me theirs was but the smallest and least powerful Home to fight in that unimaginable conflict! Yet it
prevailed!"

Matt winced at Chack's translation. Okay, so much for
not bragging. Besides, they'd "prevailed" in the sense that
they'd survived, but that was the only appropriate context for the word. Keje grinned at him ironically.

"Would you speak to them, my Brother? Perhaps you
can sway them. I'll tell them your words."

Matt nodded. For his plan to work, they had to see the
threat. But they also needed hope. How would he scare
them into joining the fight without scaring them away?
Particularly since the plan he was forming was risky, to say
the least. The irony of the situation struck him like a slap.
He remembered how unfathomable he'd thought admirals
and politicians were. Particularly within ABDA. Why they
made the decisions they did mattered only insofar as they
affected his ship, his crew, and himself. Suddenly he was
standing in similar shoes and found them most uncomfortable. He stepped to Keje's side and cleared his throat.

"I really don't know if *we* can defeat them," he said simply. Keje looked at him sharply, surprised by the dour opening, but Matt had stressed the word "we."

"I don't *know* much about them at all. Nobody does; not
even where they come from, or what kind of society sup-
ports their warlike nature. We're probably outnumbered.
Their ships aren't as large as yours, but they're much faster,
and each carries nearly as many warriors as yours since their
ships aren't Homes. They carry no families that we know of,
and they grow no food. They're meant for one thing only:
to transport warriors to battle." He paused. "That should
be both an advantage and a disadvantage to them. They
can pack a lot of warriors into their ships, but they have to
keep supplied or they can't stay in our territory long. One
thing we *do* know is they're a long way from home." He
shrugged. "They raid for provisions—Chill-chaap proves
that—but even that takes time from offensive operations,
and the more there are, the bigger that problem becomes.

"That's about all we know about their strategic situation, though. We don't know what they want or why they're
here, beyond an apparent hunger for conquest. We have

no real idea what their 'grand strategy' is. Their efforts so far have not seemed well coordinated, although Keje tells me they're better now than in the past. The best I can figure, they have several independent task forces on the loose, looking for us, and they hope to eventually overwhelm us with numbers. That's also the historical model recorded in your Scrolls.

"We too have advantages and disadvantages." Matt looked at the faces staring impassively back.

"And what are our advantages, beside the ability to simply leave them behind again?" The black-furred Lemurian's voice dripped sarcasm.

Matt regarded him coldly. "Courage is one," he answered, returning the green-eyed glare. "Thoughtful courage, not the wild-ass, charge-tanks-with-horses kind." There was absolutely no context for the statement, but somehow they grasped his meaning. All present knew, at least by description, the abandon with which Grik fought. Their attack was like a school of flasher-fish. Maybe they employed tactics, but once they came to grips, it was individual mindless ferocity.

"We also have *Walker*," he said matter-of-factly, "and nothing they have can match her speed and the range of her weapons. We'll have more weapons soon. Cannons, sort of like *Walker*'s, that'll fit on your ships. But most of all—I hope—we're smarter than they are. Smart enough to use their strengths against them. And if their strengths become weaknesses . . ." He shrugged.

"Frankly, our biggest disadvantage is ignorance." There were hostile murmurs at that. The closest Lemurian word to "ignorance" was precariously similar to "stupidity." He continued hastily on. "That's a disadvantage I'm personally sick of . . . for a lot of reasons, and one I plan to correct. It's our biggest disadvantage because of how much bigger it makes our other problems." He counted on his fingers. "First, there might be five or ten of their ships in the Java Sea right now, but we don't *know*. We don't *know* if they're part of a probe or a real push. The Scrolls describe a slow escalation, but is it just starting, or has it reached its peak? We don't *know*. Our ignorance makes it impossible to formulate a strategy to totally defeat them." He motioned

Benjamin Mallory forward. "Lieutenant, when you saw the aftermath at Tjilat—Chill-chaap, did you speculate on the nature of the Grik attack?"

"Yes, sir. It's hard to say, but I got the impression they made an amphibious assault, coordinated with an attack overland through the jungle."

"What makes you say that?"

"Well, it's just a guess. We didn't really study the battle-field, if you know what I mean, but the corpses in the jungle were in groups. Not really scattered around. Like the inhabitants were running away and ran into the Grik. Not like they were chased down and caught. It was just . . . the feeling I got."

Matt nodded. "That seems consistent—the multipronged attack. Like the tactic they used against *Big Sal*. Attack as many places as possible to split your defenses. That might even be an example of their overall strategy, writ small. If so, that shows us another one of our problems. We're way too scattered out. I know that's how you've always lived, but you've got to pull together. Believe me, we know about being all alone when the world is falling on us! The only way to defend against that sort of attack is to mass our forces. Keep them as united as possible and work to-gether as best we can. But where do we mass? We can't do it everywhere—that defeats the purpose." He looked measuringly at Nakja-Mur. "We could mass at Baalkpan—fortify the city and build a wall around it, with fighting posi-tions and maybe even cannons. We could clear the jungle around it and make a killing ground that even the Grik would fear. In fact, I think we should. But it'll take time, and that's a luxury we may not have. We don't know how much weight's behind them. It also surrenders all initiative to the enemy and sounds too much like what happened last time, if you ask me. Anyway, it all still boils down to: we just don't *know*!"

Nakja-Mur raised his bearded chin from his fingertips. "Could we defeat the Grik in such a manner?" he asked.

Matt hesitated. "No. We could prevent defeat for a time, but we couldn't win. While we sat behind our walls and fought them and killed them, and bled them white, we'd only grow weaker, while they would send more Grik. Just as it's written in your Scrolls. Eventually, they'd wear us down. The only way to *win* is to attack!"

There were incredulous cries. "Attack them? Attack where? We do not even know where they come from!" shouted the black-furred High Chief. Others yelled questions and comments as well: "We could harry their ships, but will they fight if we bring a large enough force to defeat them?" cried one. "We certainly can't catch them if they run!" "What will happen to Baalkpan if we leave it undefended?!" another asked. "He was talking about mass. Mass where?" "What's 'mass'?"

Matt listened to the uproar for a few moments longer. Finally, he spoke loudly a single word.

"Ignorance!"

Keje repeated it in the same tone. The tumult abruptly stopped and all eyes turned to the captain of *Walker*.

"Ignorance," he said again. "I'm getting pretty tired of it myself. Let's see if we can enlighten ourselves."

Even Keje blinked surprise. "How do we do that, my Brother?"

"We mass."

Keje was confused. "But you just said . . . they are spread out, they are faster—we can't mass here and wait for them all to find us, and we certainly cannot mass together and chase them down!"

"No, but we can mass defensively and let a few come to us. I don't want *all* of them until we know how many they are. And we won't do it here."

"I thought you said we should attack," said Nakja-Mur.

"Think of it as a 'defensive' attack. It won't be easy and it sure as hell won't be safe, but if it works, we ought to learn a lot about our enemy at long last."

"My people will have nothing to do with such madness!" huffed *Fristar*'s High Chief.

Nakja-Mur stood, a little shakily, Matt thought. "You may leave whenever you wish, then," he said. "My people don't have that choice." He looked at Matt. "My people . . . I . . . have never known war, but I will support this plan of yours whatever it might be. I do not want the Grik coming here." He smiled sadly. "You may have all the paint or whatever else you want if you can prevent that."

"Thank you, my lord," Matt replied, glancing around the hall. "But what we both need most right now are more warriors. 'Mass' means numbers."

Sergeant Pete Alden, United States Marine Corps, stared at the "mass" of trainees flailing at one another with clumsy enthusiasm and padded-point practice spears. Some were really trying, and the "Marines" did their best to instruct them. But to most of the newer recruits, it was still mostly a game. He cursed. Before now, the training had gone relatively well with the smaller groups he'd been dealing with. He'd applied a familiar regimen even if the exercises were different from his own experience. The rush of recruits since the Grik ship sailed right into Baalkpan Bay changed all that.

His carefully chosen, elite Marines were broken up to form a cadre of NCOs as the militia (now "Guard") swelled dramatically. Even warriors from some of the ships started to attend the drills. That was all well and good, but Parris Island had never seen a less likely draft, and he (who'd never been a drill instructor) now faced the impossible task of turning this collection of instinctively individualistic merchants, shopkeepers, fishers, and sailors into an army. And he had just a few weeks to do it. Right now, if he reconstituted his Marines, he could field two regiments of fairly well-trained, disciplined troops—and that's what he'd likely do for the captain's upcoming expedition. If they were successful, he would resume the training after they returned as veteran NCOs. Not just bright trainees who'd grasped the theory but couldn't yet teach from experience.

The warriors who came to train were accustomed to working together, but otherwise they were a pain in the neck. As "warriors" already, they had their own way of doing things. They understood that discipline was required in order to fight together—which the land folk didn't—but the close-order drill and concerted complexity of the captain's new/ancient tactics were too much trouble. Alden was having some trouble with them himself. He was a grunt, a fighting Marine, and he fully understood the concept of mass. But in *his* Marine Corps, standing shoulder to shoulder and hacking at enemies close enough to smell their breath was crazy.

He had no problem with a little hand-to-hand; he was even pretty good at it. Like many Marines, he was an artist with a bayonet—when it was attached to his holy Springfield. The dogma pounded into him as a recruit was one of accurate, long-distance riflery, backed by a bayonet and the will to use it. Standing toe to toe and hacking away was for last-ditch defense or final assault. Not for the whole damn fight.

There weren't enough Springfields, however. Hell, there were barely enough for *Walker*'s crew. Some of the better Lemurian NCOs had Krags, but his army would fight with swords and spears. For those to work, you had to be right in your enemy's face. Only shield walls and deep, disciplined ranks might give them an edge over the Grik. The captain said the shield wall and discipline set the Romans apart from the barbarians. Alden understood, but it still struck his subconscious mind as nuts. He'd have to get a feel for the new tactics too.

No Springfields, but they did have archers. In fact, every soldier was an archer of sorts. The front-rank spearmen carried longbows over their shoulders to use until the enemy came to grips—which wouldn't take long on land, considering the close confines and thick vegetation hereabouts. The problem was it took a long time to get really good with a longbow. He'd just as soon have everyone stick with the crossbows they were used to, even if they weren't as fast and didn't shoot as far. It didn't take an expert to use one of those. But his front rank couldn't wield a sword or spear while swinging a heavy crossbow, so if he wanted standoff capability, longbows it had to be. Crossbows could still be employed by females or anyone too small or weak for the shield wall. Lemurian females weren't necessarily weak, but they had the same ... encumbrances that sometimes made longbows difficult for their human counterparts. Many of Alden's best spearmen were poor archers, but he made them practice every day. Most were improving.

Right now, all were practicing their melee skills, learning to fight one-on-one in case the wall should ever break. That was also the type of fighting they expected for the upcoming operation. It was a fiasco. The parade ground looked like someone had kicked an anthill. A steady trickle of injured recruits walked or limped over to sit in the shade and be treated at Karen Theimer's "aid station." Some were really hurt, but most were goofing off.

Chack, Risa, and Lieutenant Shinya trotted up to join him. Risa was the training liaison for *Big Sal*, so she had a reason to be there, but Chack hadn't let her out of his sight since the "incident" on the pier. Alden couldn't believe she'd helped Silva with the scam. If it *was* a scam. Making Silva chew the leaves and get the screamers was a hoot, but the big gunner's mate's idea of "getting even" was ... disproportionate. Chack needed a crash course in American joke rules. The question was, did Silva's jokes *have* rules? Were they "even"? Pete doubted it. He shook out one of the cigarettes he always seemed to have and lit up.

"God help us," he muttered when they were close enough to hear.

"They have learned to march fairly well," Shinya said to console him. "And form a wall. But if it ever comes to that"—he waved at the chaos— "we'll be destroyed."

Alden smirked, but nodded. It didn't help that they'd suddenly been told to train for a different type of battle. Until now, defense had been the priority. He turned his back to the practicing troops and took a small green book from his tunic. It was an old copy of *The Ship and Gun Drills, U.S. Navy,* from 1914. He'd found it in Doc Stevens's library while rooting for something to read. It was probably on the ship when she was commissioned. Much was obsolete (even for *Walker*), but it had a rather extensive section on physical exercises, including bayonet and sword drill. The pages were illustrated, too. The bayonet drill translated easily to a short spear, but there was, of course, no mention how to combine the sword work with a shield. It didn't really matter. The activities on the parade ground were not even slightly similar to the pictures in the book.

Shinya studied the pages over his shoulder as Alden held the book so he could see. For a moment he reflected how strange it was to be working with a Nip. Sometimes it seemed perfectly natural, but other times his skin practically crawled. A lot had happened in the last few months, but nothing could erase Pearl Harbor or Cavite or the Philippines or the Java Sea. But Shinya hadn't bombed Pearl

Harbor and he couldn't help being a Jap. And every now
and then, God help him, Pete Alden caught himself almost
liking him. Not many felt the same. Bernie did, and maybe
Garrett. The captain respected him, Pete thought. But the
Chief still hated his guts. Gray was a good guy, steady as a
rock, but something about Shinya gave him the heebie-
jeebies. Alden wondered what it was.

"Damn," he said, and slapped the book shut. He handed
it to Shinya. "Can you make heads or tails out of that sword
shit in there?" he asked.

Shinya nodded. "I believe so. It seems straightforward.
Believe it or not," he said, grinning, "I actually fenced in
college."

Pete harrumphed and rolled his eyes. "Just don't teach
'em any of that Samurai bullshit. We want 'em to stay behind their shields, not run around flailing their swords in all
directions. All that'll do is confuse 'em."

Shinya chuckled. "I'm a better fencer than I ever was
a practitioner of Master Musashi's teachings. I learned
enough not to shame my father. He was very insistent. But
I doubt he was proud of my skill." His smile faded, and he
looked at Alden, expressionless. "You see, the Way is very
spiritual," he explained. "Regrettably, I am not."

"Yeah, well. Mmm. Closest thing I ever came to, looked
like a sword, is this," Alden said, grasping the long bayonet
at his side, next to the .45 holster. "Unless you count my
granddaddy's Civil War sword over the fireplace." Teeth
flashed in his bearded face. "I'm not much for this swords
and shields shit, but bayonets I can do. And I think it's
time to stir things up."

He retrieved one of the six-foot, bronze-bladed spears.
"You do the swords. Teach 'em ways to use 'em in the
open—we'll need that too, and maybe first. But also behind
shields when they've got 'em locked. Ask the captain. He
seems to know about that. C'mon, Chack." He gestured for
the Lemurian to follow. "I need your mouth."

"What are you going to do?" Shinya asked.

"Pick a fight." He motioned toward the middle of the
field, where a group of warriors from one of the ships gathered, taunting the recruits. "I'm going to show those Navy

cat-monkey types they ain't as tough as they think they are. No offense, Chack."

Chack blinked amused approval. He'd experienced Alden's "bayonet drills" himself. Together, they waded through the play-fighting troops, and Alden knocked some aside as they went. That got their attention, and some followed in his wake to see what he would do. Eventually they reached the knot of warriors, a group from *Fristar*. Alden was surprised to see them, since all their High Chief talked about was taking off. They hadn't done it yet, but it was plain that all these showed up for was trouble.

They'd formed a rough circle and were pushing and shoving any land folk who came within reach. They were enjoying their game immensely and seemed to think it was at least as effective as the training going on around them. One reached for Alden as he came close, but pulled back when he saw he'd nearly grabbed one of the "Amer-i-caan Wizards."

"Go ahead," Pete said, grinning pleasantly. "I'm a Grik. Kill me." Chack translated. The *Fristar*, a wing runner, looked aside at his fellows. One, easily the largest Lemurian Pete had seen, dipped his head. The shorter 'cat gave a high-pitched cry. He leaped at Alden with arms outstretched. The sergeant's spear blurred. With a yelping, breathless grunt, the wing runner was on his back, looking cross-eyed at the spearpoint inches from his face.

"You're dead," Alden said. "Next?"

Another troublemaker stepped forward at a nod from the "leader." This one had a few white hairs lacing his amber coat. His tail twitched back and forth. He accepted a real spear from a companion and assumed a more cautious stance.

An experienced warrior this time, Alden thought to himself. *Good.*

The 'cat held the spearpoint forward, left hand grasping near the blade. His right arm was fully extended behind him, holding the shaft like a harpoon. He crouched and took a step to his right. Lightning-fast, he lunged with the spear. Pete stepped inside the thrust, knocking it aside as he turned and drove the butt of his own spear into his opponent's midriff. Somehow the Lemurian's face showed surprise as he doubled over with a "woof!" Pete reversed the spear and made a classic thrust, ending just short of the chest. Then he turned and looked at the gathering crowd. The point he'd made was obvious. One down, one gasping for air, and Pete Alden wasn't even breathing hard.

Some of the land folk cheered in their curious high-pitched, chittering way, but Pete knew it was more who he'd bested than how he'd done it. That wasn't what he wanted to get across. "Chack, speak for me," he said. He walked in a circle, scowling. Gradually, the cheering faded and he started to speak. Before he could, the big *Fristar* Lemurian stepped forward. He was tall enough to look Alden in the eye. He wasn't as heavily built as the Marine, but Pete had to concede that he was probably stronger. Muscle rippled under the dark fur as he drove his spear into the ground in formal challenge. There was a sudden hush.

"Why do you humiliate the *Fristar* clan in front of these mud-treaders, Tail-less One? You who is a person of the Great Sea?" Chack translated as he spoke. Pete took a step closer to him and returned his glare.

"If you're humiliated it's not because of anything I've done. Your pride makes you believe you're a better warrior than you are. Besides, among my people, I'm a mud-treader too. *Walker* has clans, just like you, and we're all ruled by our High Chief. For us, that's Captain Reddy. I obey him, but I'm chief of my own clan. The Marines." He turned and looked at the gathering sea of faces. All training stopped as more recruits pressed forward to hear, and maybe see a fight.

"Among my people, Marines are *the* warrior clan. All they do is fight. Sometimes they fight at sea and sometimes on land." He grinned. "Sometimes they even fight in the sky. To Marines it makes no difference. We fight the enemies of our people wherever they are." He paused, considering. "We've made alliance with your people and we've seen the Grik for what they are. Your enemy is now the enemy of my people. That makes 'em *my* enemy and I'll fight 'em because that's what I do. In the meantime, it's my duty to train you to be better fighters. To fight like Marines.

That means fighting them anytime, anywhere, at sea or on land. That's what it'll take to defeat them.

"They aren't coming to steal your things, just to loot and plunder. If the history of your Scrolls is true, they're coming to *wipe you out*! *Walker*'s people are your allies, and that puts them in danger as well. So anything less than your very best makes you my personal enemy! Do I make myself clear?" He turned, snatched the spear out of the ground, and flung it down, accepting the challenge—the formal challenge—that meant blood could be spilled.

"There! We can fight if you want, and I promise you'll be dead so fast you won't even know how it happened." He looked at Chack. "Or you can fight him, if you're afraid of me, but he'll kill you just as fast. Because I taught him how!" He looked at the tall leader of the *Fristar* group. "So what'll it be? You want to die? Or do you want to learn how to *really* kill?"

The Lemurian returned his stare. Around them, all were silent, expectant . . . afraid. The formal challenge was rarely made, and when it was, there was almost always only one outcome. All were nervous about the political ramifications. *Fristar*, at least, would leave the fragile alliance that had been forged at the council. No one really expected the American to lose, and there was always bad blood after a formal challenge was met. The big Lemurian looked down at the spear. He put his foot beside it and, with a grunt, kicked it away, withdrawing the challenge. There was an audible sigh of relief.

"Then show me, Maa-reen. Show me how to kill."

After securing Risa's laughing promise not to fly to join her "mate," Chack left her at the parade ground to continue her studies and headed back to *Walker*. His Home. He didn't really know when it had occurred, but at some point all the ambitions of his previous life were supplanted by what he'd become. He was no longer a wing runner on *Salissa* Home. He was a bosun's mate, in charge of the Lemurian deck division on USS *Walker*, duly sworn into the Navy of the United States, just as all the accepted "cadets" had been. He had only a vague idea what the United States were, but that made no difference. He'd become a warrior and now he was a destroyerman. He loved *Salissa* and always would, but he'd changed clans just as surely as if he'd become fas chief of another Home like he once aspired to do. That was an ambition for who he'd been before. He giggled at the irony of his outrage over Silva joining *his* clan. Now he'd joined Silva's. That didn't mean he wanted him for a brother.

He was encouraged despite Sergeant Alden's gloom. Unwarlike as he once was, the people of Baalkpan were even worse. Yet at least they were trying. It took actual combat to crack his pacifist shell and his dispassionate evaluation of the land folk as warriors didn't escape his sense of irony either. He believed they would fight. Some weren't so sure, but if he could do it, they could too. A lot was riding on it. Most of the Homes in the bay had joined the alliance, but had not committed themselves to offensive operations. They'd taken a wait-and-see approach. The expedition they planned was basically a raid, a reconnaissance in force. The objective was information, primarily, but depending on what they learned, they were prepared to follow up with more attacks. Perhaps, if the Grik were as yet no more numerous than some evidence suggested, they might even defeat them—and fairly quickly. Captain Reddy hoped they could at least cleanse them from the Java Sea and establish a "Malay Barrier" behind which they could further prepare. It was a giddy thought. The captain projected cautious optimism, and Chack envied how he did that. He'd learned a lot about the fantastic war in the other world, and he knew that the mistakes and uncertainty that plagued the Amer-i-caans there now drove Captain Reddy to avoid the same issues here. If they did, they must succeed. Terrible as they were, the Grik couldn't be as formidable as the Japanese had been.

In this happy frame of mind, he ambled along, the Krag muzzle down on his shoulder, picking his way through the fishmongers and handcarts that packed the wharf near the pier. He glanced up and saw *Walker*, snugged to the dock, smoke curling from her aft funnel once more.

"Chack."

He turned, and his heart flipped in his chest. Before him stood Selass, her silken silver fur radiating sunlight. The armor she wore, much like her father's, flashed with pink-red fire. As always, she was magnificent. She was armed with a scota and was headed for the parade ground herself. He'd seen her there several times, training. Sometimes she sparred with Risa. Chack's ears lay flat and he bowed low.

"I greet you, Selass-Fris-Ar. You are well?"

"I am well . . ." She paused and blinked sadness. Chack nodded.

"You still mourn Saak-Fas. I understand. I hope the pain will pass with time."

Her eyelids flashed impatiently. "I do *not* mourn him! If I ever did, the sadness is gone. But . . . I have another sadness."

He blinked concerned query. Her eyes flashed and she almost growled with frustration.

"You will make me say it, then, I see! Has your revenge not run its course?"

"Revenge?"

"Yes, revenge! For leading you on, toying with you, and making you a fool! Don't you think I've suffered enough? Saak-Fas was the fool! Now he's gone . . . and I am glad. I was wrong about you. I thought you weak. But I also thought you loved me. I hoped you would still want me. Was I wrong about that too? I see you often, yet beyond casual greeting you have not spoken. Will you make me beg?" She blinked furiously. "Very well! I was wrong about Saak-Fas and I was wrong about you. I do want you now!"

Stunned, Chack could only stare. For so long, his fondest wish was to hear her say such words. Now, though they stirred him, they didn't bring him joy. They only brought confusion and a trace of sadness. He gently replied.

"You did not make a fool of me. I did that myself. I *was* a fool. I was what you thought I was. But I'm no more that person now than a graw-fish is still a graw-fish after it sheds its tail and gills and flies out of the sea. I admire you in many ways, Selass, and am flattered that you desire me. But I do not pine for you. I suppose I do still love you, but it does not consume me as before. I've had much else on my mind of late. Your admission and . . . declaration have come as a surprise. May I consider it? I assure you my aim is not 'revenge' or to hurt you in any way. Let us speak again, after the expedition. After we know what sort of war we face. If my answer is still important to you, I will give it then."

Shame, sadness, and consternation flashed across her eyelids, but she finally bowed and with a quick nuzzle under his chin that almost crushed his resolve, she flashed away toward the parade ground. For a very long time, he watched her weave through the throng until she was lost to view. With a stab of guilt and astonishment, he realized he'd not even thought about her in weeks. He would have to do that now.

Matt stood on the bridgewing with a cup of . . . something in his hand. He grimaced at the foamy brew. He couldn't remember what Juan called it, but it was the local equivalent of coffee, evidently. It might even *be* a kind of coffee; it came from crushed, roasted beans. Not many Lemurians drank it. They used it as medicine, as a treatment for lethargy. Matt hadn't had any before, but it had earned a following among the crew. Some just called it "java" or "joe," as they always had. A few of the die-hard factionalists called it "cat-monkey joe" or "monkey-cat joe," but just as "'Cats" was becoming the general compromise term for the Lemurians, "monkey joe" was gaining steam for the brew. It seemed to follow somehow. Whatever they called it, the stuff sure didn't look like any coffee Matt had ever seen, although the aroma wasn't entirely dissimilar. Maybe it was the yellow-green foam.

The foam slowly dissipated and the liquid beneath was reassuringly black, but there remained a bile-colored ring around the edge. He willed himself to take a sip and tentatively explored it with his tongue. *Not bad*, he decided, surprised. There was a kind of chalky aftertaste, but that wasn't unusual for any coffee Juan made. And it did taste like coffee. Not *good* coffee, but the similarity was enough to fill a dreadful void he hadn't really recognized. He smiled.

Walker was tied to the new fueling pier and the special sea and anchor detail was withdrawing the hose from one brimming bunker and preparing to fill another. Chief Gray watched their progress like a hawk, lest they spill any of the thick black fuel oil on his somewhat pale deck. Under the circumstances, Matt doubted that he'd really mind if they did. This transfusion of *Walker*'s lifeblood had raised everyone's spirits to such a degree that it would be difficult for even Gray to summon much genuine ire over a splotch on the deck.

The benevolent thunder of the main blower behind the pilothouse was almost enough to mask Matt's uneasiness about the expedition they were about to begin. An expedition that they'd planned and prepared for weeks, awaiting only this final detail. Fuel. When enough had finally been pumped, transferred, and refined, some was brought to *Walker* so she could fire up a boiler to run her pumps and get ready for the short trip upriver. All the while, the massive copper storage tanks on the shore continued to fill, awaiting her at the pier. Now, all was in readiness.

The rest of the expedition consisted only of *Big Sal* and half a dozen of the larger fishing feluccas. Together they waited, moored in the inner channel. Two other Homes had actually volunteered as well, but for this operation they would be too many. As soon as *Walker* completed her fueling she would join the task force and they'd enter the Makassar Strait. From there, *Walker* would range ahead, screening her slower consorts. Matt looked forward to being unleashed on the open ocean, where his ship could stretch her legs, but he felt trepidation as well.

It was a bold plan that he and Keje had designed and there was a lot of risk involved. But if they were successful they stood a chance of learning—at long last—quite a lot about the enemy. The lessons Matt had learned on the short end of the intelligence stick had been pounded well and truly home, and he'd managed to instill in Keje, at least, a similar obsession for information. So much was riding on this! Initially, success might accomplish little more than their destruction of the Grik ships in the strait—or the Asiatic Fleet's little victory in almost the same place against the Japanese. But he'd hoped that, in the long term, the strategic dividend would be all out of proportion to the effort, particularly if it led to sufficient information to roll up the Grik. If they knew the enemy dispositions better, *Walker* alone still had enough ammunition to wreck a *lot* of Grik ships. With victory, or even a breathing space, they could continue to strengthen their friends, look for *Mahan*, and maybe begin their search for other humans too. Those were Matt's ultimate goals. With bunkers full of fuel, they even seemed attainable.

Larry Dowden entered the pilothouse. "Skipper," he said, saluting as Matt turned.

"Exec."

Dowden glanced furtively at the other men on the bridge and lowered his voice. "Sir, I have it on good authority . . . the Mice have sneaked on board. I didn't see 'em, but I'm pretty sure they did."

Matt frowned. "Didn't they get the word when I ordered all fuel project personnel to remain behind?" Many of *Walker*'s crew would miss the expedition. None was happy about it, but aside from having necessary assignments, Matt didn't want all his eggs in one basket anymore. Letts would remain and continue coordinating industrialization efforts, aided by Perry Brister, who was also in charge of supervising the construction of defensive works. Letts had worked himself out of a job on the ship. He was too valuable in his new, expanded role. Besides, Matt didn't want a repeat of whatever had caused the mysterious shiny black eye that he wore. Officially, he'd tripped. Karen Theimer would stay and teach their growing medical corps. Matt knew that leaving the two together would only intensify the resentment of his other officers, but it couldn't be helped. One of the nurses had to remain, and Sandra simply refused. He was glad he hadn't given the order when others were around to see him back down. He was furious with her . . . and glad she was coming. As far as Letts and Theimer were concerned, maybe "out of sight, out of mind" was the best course to pursue.

"I didn't tell 'em personally, but shoot, Skipper, I never see 'em even when they're aboard. Everybody knew it, though; the order's been posted for a week. They just ignored it."

Matt shook his head. "And they can claim they never saw it and so they didn't, in fact, violate a direct order." He sighed. "No sense throwing them off. Besides, they'd just hide." He thought for a moment. "Nobody else 'deserted' back to the ship? Bradford? Lieutenant Brister?"

Dowden shook his head, grinning wryly. "Bradford almost did. He's supposed to be helping Brister with the fortifications. He is an engineer, after all, but he didn't want to miss the show. Nakja-Mur finally bribed him with a safari to hunt down a 'super lizard.' Nothing short of that would have worked, I bet."

Matt chuckled, and then his expression became serious again. "I owe him. But as far as the Mice are concerned . . . Well, I'm not going to bring them up on charges. They're too damn valuable—I can't believe I just said that!—and that's exactly what I'll have to do if I make a big deal about it. Their rig's going fine with just a caretaker now. They're no longer indispensable, just . . . valuable."

He looked at the men working on the fo'c'sle. They were having difficulty with their usual chores since the cramped space was even further encumbered by a large apparatus that Matt hoped would soon prove useful. Some of the men stared curses at the thing as they maneuvered around it, and firing the number one gun to starboard would be tough while the thing was rigged for sea. But if that gun became essential to the operation, they'd failed anyway.

"Let them stay. They've earned it. But if they pull a stunt like this again, I won't care if they learn to piss oil. Make sure that information reaches them, if you please."

"Yes, sir."

Together, they walked across the pilothouse and Matt peered over the wing rail at the water. Even this far up-river, it was getting choppy. Above, the sky was like lead: a low, monochromatic overcast with none of the flighty characteristics of the usual daily squalls. The heavens seemed to exude a restrained, pregnant power.

"Looks like Adar's right," he mused aloud. "We may be in for a real blow." He turned and grinned at Dowden.

"Perfect."

Ben Mallory couldn't believe he was flying, particularly in such heavy weather. After the conversation in which Captain Reddy told him they'd have to wait to look for *Mahan*—and why—he'd been afraid the PBY would be treated like a museum relic. He'd been wrong. If the plane could let them know what was coming—and didn't fly too far—the captain was reluctantly willing to risk it. Especially now that the radio worked.

Mallory was battling through the driving wind and rain north of a cluster of tiny, rocky islands off the southwest coat of Celebes. The world was gray, and the sea below was a roiling, foamy white. The thundering, rattling, swooping turbulence was enough to make him sick, and he was enjoying every minute. He spared a quick glance at his copilot. The young sable-furred 'Cat was peering through a pair of binoculars through the open side window. His name was Jis-Tikkar, but he liked "Tikker" just fine. He was a good companion and a fast-learning "wrench." He worked as hard as anyone keeping the plane ready to fly. On this, his very first actual flight, he was enraptured by the wonder of soaring high above the world at a measly hundred and ten miles an hour. Oh, how Ben missed his P-40E!

Whatever Ben called him, Tikker wasn't ready to *be* a co-pilot yet. For one thing, he could barely see over the instrument panel. Mallory allowed him to take the controls for a little "straight-and-level" before they flew into the storm, but it would be a while before he did it again. As soon as the little devil got his hands on the oval-shaped wheel, he'd nearly put the big plane into a barrel roll. It was all very exciting, and the flying lessons abruptly ceased. Tikker's duties reverted to observation, and keeping Ben awake with his irreverent humor. Currently, the humor was absent as the 'Cat concentrated on the business at hand.

The rest of the flight crew consisted of Ed Palmer and two farsighted Lemurians in the observation blisters. Ed sat directly behind the flight deck, checking in with *Walker* and keeping track of their navigation. He wasn't a pro yet, but he was a quick study. In his short time aboard *Mahan* he had, for all intents and purposes, been the navigation officer, since Monroe couldn't plot his way out of a paper sack. As long as there were landmarks he could identify, he wouldn't lead them astray—and they were forbidden to fly at night.

"There is the felucca!" Tikker said.

Ben banked slightly and craned his neck. Far below, a dark shape slashed through the heavy sea. The Baalkpan feluccas were fore-and-aft rigged and surprisingly nimble, but heavy weather was rough on them. "He's headed southeast! He must have run into something!" Ben banked again and dropped the nose, peering through the windscreen. The wipers flailed as fast as they could, but they only smeared the water.

"There!" said Tikker, straining his eyes through the binoculars. He looked at Ben. "The third Grik ship! It is chasing the felucca!" Through the wipers, he caught brief glimpses of a distorted red-hulled shape.

"Should we get closer?" Ed asked behind him. "I'd just as soon not get closer. Besides, they'll hear us."

"Not a chance, with all the sea noise down there and the rain," Ben replied. "All the same . . ." He began turning south. "Get on the horn . . ."

"Wait!" said Tikker urgently. "There is another . . . ! And another! Two more Grik are in company with the first!"

"Shit!" said Palmer. "Any more?" For a long moment they stared.

"Nooo," Ben decided at last. The three ships were clustered close together, and no others were in sight. "No, I think that's all."

"That's enough!" Palmer cursed and headed for the radio. He picked up the mike. "You still there, Clance? Tell the Skipper we've got *three* hostiles inbound!" Palmer transmitted in the clear. Who else was going to listen?

"Roger," came Radioman Clancy's terse reply through the static. "What's the weather like up there?"

"Moderating," admitted Palmer. "It's gone from an eggbeater to a martini shaker. Adar was right. Those Sky Priests are way better than our weather weenies were!"

"I'll say," agreed Clancy. "Lots more to those guys than reading maps and wearing silly suits. Wait one." A moment later Clancy's voice crackled in Palmer's ear again. "Skipper says to double-double-check the enemy numbers, then get the hell out."

"But Ben . . . I mean, Lieutenant Mallory, thought we might fly cover. You know, shoot somebody up if you need us."

"Negative. Captain says to get your big blue butt back to Baalkpan! It's our show now. You've done what we needed you to. Hell, you can't even set down!"

"Wilco," Ed grumbled. He clipped the mike and lurched back to the flight deck.

"What's the scoop?" Ben demanded.

"We double-double-check, then beat feet for Baalkpan. Damn, we won't even know how it goes!"

"Yeah, there're a few more guests than expected. It'll make things more difficult, but not three times as difficult—I hope."

"Well . . . what are we gonna do?"

Ben looked at him. "We're going to follow orders, sailor. But he didn't say we couldn't come back in the morning!"

The storm had finally begun to subside. It had indeed been a real blow, more violent than even Adar anticipated. The wind still blew at thirty knots or more, and the whitecaps of the heavy sea disintegrated into foamy spray. Keje stood on the sandy, desolate beach and stared bleakly at his beloved Home. *Salissa* lay at an unnatural angle, decidedly low in the water, a few hundred yards offshore. She now rested, exposed for all to see, on the bottom of the gently shoaling sand of what Matt called the Gulf of Mandar. How they'd ever managed to get her there, through the maze of huge rocks and mountainous seas, he could barely remember. All he recalled at the moment, in his exhausted, sodden state, was that the effort had been *chi-kaash*—hell.

All around him, people erected shelters amid piles of vulnerable supplies and others tended smoky cook-fires for knots of soaked, bedraggled people who'd paused from their labors to warm themselves. As far as he could see, the beach was inhabited by the debris and pitiful, helpless survivors of a traumatic calamity. Some stood as he did, staring out to sea, and some just milled about. Others waded back and forth through the surf, bearing bundles on their shoulders from one of the feluccas driven onto the beach. Another felucca still stood offshore, beating impotently back and forth, unable to risk the rocks and surf to come to their aid. Behind him, the tufted fronds of the trees beat and cracked with the wind, and the tall, skinny trunks leaned forlornly against the gray afternoon sky. Keje looked back out to sea, straining his eyes against the stinging spray. *Walker* was nowhere in sight.

Even over the thunderous surf, he heard Adar's shout behind him. "They've seen something! They're running!"

Keje wiped his eyes and peered through the binoculars Bradford had given him. Sure enough, the distant felucca was piling on more sail and slanting rapidly northeast with a grace and speed he envied. Farther away, another was racing down to meet it. The feluccas could sail much closer to the wind than *Big Sal*. Closer than the Grik. Signals snapped to the tops of their masts, and he focused carefully on them. Keje grunted. "I must return to *Salissa*," he shouted back at his friend. He'd done all he could ashore.

It was a miserable trip in the barge, damp crew folk straining at oars against the marching waves, but soon they were alongside *Salissa*, sheltered in her lee. Keje scurried up a rope and hands pulled him aboard. He glanced quickly around. Other than those gathered near, his Home seemed deserted. The forward wing clan's pagoda that they'd so recently rebuilt was intact, but the great tripod lay athwartships, its huge wing trailing over the side. Frayed cables, shattered barrels, and other unrecognizable debris were strewn across the exposed deck area. With a surge of concern, he glanced shoreward where his helpless People raced around in panic as rumors began to fly. A few tried to rally a defense, but not many. Here was a prize, ripe for the taking. The enemy couldn't possibly refuse. An entire Home of the People, loaded with food and supplies. Riches beyond calculation to any Grik raider fortunate enough to stumble across her! And her People! Their favored prey! Tired, traumatized, disorganized! There'd be no restraining them. He raced up the ladder to the battlement, and a memory of the last time he stood there, preparing thus, flashed through his mind. So much had changed since then. He raised the binoculars again.

Grik!

Three towering clouds of dingy canvas resolved themselves against the dirty-gray background, charging toward them as quickly as they dared. Already, the bloodred hulls were visible, and there was no question they'd sighted their prey. A stone seemed to churn in Keje's stomach. The Grik were as predictable as a school of flashers when a person fell into the sea, and just as remorseless.

"They've seen us," he muttered pointlessly.

For a long while he stood on the tilted platform with a

handful of his officers. Jarrik-Fas was there, as was Adar's senior acolyte. Adar himself remained ashore at Keje's command, to take charge in his absence. His daughter, Selass, was aboard as well, somewhat to his surprise. They'd spoken little since Saak-Fas disappeared, but much of that was probably his fault. He'd been so busy. They didn't speak now, and she stood nearby but apart. That may also have been because Risa-Sab-At was present. She'd been recently promoted to commander of the Forewing Guard, and there was tension of some sort between the two females.

He knew Selass had expected Risa's brother to press his suit once more, but he hadn't. He just treated her like he did everyone else—with friendly familiarity. Just as if there were never anything between them. That would have been the hardest blow of all to his prideful, self-centered daughter, he mused. To think she was that easy to forget. It would . . . do just exactly what it had: leave her sullen and introspective and less sure of herself. He wondered with a burst of clarity if that was what the former wing runner intended. In spite of the situation, he felt a small grin spread across his face. He remembered that the big Amer-i-caan, Dennis Silva, had once called Chack a "scamp." A good word. If true, good for him.

But the war had changed Chack in many ways. Not only had he become a warrior of note, but he'd joined the Amer-i-caan clan. Keje had not foreseen that, although he didn't disapprove. It just highlighted how profound the change had been. He was more serious and much more mature—his feud with Silva notwithstanding. Keje grinned again. Unlike most, he was sure that Silva and Risa's "mating" was a farce, although along with Captain Reddy, he'd pretended it was real, hoping to make them uncomfortable enough to admit the truth and let it pass. But they hadn't. He didn't even want to contemplate whether an actual mating was possible, but he was convinced, personality wise, that Silva and Risa were made for each other. Life had become very interesting in many different ways. Much too interesting to end here, today.

The Grik ships grew. Antlike figures scampered among their sails, reefing and furling in a surprisingly orderly fashion, much like wing runners of the People would have done. Half a mile away, beyond the first of the rocks that stood like sentinels around the little island, the enemy hove to. Through the amazing binoculars he saw masses of armored warriors surging against the bulwarks, waiting for boats to go over the sides. Their garish shields and bright plumage seemed dingy and washed-out, but he still felt a chill as he watched them. They didn't descend to the boats with the same enthusiasm they had when they once boarded his ship, however. Perhaps the weather was affecting them? He felt vengeful satisfaction at the thought that Grik might be susceptible to the sickness that came to some if the sea was too lively. As he watched, at least two actually fell into the sea trying to gain the boats. He was appalled that no effort was expended to rescue them. "Fewer enemies to fight," he muttered, "but by the Stars, are they not loathsome beyond imagining!" There were also three times as many as they'd expected to find in the area. Little was going as expected. Oh, well. There was certainly nothing they could do about it now.

Before long, twelve Grik longboats set out from the sides of the ships. Each was twice the size of *Walker*'s launch, and the warriors were packed to overflowing. There must be eighty or more in each boat, and as the oars dipped, it was apparent that *Salissa* would be their first target. Once they secured it, he expected they would stage the rest of their fighters aboard his Home and prepare their assault against the people on the shore. The thought ignited the stone in his stomach. Over his shoulder, he saw that a semblance of order had been restored, and a larger number of his people now stood on the beach with swords and crossbows ready. He looked back at the Grik.

Terrifying banners of red and black unfurled above the boats, each festooned with some grim image or awful beast, and they rattled downwind in almost perfect profile. Long tufts of fur or feathers bordered each flag, and he assumed they were some sort of clan device. They'd crossed perhaps a third of the distance between them now.

Keje turned to the acolyte. "I believe now is the moment we've awaited," he said. The acolyte blinked wide-eyed acknowledgment. Reaching within the folds of his robe, he drew out a large brass-framed shape with a wooden grip on one end and a black pipe on the other. He pressed a button on the side, and the pipe tilted forward. Glancing in one end, he nodded to himself and closed it up again. With another glance at Keje, he wrenched the hammer spur back and pointed the thing at the sky, slightly into the wind. There was a muffled *pop* and a bright reddish object rocketed skyward, trailing a plume of smoke that vanished as quickly as it was made. A moment later, high above, a harsh pulse of unnatural light blossomed, unheard but visible for miles around. It sputtered and glowed impossibly bright as the wind carried it away. After only a few seconds, it went out. Together, they turned back to the Grik. "Now we will see," Keje said.

For a moment the Grik hesitated, apparently startled, but when nothing happened they resumed their approach. Onward they rowed, steady and malevolent. Individual Grik, dressed gaudier than others, stood in the prows of the boats, exhorting the rest with brandished blades. It wouldn't be much longer before Keje would know if he and all his people would survive this day.

"There!" Jarrik-Fas cried out and pointed. From behind the concealing point of land about three miles to the north, a pale gray shape, barely discernible against the stormy sky, lanced into view. The tiniest wisps of smoke hazed the tops of three of her funnels and a cascade of white foam sluiced along her flanks from the knife-sharp bow. A sensation of exultant satisfaction erased Keje's dread. Their chore was bigger than expected, but they could handle that. They'd hoped for one, planned for two, but three should make scant difference. He turned and gauged the distance to the boats, now almost two-thirds to their objective. Sharp teeth were exposed as his grin became a snarl.

"They've risen to the bait. All that remains is to close the trap! Shall we reveal our surprise?" Jarrik-Fas strode to the new "jan-raal ay-laarm," a long bronze cylinder suspended in a gimbaled bracket. He struck it energetically with a heavy rod. The loud notes were clear, if somewhat flat, and experiments showed they carried well to all parts of the ship. Hundreds of Lemurian warriors erupted from belowdecks and raced to their posts along the seaward rail.

In moments, *Big Sal*'s starboard side bristled with eager warriors—not all of whom called her home. Some represented other Homes that had come to Baalkpan, like *Nerracca*, *Aracca,* and *Humfra-Dar*, but most were Baalkpan land folk leavened by Alden's Marines. Below the catwalk, five large ports opened, their doors raised by a pair of ropes and half a dozen crew folk each.

The Grik slowed their advance momentarily when they realized they faced opposition. Keje hoped they wouldn't break from tradition and cancel the attack. He'd carefully held back more than half his troops so they would think they still had the advantage. A preponderance of numbers in their enemy's favor had never dissuaded the Grik before, but they'd been doing too many unexpected things of late. He needn't have worried. With a crescendo of snarling shouts, the Grik plowed on, waving weapons in fierce defiance. Closer and closer, gnashing their teeth and pounding weapons against their shields. Their large eyes were opaque with a frenzy of rage. It was terrifying, regardless of his confidence.

He spared a glance at the Grik ships, still hove to in the distance. Their remaining crews had not yet noticed *Walker* bearing down upon them. That was understandable, since the destroyer approached from directly downwind. There was no reason on earth to suspect trouble from that direction. He grunted. Finally some lookout must have seen, because sheets were loosed and sails began to shift. The thought of the pandemonium aboard the enemy when they first glimpsed *Walker* brought a predatory smile to his cleft lips. Slowly, chaotically, the Grik sails filled, and the first ship heaved far over onto its starboard side, quickly gathering way. The other two weren't as fortunate. One attempted the same maneuver, but its head came around too far and smashed directly into one of the monolithic rocks, shattering the starboard bow and bringing down the masts in a rush of thundering, crackling devastation. It rebounded from the rock as though kicked in the nose by some terrible god and swirled away in the maelstrom, rapidly settling low.

The third ship shaped a course that might bring it in collision with *Salissa*. *Very well*, Keje thought. *An even greater test, and one just as important.* He ground his teeth and waited. The first Grik ship was clear of the rocks, but there'd be no escape. *Walker* was *flying* down upon her prey, and pure joyful wonder at her speed flooded through him. Formal supplication had been made before they set out from Baalkpan, but he sent a quick prayer to the hidden Sun and those who had gone before to watch over his friends and brothers. Then he returned his attention to the role he had to play. The Grik in the boats had no inkling of anything taking place behind. They might if the ship overtook them, but for now they were entirely focused on closing with *Salissa.*

"At my command, Jarrik-Fas . . ."

"Commence firing with the main battery, but at masts and rigging only, Mr. Garrett!" Even before the salvo buzzer sounded, Matt felt, as well as heard, a deep, muffled *whud-dump!* from the direction of *Big Sal.* He looked, but at this distance all he saw was a massive fogbank of smoke dissipating to leeward. *So far, so good,* he thought, in spite of the heavier odds. *Big Sal* would face more warriors than expected and maybe a ship as well, but *Walker*'s part remained essentially the same. He'd never really believed Letts could pull it off. The supply officer's ambitious plan to arm *Big Sal* with forty cannon had been reduced to five per side, but they were enormous thirty-two pounders—and long guns to boot. They were crudely shaped and probably heavier than necessary, but their bores were straight and true. He could only imagine what five hundred three-quarter-inch copper balls per gun had done to the Grik boats. For an instant, he even pondered later ramifications. History often showed that arming primitive people with artillery could be a very bad thing, but at this moment, under these conditions, he had no regrets. Besides, he had more pressing matters at hand. The salvo buzzer shrieked.

Three guns fired as one. Only one round struck the target, but it was a perfect hit, exactly where Matt had hoped. A single high-explosive four-inch-fifty struck dead center beneath the maintop and detonated with devastating effect. Huge splinters and pieces of metal scythed through sails and rigging, and down upon the fo'c'sle. The mast and top above the impact were entirely severed, and the whole thing fell—canvas flailing and yards disintegrating in a mad carnival of destruction. Surviving stays stretched impossibly tight and parted like a volley of rifle fire. The foretopmast snapped and added itself and everything above to the mass of debris that fell in an impenetrable heap amidships. A forestaysail billowed to leeward and fell into the sea. That, and the sails still set on the mizzen, caused the Grik to heave rapidly around to starboard and broach to, a wallowing, helpless wreck. As a final calamity resulting from that single salvo, the un-stayed mizzen sails were taken aback, and the entire mast snapped off at the deck and plummeted into the sea astern.

"Holy cow!" breathed Rick Tolson at the helm. *Walker* had closed to less than three hundred yards.

"Reduce speed!" commanded Matt. "All ahead slow. Helm, ease us in to one hundred yards and come left ten degrees on my mark." He turned to the talker. "Boarders to remain undercover, but . . ." He paused and cast a glance at Chack, standing nearby. "I don't suppose they'll surrender?" The Lemurian just looked at him, uncomprehending. The Grik never gave quarter, or asked for it. They probably didn't understand the concept. Matt doubted that Chack did, even now, after he'd so carefully stressed the need to secure live prisoners. He rubbed his nose and gave the young warrior a grim smile. "Of course not. Never mind." To the talker: "Machine gunners may commence firing if they have a target, but don't waste ammunition!"

They'd left one of the .30s at the refinery as security against predators, but both .50s and the remaining .30 were all now on the starboard side. Almost immediately, the .30 overhead began hammering. The two amidships .50s quickly joined it, shredding the dazed Grik as they emerged from beneath the wreckage. Splinters, shattered bone, and gobbets of flesh erupted along the bulwark amid a chorus of wailing shrieks. In the pilothouse there was silence. They were well within range of the Grik firebombs, but the attack came so swiftly and unexpectedly, either they hadn't prepared the weapons or they'd been buried by debris.

Walker edged closer to the rolling derelict, and the stutter of machine guns became less frequent as fewer targets presented themselves.

"Well," Matt said crisply, hoping his voice betrayed none of his nervousness. He tugged absently at the sword belt buckled around his tunic. "Mr. Dowden, you have the deck. As we discussed, lay her alongside and try to keep station as best you can." He grinned. "Mind the Chief's paintwork, though! If you have to break off, by all means, do so. But don't waste time getting back in contact." Tolson tossed a worried look over his shoulder at the captain.

"Yes, sir, I have the deck," responded Dowden grudgingly. "Should I have the whaleboat made ready to launch in case, well . . ."

Matt cast an appraising eye at the sea and quickly shook his head. "Too dangerous. If anybody falls in, try to fish 'em out real fast, but there's no sense risking people in a boat. Not in this sea." He looked at the concerned faces on the bridge, meeting each eye. He prayed that if anything happened to him, they'd be all right. But he *had* to go. "Very well, carry on. You all know what to do." He removed his hat and handed it to Reynolds, exchanging it for one of the platter-shaped helmets. He buckled the chin strap and turned to Chack. "Let's go."

Together, they clomped down the ladder to join the boarding party sheltering beneath the bridge and the gun platform amidships. The party was as large as *Walker* could carry in such seas, numbering just over a hundred. Most were the cream of Alden's Lemurian Marines, armed with swords and spears. A few destroyermen would go as well, but only those who'd shown Shinya some proficiency with a blade. They were armed mostly with pistols and cutlasses, but Silva had one of the BARs and Tony Scott carried his personal Thompson. Matt shouldered his way forward to the hatch that led onto the fo'c'sle. There he ran into Chief Gray and Lieutenant Garrett.

"Boats," he said, nodding at the men. "Mr. Garrett. I don't remember mentioning either of your names when I put this boarding party together." Gray hitched his web belt, but it stayed right where it was. It couldn't ride any higher without being let out. He met Matt's gaze with an expression of determination.

"Well, Skipper," said Garrett, "you didn't exactly un-mention us either."

Matt frowned. "Be careful, then. We can't spare either of you."

"Like we *can* spare our captain?" questioned Alden as he squeezed his way to the front of the line. The crowd parted as best it could in the cramped space. There was an overwhelming sour odor of wet fur and sweat. "Captains don't lead boarding parties. As head of *Walker*'s Marine contingent"—Alden grinned, but with a hint of reproach—"that's my job."

Matt grinned back, remembering when he'd made the appointment. At the time, Alden was the only Marine in the world. "Nevertheless, I'm going. We've been over this before." He gestured at those around, destroyermen, as well as their shorter allies. "Don't worry. These are your troops. You trained them. You'll retain tactical command if we run into organized resistance. Just don't forget the priorities."

"Right," Alden agreed. "Secure the ship, and don't let 'em scuttle. Take prisoners, but kill 'em all if we have to. Nobody speaks Grik and we'll probably learn more from the ship than we will from the crew."

Matt nodded agreement. "Don't risk anybody's life to save any of theirs. While you're doing that, ten 'Cats"—he paused, looking at Garrett and Gray—"them too, I suppose, will accompany me into officers' country. We'll try to find any papers, maps, or other documents. Maybe we'll even catch their captain!"

Alden glanced through the small rectangular window near the hatchway to the foredeck and squinted through the spray that left it almost opaque. It was nearly time. "Maybe so, Skipper. But if he was on deck, he's a goner for sure." He whistled at the nightmare tangle of heaving debris. The machine guns had stopped firing and there wasn't a living thing in sight. "What a train wreck!"

"Hell," said Gray, "they might keep him in a bucket down in the hold, for all we know. Just because that thing has stern galleries like an Indiaman don't mean their leaders stay in 'em. They're as likely to hold Hin-doo revivals there."

The men laughed, and many of the Lemurians grinned too. None, not even Chack, understood what he meant, but humor for any reason was good at moments like this. Alden moved to the hatch and turned.

"All right," he bellowed. "Listen up! We're goin' out there to activate Captain Reddy's contraption. When we do, I'll blow this whistle." He held up a chrome whistle in his left hand. "When you hear it, *go*! Single file, as fast as you can! No goofing around or gawking! It's gonna be tough for the ship to keep station in this sea, and we've got to get as many aboard as fast as we can. We could lose the bridge at any moment! If we do, those left behind will try again. There's bound to be lizards left and they're not gonna be happy to see us!" He waved at Lieutenant Shinya, about midway down the press of boarders. The Japanese officer waved back and repeated Alden's instructions to those behind. "Good luck!" Alden roared, and opening the hatch, he dashed onto the fo'c'sle. Matt and the others quickly followed.

Atomized seawater drenched them immediately as they ran to a pair of heavy cleats on the forward bridge plating. Matt looked over his shoulder at the wallowing derelict and then up at Dowden leaning over the wing rail. Dowden was gauging the distance. Suddenly he pointed at Matt with an exaggerated gesture and yelled, but the words were lost in the crashing waves. Garrett and Gray released the cables holding the "contraption" upright against the side of the bridge, and it plunged down to starboard. Matt watched it fall with a fist on his heart, hoping it wouldn't just disintegrate when it struck.

It was a corvus, a device inspired by his interest in history. Specifically, in this case, the first Punic War. A corvus was basically a long, rigid ramp that dropped upon the deck of an enemy ship so troops could sprint across. A sharp spike attached to the descending end was supposed to drive itself into the deck, holding the ships fast together and forming a temporary bridge. It *should* work. It hadn't worked well for the Romans, he reflected bleakly, but they'd never had a chance to try it.

As advertised, the weight and inertia of *Walker*'s corvus drove the spike into the enemy ship with a tremendous crash. The entire structure bowed alarmingly, but sprang back to its original shape. The frame, like almost everything else from Baalkpan, was made of the heavy bamboo. Alden blew a long, shrill blast on his whistle. Sword in one hand, pistol in the other, Matt followed the Marine across the bouncing bridge. The rest of his immediate party raced after him, followed by a closely packed line of yelling destroyermen and chittering Lemurian Marines. As soon as they gained the enemy deck, they deployed into a protective semicircle, which quickly expanded as more boarders joined them. Grik bodies were everywhere. Some were shot to pieces, while others had been crushed by falling debris. The foamy water coursing across the deck was dark with their blood.

Matt glanced back. The second wave, led by Shinya, was just starting across. The dismasted hulk wallowed horribly and the strain on the corvus was unbelievable. The spike was battering a growing hole in the deck and despite Dowden's best efforts, the bridge began to fail. "Quickly, quickly!" he shouted. They couldn't be quick enough. Ultimately, it was the attachment to *Walker* that parted, not the spike in the deck. Shinya had almost reached them when the corvus behind sagged under the reinforcements and then, with a deafening *crack!* fell into the sea.

"Grab the manropes!" Alden screamed as the spike jerked out of the hole and the whole thing tilted over. Dozens did so, and fortunately it was already so entangled in the debris of the rigging that it couldn't have fallen completely, but Matt dreaded what he would see when he looked over the rail. At least a dozen men and 'Cats dangled by the ropes. Some were actually in the water, holding on for dear life. A few disappeared astern, waving their arms in the air.

"Get them up!" Gray leaned over, snatched Shinya like a doll, and threw him on the deck. Others joined him, hauling the men and 'Cats up as fast as they could. Silva's BAR hammered. The Grik were coming up too.

Tony Scott stood by *Walker*'s rail, wide-eyed, watching the figures struggling in the water or clinging to the ropes. He'd been next to cross. His foot was *on* the corvus when it failed.

For a moment, all he could do was stand there, clinging to the chain. He would have been in the *water*! So far, none of the terrible fish had arrived. Maybe the heavy seas kept them deep or disoriented, but he doubted they'd stay away long. And there were still people in the water. One wore a helmet, like most of the destroyermen did, but seemed too stunned or injured to do more than hold a rope. With quickening dread, he saw the long brownish blond hair unfurl and stream out from beneath it when a wave washed over the helmet. He gulped.

"God in heaven! That's Lieutenant Tucker!" He glanced wildly around. No one could have known she was there! What was she *doing* there? He screamed, trying to be heard on the Grik ship, but the waves and growing gunfire drowned him out. Laney heard him, though; he was right beside him.

"Tough break!" shouted the machinist's mate with genuine remorse. Tony looked at him, appalled. But he was right. There was nothing they could do. Nothing *he* could do. Just like that, everything was falling apart. Only a little more than half the boarding party made it across. The rest were stuck on this side, with nothing to do but watch, and now the skipper's dame was in the water. He couldn't stand it. Terrified as he was, he just couldn't stand it. He saw Dowden's worried face over the wing rail and he caught his eye. He made a whirling motion over his head and pointed at the other ship. Dowden seemed confused, but within seconds *Walker* briefly nudged back within twenty yards of the derelict. Scott wound up like the pitcher he was and slung his heavy Thompson across the gap. He hoped it didn't hit anybody in the head. The ammo belt followed the gun.

"What the hell are you doin'?" Laney demanded, incredulous. Scott just looked at him, slapped him in the gut with his helmet, and leaped over the side.

The water was warm and familiar, but the memories of a lifetime spent within its comforting embrace couldn't prevent his shriek of terror when he thrashed to the surface. There, just a few yards away, was Lieutenant Tucker, eyes shut tight, trying desperately to pull herself along the rope. He looked up at the ship and saw that nearly everyone else was safely aboard or climbing out of the water. Either they hadn't noticed her or the rope was fouled and they couldn't pull her up. Something slammed into the heel of his shoe. He lunged for the rope, right in front of her, and shouted over the crashing sea: "Put your arms around my neck, Lieutenant! I'll pull us up!" He never heard her reply, but she did as instructed and he hauled against the rope with maniacal strength. In moments, he crashed against the side of the ship. Nearly stunned, he just hung for a moment. Something that felt like oak bark dragged across his leg.

"Help!" he screamed. "Help, goddammit! I've got Lieutenant Tucker here!"

Almost immediately, the captain himself was hanging above him by the wrecked corvus. Garrett and Chack and a couple of others too. Garrett was hacking at something with his cutlass while the rest tried to heave them aboard. Suddenly the rope was free, and Tony and Sandra snaked up the side and sprawled on the deck.

Scott got to his hands and knees and vomited into the water swirling around him. Then he felt himself rising, and there was Silva's grinning mug in front of his face.

"Here," he said, pushing the Thompson into his hands. "You idiot!"

Before he could respond, Sandra had her arms around his neck again, kissing his cheek. Blood thundered in his ears.

"Thank you!" she said, and kissed him again. His legs felt like melted wax. For the moment, the shooting had stopped. They must have chased the lizards back below.

"Yes, thank you, Mr. Scott!" Matt said earnestly, squeezing his shoulder hard. He looked at Sandra. The mixture of profound relief and rage on his face was something to behold.

"What on *earth* were you thinking?"

Her wet chin came up. "I was thinking, Captain Reddy, that you might need medical help over here!"

"And because of that thinking, I ... We almost lost you!"

"Captain," Alden interrupted, "we have to push 'em before they get their act together! We're a little shorthanded, and it looks like there's more of 'em crammed below than we figured."

"Of course, Sergeant. Carry on. I'll deal with Lieutenant Tucker!"

Alden nodded. "Mr. Shinya . . ." He hesitated only an instant. "Take A company. Work your way forward! Be sure and check under all this shit before you pass it by. Chack, take C company and follow 'em. Find a way below from the fo'c'sle! We'll get 'em stirred up amidships and you can hit 'em in the rear! B company, with me!"

They'd gathered near the wreck of the mainmast on the raised quarterdeck, with an open companionway gaping in front of them.

"Grenade!"

Silva slung the BAR and fished in a satchel at his side. Retrieving a grenade, he pulled the pin and lobbed it into the hole. There was a muffled *whump* and the deck shivered beneath their feet. A chorus of shrieks and snarls punctuated the blast.

"Guess somebody *is* home," Silva quipped.

"Another!" shouted Alden. "Scott, you okay? You and your Thompson follow the grenade with first squad. We'll be right behind you!"

Tony jerked a quick nod and poised himself near the ladder. After what he'd just been through, a battle was a cinch. In the water he'd been helpless. Now there was something he could shoot. Silva pitched a second grenade. More screams accompanied the explosion, and the coxswain bolted down the hatch with a dozen yowling Marines. *Bra-ba-bap! Bra-ba-bap!* roared the Thompson amid yells and screams and clashing weapons.

"Second squad, with me!" Alden cried, leading the second wave into the belly of the ship. He had a pistol on his belt, but he charged down the steps holding a spear like a bayonet-tipped Springfield. He would fight as he'd trained his Marines. Gray grabbed at Silva's satchel as he brought up the rear.

"Gimme some of those!" he ordered. Silva quickly opened the flap so Gray could snatch grenades, then he bolted down the ladder. A moment later, the heavier bark of the BAR was heard.

"More down there than we thought," Garrett mused

worriedly. "It may be a while before we can get through that way!"

One of the Marines in Matt's guard detail "oofed" and crumpled to the deck with a crossbow-bolt high in his chest. Sandra rushed to him, opening her soggy bag.

"Aft!" cried Gray. "That skylight in front of the tiller!"

Matt grabbed one of the Marines by the arm. "Five of you stay with Lieutenant Tucker and the wounded!" Sandra started to protest. "That's why you said you came," he accused harshly, opening his holster and taking out his .45.

"But I don't need that many. You do!"

"Nevertheless—" He pushed the pistol into her hand. "Can you use that?" She nodded, terrified, but not of the gun.

"Of course! But you're *not* going to fight them with just that stupid sword!"

He quickly stooped and whispered in her ear. "I wouldn't *have* to if you'd stayed where you belong!" He took a deep breath. "I think I love you, Sandra Tucker, but you're an idiot!" He flashed a quick smile and stood. "The rest of you, with me!"

Together, they rushed the skylight, hoping to make it before another bolt flew. They didn't quite, but the next went wide and thunked into the bulwark. Gray flung a grenade into the opening and dropped down beside it. Smoke and splinters rocketed from the hole, mixed with red droplets and a fuzz of downy fur.

"In!" Captain Reddy yelled, and he dropped out of sight.

Keje-Fris-Ar stared in shock at the devastation they'd wrought. The big bronze guns that Letts worked so hard to produce—along with the foundry at Baalkpan and more than a hundred helpers—had been inexpertly used, to say the least. Despite the assistance of the destroyerman named Felts and another Amer-i-caan supervising each gun, more than half the destructive force of each shot was wasted, churning up the already maddened sea for hundreds of tails beyond the target. Even so, it was more than enough. A total of fifteen shots were fired at the boats, three from each cannon, sending thousands of copper balls scything through the flimsy vessels and enemy warriors. Parts of bodies and large chunks of the boats themselves scattered among marching plumes of violent splashes and horrible, unearthly shrieks. When the smoke and spray had cleared, nothing was left of the enemy but shattered flotsam and struggling forms. Flasher-fish weren't active when the sea ran high. They couldn't sense the splashing of their prey, and the turmoil of the water was dangerous for them in such a shallow place. It didn't matter. The Grik had no more reason or inclination to learn to swim than People did. Within moments, there was no movement but the relentless march of the churning swells.

That left the Grik ship bearing down upon them. It was downrange during the firing, and its sails and rigging were savaged. The enemy aboard saw what happened to the warriors in the boats, but true to form, on they came. Tom Felts called for "round shot." The Grik bored in, without maneuver, no finesse at all. It apparently wasn't going to lay alongside and send its remaining boarders across. It meant to crash headlong into *Salissa*'s side. That might cause significant damage. Keje waited tensely while the big guns were loaded. At two hundred tails, they spoke. Massive detonations trundled the heavy guns back against their restraints. The brief "swoosh" of heavy shot ended in multiple crashes that launched blizzards of splinters and large, spinning fragments of the Grik's bow into the sea. When the smoke cleared, the Grik still came, but slower and lower in the water. The approach ended at a hundred tails, as the vessel filled. Keje saw a wisp of smoke and remembered the Grik firebombs.

"Once more!" he commanded. This time, when the massive smoke cloud dissipated, all that remained was jutting masts, rapidly slipping lower. With a jolt, the hull struck bottom, and the masts tilted crazily, almost disappearing, before they came to rest.

Then began the cheering. It was like the times before, when he'd witnessed *Walker*'s devastating powers to lay waste the hated foe. Only this time it was he and *Salissa* who'd unleashed it! It was a heady moment. With power like she now possessed, *Salissa* need fear nothing on earth!

Perhaps the time *had* come at last for the Ancient Enemy that had haunted their lives and dreams to be laid low. Perhaps even their Ancient Home, the very cradle of their race, might be restored! The name Keje-Fris-Ar would be spoken with reverence and honor as great as that of Siska-Ta, the prophet who wrote the Scrolls themselves!

Keje knew exultation beyond any he'd ever felt. He clasped Selass in a joyful embrace and capered with glee along with the others. In that brief moment, anything was possible! Most of the people on the shore couldn't see what had happened, but hearing the cheers even over the wind and surf, they began cheering too.

"Look, look!" Jarrik-Fas cried, pointing out to sea. Far away now, *Walker* grappled with the dismasted Grik. The distance was too great for detail, even through the binoculars that he hastily raised. Keje's happiness was tempered by the realization that *Walker*'s role was by far the most dangerous. He hadn't really known that when the plan was conceived, before the glory of artillery against open boats was made abundantly clear. None of *Salissa*'s numerous defenders had even had to raise a sword. Now he knew that for *Walker* to succeed, his friends—the very ones who made his victory possible—must come to direct blows with the enemy. He felt as if his own kin were at risk, and the possibility their ship might be damaged filled him with sudden dread. He chafed at the distance.

Matt landed on a shattered table and it collapsed beneath him with a crash. He rolled off the debris and scrambled to his feet, coughing from the smoke and dust. From the corner of his eye, he glimpsed movement, and he ducked as an axe whooshed through the space his head had just occupied and sank deep into the wall behind him. A Grik, snarling in frustration, tried to wrench it loose. Matt yanked his Academy sword from its sheath with a well-oiled, metallic *snink*.

Without thought, he drove it through the Grik's chest, twisted, and yanked it clear. With a terrible screech, the hideous creature slashed and lunged falteringly toward him. Matt stepped aside and thrust again, stabbing deep at the base of its throat. Blood sprayed explosively between its terrifying teeth and it crashed to the deck, its tail beating a spastic tattoo. Another rushed him from behind—already wounded, thank God—and he dodged its clumsy leap. He slashed as it passed, but the dull edge of the sword had no effect. It had never occurred to him to sharpen it. Luckily, the injured Grik stumbled or slipped on blood when it landed, and he was on it in an instant, driving the sharp point of his blade into its back. He must have pierced its spine, because it instantly crumpled to the deck, jaws gnashing, but incapable of further movement. He spun in place, sword outstretched, but there was no other threat at present.

His heart pounded with terror at his close call—and just at the sight of the things. He'd seen them from a distance, of course, and they were much like the Bali creatures, but up close like this . . . A swaying lantern hung on a bulkhead, slightly askew, its feeble glow piercing the gloom of the compartment. Blood was spattered everywhere and two more Grik lay on the deck. From the look of one, it actually caught the grenade before it exploded. Shattered bone and gray-red lengths of intestine made up its torso. There were no arms. He forced his breathing back to normal and concealed his shaking hands by sticking his sword point into the deck and resting them nonchalantly on the hilt. The remaining four Marines hopped lightly through the skylight, followed by Garrett, who helped Gray lower his more difficult bulk onto the wrecked table.

"Well done, Captain! You made short work of them!" Garrett exclaimed.

"Thanks, Mr. Garrett. Now let's check these doors. This compartment must've been their wardroom. The doors may lead to officers' quarters." He pointed with his bloody sword to another door aft. "That's the captain's cabin, I expect."

The heavy door on the forward bulkhead crashed inward and Grik surged inside, slashing with swords and ravening jaws. The Marines lunged forward with their spears and Gray and Garrett fired.

"God, this is fun!" bellowed Silva, swinging his cutlass like an axe. It caught a Grik right across the bridge of its snout and cleaved almost to its throat. Blood geysered.

"Speak for yourself!" screamed Scott, fumbling with another magazine. Silva hadn't even tried to reload; there'd been no time. He had no idea where the BAR was now. There were *many* more Grik belowdecks than they'd expected and they'd jumped into a hornet's nest. The Marines' shields were useless—there just wasn't room—so it degenerated into a melee, as Alden had feared it might. Fortunately, at least the Marines were trained in that to some degree. If they lived, some damn good NCOs would come out of this one. Scott finally locked the thirty-round stick and racked the bolt. Silva ducked. *Bra-ba-ba-ba-ba-bap!*

"I *am* speakin' for myself!" Silva replied, hacking down at a lizard trying to crawl in under the fire. He nearly severed its head and the senseless body leaped straight up and bounced against the overhead, bowling others over when it fell. He laughed. He'd killed a lot in his life, before the War even started. Bar fights and back alleys in China, mostly—although there'd been that pool shark down in Mobile too. Most had it coming, by his definition, though he might have been hasty a time or two. The Japs had it coming, and he guessed he'd killed some of them with his number one gun. But that was a team sport. He'd never killed anybody because he was "good" and they were "bad." They'd just been "badder" than he was. And sometimes Dennis Silva could be a bad man. But now he *felt* good because the creatures he killed were indisputably bad. They'd killed Marvaney (he made no distinction) and a bunch of his cat-monkey friends. Mallory said they'd wiped out a place the size of Baalkpan at what ought to be Tjilatjap. Now they were trying to kill *him*! They were mean and ugly and needed killing by anyone's definition—and utterly righteous killing had a liberating effect on Dennis Silva. He felt like the big mean dragon in the story that everybody was scared of, who swooped down and ate the evil king. Sometimes it felt good to be "good."

He almost tripped. Several Grik made a lunge for him, but Marine spears and Alden's pistol probably saved his life. With a nod, Alden reholstered the pistol and went back to his spear. For an instant Silva watched in admiration as the Marine parried another Grik thrust as simply as swatting a fly and drove his spear into the creature's belly. It screamed and intestines uncoiled on the deck. *That's one Marine I'm never pickin' a fight with*, he swore to himself. He looked down at what had tripped him. "There's my gun! Gimme a minute, Tony!"

Bra-ba-ba-bap! Bra-bap!

Silva stabbed his cutlass into a dead Grik to keep it handy and seized the BAR. It was slick with blood and rough with chunks of other things. He slammed in a fresh magazine.

"I'm almost out'a ammo!" gasped Scott. "A and C compnees should'a been here by now! If that Nip doesn't get his ass here quick, even you will be ready to play somethin' else!"

"Don't worry, he'll get here!" Dennis assured him and wondered suddenly why he was so sure. "Stand aside!" *Bam-bam-bam!*

The Grik "wardroom" was an abattoir by the time they hacked and shot their way through the initial push and managed to secure the door. It had a convenient bar to prevent it from being opened from forward. Matt wondered what that said about Grik discipline? One of his Marines was dead and Garrett's left arm hung almost useless, blood pattering on the deck to join the deep pool there. Matt wasn't wounded, but he was splashed with gore and his "ceremonial" sword was notched and bloody. Gray was tying a tourniquet around Garrett's arm, and the three Marines were wedging pieces of the heavy broken table against the door, which rattled with incessant pounding.

"Quick, let's check these other rooms!" They looked in both compartments on either side. There were no enemies, but the collections decorating each were disconcerting. Skulls, mostly. Like trophies. One cabin held nothing but rows and rows of clay pots or jars, suspended from the bulkheads by netting. At a glance, they had no idea what was in them, but the stench was overpowering. Maybe they were firebombs and the compartment was a magazine? Gray and one of the Marines guarded the door leading forward. Heavy fighting raged on the other side. It was becoming more intense, and they heard a couple of grenades and more firing. They remained there, watching the rear while Matt, Garrett, and the other two Lemurians checked the final door aft. It was locked from within.

"Stand back," Matt ordered and nodded at Garrett, who fired two shots into the familiar-looking keyhole below the doorknob. The Marines kicked it open and dashed inside. One fell back immediately, a spear through his chest. A Grik waiting beside the door slashed at the other, missing by the thickness of her fur. Garrett bellowed the first obscenity Matt had ever heard him use and fired directly through the wall. Matt lunged through the doorway and spun, raising his sword. The Grik from beside the door grappled with the remaining Marine, trying to tear out her throat. The one that Garrett had shot slumped to the deck, leaving a red stain on the wall. It was dark in the room, but blurred movement caused him to rush forward, driving his blade through a gaudily dressed Grik. It slashed at him with its claws, but they skated across his steel helmet. He yelled and stabbed it again, driving it backward to sprawl into some chairs behind it. Garrett was suddenly beside him, firing at the Grik where it lay. Together, they turned to the one fighting the Marine, and when it glanced at them with toothy, gape-mouthed astonishment, the little female Marine drove her short-sword into its belly, clear to the hilt.

Matt spun back, looking at something he'd glimpsed as he dashed inside. Seated at a dark, highly polished desk and silhouetted against the gray sea through the windows behind it, a startlingly obese Grik glared at him with intense, unblinking eyes. It was lavishly attired in a shimmering red and black silk-like robe and its fur, or plumage—whatever—was shiny and well groomed. A window was open and the desk was littered with tablets. Perhaps it was throwing things out? It snarled at him and a string of saliva foamed on its yellowed teeth. Without hesitation, it grasped a curved blade from the cluttered desk. Matt raised his sword and prepared to spring forward before it could rise. With a defiant cry, the thing drove the knife into its own throat and slashed outward, severing muscle, trachea, and arteries. Blood spumed, and the head, no longer supported by muscle and sinew, flopped backward before rebounding forward and slamming down upon the desk.

Matt lowered his sword and stared. Gun smoke eddied in the breeze through the window, but the sharp stench of blood and voided bowels was overpowering in the confined space. The female Marine, her blood-streaked sword still in her hand, retched in a corner, overcome by nausea and relief.

Gray hurried into the cabin, glancing about, taking it all in. He strode to the corpse of the Grik captain and heaved it roughly aside. It slid to the deck like a sack of wet tapioca. "Bugger was bleedin' all over the books!" he growled.

Matt shook his head and quickly joined the Chief. His eyes moved rapidly over the haul. "May be something here." He glanced at the dead Lemurian Marines, one still lying in the doorway and the other just outside. "I hope it was worth it." He reeled slightly as the ship rolled drunkenly and unexpectedly in a swell. The sound of battle had diminished, unnoticed, and there came a heavy banging on the barricaded door through the wardroom. They heard muffled shouts.

"Captain! Captain Reddy! Are you in there?"

"Who wants to know?" Gray roared.

"Why, it's me, Silva, you damned tyrant!" came the relieved, muffled reply. "Let me in! We've got the ship, or at least this deck of her. Some of them stinkin' lizards has sneaked into the hold. We're fixin' to root 'em out."

Gray approached the door while Silva spoke and heaved the barricade aside. The smoke and stench that filled the cabin were nothing compared to what wafted in from the long deck beyond. Silva stepped inside, leading a small pack of Marines. All were exhausted and their fur was matted with blood. Silva had a long cut on his forearm extending from his rolled-up sleeve to his fist. When he saw the captain, his bearded face split into a huge grin.

"Ahh, Skipper! Glad to see you well! We've killed a swarm o' them devils. I bet there was two hundred left aboard! Most fun I *ever* had! I feel like a blamed pirate!" He leered at Gray and waved his cutlass. "Arrr!" Gray's face went almost purple.

"What about our people, Silva? Anybody hurt?" Matt asked.

Silva shook his head. "I don't know how many we lost on the contraption . . ." Matt blanched. Another big mistake! "But in the fightin'?" He looked at the two dead Marines between them. "A lot of 'cats bought it. Don't know about any of our guys, past a few cuts and scrapes. It was a near thing too, when we first come down the ladders. Lizards got us backed up a mite. Then that Jap and my buddy Chack took 'em in the rear from the fo'c'sle. After that it was just pure, sweet killin'! Most of these lizards weren't even warriors, I bet. Prob'ly just ship keepers, 'cause some weren't even armed—not that they need to be with all them teeth and claws! But you should'a seen that Jap, Skipper! He's a real terror with a sword!" There was genuine admiration in the gunner's mate's tone.

"You should'a seen the Skipper!" growled Gray. "All he *had* was a sword!" Silva looked down and saw the bloody thing in Matt's hand. He whistled. Matt knew that unlike Shinya's, his own success with the sword had come from terrified desperation, not skill. But from Silva's expression, he realized he would probably be "Captain Blood" within a few days. The ship heaved sickeningly once again and he turned to the Bosun. "We have to get this wreck under tow right away, or get off it—one or the other. There're too many little islands around here for us to run into. Take some people. Try to secure a towline. Have a detail cut away all that wreckage topside. I bet she'll ride easier without it trailing over the side."

"Aye, aye, Captain," Gray responded, and started to turn. Matt stopped him.

"And check on Lieutenant Tucker." Gray nodded, and summoning Silva's companions, he picked his way through the bodies and debris forward and lumbered up the companionway. Matt turned to Garrett, who'd quietly joined them, holding his arm. "Maybe you should see the nurse?"

"I'm fine, Skipper."

"Well, see what you can come up with. Sacks, sheets, anything, and wrap up whatever looks useful. Have it ready to send across to *Walker* in case we have to abandon this ship."

"Aye, sir," he answered distractedly. "Sir, there's something you ought to see."

"What?"

Garrett flicked a glance at Silva and lowered his voice, but the tone was still insistent. "Please, Captain, just . . . look for yourself."

"Very well," he said, curious. He followed into the dead commander's quarters, paying attention to the surroundings now. More tablets like the ones on the desk were scattered on the deck. Against one bulkhead were shelves with square partitions containing what looked tantalizingly like rolled-up charts! He stepped forward, eager to examine them. "Outstanding, Greg! This may be exactly what we're looking for!"

"Sir," insisted Garrett with uncharacteristic fragility. He gestured at the heavy overhead beams. Along both sides of each, like in the other cabins they'd inspected, were many, many skulls. They were of all manner of creatures, some he knew even Lemurians ate. Matt had tacked up a few sets of deer horns himself, growing up in Texas, so he felt no innate revulsion toward taking animal trophies, even if it was creepy and bizarre to take it to such an extreme as this. What made him seethe with anger was that, by far, most of the skulls hanging in the dreary shadows were Lemurian.

He'd never seen a Lemurian skull, but by their shape, that's clearly what they were. Many were dry and yellow and covered with dust. Some were much fresher. A few were even decorated with garish painted designs, whatever that might mean. He shook his head, revolted, but from what he knew of the Grik, he wasn't surprised. *'Cats are people, damn it!* He looked at Garrett. It was clear he was shaken by what he'd seen.

"Yes. Well, make sure they're taken down carefully and with respect. We'll turn them over to our allies and they can deal with them in their way."

"Captain!" Garrett hissed, pointing directly above his head. He stood in the very center of the cabin, right in front of the desk. The gimbaled lanterns cast a crazy kaleidoscope of sinister shadows in the recess. Matt followed his gaze, and suddenly the rush of blood in his ears surpassed the crashing sea that pounded the hull outside. There above him, leering down from sightless, empty sockets, was an un-mistakably human skull.

Silva had followed them into the cabin and was leafing through a tablet he snatched from the deck. He stared as well. His happy mood and customary laconic expression were replaced by anguish and rage.

"Oh, those sorry, sick, buggerin' bastards!"

"Skipper!" called Sergeant Alden from the doorway. "All the hatches are sealed, and we're ready to go in the hold. It's not gonna be a picnic, though. There may be thirty or forty down there, and they're crazy as shit-house rats! When they knew they were whipped, it was like *Big Sal* when they jumped over the side—only these had nowhere to go but down. They're cornered, so I bet they fight like shit-house rats, too. I'd just as soon smoke 'em out, or smoke 'em period, but I'm afraid they might chop a hole in the damn hull! Besides, you said you want prisoners . . ."

Matt's face was wooden. He held up his sword and ran a finger distractedly down the notched blade. When he spoke, his voice was unnaturally calm, but his eyes flashed like chiseled ice.

"Mr. Garrett, follow my orders—and do get Lieutenant Tucker to look at that arm. Our mission is a success. We've learned as much as we need to know about the *nature* of our enemy. The documents we've captured and the ship it-self will teach us much, much more. Sergeant Alden, you said you don't speak Grik? Neither do I." He turned to look at Silva. "I don't think we really need any prisoners after all." He motioned through the door with his sword. "Shall we?"

Walker had managed to maintain close station with the madly wallowing derelict, her gunners hovering protec-tively over their weapons, but it was clear in an instant when Gray thrust his head from the companionway that they would be on their own for a while.

"Get to work clearing that debris!" he bellowed over his shoulder at the Marines following him up. He ran to a clus-ter of Lemurians helping Sandra with the wounded. She saw him coming.

"Are you all right, Chief?" she shouted over the wind. He was covered with blood.

"Nary a scratch, thanks for askin'." He saw her tense expression. "Captain's fine, ma'am." She visibly relaxed, but Gray decided now was as good a time as any to get something off his chest. "No thanks to you." He gestured at the pistol thrust in the web belt around her waist. "He could've used that." Stung, she touched the pistol with her fingertips.

"I told him not to leave it!"

"Like that made a difference! I didn't think he should even come over here, but he did and he's the captain. He figures he got us in this mess and he can't just sit back and watch. That's the kind of guy he is. But your coming was just a stupid female stunt and you nearly wound up killed." She bristled, but he stared her down. "Sure, sure, you came for 'the wounded,' but what if you'd been killed? What do you think that would've done to him? To all of us?" He watched his words sink in. Finally, he continued in a softer tone. "Look, we gotta clear this shi . . . stuff and this ain't no fit place for you or the wounded. The main deck's secure. It's a bloody mess down there, but it's out of the weather." She began to nod.

"If we can get them down there, that would be best. And Chief . . . I'm sorry."

Gray started to say something else, but shook his head. "Right."

He struggled toward a couple of Lemurians near the bulwark, clutching the chaotic mass of shrouds. They were two of the ones left on deck as a security force, but they'd obviously decided their own security was paramount. A wave crashed over the deck, knocking Gray to his knees and washing him in among the terrified forms. He reemerged from the warm gray water and grabbed one of the 'cats. A grinding and bumping was felt alongside as the ship's masts and spars, twisted in an impossible nightmare of tangled rigging, pounded against the ship as it worked.

"You useless bastards! Help Lieutenant Tucker get the wounded below!" He beckoned those behind him. "The rest of you, cut everything away!" he yelled, hoping they understood. "With your swords!" He pulled his own cutlass and laid into the cables with a will. They quickly got the idea and chopped with mad abandon at his side. Other Marines, relieved from the fighting below, arrived to add their swords. Piece by piece, rope by rope, the debris threatening to drag the ship over was released, and the hulk began riding more easily. The roll increased, but at least it was a more buoyant roll.

Gray's arm felt like lead as he swung the cutlass, huffing and wheezing with every blow. *I'm close to sixty, and too fat for this shit*, he complained to himself, but no word of complaint escaped his lips. Nor would it ever. The Bosun is all-powerful and indestructible. He has to be. He glanced at the sky. It was early afternoon when the Grik were first seen, so they couldn't have much light left. Already, it was noticeably darker. If they couldn't get a towline secured before dark, they were probably screwed. He left clearing the remainder of the wreckage to fresh, willing hands and ran to fetch something to signal the other ship.

Five grenades went down the hatch into the gloom of the hold. Each time one detonated, there was a chorus of nightmarish wails. Silva and Scott pounded down the companionway together this time, followed closely by Matt, Alden, Chack, Shinya, and a score of Lemurian Marines. They advanced through the darkness, blasting or stabbing at anything that moved and, as Alden suspected, the confined space in the bottom of the ship was working with the vermin. Footing was treacherous on the slimy ballast stones, and there were other things, barely glimpsed in the guttering torchlight. Bones. Thousands of bones intermingled with the rocks. The stench was unreal. Then, even as they fought, and their eyes became accustomed to the gloom, they entered a waking nightmare they would never forget. With the searing clarity of a lightning strike, Matt realized he *hadn't* learned the true nature of their enemy. Not till now. The belly of the ship was a slaughterhouse, in more ways than one. The gnawed and shattered bones in the ballast were mostly Lemurian. Half-butchered Lemurian carcasses swayed from hooks and all the grisly paraphernalia of the butcher's trade dangled, obscenely well ordered, nearby. Chained along the sides of the ship, conveniently out of the way but well situated to witness the horror they were doomed to endure, cowered maybe a dozen filthy, mewling, near-starved Lemurian captives. Matt knew then, that even if he ordered it, no Grik prisoners were possible.

The Marines went amok. They fought with abandon and no regard for their own lives. So, to a degree, did the humans. Scott staggered back, blood on his face, and Shinya dragged him from the fighting. Matt took the Thompson himself, firing controlled bursts at maniacally charging Grik. He burned with a towering, righteous wrath. At last there was focus for all the rage and anxiety, grief and loss he'd suppressed for months. When the Thompson clicked empty, he drew his sword again.

"At 'em!" he screamed. Once, he'd never imagined drawing his sword in anger, but now it seemed an extension of his very soul: the instrument of purification. The Marines surged forward, bronze spearpoints gleaming red in the guttering light. With a ringing whoop, Silva drew his cutlass, and so did the others. Alden knew with sinking certainty that of all the people in the world, Captain Reddy had the least business in this fight, but it was pointless to try to stop him. They charged. Without even shields, they slammed into the final, teetering Grik line and slashed it apart with a manic savagery that must have shocked even the Grik. The survivors broke. Shrieking in mindless terror, they fled farther into the darkness, flinging themselves against the hull, the overhead—anything to escape. Most had dropped their weapons. For a moment, Matt paused, leaning on his knees and gasping for breath. He started forward again.

"Captain," Alden said gently, grasping his arm. "It's done. It's done!"

Matt started to shake him off, but then stopped, shocked by the intensity of his emotions. He nodded. The Marines, still in a blind frenzy, shouldered past and slaughtered the twenty or so Grik holdouts that had fled to the farthest reaches of the dank, half-flooded hold. They mercilessly hacked apart every last Grik they found, and the Americans stood, listening, until the final shriek ended.

Chack returned from the gloom, limping and leaning on Dennis Silva. Both were drenched in blood and Chack was clearly hurting, but Silva looked like some mythical god of war. Marines filtered back into the dim light, dazed.

"Sergeant Alden, get our wounded out of here, then form a detail to release these poor bastards." He gestured helplessly at the captives.

Most of the captives had begun a shrill, keening sound. In their tortured reality they probably thought their time had come to face the knives and saws. They seemed utterly mad. Matt remained for a while, watching while they were gently released a few at a time and taken on deck to the open air, as far from their prison as possible, by expressionless, furiously blinking Marines. Once there, they were wrapped in sailcloth against the wind and spray that came over the rail. They were fed and watered and carefully tended, but their chains weren't removed. In their current state they might harm themselves or others if freed.

Silva was helping Chack through the stones (he'd flatly refused to be carried) when the Lemurian suddenly halted before a captive still chained to the hull. The wretched creature recoiled from his stare and made small gurgling sounds. Its skeletal chest heaved with terrified gasps. Matt stepped closer and regarded the creature with pity. He had great respect for the Lemurian people. He'd come to know them as stout warriors and generally cheerful, free-spirited individualists—not unlike his own destroyermen—but the things the captives had seen and endured would have broken anyone.

"Leave him alone, Chackie," said Silva, uncharacteristically subdued. "Can't you see he's fixin' to vapor-lock?"

Chack shook his head and leaned closer still. "I greet you. Do not fear," he said in his own language.

"You *know* him?" Matt demanded.

Chack nodded, a strange smile on his face. "I know him."

"Does he know you?"

Chack spoke rapidly, repeating a few words many times. A slight sheen slowly returned to the captive's flat, dull eyes and, hesitantly, he spoke. After a moment, Chack turned. "He said these were mostly survivors of Chill-chaap, but there were some from other places. He himself was transferred from another ship—as was a Tail-less One like yourself."

Matt remembered the skull. "What happened to the Tailless One?" he demanded. Chack gestured as if it was obvious, and Matt nodded sharply. "You said you know him. Who is he?"

Chack almost seemed to sigh. "His name is Saak-Fas. Daughter-Mate of Keje-Fris-Ar."

Tony Scott and Tamatsu Shinya found Gray resting in the gloom near the ship's wildly spinning wheel. He was breathing hard and futilely wiping at the salt that stung his eyes. The coxswain had a cut on his shoulder that left a bloody scrap of sleeve flapping in the wind, and his lower lip was split and swollen. He still had no helmet, but he'd tied a rag around his head to keep the hair out of his eyes. The Thompson was lovingly slung over his undamaged shoulder.

"Cambin's commimenpfs, Cheeb," Scott said, trying to talk around his busted lip. "How are eberations goin' 'or da tow?"

Gray groaned as he rose to his feet. "We're *under* tow, you nitwit. Have been for the last fifteen minutes. I was about to report to the captain myself when you interrupted me!"

Scott nodded. "'Innat cay, cambin wans you ter sounderwell."

Gray looked at him in the near-darkness. The ship rode much easier now that *Walker* was towing her and she no longer rolled beam-on to the swells.

"What the hell's a sounderwell?" he demanded.

"Sound-the-well!" Scott painfully repeated. "Vinally got da las o' dat verbin cleared out o' da hold an' da cambin wants to know if she'll f-f-vloat. I'll go vif you."

Gray nodded. "Right. I'll report to the captain first, though. What's he doin', anyway? I figgered he'd of been up here by now."

"Lookin' at fings. Charts an' stuvv . . . an' udder fings. There's . . . awful fings down dere."

Gray turned for the stairs.

"Chief Boatswain's Mate Gray," said Shinya. "May I have a brief word?"

Gray's face darkened, but he jerked a nod.

"I know you don't like me, but you saved my life today, when the corvus parted. I would like to thank you."

Gray shrugged. "There was guys behind you. I had to get your Nip ass out of the way." He turned to follow Scott, but stopped again. "You got any kids?" he asked. Tamatsu was taken aback.

"No."

"I did. A boy. Close to thirty, now. Took after his old man—'cept he was a snipe. Machinist's mate. I hadn't seen him in four years, but I was proud of him. He was my son, you know?"

"What happened to him?"

"They never found his body, so officially he was missing. But he was in *Oklahoma*'s fireroom when she rolled over. At Pearl Harbor. So don't you dare thank me for saving your worthless ass! It makes me sick! I was just pitching you out of the way." With that, he stormed down the ladder.

"Yes," Shinya said to himself, "but it would have been easier to 'pitch' me into the sea instead of on the deck."

"Well, we did what we set out to do," Matt said grimly. "We've learned about the enemy." He, Sandra, Garrett, Shinya, and Alden sat around the Grik captain's desk poring over the tablets and charts they'd found. *Walker* towed the derelict charnel house in a wide, lazy circle across the Makassar Strait, into the Java Sea. That would keep them off the islands and shoals through the long night and bring them to *Big Sal* and their friends by morning. The sea was moderating, and Gray reported they'd float as long as the rhythmic *clunk-thump* of the chain pumps was maintained.

His report was uncustomarily subdued after he returned from inspecting the hull. It sustained little battle damage, but seams had opened while she wallowed in the heavy seas and water was coming in. That wasn't what bothered him about his tour of the well, though. All of them would be haunted by the things they'd seen and survived that day, and by what they'd come to know about the nature of their enemy.

"They're worse than Japs, sir!" said Alden with conviction mixed with quiet horror. The exhausted Marine belatedly glanced at Shinya, who bristled at the slightest comparison. "I didn't mean that the way it sounded. Hell, they're worse than *anything*!"

Captain Reddy had in fact been idly searching his memory for any culture in human history to compare with the Grik. So far, his tired mind wouldn't oblige. He rubbed his eyes and watched Shinya visibly relax. "Anything," he repeated dully. "I think you're right."

It had been a long, bloody day. Eighteen Lemurian Marines were killed and almost that many wounded. Most of his destroyermen were lightly injured as well, although only Norman Kutas suffered a serious wound. That was when Scurrey dropped his cutlass down a companionway and nailed his foot to the deck. Miraculously, it missed the bones, but Kutas was off his feet for a while. Aside from the quartermaster's mate's pain, it might even have been funny under other circumstances—but nothing was funny now.

They had one of the Grik charts spread before them on the desk. Matt thought how horrified Adar would be to learn that the Grik had "Scrolls." They were looking at an overview of the western Indian Ocean, Madagascar, and East Africa up to the equator and south to latitude 30. The eastern boundary of the map was the 80th parallel. The quality of the representations was poor—about on a par with sixteenth-century maps he'd seen in history books, but they, along with the printed information, were more than adequate for rudimentary navigation. The most startling and terrible thing about the charts, however, was that he could read them.

Most of the writing, and anything added by hand, was incomprehensible and resembled a slashing form of Arabic. But many of the place-names and nautical references used recognizable letters forming English words. All the numbers were familiar too. Obviously, the Grik got much more out of their British teachers than the Lemurians did. From what they'd seen that day, Matt imagined the Grik had certainly been more persuasive.

"Madagascar," Matt said at last. "I bet old Bradford's

right about that being the original home of the 'Cats." Sandra peered at the island.

"Probably. It's been well within the Grik empire for a long, long time. In fact, every landmass shown seems to be part of their territory." Garrett glanced at Matt with a worried frown.

"They've got a lot of weight behind them, that's for sure. Way more than us."

Matt looked at Alden. "Anything from the tablets yet?"

Pete shook his head. He'd been skimming the roughly twelve-by-twelve-inch booklets while the others studied the charts. They were filled, mostly, with pen-and-ink illustrations. "Captain Grik was a pretty good drawer, or his clerk was. Mostly animals, bugs, places, and such. Must've been a naturalist like Bradford, in a perverted, lizard sort of way." Matt nodded absently and motioned Shinya to bring another chart. He unrolled it carefully and placed his cutlass on one end and a couple of .45s on the other.

At a glance, this one seemed most pertinent, at least in the short term. Even cruder than the others, it was less like a navigational chart than a map of enemy territory. It extended from the mouth of the Ganges River southward to include the Cocos Islands. From there, west to Timor, then back to Formosa. All French Indochina and the Dutch East Indies showed varying detail. The farther east, the vaguer the shapes of landmasses became. The Philippines weren't shown at all.

Matt leaned over the desk, trying to see better by the light of the swaying lanterns. He was painfully reminded he'd discovered unknown muscles that day.

"Skipper, look at this!" exclaimed Alden. He held a tablet close to his face to see in the dim light. Reversing it, he displayed the page. Sandra cried out and sprang to her feet. Matt managed only a short bark of incredulous laughter. There, on the yellowish paper, was a highly stylized but clearly recognizable drawing of USS *Walker*, down to the "163" on her bow.

"Son of a *bitch*!" Alden breathed. "This must be the one that got away!"

"Maybe," murmured Matt, "but does that make it the same one in company with the other two we destroyed?

Why was it with two more so fast—if it's the same? I wonder how many others it came in contact with."

"Quite a few," said Sandra, leaning back over the chart. Her voice was brittle. "Look. Many of these coastlines have been updated or redrawn periodically, like survey corrections. Also, see this dark splotch here?" She pointed at a spot on the map. "I'm no navigator, but that's almost the exact place we came to *Salissa*'s assistance."

Garrett squinted. "Looks like ... blood, Captain. And look! Next to it there's a little drawing of us! Just a thick line with four small lines sticking up, but I bet that's supposed to be *Walker*."

Shinya nodded. "It does look like blood. Possibly representing a place of battle? If that's the case, you may note there are many such spots on this map."

"There's one at Tjilatjap," Sandra confirmed. "Mr. Shinya may be right. There's dozens of 'spots.' If they denote battles, and the picture of *Walker* seems to confirm that, this ship couldn't have engaged in them all, or surveyed all these coastlines alone."

"That means they communicate among themselves, even from one task force to the next." Garrett's brow was creased with concern. "That means . . ."

"Right." Matt finished for him. "This may not be the one that got away. They might *all* know about *Walker*."

There was a contemplative, nervous silence as they considered the implications.

"Okay," said Matt, pointing back at the chart. "Battle here, battle here, battle here—each battle mark is accompanied by this thing that looks like a tree. Maybe that's their symbol for the 'cats." His finger traced the coast of Borneo. "Nothing at Baalkpan, so maybe they don't know about Nakja-Mur's People yet."

"There *is* such a symbol at Surabaya," Shinya pointed out, "although no battle mark."

"I bet it won't be long," Alden growled. "I wonder what these little triangle symbols mean."

Matt felt a chill, despite the dank, oppressive warmth of the cabin. "I bet those are Grik ships. And the circles around them represent their areas of operation. See? There're three in the Makassar Strait."

"Not anymore," Alden quipped.

"They're everywhere, then," Sandra murmured, her voice quiet with despair. "There must be a dozen triangles in the Java Sea alone. And all those other charts we've looked at—there're *scores* of triangles on them!"

"My God," muttered Garrett.

Alden was idly tracing the procession of battle marks up the coast of Java and Sumatra. Suddenly he stiffened. "Look," he said, his finger beside a brownish stain near the Banjak Islands. There was another thick line, but with only three smaller lines sticking out. With a rush of realization, Matt remembered a funnel that fell across a davit.

"*Mahan*," he breathed.

The storm dwindled to nothing as the night wore on, and its only remnant in the boulder-strewn approaches to the re-floated *Big Sal* was a disorganized chop. Otherwise, the sun rose bright above Celebes and the sky was blue and cloudless. All was back to normal aboard the huge ship, fake debris was cleared away and the stores that littered the beach returned. Water still coursed over the side, and it would for some time, since so much had been required to "sink" the great vessel. That was the part of the plan Matt had been most concerned about, but Keje himself suggested it as bait for the trap. He'd assured his friend that sinking and re-floating *Big Sal* wasn't difficult, or even unusual. They did it all the time.

Once a year it was deliberately done to cleanse the lower decks and "sweeten" the air. A suitable, sandy bottom in sheltered shallows was all they needed, and water was let in until *Big Sal* gently settled to the bottom of the sea. After a few days passed, she was pumped out and all hatches were laid open, allowing the interior to dry. This routine cleared the ship of vermin and insects, and washed away the foul smell of gri-kakka oil that seeped from barrels and grew rancid in the bilge.

The periodic "sinkings" were times for festivities and merriment, and contests in which younglings captured and tallied vermin that escaped to the upper decks. They never got rid of them entirely, and the little ratlike creatures were fruitful if nothing else, but for a long time afterward their numbers were diminished and *Big Sal*'s cavernous hold smelled fresh and clean. None of her previous soakings were accompanied by as much merriment and jubilation as this one, however, particularly when *Walker* appeared early that morning towing the dismasted hulk over the horizon.

Big Sal's forward wing still wasn't erected, but otherwise she was good as new when the great sweeps propelled her through the obstacles and into the open water to rejoin her ally. Hundreds of People crowded the shrouds and lined the catwalk to welcome *Walker* with thunderous roars and cheers of greeting. The great guns were loaded and fired in salute as the destroyer bore down with her prize.

Walker responded with repeated whoops from her horn. Destroyermen, Marines, and Lemurian cadets lined her rail, as did the prize crew on the captured ship. A makeshift flagstaff had been rigged atop her shattered mainmast, and an American flag streamed to leeward above the red and black pennant of the enemy.

For the first time since he'd seen the curious cloth, the meaning of the destroyermen's flag, and what it could represent, was driven home to Keje. He felt a surge of pride at the sight of it, even if it wasn't a symbol of his own People. There was also a twinge of something close to envy, and he determined then and there that one day his own People must have a flag. They had symbols aplenty that represented their clans, on the tapestries that adorned their great halls, but nothing they could look to that represented all the People everywhere. In addition to his heady dreams of the day before, it was a legacy that he thought the great uniting prophet, Siska-Ta, would surely approve of. The Americans had their flag and so did the Grik. It was time the People had one.

To cap the magical excitement of the moment, the great flying-boat descended out of the northeastern sky, thunderous motors adding to the joyful tumult of happy people. Keje watched as it skimmed low over the waves and made a proper landing for the first time, and the grace and power of the huge, flying metal contrivance took his breath away. It was a great day!

Walker hove to, her people returning *Big Sal*'s cheers. The launch went over the side and a few moments later arrived in *Salissa*'s lee, crowded with passengers who immediately climbed the netting lowered for them. An honor guard of excited Marines met them when the party reached the main deck, and a twitter of bone whistles simulated bo-sun's pipes.

Captain Reddy saluted aft, as he'd always done, and again Keje wished there was something to salute. Regardless, he fervently returned the gesture Matt offered him and then enclosed him in a mighty embrace.

"We were worried about you, my Brother," he said.

"We were worried about us too," Matt replied. "I never doubted the outcome of your battle."

Keje barked a laugh. "So certain were you? I was not! Not until the great guns spoke! It was . . . glorious!"

Matt couldn't help but catch Keje's infectious grin, but he asked a serious question. "Was the price very high?" Keje only smiled and allowed Jarrik-Fas to answer.

"We had no losses, lord. None! We slew the enemy with contemptuous ease! Our warriors never even drew their blades!"

"I'm grateful for that," Matt said, his smile fading. "We sustained . . . serious losses, I'm sorry to say, but the Marines and cadets fought bravely and well."

Keje lowered his voice in condolence. "Of course you had losses. Yours was the more difficult task and the People who were slain will find honored places awaiting them in the presence of the Maker and their ancestors!"

"Of course."

"Now!" said Keje, practically rubbing his hands together in anticipation. "What have you learned?"

Matt forced a smile, and glancing at the throng encircling them, he lowered his voice. "We have much to discuss, Keje-Fris-Ar, and unless you want to destroy the celebration, we'd better do it alone."

"You were right to suggest privacy." Keje sighed, shaking his head. "The world has fallen upon me." He sat on his favorite stool beside his simple table in *Salissa*'s Great Hall. Upon that table lay a Grik chart. He was revolted that the vile thing was in physical contact with the dark, warm wood. Other stools were occupied by his personal advisors, as well as Captain Reddy, Lieutenant Tucker, Lieutenant Garrett, and Sergeant Alden.

Adar hovered over the chart, sputtering with rage and indignation. "Blasphemy!" he hissed. "Unrepentant, black blasphemy! They desecrate the Heavens by their very existence! These ... counterfeit ... things must be burned! Destroyed! To think they take the gift of Knowledge of the Path of Stars and do ... what they do with that knowledge! It is a violation! A rape! I—" Adar was incapable of further speech.

Matt shifted uncomfortably. "Certainly you may destroy them, Adar," he temporized, "but first let's learn as much from them about the enemy as we can."

The Sky Priest looked sharply at him, and a terrible intensity burned in his eyes. "By all means, Cap-i-taan Reddy! Study them well! Do whatever you must to destroy the makers of this abomination and the doers of these evil deeds! When you have done, then I will burn these loathsome pages and I won't rest until I've helped you bring that day to pass."

Keje sighed. "You will lose much sleep." He looked at Matt, and his eyes almost pleaded for some reassurance that things weren't as bad as they appeared. Matt couldn't encourage him. "You say these three-pointed symbols represent their ships? Possibly *hundreds* more of their ships?"

"We think so. Their strategy seems clear, at long last. It's conquest, of course, but I always wondered why, if they were such a big deal, they were just trickling in." He sighed. "Your ancestors were right. They're scared of the water—at least the deep water." He pointed at the Indian Ocean on the chart. There were none of the small islands depicted. Just a large, scary-looking fish.

"Their version of 'here be monsters,' I bet," Garrett offered.

"The Western Sea is vast and deep," Adar said. "And there *are* monsters there. That is why the enemy hugs the coast and why they have taken this long to find us—to conquer their way to us—it would seem."

Matt nodded. "That's exactly right. They seem to have all the territory bordering the ... Western Sea, all the way to Singapore, although that seems a relatively new addition.

Ceylon's their closest major concentration. The tree symbols seem to indicate settlements of the People they know about. A few even have blood spots beside them. We think that shows where a battle took place."

Keje traced a claw slowly from one spot to the next. "A tree," he said bleakly. "They use a tree to represent us. How appropriate and how ... wrong." He looked up. "You said you found a human skull as well?" Matt jerked a nod. "I'm sorry to hear it, but how can that be?"

"The same way it happened to your people, Keje," Matt replied woodenly. "He was eaten."

"Saak-Fas saw it?"

Matt nodded. "He described a human being brought aboard—'one like you,' he said—but he had no idea where it happened."

"But how did they ... get this person?"

"We don't know." Matt gestured at the chart. "They know where *Mahan* is—or was. But judging by the position fixes the lizard captain noted on the chart, the ship we took was never anywhere near *Mahan*'s last position."

"You think they got this person from another ship?"

"That seems likely, as well as the information where *Mahan* was."

"Do they have her?" Keje asked.

Matt could only shrug. "They will look for her, if they have not found her already." It wasn't a question but a statement of fact.

"They must not have her!" Adar cried. "For *them* to have the power you possess ..." He trailed off.

"They must not have her," Matt agreed.

"What will you do? What must we do?" For the first time since Matt had met Keje, the Lemurian looked afraid.

"Two things," Matt responded. "First, we need help. Baalkpan's in it—they can't leave. But we need more help from Homes like *Big Sal*." He shook his head. "I really don't know what to do about that. Talk about isolationists! Otherwise, I suggest you put aside your differences, whatever they are, with the Surabayans. It looks like they're next on the list anyway. The enemy doesn't know about Baalkpan, but that can't last. The ships they sent to chart those seas have gone missing, and sooner or later they'll send more. If we help the Surabayans, it'll add depth to our defense and might gain us an ally."

"And second?"

"Find *Mahan*," Matt said, grimly determined. "We have to get her before the enemy does—or destroy her if they have her."

Keje still seemed overwhelmed. Well, that was understandable. "I never guessed the Grik could be so numerous," he whispered and glanced at Adar. "This map shows lands we never even knew to exist and all are in the realm of this evil!" He looked sadly at their faces. "Yesterday was a great day. A great victory. Or so we thought. Now I see it was less than nothing compared to that arrayed against us. We've won nothing! The fight has not begun!" He gestured vaguely toward the unseen Grik prize floating nearby. "Together, we've destroyed ten of their ships only to learn that is *nothing* compared to the strength they have! They were mere scouts!" He slammed his hand down upon the chart, claws extended. "Mapmakers!"

"It doesn't look good," Matt agreed, "but we have won a victory. We've learned what we're up against, which is more than they know." He smirked. "More than I've ever known."

Keje snorted derisively. "Yes, they face a disorganized mob that numbers less than one to their ten. An unpleasant surprise that will be!"

"No!" said Matt sharply, standing. "They face soldiers! Brave and determined! We boarded their ship with half the numbers we'd hoped—my fault—and fought them one to four! Our losses were grim, but we killed ten for one—in their kind of fight, not ours. They also face cannon, which will be a *very* unpleasant surprise. And they face *Walker*. While she floats, she'll never abandon you! I've seen evil before—at least I thought I had—but nothing in my experience compares with what I saw in the bottom of that ship. We've been friends and allies since we met, but honestly, I've often regretted getting my people involved in your war. And that's how I thought of it: *your* war. I felt kind of like a mercenary, and my men didn't sign up for that. But after last night—and *not* just because of the human skull—this war against the Grik became just as much ours as yours." He sat, leaning back in his chair.

"Now, we can sit around and mope and whine 'woe is me' or we can get ourselves in gear, make the tough decisions, and figure out how to win!" He saw Adar's predatory grin and knew he'd finally won him over. The Sky Priest probably had more swing with the other Homes than Keje did anyway.

But Keje wasn't out. He leaned forward. "Were you not overwhelmed when first you learned the odds?" Matt was guiltily aware that he'd been "overwhelmed" for the last six months. But this time it was different. The steamroller was coming and his tricycle had a flat, but he'd thrown the blindfold off. Keje huffed. "You'll hear no whining from *me*!"

Matt stood with Sandra on *Big Sal*'s battlement, leaning on the rail and watching the setting sun. Below, the victory celebration was still under way. Time enough later for the full extent of the challenge to make itself known. For now, let them enjoy themselves. They'd earned it. Adar swore the weather would remain fine for several days at least, so Matt hadn't ordered the PBY back to Baalkpan. It floated now, bouncing a little on the choppy sea but safe and snug in the sheltering lee of the massive sides of Home. Bradford cut short his safari. For such large creatures, super lizards were surprisingly difficult to find—particularly since his guides had been instructed by Nakja-Mur not to lead him anywhere near one. He'd arrived with the plane and was, even now, examining the "prize" with Spanky, Chief Gray, and a group of Naga's and Adar's acolytes. In the middle distance steamed *Walker*, festively alight from stem to stern but still screening the revelers against any approaching threat. As it should be. As she'd always done.

Matt blinked and looked around. It struck him odd that he and Sandra would have the vast expanse of *Big Sal*'s battlement all to themselves. Others had been there—Keje, Garrett, Pete, Jarrik—but he hadn't noticed when they left. Weird. Neither had spoken for quite some time, enjoying the companionable solitude.

"It's so sad about Chack," Sandra said, breaking the silence.

"Yeah, Keje's daughter too. I think she was expecting wedding bells when she saw Chack come aboard."

"Her name's Selass," Sandra reminded him. "We spoke before we left Baalkpan, and she told me her hopes and the understanding she had with Chack. She wondered what I thought he'd decide." She shrugged. "I had no idea. Now ... she's in for a rough road. She loves him, but they can't mate, no matter what he had decided."

"Why not? I thought 'cats got married and unmarried whenever they felt like it."

"Sometimes, but they seem to take 'sickness and health' pretty seriously. Selass can't 'divorce' Saak-Fas until he's well—which I doubt he'll ever be—or until he dies, of course."

It had been a heart-wrenching moment. Selass greeted Chack with a joyful embrace, but then they hoisted Saak-Fas aboard. She had her answer—the only one possible—and Chack limped into the crowd while Selass desperately called his name.

They were quiet for a long moment, and then Sandra suddenly giggled. "That Silva and Risa sure carried on—right in front of everybody—when he came aboard! They'll have everybody thinking they *are* married if they don't cool it!" She looked thoughtful. "That's probably gone far enough. They'll run it into the ground. Besides, I never figured Silva for the type to ride a joke down in flames. He's already got Chack's goat. They're just doing if for attention now."

Matt groaned, remembering the embarrassing spectacle. "I don't want to hear that man's name! As far as I'm concerned, he's restricted to the ship for the rest of his life! We'll see how married he thinks he is then!"

There was another long silence between them, and when Sandra spoke again, her voice was softer, hesitant.

"I wonder what Chack was going to say? To Selass. I wonder if he'd made up his mind. Would he"—she looked at him, eyes questioning—"have said the same thing you told me yesterday?" Matt looked confused.

"What, that you're an idiot?"

She snorted with laughter, but tears filled her eyes. Without even looking to see if anyone was watching, he took her in his arms.

"I don't know what he would have said. None of my business. But I do love you, Sandra Tucker." He kissed her on the forehead. She shuddered against him.

"I love you too," she whispered into his chest. Her breath was warm through the tear-soaked cloth. "What will we do now?"

"What do you mean?" His voice was husky. "Will we win? Will we ever find other people? Will we even survive?" He raised her chin to look into her shimmering eyes. "Will this be all we ever have?" He kissed her lightly on the lips and she returned it—hard enough to electrify every nerve in his body. For a long while they just clung to one another, each drawing strength and courage to replenish the wells they'd gone to so often. Then he brushed the hair away from her face and wiped the tears from her cheek.

"Well," he sighed sadly, "that's a whole other story, isn't it?"

Far across the water, nearly a dozen men leaned against the safety chain beside the number three gun on the amidships deckhouse. There were only two pairs of binoculars among them and they were making the rounds.

"It's about damn time," Silva grumped.

"Yeah," agreed Felts. "Way to go, Skipper!"

Silva looked at Laney. "Fork 'em over, snipe." Grumbling, Laney handed him two wrinkled cigarettes—careful to keep his distance so close to the rail. Cigarettes were the closest thing to money anybody had, and nobody ever smoked them anymore. Till now. Silva handed one to Felts and lit them both with his Zippo. They took long drags and exhaled contentedly.

"What are you so damn happy about?" Laney snarled, watching his wager go up in smoke. "There's only two dames in the whole goddamn world, far's we know, and they're both took!"

Silva looked at Felts and rolled his eyes. "Snipes' brains are like weeds. Not enough sunlight belowdecks for 'em to grow." He looked at the machinist's mate. "And some are stupider than others. It's like this, see? The Skipper and Lieutenant Tucker are nuts about each other—which everybody knows, but nobody's supposed to. But they ain't gonna *do* anything about it until they find dames for the rest of us." He shook his head. "Couple'a dopes. Anyway, that's a mighty incentive for 'em to find us some, don't you think?" After a moment, Laney grinned and lit a smoke of his own.

Eventually, the binoculars found their way to the Mice. No one knew why they were there. It was actually kind of cool on deck and they'd likely catch their deaths. Regardless, they waited and took their turn peering through the binoculars, one after the other. Then they shuffled off.

"I wonder," Gilbert said at last. "Maybe we could marry us one of them monkey-cat gals like Silva did."

Isak shook his head. "Won't work. Silva said the Skipper had his weddin' annealed, 'er somethin'." Gilbert looked perplexed.

"I thought 'annealed' means to heat somethin' red-hot an' let it cool off on its own so you can bend it."

"Yep."

Gilbert looked at Silva and cocked his head. "Didn't work."

AUTHOR'S NOTE

Every human naval vessel named in *Destroyermen* was real. On February 27, 1942, the old *Langley*—America's first aircraft carrier—was mortally wounded by Japanese planes while carrying P-40 fighters to Java. On the night of February 28–March 1, 1942, *Houston* and *Perth* stumbled upon three Japanese cruisers and nine destroyers protecting a swarm of transports. Both were finally sunk after an epic fight in the Battle of the Sunda Strait.

(The only ship in the Asiatic Fleet with radar was the cruiser *Boise*, which had long since been sent to the States for repairs after striking a reef. The Japanese had no radar either, but they did have control of the air.)

On March 1, 1942, *Pope*, *Exeter*, and *Encounter* were destroyed by a combined Japanese force, including four heavy cruisers, while attempting to escape Surabaya and reach Ceylon (now Sri Lanka). Barring any mistakes that I take full responsibility for, and a little dramatic license with the pace and sequence of events, everything that took place or was mentioned to have happened in *Destroyermen* up to that point is true. The only exception is that *Walker* and *Mahan* were not there. Neither was *Amagi*.

The addition of two "four-stackers" and yet another Japanese capital ship would have made absolutely no difference to the historical outcome of that lopsided struggle. *Pope*, *Exeter*, and *Encounter* would have been destroyed regardless; the odds against them were simply too great. The only change to the history books (minus the Squall, of course) would have been two more rusting hulks at the bottom of the Java Sea—even before *Amagi* came along. But they were real.

As designed, *Amagi* was a thing to behold. At 47,000 tons, 826 feet long, and 101 feet wide, she was larger and more powerful than most of the battleships of her time. She would have been about the same size as the much later American *Iowa*-class battleships. It's possible she would have been converted to an aircraft carrier like her sisters, but she was never completed. Badly damaged by an earthquake in 1922 while still under construction, she was scrapped.

The story of *Walker* and *Mahan* is a little more involved. More than 270 "four-stacker" destroyers were built for the United States Navy during and immediately after World War I. They were built quickly (some being launched in as few as fourteen days) and were never intended to last more than thirty years—which some of them actually did. Already outdated, they remained in service throughout the 1920s and 1930s and ultimately fought in every theater during World War II.

Many didn't last that long. Because of restrictions on the numbers and tonnage of warships agreed upon at the Washington Naval Conference, many "four-stackers" languished in mothballs for years. Over time, some reentered service when an active destroyer was lost or wore out. Some were used for parts. A lot were converted into damage-control hulks or just simply scrapped. A few were even sold into the merchant service. One literally became a banana boat. Fifty were given/sold/traded to the British at the outbreak of World War II. Most that survived to fight in World War II were modified to one degree or another into minesweepers, fast transports, convoy escorts, seaplane tenders, and so on.

The point is, by the time the Japanese bombed Pearl Harbor, even the conservative, arguably moribund United States Navy knew the old "four-stackers" were obsolete, yet they used them anyway. This is not meant as criticism of the Navy—far from it. They used what they had. It was Congress that refused to build "up" even to the restrictions imposed by the Washington Treaty. It was this policy that left antique—and, in the case of the Asiatic Fleet, WWI surplus that hadn't even been altered or updated—ships to stand against the very cream of the Japanese Imperial Navy, the most modern and powerful in the world.

Walker and *Mahan* are presented in *Destroyermen* as two of these unlucky stepchildren, but in reality—the reality of the universe in which we reside—they were two of the ones that didn't make it. After sixteen years on "red lead row," *Walker* was slated to become a damage-control hulk, but she was scuttled seventeen days after the Pearl Harbor attack. *Mahan* was scrapped in 1931. Interestingly, both ships were involved in at least one epic undertaking: They served as pickets during the Navy's historic NC-flying-boat transatlantic flights. In any event, neither ship had a wartime record, so I felt less constrained in giving them a fictional, representative one.

If there are any old destroyermen out there who served on DD-102 or DD-163, you certainly have my respect and gratitude, and I mean no disrespect toward the honorable service of either ship. Instead, I hope you will join me in engaging in a little "what if?" As Captain Reddy said, "All historians do it, whether they admit it or not."

A NOTE ABOUT
"BRONTOSAURUS" ETC.

Obviously, *Destroyermen* is set, for the most part, within the context of an alternate universe. The fascinating possibility of one or many alternate/parallel universes has long provided wonderful worlds for science-fiction/fantasy writers to explore. Even more fascinating is the growing scientific speculation that they might actually exist. Unfortunately, none of these new theories, attitudes, or even popular culture perceptions could be referenced in *Destroyermen*. The characters' perceptions of the alternate/parallel universe must be viewed from the perspective that *they* had: a perspective prevalent in the 1940s, particularly among Asiatic Fleet destroyermen. I hope I have managed to capture that.

Unlike many stories involving a similar premise, the universe the destroyermen cross to is not just slightly skewed; it is the result of a profoundly and fundamentally altered evolutionary path. The "dinosaurs" in the story are depicted somewhat from whim, but with at least a little more modern perspective than the characters are able to perceive them. We now know so much more about dinosaurs than we did even when I was a kid—we have virtually started from scratch. Compared to those destroyerman in 1942, we live in an extremely enlightened age—at least as far as dinosaurs are concerned—so before you say, "What an idiot! Doesn't he know brontosauruses weren't real?" Yeah, *I* do. But the destroyermen don't.

My childhood books depicted dinosaurs as bloated, lizard-like beasts slouching along dragging their tails, or spending most of their days bobbing about in lakes or seas because they were too fat to stand. Tyrannosaurus was cool because he had lots of teeth, but his tail was just a third leg so he could stand upright like a man. And if anybody ever mentioned a dinosaur, the first thing that popped into your mind was the brontosaurus.

We now know the brontosaurus was a myth—a hoax—an extra head bone stuck on a decapitated apatosaurus skeleton. But in 1942, brontosaurus was real. It was the symbol by which any dinosaur would be judged and identified as such. *Anything* that looked remotely like a sauropod would immediately be called or compared to a "brontosaurus"— even by someone as learned as Courtney Bradford.

In our universe, dinosaurs have been extinct for around 65 million years. In *Destroyermen*, this is not the case. Those same prehistoric creatures have not remained stagnant. Everything has evolved beyond what the fossil record teaches us—the flora, fauna, the very ecology, and, because of that, even the geography to a certain extent. The "extinction event" is the obvious diversion point between the two realities, but there have still been ice ages, droughts, floods, and other cataclysmic events that would cause other extinctions and guide evolution for 65 million years. But "brontosaurus" remains. Stunted, perhaps, but physically similar to what the destroyermen expect to see.

Brontosaurus—or whatever it is the destroyermen *call* brontosaurus—is an amazingly well-adapted creature. Nature has been trying to replace him ever since he went away, but without too much success. Crossbreed a giraffe and an elephant and we would have him, I guess. Anyway, as long as there was green, leafy stuff to eat he wouldn't have to change. He would get smaller in the jungles of Indonesia, though, just like the elephants that live there today are smaller than their African counterparts. In fact, there's evidence that sauropods—and those that hunted them—were actually smaller in densely forested regions.

The Grik are descended from one of the many species of "raptors," as they're now inclusively known. They were relatively small, aggressive, possibly even cunning creatures that may have hunted in packs. If so, that would imply cooperative and therefore social behavior. Regardless of size, this gives them a leg up, in my estimation, on the ladder to the top of the evolutionary heap.

The seas are so hostile for a lot of reasons, but mainly because the creatures that lived there 65 million years ago sure scare *me* to death, and my imagination runs rampant with how terrifying they could become if they had a little more time. Also, if they're in the water you can't even shoot them—usually.

Almost alone among the creatures of this different earth that remained unchanged are sharks, crocodiles—and the mythical brontosaurus. Sharks and crocs are still here, even after the ancient unpleasantness that wiped out everything else. Compared to that, I imagine they would manage to cope with a little more persistent competition.

Considering that competition, one begins to wonder how mammals might have fared. Not too well, according to some scientists. In the tropical regions in which the Grik thrive, an isolated domain—thus Madagascar—would be needed for mammals to evolve to a sentient level. Let's face it, if humanity did spring from Africa, our ancestors wouldn't have lasted very long in constant contact with the Grik. Let us hope they were at least thought of as "worthy prey."

But what of the cooler climes? Remember, the destroyermen that came through the Squall have been able to sample only a very small part of this new world they find themselves in. A relatively isolated and environmentally homogeneous part. What amazing discoveries might they make once they are able to do more than "float about," as Courtney Bradford would say? But again, what if?

LOOK FOR

CRUSADE

BOOK TWO IN THE
DESTROYERMEN
SERIES

AVAILABLE NOW
FROM ROC

AVAILABLE NOW

FROM

TAYLOR ANDERSON

CRUSADE

Destroyermen, Book II

Lieutenant Commander Matthew Reddy, along with the
men and women of the USS *Walker*, have chosen sides
in a war not of their making. Swept from the World War
II Pacific into an alternate world, they have allied with
the Lemurians—a mammalian race threatened by the
warlike reptilian Grik.

The Lemurians are vastly outnumbered and ignorant of
warfare, and even the guns and technology of *Walker*
cannot turn the tide of battle. Luckily they are not
alone—Reddy finally finds Mahan, the other destroyer
that passed through the rift. Together, the two American
ships will teach the Lemurians to take a stand.

Or so they think—for the massive Japanese battleship
Amagi, the very ship that *Walker* was fleeing from when
the rift took them, has followed them through. And now
the *Amagi* is in the hands of the Grik.

**Available wherever books are sold or at
penguin.com**

AVAILABLE NOW

FROM

TAYLOR ANDERSON

MAELSTROM

Destroyermen, Book III

Lieutenant Commander Matthew Reddy, along with the men and women of the U.S.S. *Walker*, are once again at war. Having sided with the peaceful Lemurians against the savage, reptilian Grik, they now find themselves scrambling to prepare for the attack that is sure to come, searching for resources to support their forces—even as they look for allies to join their struggle.

Meanwhile, the Japanese juggernaut *Amagi*, also trapped in this strange world, is under Grik control—with her fanatical commander approaching madness. And soon they will have amassed a force that no amount of fire-power and technology will be able to stop.

As the raging conflict approaches, Reddy, his crew, his allies, and his loved ones face annihilation. But if there is one thing they have learned about their new world, it is that hope—and help—may be just over the horizon.

THE ULTIMATE IN
SCIENCE FICTION AND FANTASY!

From magical tales of distant worlds to stories of
technological advances beyond the grasp of man, Penguin has
everything you need to stretch your imagination to its limits.

penguin.com

ACE

Get the latest information on favorites like
William Gibson, T.A. Barron, Brian Jacques,
Ursula K. Le Guin, Sharon Shinn, Charlaine Harris,
Patricia Briggs, and Marjorie M. Liu,
as well as updates on the best new authors.

ROC

Escape with Jim Butcher, Harry Turtledove, Anne Bishop,
S.M. Stirling, Simon R. Green, E.E. Knight, Kat Richardson,
Rachel Caine, and many others—plus news on the
latest and hottest in science fiction and fantasy.

DAW

Patrick Rothfuss, Mercedes Lackey, Kristen Britain,
Tanya Huff, Tad Williams, C.J. Cherryh, and many more—
DAW has something to satisfy the cravings of any
science fiction and fantasy lover.
Also visit dawbooks.com.

*Get the best of science fiction and fantasy
at your fingertips!*